MW01128523

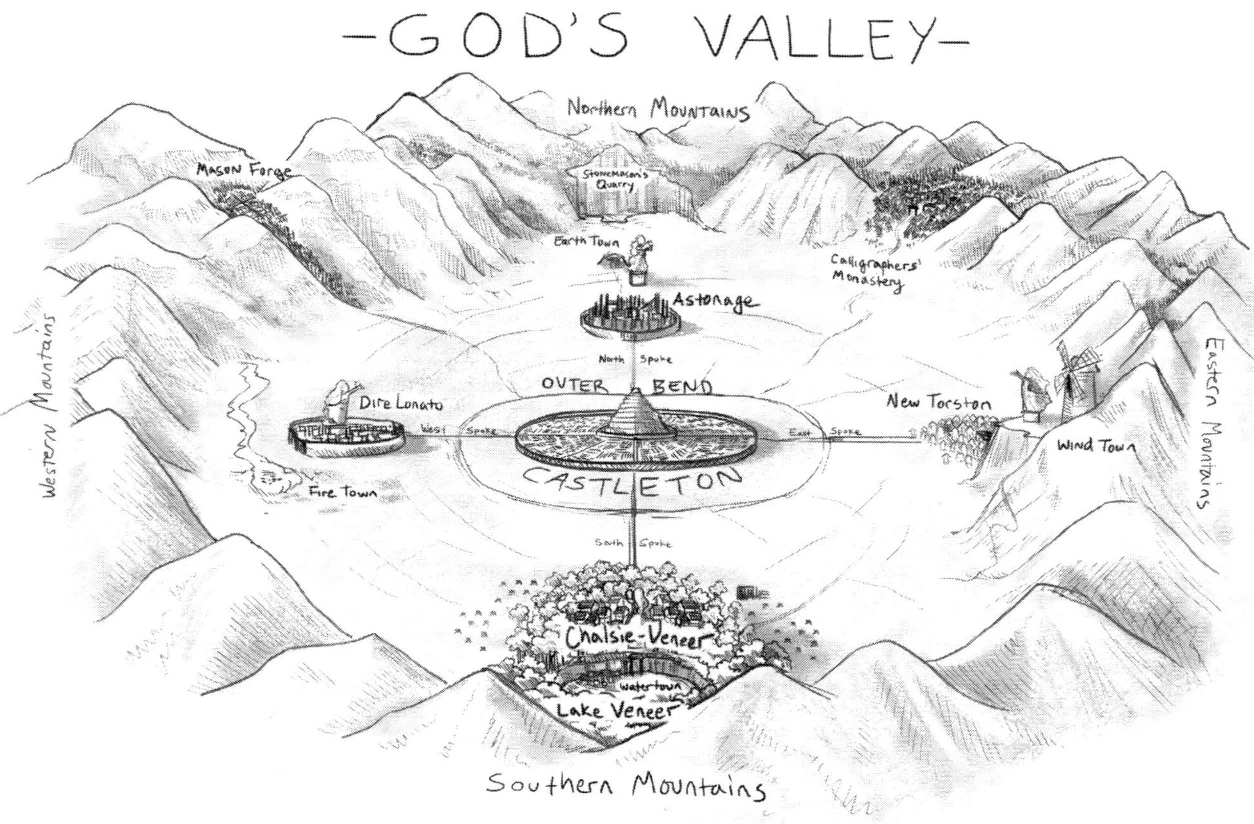

-GOD'S VALLEY-
Northern Mountains
Mason Forge
Stonemason's Quarry
Earth Town
Calligraphers' Monastery
Astonage
North Spoke
Western Mountains
Eastern Mountains
OUTER BEND
Dire Lonato
New Torston
West Spoke
East Spoke
Wind Town
CASTLETON
Fire Town
South Spoke
Chalsie-Veneer
Watertown
Lake Veneer
Southern Mountains

THREADCASTER

Jennifer Stolzer

ISBN: 978-1-5431-9859-1

Editing: Catherine Bakewell
Illustration: Jennifer Stolzer
Title text: Catherine Bakewell

Dedicated to:

The Simpson Sisters
restored and reunited
in heart, body, and mind.

Chapter 1

Cat sat in her open bedroom window, weaving a pattern of string in the cage of her hands. Her mind wandered as her expert fingers completed figure after figure. A loop transfer made the Prayer Knot; a wrist turn created the Whirlpool Spiral; crossing her thumb under and dropping her pinky loops left the Cup and Saucer, which became the Spire Mountain if she grabbed it with her teeth. It wasn't a game, per say, more like a habit introduced by her frustrated mother, desperate to keep a fidgety six-year-old still at church. Ten years later, the trick still worked. Cat drew a breath and let the familiar movements quiet her anxious mind.

Below, Mason Forge spread like a blanket over the mountainside. Residents took their time walking Main Street to shop or visit neighbors happily resting from the week's work. A group of rowdy men gathered for afternoon drinks at the town's only bar. Their laughter carried over the staircase of rooftops, ushered by dry gusts of wind from the wooded mountain pass. Somewhere, concealed beyond the Western Mountains, lay God's Valley with its complicated mess of magic, religion, and politics. Mason Forge was peaceful, stagnant, and felt less claustrophobic when Cat had a string in her hand.

The thread pulled tight. She turned from the horizon to find the first stage of the Child's Cradle taught between her palms. Her hands knew the following steps – she and Peter used to play for hours in the forest behind his house – but without someone to transfer the string to, she was trapped in a cage of wasted potential.

Dust-scented wind swept flyaway hairs about her face and stirred the sapling below her window like a tiny green flag. Cat planted the fruit tree after Peter's sixteenth birthday party. His mother saved a whole year to order peaches from Castleton, and served cake to their families with tears in her eyes. Sixteen meant Peter was a state-sanctioned adult, and officially older than the medical books said he could get. No one expected him to last another year, yet he was still with them, even though the seed they planted in his honor was already three feet tall. Cat hoped looking after a living thing would lift her spirits. After months without water, the forest in the pass was leafless, and the river was dry. The peach tree was the only green thing standing on the whole drought-choked mountainside and still it made her sad. It meant Peter was getting older, and his condition was getting worse. The thought made her physically ill.

The sapling scratched the wall beneath her window like a begging dog. Cat swallowed the lump growing in her throat and managed a smile at the little thing. It wasn't Peter, but she still knew a string game they could play together.

Cat set her opening stage with a single loop around each palm and began the steps of the Whirlpool Spiral with casual ease. Halfway through she changed her pace, carefully twisting the threads into tiny knots and lacing her exchanges more delicately than in the previous shapes. The loops braided denser and tighter, zig-zagging a line through her web until one single step remained. Cat hooked the last string in her pinky and checked the yard for witnesses. Her mother and father were probably in the living room, Sheila was likely cooking, no one was in the yard to her right – it seemed safe enough. She aimed the web at her tree and snapped the final string into place.

The thread fell across the pattern with a flash of white light. A braided chain of knots and snags glowed in the center of her tight spiral and a blast of clear water exploded from the surface. Cat locked her elbows and forced the jet down toward the tree, scattering powdery topsoil, and churning the earth around the roots to soupy mud. The force of the spell dug the string into Cat's fingers as it tried as hard as it could to shake itself apart. She fought to keep it tight, when a shout exploded from the distant townsfolk. Cat jumped and the spell uncoiled like a serpent from her hand.

She dropped below the windowsill, the soggy thread balled in her fist. If they caught her she'd be grounded, not to mention the legal ramifications. With half a dozen lies at the ready, she poked her head back through the window to see three dozen shoppers gathered in the road a block down, staring – thankfully – not up into her yard, but eastward toward the mountain pass where a black carriage had emerged from the trees. The coach was huge compared to normal delivery carts, pulled by a team of eight dark horses and flanked by six riders dressed in black tunics with white collars. Each carried a staff made of polished wood with bristles of brown horsehair cuffed at the end like a six-foot tall paintbrush.

A brand new fear charged Cat's nerves like wild fire.

"Dad!"

She raced up the hallway to the sunlit front room. Raymond Aston sprang from his seat; the law book he was reading fell heavily to the ground. "What? What is it?"

"Brushcasters!"

"Brushcasters?"

Cat swept past him out the front door and up the ramp to her neighbor's house. The door was locked. “Peter! Alan!” Cat pounded it with both fists. “Mrs. Montgomery!”

To Cat's surprise, her own mother answered the door. Mona Aston frowned. “Cat, what's gotten into you?”

“Is Peter home?”

Sheila Montgomery appeared, still holding her knitting. “The boys are out today. What's with all the panic?”

“Where did they go?”

“Brighton's, I think –”

Cat leaped from the porch. Mona charged out after her. “Stop right there, Catrina Aston! What in the world is going on?”

“Can't talk!” Cat shouted and dashed toward the street only to be caught by the arm as her father leaped from his house.

“Hold on.”

“Let go!”

“I know you're worried. Just breathe.” Raymond pulled her close and dropped his voice. “They may not know Peter's here. Use your head. Find a place to hide.”

“A place to hide.” She nodded. “Got it.”

“And Cat.” His grip tightened around her arm. “No magic.”

“Dad, not now – ”

“Promise me.” His green eyes – the ones she'd inherited – burned with an intensity that cut straight through her mania and rooted her to the spot. “I'm worried about him, too, but I won't lose you to those false prophets. No magic under any circumstances. Do you understand?”

Lips dry, she nodded again. “Yes.”

“Say you'll promise.”

“I promise.”

“I'm trusting you.” He dropped her arm. “Run fast.”

Cat gulped, riddled with panic, but thoughts of Peter brought her wits back into focus. She kicked dust as she tore away from the house, skirting porch steps and lawn ornaments until the road widened onto Cross Street. The town square was at the intersection of Main Street and Cross. Half the population congregated on the courthouse steps to greet their visitors. Cat scanned the masses, but couldn't see Peter over the heads. Below, a mass of celebrating townsfolk paraded with the carriage up Main Street. Cat elbowed through the assembly to reach the other end of Cross, where she wove at top speed through the crowd toward the river.

Brighton's Café sat across the street from town's power center with a clear view of the old waterwheel barely turning in the rain-starved current. A string of electric lights flickered above a patio dining area where a pack of weekend loiterers sipped coffee from bowl-sized cups. Peter sat at their usual table, his iced coffee garnished with a very long straw.

Although she saw him every day, his worsening appearance was still shocking. He was blond with wire-framed glasses before slightly cloudy brown eyes. His illness left him deathly pale, with swelling from head to toe. Massive arms, heavy with ten years of steady transmutation, rested limply on the table where his gloved hands cupped his drink. The wrists and elbows were wrapped in more layers of elastic bandages than she was used to seeing, as were his knees and ankles above his heavy, trunk-like feet. Below his collared shirt, his broad shoulders and barrel chest were marred with craggy tumors where juts of cold stone grew from the marrow of every bone. Peter was a fragile giant, part man and part earth. His eyes brightened as Cat approached. “Hey, I thought you were sleeping in.”

“We can't stay.” She heaved one of his arms off the table. “We have to go.”

“What's the rush?”

“Yeah, what's the deal, Cat?” Peter's twelve year-old brother Alan bounced in his seat. “The town's gone nuts! Is there a fight or something?”

“No.” She paused long enough for another deep calming breath. “It's Brushcasters.”

Peter's smile faded. “Brushcasters?”

"The Holy Calligraphers are here? So that's where my wait staff went!" A mustached man appeared, pen and notebook in hand. "You want the usual, Cat?"

"No, Mr. Brighton, Pete and I have to go."

"Relax, Catrina." Brighton laughed. "The Calligraphers are good people. They're God's messengers, you know."

"So they say." Cat gnawed her lip. "I'm not trying to be rude, Mr. Brighton. Do you think we can hide inside?"

"You know, I bet they're here to fix the river!" Mr. Brighton pointed to his flickering lights. "The power's been all wonky for months now! Bet Mayor Young called them."

"They can fix a *river*?" Alan beamed.

Cat slapped his arm. "This is not a good thing."

"Sure it is, it's the Calligraphers' job to bring miracles. Maybe they'll bless us, too. God knows we could use a blessing, right there, Pete?" Brighton elbowed Peter in the shoulder.

The blond's brow knit as he forced an uneasy smile. "Yeah, I mean, I'm a bit old to be banished at this point, right?"

"A'course ya' are! You aren't going anywhere, you're like our town mascot!"

"Yeah." Peter relaxed a bit and shrugged to Cat with one massive shoulder. "Tell them I'm your pet rock."

“This isn't a joke, Pete.” Cat squatted beside him at the table. “I know it's scary to think about, but Dad's told us how dangerous they are.”

“Your father's got too much passion,” Mr. Brighton drawled. “It's been twenty years since I've seen a calligrapher here – if it'll help y'all relax, sit back and watch the show, the drinks are my treat.”

“Mr. Brighton!” Cat glanced to the intersection where the first of the black horses pulled into view. They stopped at the crest headed for the river. Her hands shook on the tabletop.

Peter studied her a moment and slid his cup aside. “Thanks anyway, Mr. Brighton. Cat's right. We should go.”

“Aw!” Alan slouched. “But free coffee!”

“I'll buy you as much coffee as you want later.” Peter nudged his brother's knee. “Come on, help me up.”

Peter shifted forward and waited for Alan to draw his chair aside before rising with a wince. He staggered, back and shoulders cracking, until he reached his full seven-foot height and peered down at Cat with a good-natured smile. “Okay, where to?”

She sighed and took his arm. “Thanks, Pete.”

The population of Cross Street had already doubled. Farmers, dusty from the fields, arrived to the riverfront in droves. Brighton's porch was full of ogling diners who crowded the outside tables and blocked access to the door. The alleys on either side of Cross Street were full, with more revelers pushing in from the town square every second. The only clear spot was the riverbank where the Calligraphers were headed. It was a risk, but at least there she and Peter had an exit to the treeline. Cat steered her friend off the porch. “This way.”

The sick man's stride was short and slow as he balanced his uneven bulk on fused ankles and feet. Alan took the lead, shifting townsfolk out of their path. They grumbled at first but apologized when they saw Peter, and parted without complaining.

By the time Cat reached the bank, the Calligraphers' carriage was closing quickly, with its parade of locals in tow. Those who escorted them from the gate herded the crowd ahead of them like a flock of bleating sheep. The farmers along the river were shoved backward toward its edge. An old field hand stumbled and knocked Peter from behind. He staggered. Cat released his arm and took his weight onto herself. She held tight, buried in the earthy smell of his cotton shirt, until his cumbersome legs found footing.

In their pause, excitable people had flooded in from all sides, surrounding them with heat and the smells of sweat, mud, and alcohol. The jutting tumors on Peter's ribcage pressed hard into her cheek. His heart pounded through layers of skin and stone.

“I'm good.” Peter shifted back onto his heels and wrapped his heavy arm like a blanket around her back. “It's alright. I'm okay.”

The waterwheel was barely six yards to their left. The treeline, now behind them, was too crowded to reach. Alan was missing, swallowed fully by the jostling gridlock. Their saving grace was the constant movement of the over-excited crowd and the trailing slope of the dry riverbank that disguised half a foot of Peter's unnatural height.

His voice echoed through his ribcage. “What do we do now?”

Cat tightened her grip. The Calligrapher's wagon and all of its brush-toting warriors came to a stop. She tried and failed another deep, calming breath. “Pray?”

“Hah.” Peter leaned a little heavier onto her shoulder. “Right.”

Chapter 2

The Calligraphers' carriage towered ten feet over the crowd, its black polished walls matted with dust and crowned in gold molding around the top. There were no windows, but Cat could tell there were people inside from the way it jostled in place. A latch came free on the near side, facing the river, and lowed toward the ground like a platform. Calligraphers dressed in all black slid from the inside to prop up the open wall and convert the contraption from vehicle to a full theatrical stage with a heavy velvet curtain.

The six mounted Calligraphers let out a unified bark and held their brushes high enough for the bristles to catch the breeze. The six were a variety of ages and skin tones, but their black tunics and dyed black hair unified them into a single unit as they dismounted in unison and struck their heels on the paving stones. With another bark they slid their tall paintbrushes into leather holsters on their backs and stood at attention along either side of the stage.

The curtain rustled and another pair of Calligraphers emerged. The first was man with a sharp jaw and a white stole over his high collar. His teenage assistant wore a sour expression and her hair pulled into pigtails. She offered him a black, lacquered paintbrush which he raised to the crowd. “God's blessing to you all!”

Everyone cheered. Those around Cat and Peter raised their arms in response. Cat kept hers firmly around her friend's lumpy rib cage. He was trembling. The Calligrapher planted his brush handle like a flag at his side.

“People of Mason Forge! I am Trace Hayes, Senior Monk in the Order of Holy Calligraphers. It is an honor to address you today. I'm sure I speak for my fellows when I say the peace and tranquility I feel here warms me, heart and soul. It's like being home on the opposite side of the world.”

Trace gestured to his assistant, who bowed and moved upstage where she raised the heavy curtain with a thick golden cord.

"On a more serious note," Trace continued, "we come to you today, because this winter marks the five-hundredth year since the death of the Prophets and the last words from Our God."

The crowd bowed their heads. Trace paused and pressed the black brush reverently across his heart. "We in the Order of Holy Calligraphers have dedicated our lives and our honor to preserving the laws and cleansing the Valley of sin for Our God's glorious return.

"We have heard about your troubles with your rainfall and the running of your waterwheel, and I regret to inform you that the rest of God's Valley is faring even worse. The last herd of wild horses, so eagerly protected, has finally vanished from the plain, and some areas to the north haven't seen rain in over eighteen months. This is why, to honor this most sobering anniversary, our Holy Elder proposed this good-will tour to perform miracles and inspire hope in the Valley. It is my honor and esteemed pleasure to present him to you, now."

A gasp spread through Cat's portion of the crowd. "The Elder? Here?" Peter's stony arm pressed into her back and she tightened her arms around his ribs.

Trace waited for the curtain to reach its peak, drew a deep breath and stepped aside. "Ladies and gentlemen, the Holy Elder."

The townspeople fell into awestruck silence as the Elder emerged from the shadow of the stage. He was dressed in many layers black and white fabric, his face hidden by a hood. He carried a golden brush carved with a single line of flowing script that circled the handle from top to bottom. Cat's grip on Peter slacked as she stared at the brush. The words shimmered with white light, like the spells she knotted in her string. The light cleared her mind and muted her ears as it drew her toward the elder with its unearthly glow.

The Holy Elder raised the staff and the crowd burst into thunderous applause.

"Silence!"

Cat snapped from her daze as the crowd jumped and hushed. The Elder raise his head to reveal his stiff, impatient expression.

"Attention people of Mason Forge," he boomed. “I come in lieu of Our God.”

He unclasped a golden chain at his collar and dropped the ceremonial garb like a fainting woman into Trace's arms. The old man beneath was silver haired, but strong and powerful like an athlete, wearing a plain, black uniform and gold-trimmed white stole. The Elder slammed the blunt end of his brush against the stage. Cat winced as the lighted script flashed on impact.

“Five centuries ago, man chose sin over righteousness,” the Elder said. “That violation and every infraction that's followed drives the Valley further toward oblivion. Our God abandoned this place because of these. Everything that's happened, from the drying of your riverbed to the deadly plague of Curses, is the fault of sinful man.”

The crowd twittered. Cat felt Peter shudder.

"I, as the Holy Elder, am the only one in this world who's read Our God's law in its entirety. Confess the ledger of your sins to me, and I will give you a miracle."

Cat renewed her grip on Peter's chest. Those around her muttered to each other. A voice rose over the hum of whispers.

"I have a confession!" Mayor Young stepped into the ring of Calligraphers, wearing a flannel shirt and a pair of filthy work pants.

His constituents fell silent. The Elder barked to him. "Speak!"

"I've been mayor of Mason Forge for over ten years. I've attended church every week since I took office, but not once in this whole time have I said a prayer."

The crowd traded astonished whispers. The Elder extended his hand. "As mayor, it is your job to pray for your town. Begin praying tomorrow and I will forgive you your sin."

"I swear it, your honor!"

"I have a confession!" Eyes turned toward Cat and Peter's grade-school teacher. Cat's throat went dry. "I steal electricity from the school when the power is off in my house."

A farmer raised his hand. "I falsified my report to Castleton and kept extra rice!"

"I lied on my taxes!"

"I vandalized city property!"

“I favor one child over the other!”

“I cheated on my wife!”

All around, voices rose, shouting their sins. Trace wrote each violation on a long, unraveling scroll. Cat held her breath through the volley, her string tight around her wrist, and Peter's ragged breathing loud in one ear.

“Are there any others?” Trace asked in the settling lull. No one answered. The Elder nodded and Trace placed the scroll in a gold box held by his pig-tailed assistant.

“Thank you for your confessions,” the Holy Elder said. “I bring you this miracle not for my own glory, but to hasten Our God's return. Now, stand aside!"

Trace unfolded a short flight of stairs and led his Elder through the crowd toward the still river. Cat allowed the crowd to maneuver around them and tugged Peter carefully back toward the café. They made it a couple feet before the audience resettled and the two were trapped a second time.

The Elder crossed the street to the old mill where the waterwheel sat creaking in the shallow water. The wheel was nearly as old as Mason Forge itself and used to grind rice meal back when the river was high, but over time the river weakened and the mill went out of service until Cat started elementary school – about the time Mayor Young ordered the electric generator from Castleton. The transformer box for the generator sat in a wooden shed, and was grafted to the ancient wheel mechanism by a hodgepodge of metal joints and wire. The Elder prodded the mess of electrical cords with the blunt end of his brush and surveyed the river descending toward them over a staircase of low waterfalls. He puffed air over his mustache and summoned Trace to his side.

The senior monk took a silver decanter from his assistant and poured a pool of thick, white paint into a silver dish at the Holy Elder's feet. The Elder hoisted his gold brush for the audience's attention. "What you are about to see is the raw power of Our God. It may be frightening, but I warn you – do not run."

The crowd stiffened.

"Our God spoke our world into existence," the Elder said. "His voice evokes the power of both life and death. He marked the bodies of his Prophets with the names of the four elements, these words on their flesh that gave them power over magic. Our God's language cannot be spoken, but when written by hand, combined with quotes from the dictated law, and fused with the fiber of my own soul, I can use it to perform miracles as the Prophets did when they doled reward and punishment five centuries ago. This is the skill of our Order, a guarded practice few mortals may attempt without severe and destructive consequences."

Cat tensed. The Elder scanned the faces before him. "Once my circle is complete, the golem it creates will be out of my control. It will follow the instructions I write, but if it is distracted even slightly from the task I inscribe, it will turn wrathful and I will not be held responsible for the destruction that follows. Do you understand?"

They nodded in crippled silence. The Elder gripped his brush and dipped its white bristles in the paint. The cracked earth held tight to every drop as he swept a ten-foot circle around himself. He re-wet the brush and began a line of continuous text that coiled within the circle's edge until only the space beneath the Elder's feet remained. He bowed his head, stepped aside, and began again with gentle strokes.

The symbol was mathematically precise in its curves, yet free and organic. The Elder's brush added weight and form Cat could never achieve with string. He was an artist composing a masterwork and treated every bend in the braiding symbol with passion, respect, and his own reverent flair. She could hear God's whisper in the beauty of his brushstrokes.

Cat recognized the rune as 'earth' – a spell she used to conjure dirt clods and gravel for her garden. The Elder connected the last line and the symbol turned to white fire. A knot of gray stone rolled to life in mid air. It swelled and grew facets until it was larger than the circle, then shaped itself into an animal with four wide-set narrow legs, a club-like tail, and a wide, tapered head. The golem stood fifteen feet tall and still as a statue, until two glowing white eyes opened in its face and the creature came to life.

The crowd gasped as it turned its glowing eyes toward them. Cat stared back, her mind clear of thought, drawn forward with the same magnetism as the glow in the Elder's brush.

The light of the earth rune spread to the verses, burning around the coil one letter at a time like a fuse. The golem twitched and moved toward the river, shedding dust from its joints. The next verse caught and the creature rose to its hind legs in front of the waterwheel. With the next verse, it dove into the base of the hill and burrowed inward, raising the landmass seven feet upward. The golem curled into a ball beneath its earthen blanket and died, still as a statue, behind a veil of falling water.

The river water arched from its new height and splashed over the waterwheel in a steady stream. The paddles turned, the electric generator hummed, and throughout Mason Forge, power was restored.

Chapter 3

People sang praises and danced as if they'd been rescued from oblivion by the Holy Elder's miracle. Trace and his assistant escorted their leader back to the stage where the other Calligraphers drew their brushes and formed a wall against the throng of grateful townsfolk. Cheers and sobs filled the street. Some fell on their knees. Others shouted nonsense syllables like toddlers. Dozens reached through the human blockade to touch the Elder who kept safely out of reach with a twinge of disgust that Cat related to, but for a very different reason.

Peter hadn't moved since the demonstration. His shirt was damp beneath the bandages where sweat had stained it muddy brown.

"Pete!" Alan shoved toward them through the thinning crowd. "Did you see that? Real magic, just like Mr. Brighton said!"

Peter's voice was raw. "Yeah, bro, I saw it."

"It was amazing! They've got recruitment forms on stage. Cat should get one."

A wave of nausea splashed through her. "Are you crazy?"

"Why not? You already know the magic –"

"Alan," Peter snapped. "Zip it."

"What? I didn't say it loudly."

"You're not supposed to say it at all." Cat pulled Alan close enough to whisper. "Don't fall for this show like the rest of them. The Brushcasters are still the Curse-hating bad guys your mother told you about. Miracles have nothing to do with their actual holiness."

"Whatever, it was just a thought."

Peter groaned and leaned further onto Cat's shoulder. "I would like to leave now."

"Yes, let's leave." She noted the café, now clear of spectators. "How about that free coffee, Alan?"

"You don't have to bribe me, I'm not a baby."

Alan led them back onto Mr. Brighton's porch. The café owner had abandoned his post to join the festivity and those still seated did so in dreamlike reverie. Peter hefted his heavy feet up a low step onto the concrete slab and had to duck under the string of electric lights, now blazing brighter than Cat had ever seen. Behind them, a clear voice rang through the din.

"Master! Look!"

Peter froze. Cat seized his arm.

Trace Hayes stilled the crowd with a commanding voice. "Earth Curse!"

Peter drew a shallow breath.

"Turn around!"

Cat could feel the eyes of the town level on Peter. An eerie still overtook them, punctuated by the steady clack of the waterwheel. She glanced to the café door, her stomach in knots. They were so close. Cat tugged Peter forward, but he pulled his arm free and pivoted his oversized body with shuffling steps.

Trace stood outside the ring of Calligrahers with his assistant peeking from behind him. She wrinkled her nose in disgust. "What's it doing here?"

Fury replaced Cat's fear. "He's not an it!"

"Yes it is, it's disgusting!"

"Paige, quiet," Trace said. "Stay with the Elder." She scoffed and slipped between the standing Calligraphers. Trace met Cat's eye as he descended the stage. "Step aside, miss."

"No."

“This creature is sin incarnate.” Trace pulled his black brush from the holster on his back. “It's my responsibility as a Holy Calligrapher to deal with it appropriately.”

“Stay way from him.” Cat hooked her finger under the coiled string on her wrist. “I'm warning you.”

“Wait!” Raymond Aston wove through the crowd and clamped his hand over Cat's wrist, trapping the string in its place. “Don't mind my daughter, sir. She doesn't mean any harm.”

“And you are?”

“No one special. A lawyer.” Raymond swallowed hard. “Don't worry about the Curse. He's our problem, we know what to do.”

The Calligrapher's eyes narrowed. He sheathed his brush. “Apparently you don't, sir. This Curse is severely advanced. Our Order established the Curse Towns for a reason – they are supposed to leave the population as *children*. You say you are a lawyer. Law and moral principle demand Curses be removed as soon as the symptoms appear. It's the only way to keep everyone safe."

"Sorry, sir, that's my fault.” Mayor Young approached with a timid tip of his cap. "I let Peter stay. He's no harm. He's alright.”

"Forgive my boldness, Mr. Mayor, but we're the religious authority in this situation. We will tell you what is 'alright' and what's not. Choosing sin over obedience is what drove Our God away to begin with. This creature belongs in Earth Town with its kind."

“Forgive us,” Mayor Young stammered. “Pete's the first Curse we've had in generations.”

“That's no excuse for ignorance.”

“But if you'd been here back when we found out...” the mayor persisted. “We were on the tail end of a flu epidemic. Twelve people died, including Peter's father. We couldn't take poor Sheila's husband and her son in the same month!”

“I know it's difficult to break the family bond, but that's the price we pay.” Trace knit his brow. “Any child can be born a Curse; it's no one's fault, but Our God told us to reject our sin. Sympathy only delays his return.”

"Hayes!"

The senior monk spun on his heel. The Holy Elder scattered his bodyguards and stormed to the edge of the stage.

“To me! Now!”

Trace obeyed and folded himself in a deep bow. “Beg pardon, your honor. I have it under control.”

“Hardly." The Elder swept him aside with his glowing brush handle. “Mr. Mayor, I am very disappointed. I gave you an opportunity to confess your sins – how dare you ask me for a miracle while withholding such filth!”

The townsfolk recoiled at the acid in the monk's voice. Mayor Young shrank away, deflated, as the Elder traipsed the platform.

"I understand you lead a simple life up here. You are isolated. You lack good leadership and righteous examples, but that's no excuse for blatant ignorance such as this. Somehow, despite our laws and teachings, you still think this monster is a man."

Anger prickled the hair on the back of Cat's neck.

"This thing you are protecting is not a man cursed," the Elder said. "They are not *people* cursed. This mutated, impotent, bloodless, inhuman creature is the curse itself. It's sin manifested in human guise to test the strength of our faith."

A bubble of outrage burst in Cat's chest. "You're wrong!"

The Elder's glare chilled her like ice water. "You dare raise you voice to me?"

"Y-yes." She wet her lips and stepped closer to her father. "What you're saying is a lie. Peter hasn't hurt anyone."

"Then you wouldn't need a miracle."

The townsfolk muttered to each other. Friends shot uncertain glances in Peter's direction. Those who disapproved of his presence before, scowled with their suspicions finally confirmed.

The Elder addressed them with his head high. "Not only do this girl and your mayor need to repent of this. You've all allowed yourselves to be fooled, and gave in when you should have been strong. Now you are responsible for the death of the entire world."

Cat blanched. "Wait, what?"

"The Curses are a manifestation of sin," the Elder said. "They are physical evidence of the wedge between the mortal and the divine. Every Curse born proves the wickedness of the people, and to embrace one as your own is to choose sin over Our God's righteousness – the very crime that drove him from the Valley and started nature's decay. You spit in the face of all those who have suffered and sacrificed for the past five hundred years."

"Peter is not a sin!" Cat insisted. "He is my best friend!"

"And I am the Holy Elder!" The monk drove his brush handle into the stage. The white script flashed and the crowd flinched. Cat was silenced by a painful twinge somewhere deep in her soul. The Elder took a calming breath. "If this is how Mason Forge feels about Our God, then my miracles are wasted. This Curse is pure evil and I am a herald of faith. Reject one or the other, but I promise you this – Our God will not return to a world that embraces sin."

He lowered his voice. "Don't be afraid. I will not let you drive the Valley to destruction. You can still redeem yourselves in Our God's eyes."

The Elder snapped his fingers to Trace, who whispered to his assistant. The girl rushed backstage and returned with the golden box that held the scroll of the town's sins. From this, the Elder removed a leather pouch marked with silver lettering and from that, a roll of parchment tied with a white ribbon.

The Elder held the scroll aloft. “Behold! The written law!”

The townsfolk bowed in reverence. Cat scanned their bent heads, conflicted and insecure. Peter's heavy breathing rasped behind her. She tugged against her father's grip, but Raymond held firm, his eyes set on the scroll.

“Witness the words of the Prophet Amos.” The Elder unrolled and read. “To my friends of God's Valley, Our God has seen your misfortune. He wishes to save you, but knows the lessons of redemption are met more sweetly in practice. Cast out your sins and join him on the righteous path.” He released the bottom edge and the parchment snapped smartly back into a roll. “In accordance with Our God's wishes, I will give you one chance. Destroy this Curse before morning and I will ask Our God for forgiveness on your behalf. Fail and I will destroy the Curse myself, and leave you stranded on this mountainside to suffer the consequences of your selfish actions.”

“But your honor.” Mayor Young was ghostly pale. “You can't mean we should...You don't want us to...”

“The opportunity to reject your sin is long past,” the Elder said. “Bring me evidence of its death, or there is no redemption.”

Cat's heart fell to her stomach as the air in the crowd tensed. All eyes returned to Peter. The Elder smirked and spoke to Trace over his shoulder.

“Tell the monks to pack it up. This town can save itself."

The Calligraphers retreated and folded their carriage around themselves with a clatter of pulleys and gears. Peter gulped loudly as the townsfolk advanced toward him.

Cat wrenched her arm free of her father's grip. “Wait! Everyone stay where you are!”

The frightened mob did as they were told. Mayor Young stepped forward but Alan met him with his fists raised in front of his face. “She said stop or I'll hit you!”

Raymond cleared his throat. “Alan, get your mother.”

“I can fight!”

“Alan.” Peter's voice was low. “Go.”

The boy turned with angry tears, but his brother's darkened face broke his resolve. Alan wiped his eye with his wrist and ran back up Cross Street. The crowd let him pass and their attention turned again to Mayor Young.

“I- I don't know how to say this,” the mayor said. “I don't want to do it. I didn't want to do it ever – not even when you were a kid. Curses never felt fair to me.”

“Mayor Young,” Cat said. “You know he's not evil.”

“I know his soul isn't,” the mayor said. “His body though...”

“You can't be serious.”

“Young,” Raymond said. “We don't have to be drastic. If we band together – ”

"We'll be damned," the mayor said. "You've never trusted the Calligraphers, Raymond, you've said as much, but you have to trust God. This is what it says in their scriptures."

"It's what *they* say it says!" Cat grunted and appealed to the group at large. "You guys know Peter. You all raised us from birth! He's been a friend to every one of you; it's not his fault he's sick. If he were going blind or deaf you wouldn't treat him this way, but because he's turning to stone – "

"You're right, Cat, on both counts," Mr. Brighton said. "We thought we were being good and generous, but he's not sick, he's a Curse. The Calligraphers were right; the river is weak, the crops are failing, and it all started with him."

"You can't prove that."

"It wasn't like this before."

"Because there's a drought!" Cat said. "Think straight, you guys. One person can't change the weather by *existing*."

"I'm sorry, Catrina," the mayor said. "Keeping this town safe was my job from the start. If I'd obeyed the law way back then, we'd all be better off now."

"Peter wouldn't!"

"Cat," Raymond warned, but he was fighting for calm as well. "Young, please. There must be an alternative."

"I can't see one, Ray. The Elder asked for proof."

“But what you're suggesting is murder.”

“It's out of my hands.”

Raymond frowned. “Be reasonable.”

“I'm trying to do what's best.” Mayor Young blinked tears from his eyes. “I don't want to... but I'm stuck. I'm trying to help. If we don't do it gently, I don't think the Elder will.”

Cat trembled. Fear from earlier gripped her throat from within. The growth of the peach tree warned her this was coming, but she never dreamed it would be like this. The thought of Peter killed by a mob of people they once considered friends....

“It's not fair.” Cat's heart pounded as her nails clawed anxiously at the loop of string. “I'll fight – you, the Elder, I don't care who it is. You won't take him.”

“Cat.” Peter's hand pressed to her back. He drew a shaking breath. “I'll do it.”

The people stiffened at his words as if they'd forgotten he was there. Dread lanced Cat like a spear. She met heartbreak in his misty brown eyes. “Pete, you can't.”

“It's fine, I don't blame anyone,” Peter said. “I'm dying regardless, right? Whether it's today or a week from now? It's not worth hurting everyone.” He swallowed with a little difficulty. "I'm not worth fighting over."

"Peter!" Sheila Montgomery arrived with her sandy hair unkempt and tears on her cheeks. She shoved past Cat and buried her face in Peter's chest. Alan followed his mother into a family embrace.

Mona Aston also arrived. Cat ran to her mother, too full of rage and fear to explain the situation. The crowd bowed their heads like mourners, but their grief was too surreal. Cat couldn't stand it. Bile rolled up from her stomach. She held her breath to keep it down.

Mayor Young spoke again. "We'd like to send you to the next life with dignity." He averted his eyes. "We know how fragile you are. Perhaps... if we make you comfortable, the doctor can use ether or something and you'll sleep through it...."

"No." Fire burned in Raymond's eyes. "We'll do it."

Cat gaped. "What?"

"We'll do it," he repeated. "We'll kill him. At home. Without an audience."

Palpable relief settled over the crowd. Blood returned to Mayor Young's cheeks. "Okay, Raymond, if you think it's best."

" A man deserves to die in his own bed."

"Then it's settled." The mayor addressed the huddled Montgomerys. "I wish it hadn't come to this. You're a hero to us, Peter, I hope you know that. If there's anything we can do for you before you go..."

"No thanks," Cat glowered. "I think you've helped enough."

Chapter 4

Lights blazed in the Montgomerys' house. It was a cold, unfeeling light, with a buzz that hung in Cat's ears. She hated electric light, it was annoying on a good day, and now an unnatural reminder of what Peter was about to die for. The Astons and Montgomerys gathered in the front room near the kitchen with Alan left outside to watch the street for intruders. Cat bottled her outrage until the door was safely locked.

"Dad! How could you?"

"Now Cat, let me explain."

“No!” Unfocused emotion shook her until her hands and voice both trembled. “You volunteered to kill him! You gave up when you were supposed to help!”

“Cat, breathe,” Peter coached.

Sheila ignored his calm expression. “Oh honey, sit down. Your nerves...” She guided him into a sagging armchair. “There, that's better. Are you all right?”

“I'm in a bit of shock,” he said, obviously. “I wasn't expecting to be executed today.”

“Don't act like you're not bothered when I can plainly see you are.” Sheila straightened his glasses. “It will all work out okay.”

“That's right, you're safe.” Cat knelt at his side. “No one's laying a hand on you – not by morning and not ever.” She glared at her father who threw up his hands.

“No one is getting killed, I'll state that right off,” Raymond said. “Peter's not dying, not by our hand at least.”

Mona's face brightened. “You have a plan!”

“Yes,” Raymond said. “We're sending him to Earth Town.”

Cat's mouth went dry. “That's not a plan!”

“I know. I hate it, but it's the only place that's safe.”

“Dad, the Curse Towns are terrible!” Cat insisted. “We've all heard rumors – they're dirty, run-down camps of half dead people barely surviving on scraps. We can't send Peter there!”

“I like it a lot better than dying,” Peter offered.

“I like a lot of stuff better than you dying.”

“Well, sure...”

“I can't bear the thought of my Peter in that place!” Sheila whimpered. “How about we hide him? No one will know.”

“Yes they will,” Raymond said. “Mason Forge is too small.”

“Then how will you get him out of town?”

“We'll sneak the two of you out after dark,” Raymond said. “You're his mother, so Young won't question your absence – he'll think it's a mourning period.”

Peter frowned. “And from there we walk?”

“You can take a horse and wagon.”

“You have one?”

“I'll buy one.”

“I suppose it's the only way,” Sheila said. “If he must go, I'll stay with him. I won't leave him alone in a place like that.”

Peter's feigned enthusiasm failed. “Mom, you can't do that.”

“No more than I can abandon you in the desert!” she replied. “Perhaps I can't live with the Curses in Earth Town, but I can make a home nearby. I'm sure there's some work or something for me in Astonage. They have factories there.”

“But Mason Forge is your whole life,” he said. “Dad's family built this place. They take care of you. And what about Alan? I'm a seventeen year old Curse, I've got a year left at best. I can't ask you both to give up everything for that."

"I don't recall it being a question."

"What about the proof?" Peter asked the rest. "The Brushcasters needed proof. What does the plan say about that?"

"Cat will provide the proof," Raymond replied.

She started. "Are you suggesting I use magic?"

"Peter's mostly stone. You can use your string to make enough to substitute for a body."

"We'll put it in his clothes!" Mona said. "We can add animal meat and blood! The monks will believe us if it's fresh."

The image churned Cat's twisted stomach. It was an awful plan full of horrible outcomes, but it would get Peter out of danger. Still Cat, like Sheila, couldn't bear the thought of her dearest friend dying in a slum. If Mason Forge would not accept him, perhaps someplace else would.

"Alright, fine." Cat said. "I'll use my string to make the evidence, but only if I take him to Earth Town."

"Cat, no," Mona said.

"Peter wants his mom to stay, and I don't want to leave his side." Cat stood, her hand on his shoulder. "I'm sixteen years-old, I'm technically an adult. It's my decision. I'll take Sheila's place in the wagon and in Earth Town, as well. I'll stay with him as long as he needs me."

"No," Raymond reached forward. "I forbid it."

"Dad, stop." Cat stepped away from his hand and looked into his fearful eyes. "You've been telling me what to do for long enough. I know when it's safe to use magic. I know to be careful around the Brushcasters. It'll be okay."

"How?" He lowered his voice and took her hand more gently than first intended. "I know you're brave, and strong, and wholly capable, but I won't lose you like this. Peter isn't your responsibility. The Montomgerys are his family."

"Dad." She met his eye. "He means more to me than anyone."

Raymond clenched his jaw and nodded. Mona peeped a sob.

Peter's brown eyes glistened behind his glasses. "I know I should object but..." He warmed with a grateful smile. "Thanks, Cat."

Her heart swelled, his genuine smile scattering any residual doubt. "My pleasure."

"Is that okay, Sheila?" Mona asked with a sniffle. "Can Cat take your place?"

"I – I suppose." Sheila wept. "Just... write us so we can visit."

Cat smiled. "I promise."

With only a few hours to nightfall, the families got to work. They converted a bookshelf to a coffin and laid it in the family room near the door. Cat set her jaw and readied her string. Her hands twitched from nerves and general weariness, but she threaded the opening stage and began the careful process of knitting the symbol. The earth rune was blockier and squarer than the water one, and built at a skew so that she had to twist her wrist to actually complete it. The surface flashed and a rain of grayish dust and gravel cascaded from the spell. It took three runes to fill the box. Peter changed and the mothers shoveled the pile into his dirty clothes. Cat felt ill at the sight. She retreated to her room to pack.

She didn't have a lot of travel clothes – her father moved to Mason Forge before she was born and outright refused to leave – but she did have hiking boots and options for layering. She chose a heavy skirt and vest, a checkered headscarf she tied around her waist at the hip, and her grandmother's heirloom comb to pin her hair back in a bun. There was no telling how long she and Peter would be on their own. They could live like nomads in the plains as long as they could find food. She filled a knapsack with her lightest outfits and all the money she could find – there wasn't much, but she had some jewelry and small keepsakes she could sell. With the bag on her shoulder, Cat gave her childhood bedroom a final scan and left for the Montgomerys', feeling nervous and unprepared.

Everyone but Raymond stood in the front yard. Mona and Alan stacked cardboard boxes full of food for the journey; there was enough to make it to Earth Town but not much further than that. Sheila stood on the front ramp pressing Peter's favorite atlas into his chest. “Don't argue with me. I said take it.”

“It was dad's.”

“But you love it.”

“Mom.” He bowed his head. “I won't have book shelves or a map collection in a place like Earth Town. The book has value. Sending it with me is like throwing it away.”

“Don't say things like that. You have value.” Sheila sniffled with fresh tears. “At least... you do to me.”

“I'll take it, Sheila.” Cat offered.

The woman dabbed her eyes. “See? Cat knows how it is. She'll look after it.”

“Of course I will.” Cat wedged the leather volume in her bag. “You ready, Pete?”

“Not really. How about you? Regrets?”

“Still too angry for that.”

Mona dusted her hands and straightened the pink comb in Cat's unkempt brown hair. “I can hardly believe it... my little girl all grown up and moving away. I always knew you'd do great things with that talent of yours. You stood up for what you believed in. I'm very proud of you."

She blushed. "Thanks. I wish Dad was."

"He is. He just has a strange way of showing it." Mona nodded up the street. "See?"

Raymond rounded the far corner driving an open-bed wagon with thick rubber wheels. The body of the vehicle was metal, probably chosen for the coiled spring shocks, with wooden walls and padded benches in front and along the sides. The rig was pulled by a copper-colored draft horse with furry hooves and a pale mane that draped past its eyes.

Raymond parked in front of the house. "What do you think? Her name is Strawberry."

"Where did you get her?" Cat asked.

"She's a farm horse that I rescued."

Mona grimaced. "You didn't steal her, did you?"

"I'll compensate them later."

"Did you rescue the wagon too?"

"No time for details." He hopped from the driver's seat with a grunt. "Everyone's gathered at the church including the Brushcasters. You'll have to take the nature trail down to the gate. Do you have everything?"

Cat adjusted the bag on her shoulder. “Everything I could think of.”

“I guess this is it, then.” Raymond handed her the reins, his face tight and reddening especially at the eyes. Cat kissed his cheek and let him hold her until Alan finished loading all the boxes.

Peter and his family said their “I love yous” and “goodbyes.” Cat hugged her mother and father with a promise to write and a kernel of guilt swelling in her chest. She took the driver's seat, Peter slid in the back, and the two headed out.

They rode downhill in silence, haunted by distant voices and the steady clop of Strawberry's hooves. Squares of light shone from the houses and shops. In the twilight, Cat could see the silhouette of the church and schoolhouse where she and Peter used to learn. Part of her wanted to miss them, but a conflicted churn of emotion dulled any nostalgia to a dull ache. She drove the wagon through the town gate and along the mountain pass until Mason Forge vanished amid the crumbling boughs of the dead forest.

Darkness fell to near blackness as the two continued without speaking. Cat kept the reins loose, growing wearier and more hollow as they went. Peter sat behind her on the bench, facing away. Their backs pressed each other. Perhaps he was asleep, or deep in heavy thought; either way she couldn't blame him. The knobs of stone along his shoulder blade poked below her ribs. Cat adjusted herself but kept their backs touching to let him know she was still there.

Leafless branches arched like black veins against the star-filled sky. The last time they traveled the forest was the summer before grade school. Peter was as strong and able as any other kid, and the two of them would race through the woods, imagining fairy trees and crystal caves until their mothers called them home. There was no way to guess back then that the coming winter would teach them about death, or that the next time they sought adventure it would come at such a price.

As a child, Cat imagined God's Valley as a green field of waving grass. Peter's atlas described windmills and herds of wild horses, but that was over a century ago, and as the pass widened, Cat beheld crumbling badlands ringed in a full circle of snow-less mountains as far as the eye could see. Nothing moved, not even insects. The Valley made no sound. A dusty haze settled in the moonlight, prefaced by a carpet of long-dead shrubs and brittle grasses that barely twitched in the cold breeze. Cat stopped Strawberry on the roadside and stared for what felt like forever as reality dismantled the foundation of her secret plan.

“What's wrong?”

She jumped. “Pete, you're up.”

"Yeah, I'm up." He slouched. "Don't think I'll be sleeping much at all, to be honest."

"I can understand why." She nudged him. "Are you okay?"

"I didn't want to say it in front of Mom and Alan but... I'm scared, you know?" His arms lay heavy in his lap. "I grew up terrified of Earth Town. Kids would tease me and tell me I'd go there if I was bad or that the mayor would change his mind and I'd never see my family again. I had this vision of a huge jail house where all the Earth Curses were kept in cells with bars on the windows. It made me cry every time."

"I remember. They were jerks."

"They were kids; I was an easy target. And I know Earth Town's not like that, but it still scares me." He sighed and stared at the stars. "Today was the worst day of my life. Worse than Dad dying. It was horrible."

"Mine, too."

"Thanks for coming with me. It feels better." He paused. "Finally going to Earth Town isn't so bad with you along."

Cat pressed her lips and swung the loose end of the reins back and forth between her hands. "We aren't going to Earth Town."

Peter frowned and straightened. "What?"

"I agreed because Dad was sure it would work, but that's not where you belong."

Peter paused to think, tentatively hopeful. “Where are we going instead?”

“I don't know.” She kept her voice low. “Live off the land?”

“How? The Valley's ruined because of the drought.”

“I've still got magic.”

“Do you know a spell to make bread?”

“I can make water and fire.”

“At least our clothes will be clean.” Peter pulled a slow grin. He leaned toward her over the wooden divider, with one thick elbow propped on the wall. “Get the map out. We're not in a hurry. Let's see what's still around.”

Chapter 5

The roads of the Valley resembled a giant wheel with spokes carving straight lines from the mountains toward the Outer Bend beltway running a ring around center. The road to Mason Forge joined beltway at a place called "Cartographer's Junction," a good fifty miles in. The wagon followed side roads, past abandoned overnight stops, dead-end driveways, and fences with faded "for sale" signs on the gates. By dawn they found a small roadside town devoid of life. Cat parked in a dusty stable and checked for inhabitants, but every door and window on the main street was boarded up. The general store had a big "Moved to Castleton" sign on the front door. Cat ducked beneath it into the door to find every shelf bare.

She returned to find Peter on his feet, stretching his massive shoulders. Cat sighed. "I don't think anyone's home."

"The farms are all dead. No reason to stay."

"The store relocated, too. Did everyone go to Castleton?"

"It's the largest city." Peter shrugged. "A business needs customers and that's where all the people are."

They caught a few hours sleep and were back on the road by morning. It wasn't long before the dry heat grew unbearable. Without a cool breeze from the mountains or the shelter of trees, Cat could actually feel moisture evaporate from her skin. There were no birds or insects, and no travelers to be seen.

Two ghost towns and several hours later, Cat reached the Cartographer's Junction with a debilitating headache. A tall wooden signpost stood at the intersection with the names of a dozen towns carved on arrows pointing north and south. All but four were marked out with scratches or paint. Remaining were Mason Forge to the west, Astonage and by extension Earth Town to the north, Dire Lonato to the south and Castleton, gleaming straight ahead of them atop the Valley's only hill.

Peter looked up from his atlas. "Taking a break?"

"Yeah."

"Want me to drive?"

She pursed her lips. "Can you?"

"I'm a Curse, not an invalid."

"Okay, when you put it that way...."

Moving made her head pound, but Cat managed to disembark. She poured water for Strawberry out of the tank in back, then pulled the string off her wrist and knitted a quick water spell to refill it. "At least we won't die of thirst."

"We'll need to find other supplies somewhere, though." Peter hooked his heavy foot on the running board and levered himself into the driver's seat. "We only have enough to get us to Astonage, and we spent a lot of time zig-zagging around. Assuming the sign's correct about the rest of these towns, we might run into problems."

"Maybe we'll run into another traveler we can trade with."

"Hopefully not while I'm driving."

Cat draped the reins over his hands. He pinched the strap beneath his thumbs and settled into the padded seat. She climbed in back. "So do we go north to the sure bet or take a chance and go south to say as far away from Earth Town as possible?"

"Not going to Earth Town sounds great."

"Southbound it is."

Peter used his knees as fulcrums to give the strap a tiny flick. Strawberry snorted and plodded into the baking sun with her head drooping forward. Puffs of fine dust rose like smoke at each step.

They traveled the rest of the afternoon with no travelers or towns. The metal cart squeaked in time with the hoof beats. Cat listened to the rhythm, her eyes barely open. Exhausted by heat and emotional rawness mixed into nausea, she reclined on one of the cushioned benches and stared at the cloudless blue sky. A high wind whistled faintly. She closed her eyes and let the rock of the wagon lull her into an uneasy sleep.

Cat woke beside a field of sunflowers. At first, the intrusion of yellow and green was staggering. She sat up in the wagon, dazed and confused. A sign hung on the tall metal fence declaring it "Electrified" and "Property of Lord Creven."

A wooden signpost displayed the same town names crossed out with slashes of paint. The placard indicating Castleton pointed past the sunflowers up a road lined with fields field of fruit trees, corn stalks, vine rows, and vegetables sealed behind chest-high fence. Tarnished pipes large enough to crawl into ran along the inside edge of the barriers, spraying fine jets of sparkling water over the crops. The pipes snaked up the incline to Castleton proper.

Peter slept in a sitting position beside her, his chin folded to meet his chest. Cat tousled his hair and climbed along her bench toward the front where Strawberry dozed beside the signpost, her hair obscuring her eyes. Her supply of oats was empty. So was the tank of water. Cat eyed the irrigation pipes and stitched another water rune to quench Strawberry's thirst.

Peter's atlas lay open on the driver's seat beside her with rough pencil squiggles denoting their stops. A big “x” marked the current location at the intersection of Outer Bend and West Spoke. It was only five miles into the city, and another fifty to the nearest town. Cat glanced from her soundly sleeping friend to the towering central city and picked up the reins.

Lush fields rolled like a quilt of colors, each with its own acreage, farm house and barn. Cat noticed a farmer tilling with a horse-drawn contraption. He spotted Cat and waved. She smiled and waved back.

Morning activity was in full swing when they reached the city wall. Hundreds of people milled around the ten-foot retaining wall. Beggars and campers sat at the foot, while fruit-laden wagons queued outside the arching outer gate. Cat pulled Strawberry to a jarring stop when she saw the wealth of people. The jostle woke Peter who stretched with a pop. “What time is it?”

“Hush,” Cat reached blindly behind her and patted the side of his head. “Get under a blanket or something.”

“Do what?” He recoiled at the crowd. “Whoa!”

“I know.”

“Cat, what are we doing here?” He peeked over the partition behind the driver's seat. “I parked us at the edge.”

“I thought I could hop in and buy groceries.”

“We can't 'hop in' to a place like this.” He fretted. “There's ten thousand people here!”

“I know!”

“Someone's going to see me!”

“I know!”

“We should have waited for dark.” His voice quivered a bit. “We don't have supplies to last until dark. We could steal some – stealing's bad but better than getting caught – and getting arrested would kill me for sure.”

“So would the fences. They're electric.”

“They have power for fences, they can grow these crops... what kind of place is this?” He sat up. “Cat, behind us!”

A farmer driving an ox cart approached. Cat steered Strawberry off the road and around the corner to let the team and its heavy cargo of apple barrels pass.

The crowd massed all around them with wagons and carts. Peter found a vinyl tarp and stretched it awkwardly over his legs. "Okay." He patted the cover with a crackling sound. "This could work. Here's my plan: if you leave the wagon here you can get into the city, buy what we need, and bring it back out without anything going wrong."

"Leave you out here? By yourself?" She took another scan of the crowd. Nerves clenched her gut like a warning. "Absolutely not."

"I can hide under the tarp."

"You're not leaving my side." She tightened her grip on the reins. "Keep your head down. Let me do the talking."

He pressed his lips. "You sound so confident."

"That's what makes the difference." She shot him a smile. "You hide under that tarp, we'll hit the vendors and get out quick. No one will even notice you're here."

"I don't know, Cat. I'm pretty hard to miss."

Cat lashed the reins and joined the other wagons. Despite the size, the line advanced quickly around the paved courtyard and through a stone archway where a checkpoint station separated the crowd from the city. A drowsy man in a uniform scratched tic-marks on an official-looking clipboard. He surveyed the cart full of beets ahead of them. "Make quota?"

"Yes sir," the beet farmer answered.

“Ahead on your right. Next!"

Cat pulled forward.

The sentry noted her face and turned a page on his clipboard. “Business or pleasure?”

“Um...” Cat scooted a bit to hide Peter from view. "Business.”

“Quota?”

“No, I mean, I'm not a farmer. I'm here for supplies.”

The sentry grunted and flipped a couple more pages. “Name?”

“Catrina Aston.”

"Aston..." He scribbled it on several pages before peeling a sticker and smacking it on the wagon rail. A speech rolled, rehearsed, from his mouth without cadence or punctuation. “As newcomers to Castleton it is my duty to inform you that livestock and other large animal species are not allowed within the city limit a complimentary stable system has been provided for your convenience ask our friendly staff for more details on Lord Creven's generous refugee contracts and long-term residency enjoy your stay in Castleton.” He waved them along. “Next.”

A cold sweat broke under her collar. “Wait? A stable?”

“Ahead on your right.” He shouted louder. “Next!”

Cat urged Strawberry into the bustling city. Hundreds of buildings like staircases climbed the steep slopes along slate-paved streets. Morning colors mixed to rosy pink on the white walls above farmers shuffling payloads along a block of numbered warehouses. Staff members in buttoned overalls shuffled the wagons into various lines. A young woman dashed to Cat's wagon, noticed the sticker on the sideboard and grabbed Strawberry's bridle.

“Hey!” Cat stood, but the girl replied with a tug and the wagon rolled into the stable with Peter cowering in the back.

The building was larger than any structure in Mason Forge, full of barn sounds and the smell of manure and wet straw. Attendants in overalls swarmed the cavernous building moving vehicles and animals in and out of stalls. Several black horses with well-laden saddles were tethered along a water trough near the entrance. The girl left them in front of the office where an old man with a sun visor lowered his reading. “You here for a board?”

“Apparently.”

The stable master hoisted himself to standing position. He hobbled to Strawberry and clapped her on the neck. “’E healthy?”

“Yes, very.”

He checked Strawberry's hooves, teeth and eyes. "A'right, that's fine." He pulled a warped pad from his back pocket and readied his pen. “Short term or long.”

“Short, definitely.” Cat eyed to the black horses. “Are there Brushcasters here?”

“There's always at least one around. Need a miracle?”

“Not one of theirs, no.”

“Okay then.” He scratched across the pad. “Price is twenty up front and ten an hour after that.”

“Twenty? That's robbery.”

“Ten for the wagon and ten for the horse.” He shrugged. “Space is at a premium, miss. More people show up every day.”

She opened her satchel and thumbed through the tiny wad of paper bills. Even if she knew where the market was and back and forth at full speed, twenty was a huge chunk of her monetary supply. God forbid she try to pawn something, they might be stuck in town for hours and every cent she got would go into the stable master's hand. “Is there a cheaper option?”

“Are you a refugee?”

“I am if that means I'm broke.”

The man winked. “Refugees get special treatment around here. Free parking and storage up to twenty-four hours. Lord Creven's invested a ton in his charity land contract program.”

Cat raised her eyebrows. “Land Contract?”

“It's for farmers who had to move in from the country. They get free land, free housing, free electric, heat, and water, and a really nice fence all in exchange for working a plot of Lord Creven's land.”

“He gives all that for free? How?”

"Oh, Lord Creven's loaded. He's the last land baron in the Valley – bought everyone else out of business decades ago. Everything inside the Outer Bend belongs to him."

"And he gives it all away?"

"He could afford to hire folks, I guess, but instead pays in utilities and provides homes for people who lost everything to the drought." The man tipped his visor. "He's a modern hero, miss. Gave my brother a place to live when his homestead dried up. Our folks live out there with him, it's a real peaceful place."

"That sounds nice." Cat leaned back to stealthily poke Peter in the shoulder. "And he leaves your brother alone out there?"

"Yeah, as long as he keeps up his farming quota."

"What did he do to get a contract?"

"Just walked up there and asked!" the stableman said. "Lord Creven lives at the top of the hill; you can see his mansion from here. Walk yourself to his gate and ask for help. Once you sign a contract he'll give you some land. Bring the claim back here and I'll waive all your fees and show you where to move in."

"That's amazing," Cat said. "Okay, let's do the refugee thing."

"Sounds good to me."

She hopped down and poked Peter through the rail. "Get out."

"Are you crazy?" he hissed.

"Don't you think it's a good deal?"

“Fishy deal or not, I'm not walking through this city.”

“I can't take the wagon with me!”

“Then pretend I'm a load of gravel.”

“You're not for storage. Besides, Brushcasters are here.”

The stable master snapped his fingers and two attendants dashed toward them across the barn.

Cat gripped his wrist. “Please, Pete.”

He grimaced, but slid to the end of the wagon and planted his thick feet on the ground with a wince.

The stable master gasped. “Is that a– "

"No." Cat hurried Peter away. More wagons were headed toward the open stable door. She steered Peter right and into an alley between two buildings only to find themselves standing in a river of humanity. Aristocrats, city folk, peasant farmers, and weary travelers of all types congregated around shops and vendors. Children ran in small packs carrying bundles of school books. Somewhere deep within the city a church bell rung the hour.

Peter froze stolid. "This is bad.”

She hugged his arm across her chest. “We're none of their business."

"I should have stayed with the wagon."

“We can't go back now.” The city rose like a pinnacle behind the outer wall. Whitewashed shops and houses lined the slopes, their copper-colored rooftops gathering to a point where Lord Creven's manor perched, shining like a temple to an earthbound god.

Peter cleared his throat. “There's so many people here.”

"If we sneak, no one will notice."

“I don't like this at all.”

They stayed near the storefronts, ducking under covered awnings and darting past windows as fast as Peter could manage. He stumbled on the incline and paused often to catch both his breath and his balance. Shocked gasps echoed all around.

"Cat, they're noticing."

"Ignore them."

His arm shivered across her chest. A man and a woman with black hair and brushes appeared a block ahead. Peter stumbled backward.

“Cat look – ”

“I see them.”

“But Cat...”

She turned to find him chalk-white and trembling, beneath stripes of muddy sweat.

“Whoa!” Cat hurried him into the narrow gap between two buildings. His eyes darted and his feet shuffled. She leaned him against the wall. “Pete, calm down.”

“This was a mistake.” He shook his head. "They keep looking at me. They don't want me here."

"It's okay. Relax."

"I should have stayed with the wagon." He kept his eye on the street. "I should have – "

“I'm not leaving you alone.” Cat tugged his shirt and met his eye with unshakable determination. "You trust me, right?"

He calmed a bit. "Yeah."

“Take a deep breath. I won't let anything happen.” She wadded the hem of her sleeve and wiped a brown smear from his cheek. "Can we do this together?"

“Together?” He released a shaky breath. "Maybe.”

"I can set people on fire, you know."

He managed half a smile. "Immolation's not the answer."

“Then snarls and glares will have to do."

Their narrow alley connected to an equally narrow service road where one of the copper irrigation pipes ran parallel to the street. The two inched along the gap beside the sweating pipe and rejoined the thoroughfare at the next cross street. The Calligraphers were gone, and the side roads almost clear. Cat waited for the stragglers to clear and drew Peter out of hiding. He took one step and stopped. The stone deep in his fused wrist squirmed against her palm.

“Ah!” Cat dropped the arm and found him frozen in place, staring intently at an alley on the opposite side of the street.

A figure stood in the shadows wearing a heavy hooded cloak. Two black eyes stared daggers from beneath the hood. Cat was caught in their magnetism. Time seemed to slow as she was drawn mentally and spiritually toward the dark pupils.

The stranger blinked. Cat snapped like a rubber band from her daze. The alley where the man stood was now empty, but a chill lingered in her heart. Peter's eyes were clouded with a muddy film. He stared blankly forward, like a statue. She tugged on his arm.

“Pete? You okay?”

He wasn't breathing. She seized him, again.

“Pete!"

He inhaled with a start. “What? What is it?"

“I don't know. You scared me to death.”

“Sorry. I thought I saw something...” He trailed off again, his eyes on the empty alley.

A pair of local policemen appeared at the far end of the street. Cat strengthened her grip. “Never mind, let's go.”

Chapter 6

High-class estates covered Castleton's heights. Cat and Peter slowed their ascent but kept their guard up as they navigated the garden walls, green lawns, and thankfully empty streets. They arrived at Lord Creven's manor, winded but significantly more at ease. Peter leaned against the white-washed garden wall in utter exhaustion. "Think we're safe?"

"For now." Cat panted. "You alright?"

"Better. I've decided I don't like the big city."

Cat patted his arm. "Agreed."

A decorative gate blocked Lord Creven's manor from the street. Inside, the alabaster mansion stood elevated atop a thirty foot marble staircase. A cascade of tiered flowerbeds connected the manor to a wide, encompassing garden rich with lush grass, sculpted topiary, and hanging vines. Birds chirped in large cages and rabbits hopped about fountain where sculptures of four dancing women shot clean water toward the sky.

Cat gaped a moment. "Is this place for real?"

"It could be a joint hallucination."

"I almost hope it is." Cat gulped. "I don't know, Pete. Perhaps this was a bad idea."

"After all we've just been through, not trying would be worse."

Cat took a deep breath and jiggled the gate. "It's locked. Do you see a bell?"

"I see this." He nodded to a jeweled tassel hanging just inside.

Cat rolled her eyes. "If fairies answer, we're leaving."

The lever caused a gong to sound, stirring the birds to squawk and flap in their cages. A small door opened in the side of the massive staircase, releasing a short man in a blue waistcoat and a powdered white wig. Peter ducked out of sight, snickering in spite of himself.

The tiny doorman raised an eyebrow. "Who goes there?"

"Hello, sir." Cat folded her hands. "My name's Catrina and this is my friend, Peter."

The Curse barely peeked around the door frame. "Hi."

"We're here for an audience with generous Lord Creven."

The doorman wrinkled his nose. “The lord is dining and will not be disturbed.”

“It'll take two minutes.”

“Ma'am, he is indisposed.” the doorman said. “Lord Creven is not a service. He a very busy man. Come back tomorrow.”

“Tomorrow?” Cat grabbed the bars. “Where are we supposed to go until tomorrow?”

Peter cleared his throat and called from behind the wall. “What she means is, we're refugees.”

“Yes! That's right.” Cat sweetened her voice. “We heard at the town gate how very generous Lord Creven is to homeless people. I'd hate to think we were misled by his reputation.”

The doorman rolled his eyes and pulled a silver watch chain from his cummerbund. “I suppose I could *ask* Lord Creven if he's willing to see you.”

“Yes, yes please!” Cat urged.

The tiny man pocketed his watch and scuttled back up the drive to the staircase where he shut the service door with a slam.

Cat leaned into the gate and exhaled against the bars.

Peter slouched. “So you think he's coming back?”

“I hope he's coming back.”

“Well sure, we can hope.”

She glanced to Peter's bandaged arm. “What are we going to do when he does?”

“You go in and state our case.”

“And leave you out here?”

“I can hide.” He sucked his teeth and checked the cross streets. “Somewhere.”

Cat checked over each shoulder. Lord Creven's wall extended as far as she could see in either direction, likely capping the entire hill. The nearest mansions were behemoths of red brick and wooden siding, each with a ten-foot wall of their own. “No alleys up here.”

“At least there's no traffic.”

A slam signaled the return of the doorman. Cat met him at the gate. “Well?”

“You're lucky, miss.” The doorman produced a gold key and inserted it into the back of a lion-shaped lock in the center of the gate. He pulled it open and bowed. “If you and your friend would please follow me.”

“Er...” Cat glanced to Peter. He backed away, shaking his head.

The doorman cleared his throat. “Miss?”

“My... uh... my friend had to go.”

“Go?”

The Earth Curse crossed his thick wrists over his stomach and pretended to gag.

“He got sick,” Cat muttered. “Heights.”

The doorman raised an eyebrow but didn't question. He allowed Cat to enter and locked the gate behind her. “This way.”

Cat lingered at the entrance as the doorman marched up the gravel walk. The wall seemed taller knowing Peter was alone on the other side. She ran a finger under her string, heart beating like the feathers of the birds against their cages. “Pete?”

He peeked around the corner. “Yeah?”

“Be careful.”

“Be quick.”

She gulped and nodded. He vanished again and she trotted after the doorman, full of sudden regret. They rounded the sculpture fountain and ascended the towering staircase. Cat zig-zagged up the flights, legs sore from her climb through the city and struggling to keep pace. Above her, the mansion's grand entrance gleamed in the harsh desert sunlight. White columns crowned with female imagery supported a capstone of gold and bronze. She stopped at the top and looked out over the city. The cascade of buildings spread into a colorful patchwork of farmland and out into brown, shapeless desert. She noted the Outer Bend littered with the dark patches of townships she and Peter passed through the day before. The pass into Mason Forge was hidden among the Western Mountains. They'd come so far, but still looked so small. The doorman cleared his throat again and ushered her inside.

Ten-foot oaken doors led to a cavernous reception area lit by high windows and draped with tapestries. Servants moved about the second floor balcony in blue uniforms and powdered wigs. She continued left off the main foyer, down a hall filled with portraits of dead Crevens all wearing the same pout.

“I'll announce you,” the doorman directed. “Freshen up.”

There was hardly time to ruffle dust from her bangs before the double doors opened, revealing a luxurious dining hall hung with chandeliers and lined with servants. The portly Lord Creven and his willowy wife sat at the far end of long table, surrounded by more food and spirits than Cat had ever seen in one place.

Lord Creven gestured heartily. “Please, my dear, join us!”

A footman drew Cat a chair at Lord Creven's right. She walked the length of the hallway and sat across from the lady, perched in her chair like a buzzard. The sallow woman's eyes blazed menacingly over the remains of a well-carved turkey.

“My my, you're younger than my servant implied,” the Lord said. “We don't often have pretty girls for lunch guests, do we Orella?” Lady Creven slid him a glare. He ignored her and poured Cat a tall glass of wine. “Miss Catrina wasn't it? Tell us your story.”

“Well,” Cat ran her finger under her string. "I'm from a town called Mason Forge – ”

“Roll?” The Lord held a basket of bread. Cat lifted a bun with two fingers and set it on her plate. His eye followed it to its resting place, lingering uncomfortably at chest level as he placed the dish before his wife. “You were saying?”

“I, uh... I'm a refugee from Mason Forge – ”

“I'm told you're here about a land contract.”

“Yes,” Cat said. “Yes, I want a contract.”

“Ah good! Always room for more workers!” Lord Creven gulped some wine and wiped his mouth with the silk napkin in his lap. “How old are you, my dear?”

“Excuse me?”

“Well, you can't expect me to enter a business deal with a minor. You couldn't be a day over sixteen, could you?”

Cat fidgeted. “Sixteen and a half.”

“Ah! I knew it!” Lord Creven congratulated himself with more wine. “Fresh out of school, huh? Anxious to get out of the house? I believe we can come to some arrangement.” He planted the glass triumphantly on the table and leaned a little closer. “Don't worry, I never ask for money up front; just a signature and ninety percent of your yield in exchange for all your necessities. How's that sound?”

“It sounds – ”

“Of course it does!” He tore the leg off the turkey. “So do you have any experience? Any special talents or tools?"

Cat thumbed her string. "I'm pretty capable."

“I wouldn't want to worry about you out there,” Lord Creven grinned. "A teenage girl living and working alone..."

"I won't be alone."

"No?" His grin broadened. "Now I'm even more interested."

"I'll be living with my friend. A man. A big, strong, man." Cat regretted the words immediately. "Solid. Very solid."

"He sounds like a brute," Lord Creven said. "We'll have to find something to keep him occupied."

"No, he'll be in the house," Cat said. "With me. All the time."

The Lord searched his wife's face a moment. She passed him a scathing look. He lost his smile. "You're lying."

"I – what?" Cat stammered. "No, I'm totally honest."

"I have little patience for liars, Miss Aston, and I'm too good a businessman than to sign a contract with a cheat. I suggest you change your tune right now."

Cat gulped.

"Tell the truth or any chance of our deal is off."

“The truth..." Cat grimaced. Lady Creven was staring straight through her. "The truth is... my friend is not real. I lied.”

The lord leaned forward. “And?”

"And..." The string itched around her wrist. "I know some self-defense tricks."

Lord Creven frowned. "Tricks?"

"Secret...mountain... things." Her heart raced. "Like making fire and using the wind and water and... stuff."

The lady's thin eyebrows arched. "You can use the elements?"

"Well uh..."

"Are you implying magic?"

Cat paled but Lord Creven heaved a hearty laugh. "That's rich! Orella, when'd a sense of humor sprout in you?" He dabbed his eyes. "Magic... you're hardly stiff enough to be a Calligrapher, Miss Aston."

"No," she stammered. "I didn't mean– "

"Don't be modest, girl!" Lord Creven grinned. "You're some kind of performer!"

"Yes!" She nearly cheered. "You guessed it; I'm a performer. I came from a circus. I can juggle and cartwheel and spit fire – all sorts of crazy things."

"You'll have to give us a show, then!"

Cat folded her hands. "First let's talk about the contract. I was hoping for a field far outside the city... like on the very edge where everything's super peaceful and no one will bother me. Ever."

“I'm sure we can find something like that.” He clapped the table. “You know, I've got an apple grove all ready to plant. That sound alright?”

“Oh yes, sir! I love trees.”

Lady Creven's hooded eyes studied Cat over the table. "You're not a performer. That's not what you meant.”

Her husband turned. “I'm sorry?”

“You know magic.” The lady's face tightened. “Actual magic.”

“Orella, don't be foolish, only monks cast real magic."

"And your friend,” the lady persisted. “He's real too. You're trying to hide him. Could he be... is he a Curse?”

“What? No!” Cat fumbled. “I mean, what are you saying? No one'd bring a Curse here, that'd be insane!”

Lord Creven rounded on her. "You brought a Curse to my mansion?"

"No, I – "

"You said you were from the mountains,” Lady Creven said. “Were you were born there?”

"No! I mean yes, but what does that have to do with – "

"Orella!" Lord Creven toppled his wine glass, staining a red gash across the lady's silken dress. “Enough! Get out of my sight!”

Lady Creven spun to retort, but he raised his hand to strike. She gathered her skirts and escaped the room as fast as she could.

Lord Creven rounded on Cat with his plump face twitching in purple rage. “You little liar! You dare bring a Curse around here? Take your fake magic and your walking sin and get out of my town!”

“But sir!”

"Security!" he shouted. The blue-coated servants scrambled through the dining hall. “I want her out and the gate locked behind!”

"No, wait! Listen to me!" The guards grabbed her under the arms. "This isn't fair!"

She shouted all the way down the hall, out the main door, down the steps, and back to the entrance. Peter appeared in time to catch her on the other side of the golden gate. “Cat!”

She sprang from him and grabbed the bars. “You can't get rid of me like this. Let me back in! I said let me in!”

“Cat, stop!” Peter scooped a thick arm under her ribs and swept her back behind the wall.

She fought against the weight, then noticed what held her and focused on his face. “Pete?”

“Hi.” He released her. "What happened?"

"They threw me out!”

“Yeah, that part I saw.”

She clenched and unclenched her fists with stress-fueled tears in her eyes. “He wouldn't let me talk! I keep trying to explain. And his wife! They just..." Peter's massive shoulders sagged. A sharp pang of guilt replaced her rage. "Oh, Pete, I'm sorry... I failed completely."

“It's okay. It was a long shot.”

“We'll think of something else.”

Cat jumped as the golden gate rattled behind them. An attendant in blue cowered on the other side. “Are you Catrina from the mountains?”

She took Peter's arm. “That's me.”

“My name is Kaleb.” He unlocked the gate. “Follow me.”

“Both of us?”

Kaleb licked his lips and nodded. “Quick, before you're seen.”

Chapter 7

Cat and Peter followed the young attendant through the lush garden to the service door under the stairs. Kaleb shot fevered glances to the gate and the stairs. “Stay close to me. Don't make a sound.”

Cat tensed. “I don't understand.”

“Shh!” He checked the hallway beyond the door and beckoned Cat and Peter inside. They followed through a network of branching corridors past offices, servant quarters, and storage rooms. Kaleb advanced them one block of doors at a time, taking care not to be seen. They dodged left and right to avoid other servants in wigs and tail-coats. They passed another servant with natural hair, like Kaleb, who bowed to them and rushed ahead to make the path clear.

A half-dozen turns and close calls later, they arrived at a dead-end hallway with a single padlocked door at the end. Kaleb opened his powder blue coat and removed a small key. “This way, your honor.”

Cat's eyebrows arched. “Your honor?”

He blushed and held the door. “Please wait inside.”

Cat and Peter exchanged a glance and did as they were told. The room beyond the padlocked door was dramatically different than the hallway that led to it. A set of double doors with heavy iron knockers waited at the far end of an arching stone antechamber. Sconces designed for torches held electric lamps trailing wires. Hairs rose on Cat's arms as the temperature dropped ten degrees. The gloom darkened further when the attendant closed the hallway door, trapping her and Peter inside.

Cat hugged her arms close. "This might have been a mistake."

“I don't like this place.” Peter shuddered. “It feels strange.”

A heavy clack echoed off the stones and the double doors swung toward them. Waiting on the other side was the skeletal silhouette of Lady Creven, wearing a black lace dress and a veil before her sunken eyes.

"Miss Catrina from the mountains?"

"Yes.”

“I am Lady Orella Creven.”

“Yes, I know.”

“And this must be your friend.” Lady Creven removed her hat and pressed it to her heart. “You poor burdened creature. You really are a Curse."

Cat wedged between them. "What exactly do you want?"

The lady resumed a professional air. “I apologize for the scene upstairs, Miss Catrina. I doubt the interview with my husband went as you planned. The lord knows how to take and build power, but he is a fool. I know an opportunity when I see it. Please follow me inside.”

They entered a cavernous library lit with warm, welcoming light. Shelves full of leather cases lined the walls. The volumes were shallow and tall, like the one the Holy Elder brought with him to Mason Forge. The hundreds of spines were marked with dates and names in fine silver leaf. The lady lifted a candle from a desk in the center of the room. “Do you know where you are, Miss Catrina?”

She shook her head.

“This library holds a copy of every scripture written by the Prophets.”

Peter gasped. “These are the laws?”

“Not all are laws. Most are correspondence between the Prophets and the people. Some predict the future. Very few are direct commands from Our God. Those scriptures are reserved for the Calligraphers' highest library."

"This is a Brushcaster library?" Peter gaped. "Have you read it? How did you get copies? Do the Brushcasters know it's here?"

"Calm yourself, please," the lady bade. "Emotion makes your condition worse."

Cat bristled. "Answer the question."

"Yes, the Calligraphers know it is here. The library is an heirloom of my husband's family. And no, they do not know I have read it." She lifted the candle, casting light onto the many spines. "Twenty years ago, I was a naive young bride, curious about my new riches. The servants told me about the Holy Elder's secret visits, one night I followed he and my husband to this archive. It didn't take long for the servants to procure me a key to copy. Inside, I found the truth of my husband's concealed but significant ancestry, but these scriptures were the greater discovery. I stole away every chance I could get and devoured every scroll. Then I found this..."

She pulled a case from the the bottom corner of the most distant shelf. The spine read "Malachi" in gold letters.

"This is the last document written by the last Prophet. It's part of the Calligraphers' highest library, intended for the Holy Elder's eyes only." The lady extended the case to Cat. "You should read it."

"Why me?"

"You'll understand when you do."

The case was deceptively heavy. Inside, a parchment scroll lay on a bed of white silk. Cat untied the ribbon and read the words aloud:

"I, Malachi, God's chosen, write this letter with words he revealed to me."

Her voice caught on a lump in her throat. Peter leaned over her shoulder and she continued.

"Our God, my friend whom I respect and love, shared a fearsome vision with me today. Words cannot convey the urgency I hear in his voice. I will relay the message as accurately as I can.

"Some day soon, he said, man will betray him. Humanity will steal the magic of nature from our God. God despairs, for there is no greater punishment than to give humanity what it wants. The moment magic is stolen, he will remove himself from his valley, and mankind will be left with power over nature, and the consequences that result.

"The theft will give mankind magic but rob the land of all life, both plant and animal. The sacrifice of the Prophets will fall on the sinner's children and grandchildren. All the world will bear this burden, but our God assures us there is hope.

"When the blood of the sinner is spent, a new Prophet will rise. This is my vision:

"A youth – born of sinners and friend of the cursed – will come to God's Valley from the mountains. This stranger will return to

the place magic was stolen and offer a settlement of life and magic incarnate. This sacrifice will absolve the peoples' guilt, and return magic to it's rightful place."

A gap of two lines broke the passage in half. When the words resumed, they were smeared by Malachi's shaking hand.

"I can feel God's voice trembling in my heart and in my mind. When I dream, I see visions, but the facts are purposefully concealed. I'm terribly afraid. God is shielding something from me. He's never done that before. He asked me to send this letter as a warning to everyone. He's worried for us, yet the promise of this future reconciliation gives me reason to hope.

"Our God, as always, sends peace and great love. Hold tight to these, my brothers, for they are my words as well. In faith, your humble servant, Malachi."

Cat lowered the scroll, heart pounding, although she wasn't sure why. "Is this real?"

"Terribly real," Lady Creven answered. "Malachi was murdered a week after writing this letter. That was the crime Our God mentioned to him – his own death."

Lady Creven drew a chair and sat at the desk. "You see, being a Prophet is not a job, like being a Calligrapher or a lord. It is a physical merger of magic and man. Each Prophet was born with the names of the four elements stained into their skin. These marks were always to be hidden – they gave the Prophet a direct connection to Our God. With them, they could use his powers, hear his voice – some said they could see his face. The symbols are the same runes the Calligraphers use in their casting circles. When the murderer killed Malachi, he copied the symbols for himself.

"Malachi's death sent nature into an uproar. Geological records report violent earthquakes from one mountain range to the other. A wide chasm sliced deep into the earth a hundred feet below this room. I have been there. It's full of magic... and anger." Lady Creven shuddered. "My husband is descended from the original thief who used his new-found magic to cover the evidence of his crime with the same hill we now live on. My husband uses the magic of the rift to power Castleton – that is how he became so wealthy. He creates water, wind, earth, and fire to fuel homes and water crops. He feeds off God's Valley like a leech, not caring about the consequences. Meanwhile the Valley has shriveled. He's likely the reason your friend was born as he was."

Cat frowned. "He's making Curses?"

"The Curses are visible evidence of magic's use," Lady Creven replied. "Evidence of sin, as they say. The Curses are what happens when mortals play god. Those who use magic today were not marked like the Prophets were, therefore the marking happens elsewhere and in terrible, terrible ways." She glanced to Peter's swollen limbs. "I am so very sorry."

"But... I use magic." Bile gurgled in Cat's chest. "If any spell makes Curses, then since I was six years old I have..."

"Not you," the lady said. "If I'm right, that shouldn't matter."

"What do you mean?"

"Once I realized what the Crevens were responsible for, I began searching for the new Prophet Malachi mentioned. I've hunted for candidates almost twenty years. There were many tries."

Cat sucked her lip. "And?"

"I interviewed travelers, scholars, and monks – even some of my own servants. A couple tried to attempt the sacrifice, but were killed in the process or on the journey."

"Killed?" Peter asked. "By Brushcasters?'

Her face tightened. "By those who would rather magic stayed where it was."

The sick feeling returned with a vengeance. A wave of cold sweat dampened Cat's collar. "You sent people to their deaths?"

"Not me alone. The sacrifice has been attempted five times over the recent centuries, but hundreds have died in this pursuit – not to mention the children who were born as Curses in the time that elapsed." Lady Creven's sunken eyes widened as they met Cat's across the table. "Every candidate I've approached fit Malachi's descriptions to a 'T,' but you... you came down from the mountains. You can use magic... and you have an Earth Curse."

"Whoa, hold on." Cat backed away. "I am *not* a Prophet."

"You fit the descriptions."

"I'm not marked with the element symbols."

"Then how did you learn them?"

"I don't know. On accident?" Her hands shook. She raked them through her bangs. "I was a kid. I was playing."

"And in your innocence, you mastered something the Calligraphers study their whole lives to possess." Lady Creven narrowed her eyes. "The symbols were in you. Perhaps your skin didn't hold them but they existed in your mind. That's not an accident, Miss Catrina. "

"But it was, though."

"What are the odds of such a thing?"

Peter shifted his weight. "Lady Creven makes a good point."

Cat wheeled on him. "You're on *her* side?"

"Cat, you were six." The Curse pressed his lips in apology. "I mean, how could you know magic when you barely knew what a Brushcaster was?"

"How? You saw! You were there!"

“Yes I was.” He frowned. “We were playing the Child's Cradle game on your back step when, on your turn, you twisted a bunch of knots and set the yard on fire. Would you call that normal?”

“I never said it was normal.”

“Well it wasn't luck!” Peter cried. “Within weeks you were making water the same way, and after that you were making wind. We filled the whole bathtub full of gravel by the time your dad found out. You taught yourself four super complex symbols in less than a year without any instruction at all.”

“I was just twisting string.”

“And even that,” Peter said. “Brushcasters don't use string, as far as I know no one's ever used string for magic. You did that by yourself, too.”

“Peter, seriously.”

“It's a sign,” Lady Creven interrupted. “If you are the new Prophet, that means you can offer the sacrifice Malachi described and end our punishment.”

“Whoa whoa whoa whoa.” Cat backed away from them. “I haven't agreed to do anything.”

“Catrina.” The lady sounded grave. “Don't forget what we would gain. No magic. No Curses. No Holy Order of False Prophets using power to frighten and control. Wicked people like my husband will be defeated and life – life itself – will come back to the Valley.”

"Will Peter get fixed?" Cat asked in challenge. "Will life coming back fix him?"

The lady blanched. "Curses are being transformed by magic. I assume giving magic back would make it stop."

"But would it fix him?"

"I..." The lady hung her head. "I don't know how it could. The transformation isn't an addition of matter, it's a changing the flesh into whatever element the Curse is. If magic stops the stone would remain, or if it did vanish, what little that was left wouldn't be –"

"Then there you go." Cat grunted. "Getting God back to the Valley sounds great, but nowhere in that scripture does it say it's my job. I came here to look after Peter; that's my purpose, and my final answer."

"Would you really be so selfish?" Lady Creven asked. "To choose one person over the world?"

"Suppose she says yes," Peter interrupted. "What kind of sacrifice will it take?"

"Life and magic incarnate," the lady replied. "The living elements."

His brown eyes flashed. "You're talking about Curses."

"I believe so."

"Curses?" Cat squeaked. "*Curses* are the sacrifice?"

“The Prophet was a combination of magic and flesh. Each Curse is one element combined the same way. There is no medical reason why these people should survive, but modern research proves the Curse symptoms germinate in the blood. The veins and arteries carry the cancer to the whole body, transforming the soft tissues into whatever element the Curse is. Areas with more blood flow are affected first – internal organs, hands, and feet – and injury or excitement make the symptoms worse. Science has no explanation for what keeps these people alive, proving that it is magic that both gives the Curse life and turns them into what they are.”

Peter's brow furrowed. “And that's why you think spilling Curse blood fills the requirement Malachi spoke of.”

“Don't sound so professional about it,” Cat snapped.

“I'm trying to understand.”

“Don't bother, it's ridiculous,” she said. “This was written five hundred years ago, before Curses even existed.”

“The scripture was a vision from Our God!” Lady Creven exclaimed.

“Yeah, well, God's gone,” Cat said. “God's not here. Curses aren't human sins. I'm not anyone's savior, and I'm absolutely not killing anybody.”

“It's a sacrifice, not a slaughter,” the lady replied. “They will die, that's true, but it's their choice, not yours. They are willing and you'll lead them.”

“Nope, sorry, I won't.” Cat took Peter's elbow. “Let's go.”

He resisted. “Hold on.”

“Pete, let's go.”

“Cat, let me think!” He stepped away with a rattling breath. "If you really are the right fit for this mission, and Lady Creven's right about the Curses, then that means I can help you."

“No.”

“I'll be the Earth element. My blood can save the world.”

“No you won't and no it can't!”

“It might as well. What other purpose do I have?”

“To *live*, Pete!” she shouted in tears. “We came here so I could save you!”

“You can't keep me from dying, Cat.”

“Don't!” she cried. “We're not talking about this!”

“We never talk about it!” He snapped. “Deny it all you want, I'm seventeen. I have less than a year to live. If I don't fall and break to pieces by then, the stone will grow through my organs and I'll be crushed by my own bones. No matter what happens, it's got to be better than that.”

“Stop.”

“You can't pretend anymore.” He paused to calm the tremor in his voice. “I know I get around pretty well – I try not to complain – but wrapping bandages on my arms and legs aren't a cure.” Tears stood muddy in his eyes. “It hurts.”

Cat's anger faltered. Peter took a step toward her.

“It aches, Cat. My whole body. It hurts to stand, to sit, to breathe... even gravity hurts. Everything's so heavy.” He looked away. “I know you're scared. We didn't come here to risk our lives, but think about what we could gain. If succeeding makes the world better for you and Mom and Alan, I don't mind ending my life a little early. Even if it doesn't, I'm willing to try.”

Cat shook her head. “You were always the noble one, but I can't let you die for this world that hates you. The scripture needs a Brushcaster or a scholar or something – someone who knows what they're doing. I came here for your sake. We were supposed to have more time...”

Lady Creven bowed her head. "I'll give you some time to think. My attendant will in the annex; send him to me when you decide.” She swept her dress in a curtsy. “Good day, your honor.”

The door latched and Cat dropped into Lady Creven's abandoned chair. “Why has this happened to us?”

“I don't know if there is a reason, unless that reason is you're a Prophet.”

“I don't feel like a Prophet.”

“I admit you're not what comes to mind with the title, but maybe that's a good thing.” Peter leaned on the desk beside her. “I'd rather people follow your example than the Brushcasters.”

“Oh please.”

“Think about it. What if this *was* part of God's plan? Everything that's happened; you finding the symbols, us being run out of town, even me being an Earth Curse suddenly makes perfect sense.”

"I'm not here to be a hero, Pete. I came to keep you safe... to keep you *alive*.”

"I know.” He slouched. “It's always the same. I've always been the burden. You'd still be in Mason Forge if it wasn't for me.”

"This isn't your fault."

“Maybe not, but if this wasn't according to a plan, then it was all my bad luck.” He studied the nearby shelf for a moment. “If we stay here, I'll only get worse. The Curse will progress until I'm a paralyzed, deformed, lump of stone lying in bed with you feeding and changing me." He shuddered. "Waiting to die."

She felt ill. He shifted to face her.

"If we say yes, I die a full person. Even if Lady Creven's wrong, at least I tried to make a difference. The future is going to be full of Cat and Peters – kids growing up sick and families having to lose them. We'll break the cycle. I hate seeing you upset because of me. This is my chance to take care of you, and if we succeed, I save everybody." The sincerity in his voice was more convincing than the words. Candlelight flickered in his glasses. “I know it's a risk. The odds are against us, but we've dodged odds before. We've come this far without getting arrested.”

She 'hmph'ed.

“Let's call it an adventure, like when we were kids. Except this time we'll actually go places and see the things written on all the maps. And at the end, when it's over, you'll save the world, and me..." He paused. "I'll finally stop worrying about you."

Cat breathed in deep and exhaled a sigh. "I'm scared.”

“I know.”

“It feels awful.”

“But it's worth it.” He waited for her to make eye contact. “Cat, this is how I want to die.”

They stared at each other as Cat fought to still the trembling in her chest. “Okay.” The word released the dam holding tension and doubt in her heart. She laced her arms around his elbow. “At least we can try.”

Chapter 8

Lady Creven wrung her hands. “We don't have much time. The world suffers more every day. Every minute counts. Here.” She pressed an envelope into Cat's hand. “Some of my husband's blood money paid back.”

“Thank you.”

“And this.” She handed Cat the leather case with Malachi's letter inside. “Take it with you. Perhaps it will help you find volunteers.”

“We'll need all the help we can get.”

The lady's attendant, Kaleb, appeared in street clothes with his brown ponytail tucked in a cap. He bowed to Cat. “I'll escort you out of the city, your honor.”

“Don't call me that.”

“Sorry,” he stammered. “Ma'am?”

“'Your honor' is appropriate for a Prophet.” Lady Creven pursed her lips. “You are a Prophet, are you not, Miss Catrina?”

“I'm not sure.” Cat tucked Malachi's scripture in her pocket and took Peter's hand. “But my friends have faith in me, and that's enough for a start.”

The lady bowed her head a moment and spoke again. “I won't lie to you. The road will be difficult; once you leave, you won't be able to contact me, and you can't use my name in the cities you pass. My husband owns most of God's Valley, including its leaders. Neither he nor the Calligraphers can find out your purpose. If their power is threatened, they'll strike with all they've got.”

“We'll be careful.”

The lady studied them, her face taut. “I will watch for your return. Peace and great love to you both.”

“You, too, Lady Creven,” Peter said. “Thanks for trusting us with this.”

The halls were empty as Kaleb led Cat and Peter out of the mountain. They exited the door under the stairs into cold night air and kept close to the wall as they traversed the sleeping garden to a loading area in the back of the house. Waist-coated attendants stood watch over wagons full of cargo. Kaleb signaled to the nearest guard and directed Cat and Peter to an unassuming horse and buggy piled with unmarked boxes.

Kaleb held the door for them. “Is there anything you need before you leave?”

“Yes. Here.” Cat pulled Strawberry's claim ticket out of her pocket. “All our things are there.”

“As you wish.”

The buggy was a tight fit for Peter. Cat wedged in beside him and watched the mansions pass through a tiny oval window. The world looked different after reading the scriptures. Each home and business ran on stolen magic, from the manicured lawns to the streetlamps and plumbing. How many Curses were born to light the windows? Or heat and cool the buildings? Or grow all the crops? Was the humble family home at the last cross street lit by Wind Curses or by Water Curses, and how much money in utility bills was Lord Creven charging on top of it?

The road leveled out in the warehouse district where the last of the farmhands unloaded their carts. They rolled past the free stable to the guardhouse where the same guard from the morning stood sleepily with his clipboard.

“Name?”

“It's me.” Kaleb disembarked. He whispered something and the guard replied in anxious tones. Kaleb appeared at Cat's window. “The gatekeeper is going to watch you until I get back. He and the other keepers are part of Lady Creven's network. You can trust them.”

“Okay.”

“Please wait here.”

The city around the buggy grew still. Cat felt small and vulnerable wedged next to Peter. He cleared his throat.

“Are you okay?”

“I'm fine.”

“You don't sound fine.”

Cat sighed. “I'm overwhelmed.”

“The whole Prophet thing?”

She dropped her head against the window pane. “It doesn't feel real. One day I'm a nobody in a no name town, then suddenly I'm everyone's savior with the fate of the world on my shoulders.”

“There's no 'suddenly' about it,” Peter said. “You've always been a Prophet. It's like me being a Curse. I was born with the illness, but it took a swollen ankle in first grade for anyone to notice. Just because you found out today, doesn't change who you were all along.”

“I find that hard to believe.”

"Malachi didn't," he said. "God foretold your coming five hundred years ago."

"It's more than that." Tears welled despite resistance. "I can't deal with you dying, Pete. I hate that it's true, and that it's not fair, and I can't stop it." She wiped her nose on her her sleeve. "I don't want to be a Prophet because I don't want to be the one to cause it."

He shifted against her. The protrusions deep in his arm poked into her shoulder. "Do you remember the day I was diagnosed?"

A knot tightened in her throat.

"We were six. Mrs. Smith announced what I was to the whole class and all the kids avoided me except for you. Mom couldn't look at me without crying, but I was okay because you were there to hold my hand or talk to me at night through our bedroom windows. You've saved my life a hundred times... that's not even counting this week with the Brushcasters. My life is so much better because of you."

"That doesn't make me special." She bit her lip to keep it from trembling. "You're my friend. I wanted to."

"A friend, yeah, but it takes a hero to give up everything they have for someone else. You've always been like that – you were made that way." He smiled. "I'm lucky to have you."

Her heart swelled warm in a chest tight from suppressing emotion. She met his gaze and wiped her eyes. "Likewise."

Kaleb returned with Strawberry and their wagon in tow. He signaled for them to get out and held the horse while Peter slid in the back and Cat climbed into the driver's seat. She took the reins and spoke to Peter. “So, where first?”

“Fire Town is at the end of this road,” he replied. “We might as well start there.”

“Fire Town it is, then.”

“Wait, your honor.” Kaleb wrung his hands. “I mean Miss Catrina. Um, I don't want to impose but....” He licked his dry lips and averted his eyes. “When you get to Fire Town, if you happen upon a boy named Kory could you tell him I said 'hi'?”

Cat watched him fidget. “Is Kory your brother?”

He nodded.

She softened with a more genuine smile. “Okay, Kaleb, we'll tell him.”

“Thank you, your honor.”

She said goodbye with a nod, gave Strawberry a flick and steered the wagon westward into the starlit desert.

They drove all night, past patchwork fields and darkened homesteads with Castleton at their back. The scripture case poked Cat's leg through her skirt pocket.

They traded drivers at dawn. Farmers moved on the West Spoke behind them, but no travelers crossed the desert beyond the

Outer Bend. Cat laid on her back and watched morning spread in pinks from the distant mountains. Kaleb transferred the supply boxes from the buggy to the back. Cat snacked on jerky, grateful for a sense of safety and a chance to process a mind full of prophets and sacrifices.

She read the scripture over and over, and noticed new details each time; the fact that Malachi could hear God's voice tremble, the way the pen quivered when he wrote of his own fear. Her heart clenched. Such a sincere young man murdered for magic – the power didn't seem worth it, yet the Calligraphers let the world die to keep it for themselves. She was glad God kept the truth from him; at least he died with hope. His letters enlarged when he mentioned the new Prophet, and her sadness turned to butterflies. Cat put the scroll back in its box and wove string instead.

She moved through her collection of patterns and shapes; each held a memory of simpler times. Her mother taught her the Cup and Saucer when she was four. The Striped Star was the first one she invented herself. She knitted broomsticks and animals and three different diamonds until she found herself holding first stage of the Child's Cradle.

Peter noticed the pattern over his shoulder and grinned. "Not while I'm driving."

She smirked back. "I was thinking of home."

He glanced north along the Western Mountains. "I feel like we've been away forever."

"A lot has happened."

"I hope Mom and Alan are okay."

"We could always swing by?"

"No." He slouched. "Not after all that."

"We can prove the Brushcasters were wrong. We have the evidence right here. If we go back, they'll have to listen."

"Would that do any good?"

"It would clear your name." She raised an eyebrow. "Don't you want justice? At least you can say goodbye."

"I already said my goodbyes." He swallowed hard. "You can tell them about it when we've fixed everything."

They traded drivers three times along the West Spoke and once more when the road branched left toward the city of Dire Lonato. Cat perched in back and kept a look out for pursuers in black. The Calligraphers didn't know about their mission, but that didn't mean they weren't around.

The flatland changed from cracked earth to rolling foothills covered in brittle grass. Broken fences and long-abandoned farmsteads lined the rocky path as the setting sun cast the mountains' shadow like teeth across the land. Cat started to doze when Peter leaned over. "Hey."

“What?”

“Look.”

Two tiny figures occupied the road ahead of them – a hunched older woman and a young girl under ten. Cat narrowed her eyes. “Why are they walking?”

“The little girl is a Curse."

The girl wore a tattered dress covered in black patches and stains. A dull glow peeked through her mattes of dark hair and along the edges of the stiff bandages clinging to her inflamed skin. She walked on the outsides of her bandaged feet with an obvious limp.

Cat cleared her throat as the wagon approached. "Excuse me?"

The hikers ignored her.

Cat cleared her throat more loudly. “Hello?”

The girl twisted over one shoulder to peer through her stringy hair. Her face was rosy, with swelling around her mouth and eyes. She spotted Peter's bandages and gasped. “Mommy, look!”

Her mother tightened her grip on the child's hand. “Ignore them, honey.”

“But that's an Earth Curse!”

The mother peeked over her shoulder and reeled. “What in heaven is that?”

“Calm down, ma'am,” Cat said. “We don't want to hurt you.”

"That's a Curse!" The woman pointed. "You have a full-grown Curse in your wagon!"

"Yeah, Peter's a Curse like your daughter is."

"He is *not* like my daughter." The woman yanked the child behind her back. "Keep away from us."

"We're trying to help –"

"You're a sinner!"

Cat fought to remain pleasant. "We're travelers going the same direction you are, who thought you'd appreciate a ride."

"I don't want a thing from you!" the woman spat. "I'm taking my daughter to Fire Town."

"I guessed as much."

"You won't stop me!"

"I'm not trying to."

"A likely story!"

The girl tugged the woman's apron with pleading brown eyes. "Mommy, please?"

"No."

"My feet hurt."

"We can't stop."

"How about we share camp?" Cat interrupted. "It's dark. You need to rest. Share our food and our fire. You can even sleep in our wagon – it has cushions."

The girl's eyes shone. "Mommy, please?"

"No!" The woman ground her teeth, speaking more to herself than anyone else. "I am doing my duty. My daughter is sin incarnate. I'm taking her to Fire Town. I'm being faithful."

Cat climbed from the wagon. "I know you are – "

"Leave me alone!" She hurried away. The young Fire Curse was tugged after, but tripped on her bandage. She fell with a cry. Her mother dragged her up.

"Are those tears? Do you want to die?"

"... No."

"Then stop it right now!"

"Stop it!" Cat pulled the girl free of her mother's grip and tucked her behind her back. The mother clawed the air where the child once was, her mouth opening and closing like a fish.

"Are you okay?" Cat asked.

The girl trembled, cradling her arm. Bright streaks of red cracked along the sides of her face, and the corners of her eyes burned like small embers as she did her best to fight tears.

"Give my daughter back." The woman stammered. "She's my burden. She's mine."

"She's still a child."

The woman raked her nails down her face. "Give her back."

"You have to let her rest."

“She's mine.”

“I'm not trying to take your daughter away. You were hurting her.” Cat heaved a frustrated sigh. “I think you both need some sleep. Share camp with us. Some food and a fire, and I bet everyone will feel a lot better.”

“Sleep?”

“Yes, sleep.”

“Another night.” A war of emotion played across the woman's dirty face. She tugged her hair. “One night. One more night.”

“Yes, ma'am, one more night.”

“We will stay one night.”

The little girl smiled, her face aglow with faint subcutaneous light. “Thanks, Mommy!” She hurried onto the padded wagon seat and straight beneath a blanket.

Cat looked the woman in the eye. “Thank you for agreeing. We really are trying to help.”

“You're a sinner,” the woman seethed. “My daughter is sin incarnate; I'm not supposed to take pity.”

“The Brushcasters told you that.”

“The Holy Calligraphers are messengers! They read the words of the Prophets.”

“They manipulated them.”

“Blasphemy.”

“Our God doesn't want to destroy families,” Cat said. “I've read the Prophets, too. Your sin has nothing to do with whether or not your daughter is a Curse and mothers are supposed to love their children.”

“Do you have any idea what I've been through?” the woman yelled. “I didn't ask for this task! I'm faithful and obedient like the Callgraphers ask. I want Our God to come back. If you cared about other people, you'd do the same!”

“I'm not the one being selfish here!”

The woman pointed at Peter. “Yes, you are!”

Cat's face flushed. “Leave him out of this.”

“You disobeyed the law,”

“Shut up.”

“You're killing the whole world.”

“Shut up!” Cat shouted.

The Fire Curse flinched with a peep. Cracks burned in the creases of her fingers as she tugged the blanket over her head.

Cat fixed the woman with a critical stare. “I want you two to stay for your own sake, but don't say another word against Peter. He's none of your business.”

“And Edana's none of yours.”

“Fine.”

They broke to make camp. Cat started a small fire and laid more blankets out for their guests. Peter got Strawberry food and loosened her harness for the night. He was stiffer than normal, his face steely and his eyes narrowed beneath a deep, heavy brow. His gloved hands pinched at the buckles of Strawberry's harness, but the task was painstaking and his arms shook with the effort. He ground his teeth as the buckle slipped from his grasp.

Cat put a hand on his wrist. "Let me try."

"I can do it."

"Yeah but I'll be faster – "

"Don't." He yanked his arm free of her hand. Cat met his eyes and drew back. His pupils were clouded and the whites were bloodshot with brown veins. He saw her fear and the dirt vanished along with his anger. "Sorry."

"Are you okay?"

"Yeah."

The mother and child huddled in the back of their wagon, eating dry crackers from a crumpled paper bag. "Is this about what she said?"

"Yeah."

"We know she's wrong."

"That's not the point," he muttered. "Hundreds of kids have been through this. Maybe thousands. I would have – " He stopped himself. “I hate that she's tormenting her little girl this way and I hate even more that she's doing it for the right reasons.”

“Come on, Peter, you know that's not true.”

“It's true that my mother broke the law by keeping me.”

“Yeah, but we hold to a higher authority.” Cat pulled the scroll from her pocket. “My sources say you're a victim, not a plague. Who do you trust more?”

“It's just like going back home.” He slouched, appearing more burdened and misshapen than ever. “We might know the truth, but what does the world believe?”

Cat rubbed a hand along the back of his arm, noting every bump along the way. They seemed more pronounced, somehow, unless in her exhaustion she was imagining it. “It's been a rough couple days. Go sit down, I'll loosen the harness.”

“No, I can handle it. I want to.” He nodded to the wagon. “Edana's the one who needs your help.”

“Apparently she's none of my business.”

“Since when has that stopped you?” He leaned into her side. “You remember me at that age. Scared and lonely? I think she could use a friend.”

“And I'm all she's got?”

He softened with a slow smile. “You come highly recommended.”

Lord Creven stared out the window of his plush office, watching his reflection against the coming night. A wigged attendant opened the door behind him. "Your Lordship?"

"Yes?"

"A guest to see you, sir."

"Right. Send him in."

The attendant bowed deeply and snapped to stiff attention as the Holy Elder entered in his ceremonial black and white robes. He waited for the assistant to leave before speaking. "Horace."

"Artemis. Welcome." The Lord gestured to a seat by his desk. The Elder declined and Lord Creven sat anyway. "I'm honored you replied in person."

"I got your note on my way through town. What's happened?"

"Nothing important." Lord Creven pulled two glasses from the desk's top drawer. "Wine?"

“Never," the Elder said. "Stop offering."

"Art, you're such a stiff!" Creven filled both glasses. "I hope I'm not keeping you from some 'God thing'."

"All our things are 'God things', Horace,” the Elder seethed. “I must return to the Monastery. Tell me what you've found. Did you read something in the scriptures you want me to clarify?"

"Hah!" The Lord drank from his glass. "You know I don't read that stuff."

"A waste." The Elder stood over the desk, hands folded behind his back. "Since the first son of Uzzah made his home in the Northern Mountains, the Holy Calligraphers collected and guarded scripture. Your lineage allows you to keep your family library, although I often wonder why you should."

"Don't give me any of that duty crap, Artemis." Creven coughed. "You were elected, but I inherited this magic stuff. I don't have to care about it, I just get to use it. That's why I let you take care of all the protocol. You've got a real drive for the book-smarts. I respect that in you painters."

"You have no respect for anything," the Elder said. "Out with it, Horace. What did you call me here for?"

"Oh." He finished his wine and grabbed a paper off his desk. "A girl came through today. Cute thing, but real suspicious. She claimed she could cast spells."

"And you believed her?"

"Orella sure did," Creven said. "She about went mad. That's the reason I called you. Orella has all the emotion of a corpse in a dress, but she's my test for liars. She was so startled I had to remove her from the room. If she believes the girl that strongly, then I trust her implicitly. It's all she's really good for nowadays."

Artemis pouted and knocked a knuckle on the gold brush behind his back. "Where is this girl?"

"Gone." Creven handed him the papers and poured himself another glass of wine. "That's the West Gate manifest from this morning. Her name's at the top. I kicked her out for bringing a Curse here. Whether she can actually do magic or not, it's probably best to keep her as far away from here as possible."

The Elder read the name on the gatekeeper's notes with a long pause. "Catrina Aston."

Creven stopped mid-pour. "You know her?"

“No.” The Holy Elder cut his host a halfhearted smile. "Don't worry about this, Horace, I'll have someone on her trail tomorrow."

“Tomorrow, eh? Guess it qualifies as a 'God thing' after all."

The Elder dropped the smile. "You're not the only one in this Valley who has inherited magic."

Chapter 9

Cat woke in a ball under the wagon with her checkered scarf tight around her arms. Predawn tinted the desert pale lavender. She crawled out into the meager daylight, shivering with cold. Peter was sound asleep in a sitting position against the front tire with his arms splayed out wide and his chin on his chest. Cat straightened his lopsided glasses for him before knotting her scarf back on her hip and checking on their guests.

Mother and child huddled against the rails on the padded benches. The older woman twitched and mumbled in restless sleep beside Edana, buried in a pile of blankets. Cat gave the girl-shaped lump a sympathetic look, pulled a box of cookware from beneath the right-hand bench, and tiptoed past Peter to find an open space for breakfast.

The firewood from the previous night still had potential. She carved some of the charring away with a frying pan and readied her string. Lady Creven said Cat was exempt from the rule because she was the new Prophet, but that didn't change the fact that she didn't have the symbols written in pigment on her body or God's voice in her ear. She was using power for the sake of power and had been since she was little. If it was always God's plan, her cooking fire a miracle, but if it wasn't...

“Good morning!”

“Ahh!” Cat fell backwards off her knees.

Edana clapped a bandaged hand over her own mouth. "Sorry!"

"No, it's okay!" Cat checked to see if Peter was still asleep. “I didn't hear you get up.”

"I tiptoed," the girl whispered. “What are you doing with that circle of string?"

“This?” Cat wadded the unfinished spell in her hand. “Nothing. It's a game I play sometimes.”

“What kind of game?”

“My mom called it threadcasting. You make patterns by twisting loops.” She weaved a pair of cat whiskers and held them to her face. “See?”

Edana laughed behind her hand. “Okay, I get it.”

“Peter and I used to play all the time. Our favorite game was called 'Child's Cradle.' You need a helper to do it. Want to try?”

“I don't know.” Edana wrung her hands. “The string might hurt my fingers.”

Cat glanced to the yellow gauze and dropped the loops. “Oh, yeah. Sorry.”

“It's okay, I can't do a lot of things,” Edana said. “I haven't had a bath or washed my hair in weeks. The doctor says I can't run or play anymore, and I can't get sad or mad because it makes the fire worse.”

“You can't get mad at all?”

“I can't get too happy either. My blood burns when it moves fast.” Edana chewed a bit of dead skin on her chapped lip. “When I get upset I usually hold my breath. It's hard to do sometimes.”

“I know how that feels. I've been upset a lot on this trip.” Cat wound the string back to her wrist. “Want to help me cook breakfast?”

“Okay.”

Cat searched the box for matches while Edana re-stacked the wood into a tower. They got a small fire going and set the pan on embers to warm.

Edana poked a spoon at the coals. “Thanks for convincing my mom to let us stay.”

“You're welcome.”

“It's really nice talking to someone. Mommy barely looks at me. She doesn't let me do anything.”

“It's been hard, huh?”

She nodded. “We've been walking for a long time.”

“Where are you from?”

“Sage Hall. It's by Astonage.”

“I know where that is. Peter and I were going to go there. It's pretty far from here.”

“My daddy worked in the city. We visited him sometimes before... stuff.” An ember popped from the end of Edana's spoon. “I hadn't seen a Fire Curse before I was one. I saw a couple Earth Curses, not one as old as Peter, though. Is he your brother?”

“He's my best friend.”

“Why isn't he in Earth Town?”

“He didn't want to go.”

“Lucky. Nobody asked me.” Edana blew at her bangs with a puff of steam. “Do you live in Dire Lonato?”

“No, we're on a journey.”

“What kind of journey?”

“A long one.” A lump knotted in her throat. “We're traveling all over, meeting new Curses.”

“Like me?”

“Yes, like you.”

“Can I come along?”

“No.” Guilt snaked through Cat's gut. “I mean, I don't think you'd enjoy it.”

“Why not? I want to meet Curses.” Red blotches spread across her face and scalp. “Don't you like me?”

“I like you a lot. There's more to it than that.”

“But I don't want to go to Fire Town!” The splotches swelled to blisters under her eyes. “I hear it's dirty there and people burn up right in front of you! You didn't make Peter go to Earth Town; I'll be as good a friend as he is, I promise!”

A grunt came from the wagon. Edana shushed herself and stared at her hands. Peter stretched with a pop and a grimace. "What time is it?"

“Early,” Cat said. "Did you sleep well?"

“No. I think there's a rivet-shaped dent in my ribs."

“Does it hurt?” Edana asked.

He smiled. “It's fine. I'm just complaining. How'd you sleep?”

“Way better than on the ground.” She crawled a little closer. “Do you wear bandages because of your sores?”

“I don't have a lot of sores.” He offered his hand and she scurried over to inspect it. “They're pressure bandages. They bind everything nice and tight.”

“Does tight keep it from hurting?”

“A bit. More importantly, if I didn't wear them, the stone in my bones would grow all different directions and I might not be able to move as much as I do.”

“You don't have any on your chest.”

“I don't want them growing into anything important.”

“Oh okay, I understand.”

Cat plucked at her string while the two Curses chatted. It was good to see Edana happy, and Peter back to his relaxed, genuine self. She remembered when Peter's brother Alan was little. The little tyke was a ball of energy, but always gentle with his fragile older brother.

Edana cradled Peter's arm against her chest and lay it carefully in his lap. ”Cat and I were making breakfast! Do you want some?”

“What are you making?”

“Probably toast.” Cat shrugged and unwrapped their bread. “I could crack an egg on it if you want.”

“No, dry is fine.” He hooked one elbow on the tire and levered up, scraping his ankles through the dust. Cat tensed until he was safely upright and slouching against the rail. “I could use a drink of water first. Where's the canteen?”

“I'll get it!” Edana scrambled back in the wagon and rustled through the boxes.

The movement woke her mother, who sat up, dazed. She blinked at her daughter. “What are you doing?”

“Helping.” The girl fished the canteen from its box by the shoulder strap.

The woman shrieked. She snatched the canteen and sent it sailing across the campsite. "What do you think you're doing? Trying to kill yourself?"

“Whoa, whoa!" Cat rushed over. "She was doing me a favor.”

"You?" The woman staggered in the rocking wagon. “You... you tried to kill her! You wanted her to kill herself!”

"No, of course not!"

“You're evil." Her face twisted from anger to wide-eyed realization. “You're a test!”

“What?”

“You're testing me!” The woman flailed her splayed hands. “You're a hallucination or something meant to send me astray, but I won't go astray, I'm a good person!”

Strawberry sensed the agitation and shook her mane with a deep snort. The frantic woman whirled toward the sound so fast she lost the bandana around her wild, graying hair.

“Mommy?” Edana cowered. “Are you okay?”

"Sit down!" The woman grabbed the girl by the collar and plopped her onto the bench behind the driver's seat. "We have to get to Fire Town, then everything will be right!"

The mother clambered over the partition, scooped the reins off the footboard and gave Strawberry a sharp smack. The plow horse whinnied and bolted. Peter staggered as the wagon leaped from behind him. Cat grabbed him under the ribs, eased his weight back on his feet, and sprinted after the escapees as fast as she could go.

The wagon bounced and pitched on the stony path, tossing supplies like confetti out the back as it went. Dust rose between them. Cat breathed the dirt and staggered, coughing, to a stop. The wagon lurched toward the city, Edana screeching for Cat and Peter at the top of her lungs.

Cat bent over her knees, eyes watering and lungs ablaze with irritants and cold air. Peter laid an arm across her back. "You okay?"

"No." She started walking. "We have to catch them."

"Cat, they're gone."

"But we *have* to."

"On foot?" He gestured to his bandaged legs. "We know they're headed for Fire Town. We'll get our wagon back there."

"We can't wait." Cat wiped her face. "Edana's our Fire Curse."

"What?"

"Edana's our Fire Curse."

“*Our* Fire Curse?” Peter stared in a wash of shock and disbelief. “You can't bring a child on a suicide mission!”

“I didn't say I wanted to.” Her voice caught on unexpected emotion. “She likes us, her mom is crazy, she doesn't want to go to Fire Town, so I thought – ”

“Cat.” Peter stepped closer. “I know it's why we came here, but Curse lives are short already; we can't use kids. It's wrong.”

“You said dying for the cause is better than dying in a bed.”

“I know, but... it's hard to explain when you're not living through it."

“I am living through it, Pete!” she snapped. “It's not the same as being a Curse, but I'm still feeling the effect. I still wake up sobbing sometimes.”

“I didn't mean it like that.”

“I can't do this.” She pressed her fists to her face and lowered to her ankles in the dirt. “I don't want to be a Prophet. I'm trying really hard, but I don't like what it's done to me. The old me wouldn't hurt people.”

“You're the same you, and you're not hurting anyone.” He leaned over. “I volunteered for this. That's not your fault. We're looking for adult minds able to understand what we're asking. The choice makes us heroes, not victims.”

“It feels awful.”

"That's why we can't take Edana," he persisted. "She doesn't know what she's losing. Even if she only has ten years to live, that's half her life. We can't rob someone of that."

"Yeah, I agree."

"Let's make a rule, then. No kids, no kidnapping – no matter the situation."

"No kids. No kidnapping." Cat wiped her nose on her sleeve. "I'm better with that."

"You're better?"

"I'm better."

"Me too." He offered his arm. She hugged it to her chest and let him pull her up. "So what did they steal? Food, water, clothing?"

"Your atlas."

He drew a sharp breath. "What about the scripture?"

She patted her skirt pocket. "Right here."

"That's good at least."

"I'm the worst Prophet ever."

"But you're calling yourself a Prophet." He chanced a smile. "That's some progress, anyway."

"Some will have to do. We've got a long way to go."

Chapter 10

It took three hours at Peter's pace to cover the mile and a half to Dire Lonato. He dragged his feet along the rocky pathway, muddy sweat soaking his cotton shirt. Cat gathered their strewn belongings in the cooking supply box as they went. The canteen tossed by Edana's mother was still full and intact. With frequent rests for food and water, they made their way to town.

The city was hidden behind by a high clay-brick wall. Ten-foot doors stood open on either side of an abandoned sentry station. Strawberry munched blades of grass from the patch at its base.

"Pete, look!" Cat set her box down and grabbed Strawberry's bridle. The horse was exhausted, her matted coat striped with rows of sweat and mud. The harness that once connected her to the wagon hung limply from its yoke. The belts were unbuckled, not broken and a scan of the desert revealed the wagon parked awkwardly in the shadow of the western wall.

"The straps were still loose from last night." Cat touched the sore places on Strawberry's flank. "I guess the wagon broke free and they abandoned it."

"That's good news for us." Peter ran the back of his hand over Strawberry's tangled mane. "I'm sorry, girl. It was an accident."

"Think she'll be okay?"

"She'll be fine. I'll get her water. Is anything stolen?"

"I'll check."

Boxes lay strewn about the bed of the wagon. Cat rooted through the remnants. "I can already tell we're missing food. Our money is gone but we've still got our clothes and stuff. Hey, first aid!" She clicked the metal case open. "Elastic bandages, Pete!"

"Isn't that something Edana might need?"

"Guess that awful woman didn't think of her daughter while she was robbing us." Cat sifted further. "My personal stuff is still here. All the thefts were from the top boxes... and look at what else!" She held the leather atlas aloft.

Peter slouched in relief. “Hooray, my one possession.”

“I'm sure it missed you, too.”

Cat hooked Strawberry back to the cart and headed into town. Square stucco shops and houses lined the narrow streets. No one was out, save a couple vagrants sleeping through the heat of the day in side alleys or boarded up doorways piled with dust.

The main road forked into three unmarked paths, lined with more stucco buildings and draped with colored awnings. Outdoor signage declared the storefronts open, but no one moved between them. Cat whispered to her companion. “This is eerie.”

“Tell me about it.”

“Which way to Fire Town?”

“I'll check the map.”

She pivoted. “That book is a century old; would the streets be the same?”

“We can look.” He flipped pages with the heel of his bandaged hand and arrived at Dire Lonato. The egg-shaped city was full of circular courtyards and squares. She spotted the front gate on the eastern side and the fork where they stood. Peter squinted at the page. “Go straight.”

“You're sure?”

“Sure enough to try.”

The road snaked deeper into the city, past empty storefronts and darkened houses with carts covered in Castleton checkpoint stickers. Thirsty-looking donkeys pawed the dust in narrow alleys while their equally destitute owners fanned themselves in open windows. Market bustle filtered through the buildings from somewhere nearby, but faded as they continued westward toward the back gate.

After a wide, sloping curve, the wagon emerged in a brick square surrounded by dilapidated buildings. Scorch marks and stains spotted the walls. In the center stood a twenty-foot alabaster statue in the shape of a young woman holding a plume of fire eastward toward Castleton. Her face was oddly familiar, despite centuries of weather and steady erosion.

Cat stared in awe. “Wow.”

“That's the Fire Goddess!” Peter grinned and boosted himself onto a bench. “She's one of the oldest things in the Valley. There are four of them – one for each element, set at the four cardinal directions. Legend says they were carved as an apology to God, but more commonly they're supposed to mark the locations of the Curse Towns. That's why the elements are spread out like they are.”

“Okay.” Cat checked the street. “So where's Fire Town?”

Peter frowned at the abandoned buildings and checked his atlas. “I don't know.”

Cat disembarked and ventured into the square. The buildings were stone instead of the expected clay and stucco. Gusts of cold wind stirred soot and loose garbage over the cobblestones, and batted shutters held closed by knots of fraying string. Behind the statue, a ten-foot black gate stood locked with a crossbeam. Pale smoke wafted in a column from somewhere beyond, like a massive chimney hidden by the towering city wall.

Peter studied a damaged panel in the front of the Goddess; a large, circular portion of the marble was missing at the figure's feet. A metal plaque was riveted in the center of the void.

“Attention,” Cat read aloud. “For the beautification and cleanliness of Dire Lonato, Fire Town has been relocated. Cordially, the Mayor's Office.” She groaned. “Beautification? Seriously?”

Peter didn't reply. His whole body tensed. He paled and scanned the rooftops.

“What's wrong?”

Still no response.

“Pete, you're scaring me.” She took his arm. The tumors below his bandages trembled against her hand. “What's happening to you?”

“We're being watched.”

“Watched?”

“I can feel him moving.”

Peter tracked the unseen figure around the square. Cat shuffled with him in a circle, but saw no strangers on the skyline. They stopped with their backs to the Goddess and stared back the way they came. A cheer rose somewhere distant, followed by heavy footsteps. Orange light warmed the far end of the curving road and a ten-foot fire golem appeared around the bend.

The creature walked on thick muscular forelegs and squat, bowing, back legs beneath a heavy torso. Revelers swarmed around it, singing hymns. Memories of Mason Forge flashed through Cat's mind. She inched toward the wagon, but Peter stood shaking, too frightened to move. The golem stopped before the sculpture and stared with tunneling, white eyes as townsfolk flooded into the square.

A pair of Calligraphers followed their golem on horseback. The lead monk regarded Cat, bemused. “So we meet again.”

She pulled the string off her wrist. “It's you.”

“Senior Calligrapher Trace Hayes." He dismounted and transferred his black brush from the holster on his saddle to the one on his back. "You recall my assistant, Paige Waverly, from our first meeting in Mason Forge.” His eye flit to Peter. "You're a long way from home, Miss Aston."

“Stay away,” Cat challenged. “I won't let you near him.”

"I didn't ride from Castleton to kill a Curse.” Trace straightened with commanding tone. "Catrina Aston, by the authority of the Holy Elder, I charge you with the crime of heresy and place you under arrest."

The crowd gasped. Cat stammered. "You what?"

"The Elder heard what you said in Castleton," he replied. "You threatened Lord Creven with unholy miracles."

"I didn't threaten him! I was protecting myself."

"With lies?"

"I wasn't lying!" She gulped. "I mean, maybe a little, but that was to save Peter."

Trace glanced between Cat and Peter and folded his hands behind his back. "You seem like a nice girl. I can tell you care about your friend. How about we make a deal'?"

"What do you mean by 'deal?'"

"The Elder sent me after you because you claimed to perform magic. Using magic without permission is a violation of moral and religious law. It usually happens when monks desert the order, or when citizens find a way to copy the symbols we paint in our spells. I assume that's what happened here – you made note of the earth symbol our elder painted in the moment before it was consumed with holy fire and thought you could use it, yourself."

Cat wrinkled her nose. Trace sweetened his tone and took a step forward. "I don't think you're wicked, Miss Aston. You only want to protect your friend. If you confess your sins and pledge yourself to a life of piety and service, I'll see he gets safely to Earth Town and put your interest in magic to good use."

Cat frowned at Trace and his assistant. "You want me to be a Brushcaster."

His smile faded. "The Order of Holy Calligraphers welcomes all who desire Our God. If you repent, heart and soul, you will be absolved of sin, and with the proper education, you may be accepted as an acolyte and in time, perform miracles as we do."

"You don't perform miracles," Cat said. "You trick people with shows of power."

He stiffened. "We help people."

"You control them." Cat stepped forward. "You listen to *me*, now. I know more than you think. God never gave you magic, you took it from him."

"What did you say?"

"You stole it!"

The fire golem's eyes flashed. Flames spiked blue along its spine, but Trace was too livid to notice. "You're treading dangerous water, Catrina."

"You don't scare me," Cat said. "I'm not going with you and you won't touch my friend."

"You'll come with us quietly or I will bring you by force."

"With what? Your horrifying fire monster?" She pointed at the twitching golem. Trace followed her finger and recoiled.

"You're not doing God's work." Cat raised her voice for the crowd. "Your magic's the reason he left in the first place!"

Trace raised his hands to her. "Calm down, now."

"Why? It's the truth!"

A mouth of white light ripped the golem's flaming face. It reared back, clubbed forelegs in the air, and slammed its full body weight into the pavement. Cobblestones dislodged, dirt rained from the arms of the Goddess, Strawberry whinnied and bolted as locals scattered in all directions. Paige was thrown as the black horses retreated from the chaos. Trace pulled her up and backed them both away from the golem. "Everyone freeze! No one run!"

The golem crouched on its flaming knuckles as the crowd staggered to a frightened stop.

Trace leaned to his assistant. "Get our horses back."

"But – "

"Do as I say – and be careful."

Paige backed away from the circle. Trace shot Cat and Peter a warning glance and raised his brush for attention. "People of Dire Lonato! We don't have much time. This heretic has turned my golem wrathful with her lies. What stands before you is the anger of Our God. It does not obey my commands, and I cannot paint another while this still creature lives. To kill it, I must destroy the circle I painted in front of the church. I need you all to stay calm. The golem exists to destroy sin, but can only hunt by sight. Stay hidden until I return."

The creature bellowed and charged. Trace threw Cat out of the way and it struck the pedestal near where Peter stood, splitting deep cracks around its fist and up the Goddess's side. One of the sculpture's upraised arms dislodged and fell like a timber. Cat sprang clear and the limb crashed to pieces where she'd been.

"Pete!"

The golem drew its fist from the smoking crater to reveal Peter cowering a couple feet from death.

Cat made eye contact and stretched her string. "Run!"

He ducked around the pedestal. The golem pursued. Cat shoved to her feet, rushed through a water rune, and speared the creature through its heart.

The golem roared as steam hissed from its wound. Cat checked the square for Peter but Trace grabbed her from behind. "What? Was that a water spell?"

The golem spun, seething, its attention on Cat. Trace put her behind his back and spoke over his shoulder.

"Catrina. I don't know how you cast that, but listen carefully. A wrathful golem not only lives to end sin, it destroys other magic. It will kill your friend, but you can lead it away. Make for the rear gate. You can save innocent people and buy me some time."

"You're using me as bait?"

"Don't argue!" he snapped. "I'm saving your life."

Paige rode up with Trace's horse. He swung into the saddle and kicked hard. Cat ran for the back gate with the golem right behind. Embers flew from its footfalls. Heat rippled as the golem herded her along the outside of the square where frightened locals cowered in alleys. Cat threaded her string and threw another water spell over her shoulder. The creature reeled. Steam poured from its face and it swung its arms into the nearest building, drawing screams rose from those trapped inside.

Cat sprinted back to the square and searched for Strawberry among the chaos. The wagon was nowhere to be seen. She spotted Peter staggering beneath the Goddess to her right. He motioned for her to run, but the golem charged and she fell. The thread twisted beneath her palm as it scraped across the stones. She regained her feet and sprinted for the back gate.

Cat wedged her shoulder under the crossbeam and hefted it off its pegs. The golem leaped and slammed its flaming shoulder into the gate above her. The demon burned a stripe across the wood and prowled closer, shoulders hunched. Heat baked through her clothes and burned in her lungs. She scooted backward along the city wall, clawing at the tangled string, but her fingers were sticky with dirt and evaporating sweat.

The monster raised its fist for a deciding blow but stopped with a spasm. The ground below it exploded in a blanket of steam.

From the paving stones rose a fountain of diamond-clear water. The magic gurgled ten feet into the air and swallowed the golem in a sparkling prison. The creature writhed, its death throes muffled by the wall of water until it withered into nothing. The column receded, leaving a damp, black stain.

A cloaked figure stood atop the city wall, one hand outstretched. A white circle glowed in the stranger's cupped palm. He snuffed the light in a fist and lowered his arm. Cat stood mesmerized at the power and mystery, drawn by the stranger's coal-black eyes.

Someone struck her in the side of the head. Cat hit the wet pavement and was surrounded by a mass of faces. Through a starry haze she saw a crying child, a bloodied policeman, and the city gate standing open with no cloaked stranger in sight.

Chapter 11

Cat shielded her face from her attackers as they surrounded her in a blur of scrapes and burns. They kicked dirt on her and spat, swearing and jeering. A man in a wig and decorative waistcoat grabbed her by the wrist. “I have her! She's caught!”

The people cheered. Cat struggled as two bloodied men twisted her arms behind her back.

“You are under arrest for crimes against Dire Lonato,” the waist-coated man said. “As mayor, I declare you guilty and bring sentence upon you.” He raised his voice to the crowd. “She goes to the Calligraphers. They'll bless us for catching their heretic!”

The mob raised bricks and fists in agreement and marched her across the square. Cat dragged her heels and tugged the knots of her string behind her back. They passed a policeman with a head wound holding Strawberry's reins. Cat measured the distance between the wagon and the open gate and pulled forward with a twist. One arm came free. She jammed her thumb into the back of her second captor's knee and he buckled. New assailants took his place, lifting her by the arms and legs.

A greasy-haired child parted the spectating crowd. “Cat!”

“Edana!”

The townsfolk dropped Cat in time for the Fire Curse to jump in her arms. The wounds on Edana's papery scalp oozed hot against her cheek.

Peter appeared, panting, with his glasses askew. “You okay?”

“Yeah,” Cat said. “How about you?”

“I'm in one piece.” He scanned the square. The crowd shrank away, like roaches from a wandering light. Peter's heaving shoulders squared, his panic hardened to a steady calm. “Stay behind me.”

Edana's haggard mother elbowed into the circle, her eyes red and less wild than the last time they met. “You!”

Cat leveled her brow. “Yes.”

“I thought you were a dream.”

“I'm afraid I'm very real.”

"Woman!" the mayor barked. "Are these yours?"

She blinked and searched his face "What?"

"The Curses – are they yours?"

"No, I... "

"And the heretic? Do you know her?"

"I – I met them on the road." The woman knotted her fingers in her hair. "I thought it was the stress..."

"You're not imagining things," Cat said. "Peter and I are on a quest to bring the Curse cycle to an end. We're going to ransom God back to his valley. It's a peace mission. We don't mean you any harm."

"Blasphemer," the mayor snarled.

"I'm telling the truth."

"The truth?" Edana's mother stared tearfully through her tangled hair.

Cat loosened her grip on Edana. "What's your name?"

"Name?"

"Yes. Your name?"

"Dolores," she mumbled. "Dolores Preston."

"Dolores," Cat said, "you've been living a nightmare, I know. You've forced yourself to do something you never wanted to do and it's killing you, but Pete and I want to show everyone you don't have to listen to the Brushcasters any more. They've been lying to you."

"But... they speak for Our God."

“No they don't,” Cat rose. “I do.”

The mayor lost his scowl. “You what?”

“I've read the scripture for myself.” She pulled the scroll box from her pocket and held it high. “I can tell you what it says.”

“You're...” Dolores' eyes widened. She lifted a shaking hand to her face. “You're...”

Cat nodded. “I'm a Prophet.”

The mother pointed from Cat to the one armed statue overhead. “You're the Goddess!”

“What?”

“She's the Goddess!” Dolores cried. “Look! Everyone, look!”

Half the crowd gasped in agreement. The other half growled in anger. The words “prophet” and “goddess” echoed through them in waves. One local punched another deep in the crowd and ignited a brawl. Neighbors already bloody from the golem attack, shouted insults and debate over Cat's head. One called another an idiot, then turned their fiery eyes back to her. “Get the liar!”

“Pete, run!”

Dolores picked up Edana and followed Cat and Peter to the waiting wagon. Cat shoved the policeman holding Strawberry's reins. He readied a punch, but fled in horror when Peter appeared beside her.

Dolores pressed Edana back into Cat's arms. “Take my daughter.”

"What?"

"The priest said to take my daughter to the Goddess because she was chosen by Our God." Dolores smiled through tears. "I know you will care for her. You came to me as a miracle! Forgive me, your honor, for not seeing it before."

Voices rose from the chaos. "They're getting away!"

"Run." Dolores kissed Edana's face. "Thank you!"

A burly man swept in to attack, but Dolores slapped him across the face. He landed a blow against her cheekbone and she dropped like a rock. Edana screamed. Peter slid in the wagon bed and Cat dumped her, squalling, into his lap before leaping to the driver's seat and lashing her hard. The back gate revealed wide, untamed desert through its open doors. Cat charged out and away from civilization as fast as they could go.

"Go back!" Edana shouted as the town receded. "Please! I didn't get to say goodbye!"

"It's too late," Peter whispered. "I'm sorry."

The Calligraphers' casting circle glowed on the pavement before a white limestone church, surrounded by priests and deacons in prayer. White light danced in slow waves like the surface of a river, dappling the priest's black cloaks and glinting off the small calligraphy brushes attached to beaded ropes about their necks.

A muffled roar bellowed over the stucco rooftops. A priest looked up, but a sharp look from his senior sent him back into prayer. The slow dance on the ground before them increased speed and intensity. The smell of spice and burning incense rose from the cursive lines with a steady hiss until the paint ripped itself from the ground and scattered into a thousand tiny flakes.

The priests stopped praying with worried looks. Trace thundered toward them from the main road with his brush wet and ready to strike. The paint chips scattered on the wind as he arrived.

"Sir!" the head priest cried. "We don't know what happened!"

"Hush!" Trace dismounted and dropped to a crouch within his ruined circle. "When?"

"Just now."

Paige lowered to the ground beside him. "Why did it break?"

"The golem's dead," Trace said. "She killed it before we could destroy the spell."

"How?"

He brushed his hand through the sooty remnants. "Magic."

Paige tossed her pigtails with a scoff. "You sure you didn't paint a bad spell?"

"I do not paint bad spells."

"You painted a wrathful golem."

"Paige!" Trace rounded on her. "I am a senior monk and your master. That girl can use magic – this was not my mistake."

She rolled her eyes. Trace shook his head and smoothed his black hair back into place.

"Was it our fault, sir?" asked the head priest.

"No, Father," the monk replied. "You did very well. Tell your parishioners Catrina Aston of Mason Forge is now dubbed a False Prophet. She is a mortal playing god; the sin for which the Order of Holy Calligraphers was founded centuries ago. She is not malicious, of that much I'm sure, but she's waging a passionate war for a radical cause and that makes her dangerous."

The priest gulped. "What should we do?"

"Your city met an unexpected evil today, one that may spread throughout God's Valley. Care for each other and your city. Leave Miss Aston to me. I will see her caught and brought to justice for all of her crimes." Trace sheathed his brush. "May Our God's entrusted will be done."

Chapter 12

Thick white smoke wafted from somewhere between Dire Lonato and the towering Western Mountains. Cat kept their frenzied pace until they found a dry riverbed where the raised banks hid the wagon from view. The rubber tires rolled softly over smooth stones and buried driftwood rubbed smooth by course wind and ancient currents. The gentle rocking lulled the passengers behind her into a light, exhausted sleep, although Edana continued to whimper. Cat let the reins slack and took a moment to reflect.

The world knew she was a Prophet, false or not; the Calligraphers were after her; a mysterious stalker saved her with magic, but left her to fight off a mob; and she and Peter were alive despite it all. Cat tried to be more grateful, but worry left her tense.

Peter shifted in the seat behind her. “Do you think it always happens like this?”

A knot tightened in her throat. “You mean Prophet missions?”

“I mean kid abandonment.”

The one thing Cat hadn't dwelt on was Dolores. They left her unconscious in the street. Would the townsfolk show her mercy? Was she in jail or in a hospital? Would she find her way back home?

“Do all the parents go crazy?” Peter continued. “I mean, she thought we were hallucinations. She thought you were a goddess.”

“They were walking for a long time, and they weren't carrying a lot of food or water. They probably didn't get much rest, either. That can make you pretty sick.”

“So your answer is 'yes,' then. All parents go crazy.”

“I didn't say that.”

“If Mom obeyed the law back with me, she'd be the same way, right? Babbling nonsense and quoting the Brushcasters.”

“Dolores isn't your mom.”

“You're right, Mom would pack better,” he huffed. “Even then, would the same woman come back for Alan? He was just a baby.”

“Pete, don't.” Cat eased Strawberry to a stop and climbed the partition to sit beside him. “It doesn't matter what might or might not have happened. Your mom is a wonderful person and your brother's an awesome kid and *you* are an important part of their lives."

He turned his face but couldn't hide the muddy stains on his cheeks. Cat balled the cuff of her billowing shirt sleeve and wiped away the lines. He slouched further. "I'm still helpless."

"No you're not. You were really brave back there."

"Then why do I feel bad?"

"Because you know this is wrong." Tumors on his cheekbones poked like rivets into her hand. "People aren't supposed to be Curses, and parents aren't supposed to abandon their kids. It doesn't have to be this way. Even if the scripture's wrong about me, it's definitely right about that."

"It *is* right about you."

She sucked her lip. "It's right that I've got tools most people don't, and I want to fight against the Brushcasters. This whole Curse Town system needs to stop."

"What about her?" He tucked a murmuring Edana against his side. "I feel like a hypocrite, but it's not like she can go back home after everything that's happened. Is it right to leave her in Fire Town? I mean, she's getting worse. I can feel how much warmer she is through my clothes."

Edana's face twitched behind her stringy hair. New blisters peppered her face, especially around her eyes where the old ones were burst and swollen. A flake of white fluff stuck to her hair. Another flake floated between them to land on Peter's leg as the white column bent toward them on the changing wind.

A flurry of tufts swirled on a sweet smelling breeze. Cat reached out, expecting cold, but found fine powder instead. The flakes crumbled into soot in her hand "It's ash."

Peter sighed. "I guess that means we're close."

They resumed their journey westward through a thickening haze. Fog filled the riverbed and soured the sweet air into a putrid musk. Visibility worsened as gusts stirred the ash into whirlwinds, littering Strawberry's mane with flakes and casting fine grit into Cat's eyes. She bowed her head against the flurries, but breathed soot into her lungs and could taste the acrid scent in the back of her throat. The storm lifted a bit as the riverbed widened and emptied the wagon onto the bank of a dry lake where twelve dug-outs sat clustered in a small clearing surrounded by a carpet of low-burning coals.

"Fire Town," Cat directed. Peter leaned around her for a look. The coal field stretched a full acre within the lake bed, emitting ash and bits of flame in crackles and pops. Bands of live fire striped the hillside and fed the rotating column overhead with a constant stream of white smoke. Strawberry shied from bursts of steam, but Cat kept the reins taut and eased them toward a narrow footpath, snaking away from them through the field.

The wagon crunched coal smoothly at first, but started rocking as the scattered clods increased from bricks to blocks. Smoldering mounds burst to ember under their weight, scattering motes of flame into the driver's seat and through the open rails. Heat baked from below and through Cat's heavy travel clothes, sticking them to her skin as sweat pooled in her boots. Strawberry panted and fought to turn, but Cat kept her moving forward. Fire Town waited a dozen yards away.

The burning husks were larger and tougher near town. The wagon jostled over obstacles, tossing the passengers from side to side. They rose half a foot on the back of a stubborn bolder, then dropped with a flurry of ember and a loud wince from Peter in back. Strawberry dodged a crumbling log in a sack, then a pile of singed hair wrapped in colored fabric. Another hair pile had a ribbon on it. Then Cat saw a face.

Bodies. Every mound of blackened garbage, every crumbling husk and open flame was part of a person. Eyeless skulls stared with fiery sockets. Fingers curled from amputated limbs. Rib cages glowed in stripes within piles of charcoal still wearing the pants and sleeves they had in life. Cat breathed in human soot and gagged. She dropped the reins to cover her eyes, but her mind still saw the horrors. Strawberry threw her head and rushed the final yards into town, churning loose remains under their wheels before skidding to a stop.

Twenty people watched from the lips of their dug-out stairwells, with tiny motes of yellow firelight glowing in the pupils of their eyes.

The Fire Curses' faces were leathery masks covered with open sores and layers of scar tissue. Each wore a colored scarf like a hood to protect their damaged heads from the sun. One wearing yellow climbed into the courtyard. Cat guessed from the hint of body shape beneath the stained smock and pants that the Fire Curse was a teenage girl, but other distinguishing features like complexion or hair color were completely burned away.

“Who's there?” the girl asked.

“I'm – ” She coughed, throat raw. “My name is Cat.”

The teenager's forehead creased in lines as she raised a hairless eyebrow. “I don't recognize your voice. Are you from the church?”

“Not really.”

“If you brought rations, leave them there.”

“We didn't bring rations. We brought another Fire Curse.”

“Oh.” The girl cupped her hands and called back to her dugout. “Ildri! Another one!” She tightened her yellow scarf and and limped toward the wagon. “Okay, let me see.”

Peter sat in the bed, shielding Edana with one arm. The teenager in yellow spotted him and backed away, cracks of light splitting in rings around her eyes. “What is that?”

“I'm an Earth Curse,” Peter replied. “This is Edana. I think she's sick.”

The teen's face flared under her hood. She climbed into the wagon and pressed a bandaged hand to Edana's forehead. “How long has she been like this?”

“A couple hours,” Peter replied. “We rode from Dire Lonato.”

“They didn't use water on her, did they?”

“No.” Cat cringed. “They do that?”

The older Fire Curse carried the younger out of the wagon. Edana whimpered and fidgeted. She pried her eyes open, saw the face beneath the yellow hood, and screamed at the top of her lungs.

A Fire Curse wearing a purple scarf appeared beside them. “What happened?”

“Ildri, finally!” The first struggled to hold the thrashing child. “Help me!”

“Come here, baby,” Ildri cooed. She dabbed Edana's tears with the hem of her smock and rocked until the child slipped back to unsettled sleep. Ildri whispered to the girl in yellow. “You okay?”

“Could be worse.”

“Is Edana all right?” Cat asked.

“She's overheated. She needs rest,” Ildri answered. “Are you her parents?”

“No.” Cat glanced to Peter. “We found her on the road.”

Ildri noticed the Earth Curse with start. “Whoa!” A blush inflamed the blisters across her peeling nose. “Sorry.”

“I'm getting used to it.”

“I'm Ildri,” she said. “This is Sera.”

The girl in yellow crossed her arms.

“Thank you for bringing Edana to us. It's rare strangers are willing to help.” Ildri stared at Peter's bandages. “Although you're unusual in a couple ways.”

“We just want her to get better,” Cat replied. “Besides, we were coming here anyway.”

“You were?”

“Yes, we have something to say to your town.”

Ildri's pleasant tone strained. “I thought it was against the law to talk to Curses.”

“We don't care much about the law.”

Sera side-eyed Peter. “Apparently.”

“What's going on out there?” A gruff male voice rumbled from one of the far bungalows. “Are the healthies leaving yet?”

Both girls turned red. Ildri grit her teeth. “They will, Tyson! Stay inside!”

“Our Absent God, Ildri!” The man marched up the stairs. He was tall and lanky for a Fire Curse, and wore his green hood loose and tattered. Cat could see the deep scars that split his face from the other end of the compound.

"Here!" Ildri hurried Edana into Sera's arms. "Get her inside."

"Don't piss him off."

"I'm not trying to!"

A man in a gray hood followed Tyson out of their house. He caught the taller man by the shoulder. Tyson slapped his hand aside. "Buzz off."

"Don't do something stupid." The other Curse warned.

"Tell that to your girlfriend!"

The two launched a muttered argument. Ildri exhaled a puff of steam and turned to Cat. "You need to go."

"Not yet."

"Aiden's buying you time." Ildri pulled her hands into her sleeves and shoved Cat toward the driver's seat. "Get out before you hurt someone."

"Ildri!" Tyson snapped. "Stop catering to the healthies!"

"I wasn't – !"

"I said, leave her alone." Aiden took his shoulder. "You're overreacting."

"Get your hands off me!"

"Don't yell at him, Ty."

"I'm not! I'm yelling at *you*!"

The rest of Fire Town rose to the surface like bodies from their graves. Cat mapped the progression of the illness through the gathering, from children covered in blisters to young adults with peeling burns and open sores. The worst of them were missing fingers, or had fire actively burning patches in their skin. The group muttered to each other in different accents, asking questions, and making demands.

"What does the healthy girl want from us?" a child Edana's height asked.

"She doesn't want anything." Aiden raised his bandaged hands. "Don't worry, it's nothing weird! Everybody go back inside."

Cat dodged Ildri and rushed forward. "Hi everyone, my name is Catrina Aston. You can call me Cat."

The Fire Curses recoiled. Aiden turned with an angry flash in his black-ringed eyes. "What the hell do you think you're doing?"

"I'm unarmed, look." Cat turned her hands. "No water, no weapons. I'm a friend."

"There's a big gap between being unarmed and being friends," Tyson snarled. "Does being healthy make you stupid?"

"I didn't come here to fight," Cat insisted. "I'm trying to help."

A glow spread across his face and down his neck. "You? Help? Like you did when you drove us out of our family homes? Do you know how many of our friends died thanks to your help? How many little kids?"

Cat blanched. "I didn't drive anyone out."

"No, you scooped a kid off the road, didn't you? So that makes it all better. Bet you feel so good about yourself, now. You can leave here and sleep super well in your soft bed in your warm house."

"Tyson, stop it," Ildri said. "She hasn't done anything to us, leave her alone."

"See!" He appealed to the crowd. "She's on their side!"

"No I'm not!" Ildri stopped herself with a long deep breath. "Tyson. Stop working everyone up. You'll overheat yourself again."

"Don't baby me, Il."

"Everyone should be calm," Cat agreed. "I know Fire Curses get bad when they get agitated – "

"Get *bad*?" Tyson roared.

"No!" Cat said. "I mean – poor choice of words!"

"Let me try." Peter slid out of the wagon and straightened to full height. The Fire Curses fell silent. The lighted dots of their eyes darted from Cat to Peter, befuddled.

Tyson's face flushed red. "What are you supposed to be?"

"A Curse."

"I can see that."

"Drop the attitude," Peter said. "I've had a really long day."

“You're not a Fire Curse,” a child in an orange scarf said.

“No, I'm an Earth Curse,” he answered.

“What are you doing here?” a teen in red asked.

“I came because of Cat.”

“What's your name?” asked a girl in black.

“It's Peter Montgomery.”

“Montgomery?” Aiden leveled his scabbed brow. “You kept your family name?”

“Of course.” He rested his massive arm against Cat's back. “I kept my family, too.”

Her heart swelled beneath the comforting weight of the limb. Aiden studied them, his lighted eyes flashing in thought as the other Fire Curses pressed forward with more questions and observations. Cat gestured for quiet. “Okay, one at a time.”

“Is he really your brother?”

“He might as well be.”

“And you don't want to hurt us?”

“I promise I won't.”

“Where did you come from? Did you bring us something? Is that Fire Curse your sister?”

Ildri spoke in her sweeter tone. “It's nice all of you are curious, but the healthy girl's not staying. She said she wants to tell us something and then she will be gone.”

"Yeah, what's so important, healthy girl?" Tyson crossed his arms with a cynical smirk. "What wisdom does one of Our God's perfect children have for us degenerates?"

The Fire Curses waited at attention, but a lump lodged in Cat's throat. She had to be convincing, but no matter how kindly she phrased it, she was asking one of the damaged people before her to die. Cat ran a finger under her string. "It's kind of complicated, actually. Peter and I are on a mission. We're trying to end the Curses."

"*End* them?" Ildri asked.

"Cat's the new Prophet," Peter said. "We're getting God back to the Valley so he can take control of magic again."

"A Prophet, huh?" Aiden's brow knit. "So that means Our God speaks to you?"

Cat blushed. "Well, no..."

"Our God's supposed to inhabit his Prophets, how can you be one without hearing him talk?"

"He can't because he's gone," Peter said. "But he predicted she'd be coming. She's got a scripture in her pocket that explains it."

Tyson groaned. "Sure, of course she does."

"It's true." Cat pulled it free. "I got this from a scholar – "

"We've heard all of it before," he said. "Priests and Brushcasters quoting scrolls to explain why they threw us out like trash. You healthies think God put your sin in us so you don't have to deal with it. Well, deal with this, girl!" He shoved Aiden to one side and balled his bandaged fingers. "The God you want back is dead! He died forever ago, and us Curses and the Brushcasters are the scraps that we've got left. If you think killing us is gonna fix anything, you're dumber than my fist – at least it knows not to hit innocent people."

"That's not why I came," Cat appealed. "I won't hurt you."

"Get the hell out of our town!"

"Tyson," Ildri warned, "please..."

"No." Cat said. "He has a right to be upset. You've been mistreated, and I'm a symbol of everything you hate, but I'm right, too. I am a new kind of Prophet – one that's as lost and confused as you are, but I can make miracles like the old Prophets. Let me do one to prove I'm honest. You don't have to listen to me until then."

"You know magic?" Ildri gaped at her. "Real magic? Like the monks use?"

"My miracles don't come out as monsters." Cat pulled off her string. "I'm not a Brushcaster, but I can do magic. How can I help?"

"Don't fall for it, Il," Tyson said. "She's playing you."

"But if she can make real magic..."

"She's lying to your face," he insisted. "Only Brushcasters do miracles."

"I've heard of other people doing them," Aiden said. "Of course, they got arrested and were hanged."

“See? All the more reason to kick her out!”

“Rejecting people for what they are is something healthy people do,” Ildri said. “A miracle is a miracle. Either she can do one or she can't.”

Tyson puffed the frayed hem of his scarf. “When did you get so bossy?”

“I... I can tell this one is different.” She studied Peter's limbs from the corner of her swollen eye. “If she really cares about us Curses, we should give her the chance to show it.”

Chapter 13

Ildri led Cat, Peter, and the Fire Curses past the cluster of bungalows to the edge of town, where several empty wooden barrels waited under ashy tarps.

"I don't know how much you know about Fire Curses," Ildri started. "Water is dangerous to our skin, but we still drink it to survive. Dire Lonato sends what the Brushcasters force them to, but it's been hot this summer and we keep running out. The ground is dry. There's not even a well – not like any of us are healthy enough to dig one, either way."

"So you want me to make you some water," Cat finished.

Ildri wrung her hands. “Can you?”

“Easily.” Cat readied her string. "Tell everyone to stand back."

“Back?”

“Really, really far back.”

Ildri herded her fellow Curses behind the earthen bungalows. Peter set his back against a building with a reassuring nod. Cat smiled, threaded the opening stage and closed her eyes to pray. She wasn't sure what praying felt like – she never did it much as a normal citizen – but if God was somewhere listening, perhaps the effort was enough.

“Please don't let me screw this up.”

She moved through the steps of the water rune reverently, crafting the symbol as an offering with every string precise. She recalled the sapling under her bedroom window and how her magic drew life from the barren soil. This miracle brought life to a dying people, it probably made God happy. She hoped it did. Hand steady, she took aim at the nearest empty barrel and dropped the last string into place.

The symbol at the center of the string flashed white and a thick column of water exploded from her hands with devastating force. The jet writhed and bucked, chafing hard against her hands. She overcompensated for the force and carved a trench into the ground. The Fire Curses screamed. Cat threw herself over the lip of a barrel and forced the spell inside. The stream hit the flat bottom and ricocheted high into the air. Water fell from the fountain in fine sheets of rain. It filled all the waiting barrels and painted wide, slanted rainbows across the late afternoon sky.

The spell weakened the longer Cat held it. She topped each barrel off and pressed her hands together. The miracle ended as the strings slipped peacefully out of alignment.

The people of Fire Town stared in silent terror from the shelter of their homes. Tyson emerged, fires blazing. “What on Our God's dead earth was *that*?”

“A miracle?”

“A death trap!”

She grimaced. “It's still a work in progress.”

“You're trying to kill us!” he cried. “I mean, true you've got magic, but damn!”

“I can't believe it's real.” The fires sparkled like stars in Ildri's eyes. “You have Our God's power, just like you said!”

“It's not what you think,” Cat said. “I am not a Prophet the way the Prophets were in the past. I am not a magical being, and the Brushcasters aren't either.”

The child wearing orange peeked out from behind Peter. “But the Brushcasters have their paint and stuff.”

"They know the symbols for the elements like I do," Cat said. "The difference is they use their magic without God saying so, and that's why you all are cursed."

"Wait." Aiden stepped to the edge of the damp earth. "My parents worked for our city priest. I know the Brushcaster laws back to front, and they don't say anything about us being cursed by magic. We were born this way as an offering."

"That's what they tell you to believe," Cat said. "We were taught that stuff, too, but we have a real scripture and it says what I just told you."

"They said they had real scripture, too."

"Take me as evidence then," Peter said. "My mom kept me when they found out I was a Curse; it didn't cause storms or sickness or any of the stuff you hear horror stories about. The Brushcasters are lying to everyone because their magic is ruining the world, and they'd rather pin the blame on people like us than accept it on themselves."

"That's real nice," Tyson lilted. "Brushcasters are the worst, sure. That sounds like what we want to hear. What did you really come here for?"

"Yes, you said you had a mission!" Ildri said, anxious but encouraged. "Your scripture tells you how to end the Curses. What do you need? How can we help?"

"Well...." Cat met Peter's eye and pulled the leather case from her pocket. "This scroll is the last thing God said to the Prophets. Long ago, the first Brushcaster stole magic; that's what gave them powers and made the first Curses. We can keep more Curses from happening it by giving the magic back."

Aiden's blackened eyes narrowed. "What do you need us for?"

Cat swallowed hard. "You're the magic."

Tyson glowered. "What?"

"For the sacrifice."

Ildri's brow knit. "Sacrifice?"

"I need one of you..." Cat swallowed, her mouth dry, "to come on a journey with me."

"And?"

Her hands shook. "And..."

"Wait." Tyson heaved a raspy laugh. "Oh... oh no!"

Ildri turned. "Ty, what is it?"

"She's gonna sacrifice us to get rid of magic." He stared at Cat with fierce intensity. "You *did* come to kill us!"

"I swear I don't want to!"

"Why didn't you blast us with water, then? You've got enough to fill this lake back up. Why'd you bother bringing that new girl here? Need us all in the same place?" His voice cracked as it gained volume. "You gonna murder us right now, healthy girl?"

"I didn't say anything like that!" Cat backed away. "I need a volunteer from each Curse Town. Life and magic incarnate, that's what it says. When God comes back, magic will leave and everything ends – the Brushcasters, the Curses, even the drought! The whole world will be better."

"You mean better without us."

"I didn't say that!" Cat reached forward. "Please! Listen!"

"I'm not part of your human scavenger hunt." A fresh wound split at the corner of Tyson's mouth.

Aiden noticed with a gasp. "Ty – "

"Shut up!" Tyson roared with a flash of fire that opened wounds at his temples. The Fire Curse shuffled away as he rounded on Cat. "How dare you come here after everything you've done to us? How *dare* you!"

Sweat prickled the back of her neck. "Please..."

"You already took my home, my family, my dignity...." The fresh wounds peeled paths along his cheekbones. "I won't give you my life! It's all I have left!"

Flame kindled in the back of Tyson's mouth and deep in his sinuses. Sores oozed in raw skin around his nose and eyes. His fellow Fire Curses stared in fear as the fire ignited the veins and arteries in his face, tearing swollen gashes on either side of his neck. Blisters bubbled from his jaw to his collar. Cat stared into his flaming pupils as she did with the advancing fire golem; crippled and helpless in the face of supernatural horror. “Please... don't this to yourself.”

“Get out of our town!”

He swung a skinless fist, but Aiden tackled him from behind. The two Fire Curses hit the damp earth with a hiss and a scream. The other Curses scattered, some to the safety of their houses, others to the fight. Younger ones stared in shock. Older ones tried to interfere. Fiery cracks like shattered glass ripped open along the sides of Tyson's face. Heat burned black marks on his linen tunic. Aiden dragged him onto his back, kicking and thrashing. Tyson covered his face and shrieked into his palms.

“Aiden!” Ildri cried.

He gestured to Cat. “Get her inside!”

Ildri's eyes swelled. She grabbed Cat's sleeve and yelped at the damp fabric. “Ow!”

Cat hugged the scripture case. “I'm sorry!”

“No, I am!” Ildri pulled her hands into her sleeves and slammed her shoulder into Cat's chest. Cat toppled backward, down a staircase, and through the door of the nearest hut. The scripture case skidded away as her head struck the earthen floor and the domed room spun. The child in an orange scarf bounded from the stairs and lifted the case from the dirt.

Sera ran from a back room. “What's happened?”

“There's... a fight.” Cat winced as the sound of her own voice lanced pain through her head. The sifting world settled as she blinked the stars from her blurry eyes. “Peter!”

“Sera!” Ildri barreled down the stairs. Peter followed, uneasily, his wrist wrapped in her arms. She tugged and he faltered. His feet slipped on the final step. Cat shoved Ildri aside and grabbed him under the ribs. Stone dug into Cat's arms as his weight fell into her embrace. She buried her face in the ridges and flattened his back against the nearest wall.

Peter wheezed. “Wow.”

Cat held tight. “You okay?”

His heart pounded in her ear. “Sure, yeah, fine.”

Ildri slammed the wooden door and threw down the lock.

“Our God, Il,” Sera cried. “What's going on up there?”

“The Prophet made us water,” the child in orange said. “Then Tyson blew himself up.”

Sera blushed orange. “He did what?”

“Aiden's looking after him,” Ildri said. “It looked bad –”

“Out of my way.” Sera reached for the door but Ildri stopped her. “I said, let me though!”

“It's not safe for you.”

“That's not fair!” The veins reddened in Sera's throat. “You'd go if it was Aiden!”

"I'm sorry." Ildri took Sera's shoulders. "Take a deep breath."

Sera ground her teeth, face twitching as her color slowly returned to normal. The child turned to Cat. "Here's your box."

"Thanks, kid." She took the case with a weary smile.

Ildri flit a worried look to Cat and Peter. "Don't talk to them, Kory." She took the boy's hand. "Come with me."

She whisked the child with her to the back bedroom.

Sera narrowed her eyes and spoke in a restrained, voice. "What happened?"

Cat's stomach clenched. "We just wanted to talk – "

"Can it with the diplomacy. What did you say?"

"Here." Cat pulled the scripture from its box. "I'm the New Prophet. We need a Curse of every type for it to work."

"It?"

"The sacrifice."

Sera unrolled and read slowly, mouthing the words as she went. Her bandaged fingers left ashy prints on the back of the parchment. She scowled at Peter. "This is that's why you're here, right? You're her first victim?"

"I'm not a victim. It's my choice."

"Uh huh." Sera leveled her brow. "You really thought this would fly in Fire Town?"

"I didn't mean to hurt people."

“What's that matter?”

“I'm trying to save the world.”

“Curses don't have a *world*,” Sera seethed, “just time and someone to drag us to the embers when we die.”

Muffled voices moved past the skylight overhead. Sera heaved a sigh and dropped the scripture on the kitchen table. “Look, you can stay here until morning. Leave before everyone wakes up. You're not getting what you came for.”

She crossed to the bedroom and closed the door behind her. Cat tugged her bangs and paced the floor of the tiny front room. Peter cleared his throat. “I know this looks bad...”

“They hate us.”

“I wouldn't say that.”

“Did you see the way he looked at me?” She turned. “Did you see his eyes? It was like the inside of his head was on fire!”

“He was a loose cannon.”

“He was a Fire Curse,” she growled. “He hated me so much it almost killed him!”

“Don't yell. They can probably hear you.”

“Who cares?” Cat stopped by a wall covered in children's drawings and charcoal smears. “Everything's ruined. We've failed.”

“Don't lose hope already. It was only your first try.”

“It was my only try. There's not another Fire Town to go to.”

“Perhaps we'll find a Curse somewhere else?”

“Don't tease me.” She rolled her eyes. “We said no kids.”

“Then maybe we'll find an older Curse.”

“Sure, and maybe God will come back without our help.”

“Now you're just being stubborn.”

“Yeah, Pete, I am,” she fumed. “I was willing to give this Prophet thing a try for your sake, but obviously you were wrong. It's like back in Castleton when I thought I could be a farmer for ten minutes – and I considered *that* a sacrifice. What a laugh.”

“So you're saying we quit?”

“It's not quitting, I failed!” She threw up her hands. “Story of my life! I have no idea why I let you convince me God thought I was a Prophet. Everywhere I go I get yelled at and attacked – I've been run out of four towns in four days; who gets treated like that?”

“A Curse.”

She glared. “That's not funny.”

“Who's being funny?” His brow leveled. “Curses live with being unwanted every day. You can't lose your mind over one stumble, that's stupid.”

“So I'm stupid, now?”

“Cat, stop it.” Peter rose from the wall; his size and height blocked light from the skylight overhead. “I get it. This is hard. You got your feelings hurt, we caused some accidents, I think I broke a rib

– today sucked – and you can act selfish and play the victim like people have for centuries, or you pick up that scroll and do something about it."

Cat's anger turned to guilt. She couldn't speak without stammering, so she turned her back to pout.

He grunted. "Fine. Be that way."

Peter moved to a bench carved into the wall beneath another skylight. Friction hung in the air between them. Cat hated the feeling more with each passing moment. A deep ache clawed through her, dismantling her pride. Somehow, after everything they'd endured, the one thing that split them apart was herself.

Cat filled her lungs with the burnt smell of Fire Town and exhaled with a sob. "Pete, I..." Words fell in a rush. "Please don't be mad at me. I don't want to fight. I didn't mean it."

"I know."

"You're the only thing that makes sense on this mission. And I trust you, I mean it, but I get so confused..."

"It's okay."

"I'm sorry."

"Me too." He offered a patient smile. "You won't run me off, you know. We're doing this together."

She blushed and returned the smile. "Right."

He nodded to the space beside him. "I saved you some room."

Cat wiped her nose and climbed onto the bench beside him. Peter laid his arm across her back and nudged her closer. He was warm and smelled earthy like her garden in spring. She welcomed the rest and nestled her head against his shoulder. Stone barbs poked into her cheek, reviving her dull heartache but reminding her of home.

Trace stood in the desert outside Dire Lonato, contemplating the ring of glowing white script at his feet. Behind him, two black horses waited with travel-ready saddles. The sun dipped below the Western Mountains. Paige hugged her arms for warmth. “Master?”

He didn't respond. She tried louder.

“Master?”

"Hm?" Trace looked up. "Sorry, were you talking?"

“No, but...” She gestured to the darkening sky, but Trace was refocused on the spell. Paige raised an eyebrow. "How long do you plan to wait here?”

"Until the message is received.”

“It's been hours. The Holy Elder has better things to do than read your reports."

"We've encountered the first False Prophet in three hundred years.” He leaned on his brush. “I don't want to do this wrong.”

“Whatever.” Paige shivered. “Can we go back to town?”

“Not without Catrina Aston. Make camp.”

"Camp?"

"You heard me."

She grumbled and unpacked supplies from the horses, including two bedrolls, a field kitchen, and a satchel of firewood. She dressed the dry logs with kindling and struck a flint lighter.

Trace watched her toil without a spark. "You're not used to this, are you?"

"I don't have to make camp in the dormitories."

"Monks are traveling sages."

"That's why we get free lodging." The lighter slipped and pinched her hand. "Ow!"

He suppressed a smile. "You won't always be in a fancy hotel. It's my job to teach you the ways of the world. That's the point of an apprenticeship."

"The point of an apprenticeship is to become a monk," Paige retorted. "The other acolytes aren't sleeping in dirt – their masters are noble and civilized. They repair houses and fix windmills and are worshiped by hoards of grateful followers." She struck the flint more ruthlessly. "Why am I the one stuck in the middle of nowhere with a useless know-it-all?"

Trace lost his humor. "The others may have grander miracles, but I'm still a Senior Monk. I've memorized the lower library almost entirely, and written more extensively than any of my peers."

"Good for you," Paige replied. "Studying won't bring Our God back, though."

"Maybe not on its own." Trace watched sparks fly from her flint. "Can I help you with that?"

"I can do it."

"Okay." He considered his brush, breathed deep, and held it out to her. "Show me."

Paige dropped the flint. Her eyes locked on the staff. "Me?"

"You said you wanted to be a monk." He nodded to his glowing circle. "I can't paint more than one at a time."

"But... Me?" She looked from the handle to his face. "With a monk's brush?"

"Don't worry, it's not complicated." He tossed the staff and watched Paige scramble to catch it before it hit the ground.

The brush was surprisingly heavy, made of polished hardwood, metal, and horsehair. She turned it in her hands and studied her master. "You're not trying to trick me somehow, are you?"

"I wouldn't trick you," he said. "Circle first. Make it big. You don't know the size of the verse you're going to need."

She poured some paint into a bucket and filled the bristles with white, then hooked the brush under one arm and swept a shaky, elongated circle in the dust.

Trace grimaced a little but smiled when she finished. “Now we'll tell the golem to sit.”

“Do I just write 'sit'?”

“Not quite.” He grinned. “Use scripture. Golems are living creatures made of magic. They have wills of their own, but we can instruct them by quoting the word of Our God.”

“So at some point in scripture Our God told someone to 'sit'?”

“About thirty places, actually.” He pulled a battered, black notebook from the inside pocket of his tunic. “You can use any verse, but it takes a smart Calligrapher to pick the strongest quote for each particular situation. Here.” He turned the page toward her. “This one is from the early letters of Malachi. It'll do for now.”

“Why Malachi?”

“He's famous for his conversational approach,” Trace replied. “He translated the words of Our God as frankly as possible. It's not poetry, but makes for good, solid, casting. That's why so much of his writing is in the highest library.”

Paige squinted to read her Master's scribbles in the dark. “*And God bade me sit*.” She raised an eyebrow. “That's all it takes?”

“That's all. As long as Our God said it, it counts. Talented Calligraphers can interpret and draw Our God's commands from long blocks of text. Those instructions tend to be more subtle, they carry the connotation of the message – the difference between sitting and sitting at attention – but it takes a lot of study and a lot of memorization. Verses without Our God's voice in them will kill a golem or worse."

"Can you do it?"

"Of course, that's why I'm a senior monk." He nodded to her unfinished circle. "Start with a 'stop' command. The word 'dismissed' is fine, the first Prophet coined that. Then lay a fuse line down to extend its life a bit. Write Malachi's verse exactly as you read it. Even the punctuation matters."

Paige filled the brush with paint and did as instructed. She looped a spiral within the circle and wrote the scripture, leaving enough room at the center for the elemental rune. Her hand shook drops from the bristles as she paused over the blank space. "Fire?"

Trace softened. "Have you painted golems before?"

"No." She averted her eyes. "I mean, I've seen the symbols performed, but I didn't want to paint something wrathful...and I never felt worthy."

"No man is worthy," Trace said. "You'll probably always feel that way, even as a monk, but the Order exists to better understand Our God. We have to trust the words in His scriptures and do our best to follow them."

Trace opened the notebook to a pattern of interlocking shapes and curves. It was mathematically perfect and deceptively simple, with sharp angles and blades like the rays of the sun.

Paige gulped.

Trace put a hand on her shoulder. “You know, my master was a very strict man. He said apprentices were to assist, not emulate. This is your head start. Don't be nervous. Paint it as accurately as possible. The spell is a prayer. Do your best.”

She chewed her lip and nodded. The brush shook along the first line, but evened out as she continued. The symbol wasn't perfect, but she could feel the power growing as she drew, and when she closed the interlocking line, the whole ring flashed white. A ball of orange flame boiled to life in mid-air.

The fire expanded, forming two spindly legs, a long tail, and narrow stalk-like neck. The creature opened its eyes and unfolded a pair of blazing wings from its back.

Paige dropped to her knees for a closer look. “Whoa.”

“A bird.” Trace joined her on the ground. “Unexpected.”

“What does it mean?”

“The golem shape is unique to every Calligrapher,” Trace explained. “It's drawing life from your life, defined by your spirit, and shaped by your specific handwriting. It's an extension of yourself. The ancient monks believed it was the shape of your soul.”

“The shape of my soul...” she marveled. “Is that why we can only paint one at a time?”

“In a sense. The highest library has verses for casting many golems at once, but those are reserved for the Elder himself.”

“So he can paint the Living Golem.”

“That's right.”

“I was at the Elder's ordination, you know,” Paige said. “Of course I was six, so I didn't understand much.”

“I was seventeen,” Trace said. “I'd already finished my apprenticeship, and the Living Golem was the most astounding miracle I'd ever seen. It was the defining moment of my life.”

“I remember he told it to sit,” Paige said. “I'd never seen someone speak to a golem before.”

“The verse for verbal command is in the highest library,” Trace said. “The Living Golem is comprised of sacred verses to demonstrate the new Elder's mastery of the text. Its 'stop' command is tied to his life. It remains awake and active so that a fragment of the Elder's soul can watch over the monastery while he's away. When the Elder dies, the beast goes dormant and becomes a statue in the Hall of the Elders.” Trace sighed. “It's a beautiful symbol.”

“You're really into this stuff, huh?”

“I love it,” he said. “I'm amazed the residual power of Our God. Even though he's gone, a quote as simple as 'sit' can still control the the forces of nature. We already know so much, but there is so much left to learn. Why did he leave? When will he return? Someday I'll reach the highest library and learn everything there is to know."

"You want to be Elder?" Paige asked.

"Is that so hard to believe?"

She scoffed. "Yeah."

Trace reclaimed his brush with a smirk. "Mark my words, my dear apprentice, if we catch this False Prophet, I will be a hero and you'll tell your students how you painted your first golem under the direction of the holiest man in the Valley."

The white light of Paige's spell finished burning through Malachi's verse. The golem drew to attention, folded its wings and sat peacefully in the center of the circle.

Trace smiled and clapped Paige on the back. "They don't allow *that* in their fancy hotels."

She smiled to herself. "Whatever."

Cold wind swept dust through the camp, followed by a powerful gust as a mirage-like wind golem appeared from the darkness. It had four willowy legs, a pointed head, and a thick, club-like tail. Breath wheezed through its astral lungs. A man floated atop it, wearing a faded Calligrapher's uniform, and a glowing, golden brush strapped across his back.

Trace's message spell broke apart between them.

Paige gasped and bowed. “Holy Elder!”

"Dismissed!" the Elder barked. The golem let him slide down its leg and vanished in a puff of smoke.

“Master!” Trace jerked into a bow. “I didn't expect you to come in person – “

“And I didn't expect you to fail.”

“There were complications, your honor,” Trace said. “Catrina's more than a heretic, she's a False Prophet.”

“And you let her escape.” The Elder backhanded him across the face. Paige flinched, but Trace set his jaw and stayed at attention. The Elder frowned. “When I say 'arrest Catrina Aston at all costs', I mean 'at all costs'. She should be in a cell; I don't care how many towns you flatten.”

Trace tried to recover his composure. “I wasn't prepared.”

“You've never been able to follow rules, Hayes. You were useless as my apprentice and you are useless to me now.” Paige glanced between them. The Elder spotted her as if for the first time. “Acolyte!”

“Yes!”

“Make ready those horses. There's no rest tonight.”

“But sir,” Trace protested. “Miss Aston escaped to the desert. We'll be more effective in daylight.”

"Do you know where she's going, Hayes?" the Elder asked. "Have you the faintest idea what's actually going on?"

Trace paled.

"Of course you don't. I'm the Holy Elder; keep your mouth shut and follow orders. Maybe you'll finally learn something."

"Yes, sir."

Paige returned with the horses. The Elder hooked his rucksack onto Trace's saddle and spotted the miniature fire golem trembling at his feet. He unsheathed the gold brush from his back and sliced through its fire symbol with one angry stroke. A chill shivered up Paige's spine as the bird golem shrieked and vanished with a tiny hiss.

Chapter 14

Cat woke the next morning in a cold sweat. She was draped across Peter's chest with her arms about his middle and a jagged stone knob wedged into her cheek. She tightened her grip and listened to his rattling breaths until he moved his arm against her back.

"You okay?"

"Yeah," she peeped. "Nightmare."

"The fire golem?"

She nodded.

"Me, too."

“I'm sorry,” Cat muttered. “I shouldn't have lost my temper yesterday, I put you in danger when I promised to protect you.”

“You can't take credit for that, talking to Brushcasters would set anyone off.”

“Hmph,” she snorted. “Have you been up long?”

“A bit.” He flexed his broad shoulders. “This bench is murder on my back."

“Then let's get you out of it.”

He winced and lifted his arm to let her up. Cat straightened her vest and took his hand. Dozens of unfamiliar growths dotted his swollen forearm. She dropped it with a gasp.

Peter grunted. “I know."

“Pete, it's awful.” Cat ran her hands over his arms. Every inch was covered in new lumps and tumors, some larger than any she'd felt in him before. She cupped her hand around a mound growing from his spine. “Is all this from yesterday?"

"It's not a big deal.”

“Yes it is!” she cried. "Are you in pain? Can I wrap it?"

"It's fine, really.” He feigned a laugh. “I mean, as long as I can still feel my legs, right?”

Her stomach turned.

“Cat.” Peter's brown eyes softened. “It's fine. I've been turning to stone since the day I was born. Nothing's changed.”

“I know, but – ”

"I'm okay." He sidled close as she lowered back to the bench and fit the bruise in her check back to the growth it remembered. “This isn't your fault."

“Cat!” Edana rushed in from the bedroom wearing a clean, blue headscarf.

Cat bent forward to greet her. “Wow! Look at you!”

“Sera said you were asleep, but I wanted you to meet somebody.” Edana smiled through fresh face wounds and retrieved the boy in orange from the bedroom. “This is Kory.”

“Hi, Kory,” Cat smiled. “I remember you from yesterday.”

He twiddled his fingertips. “Hi, Prophet Lady.”

“This is Cat, Kory, she saved me,” Edana said. “Kory and me are best friends now. We talked all night about our moms and dads and stuff. He's from Castleton.”

“I bet this town feels really small compared to a big city like Castleton.” Cat sat on her ankles and studied the boy's mousy features. “Do you have an older brother, Kory?”

“Yeah.”

“I think I may have a message for you, then.” She grinned. “Kaleb told me to say 'hi'.”

Kory gasped. “You know Kaleb?”

“Yeah, he was our guide when we were in the city. Would you like me to say 'hi' back when I see him again?”

“Yes!” Kory squirmed in excitement. “Tell him I miss him!”

“You bet I will. And I'll tell him all about how helpful you were yesterday.”

“Um...” A rosy shine warmed Edana's cheeks. “Cat, I know I asked you take me with you before, but is it okay if I stay here, instead? Kory promised to show me around.”

“I think that's a great idea,” Cat replied. “I know how important a friend can be.”

“Not so important that you won't sacrifice him to an absent God.” Sera leaned on the open door frame behind them. “It's dawn. Time for you to go.”

Edana's brow knit. “Do they have to?”

Sera sucked her chapped lip. Across the room, the front door creaked open. Ildri slipped in from outside, her eyes red and puffy. She wiped her face on her sleeve and spotted the group with a start. “You're all awake!”

“Where have you been?” Sera asked. “Were you crying?”

“No I was...” Ildri cleared her throat. “Talking with Aiden.”

“About Tyson?” Sera pressed forward. “Is he okay?”

“Well...”

Sera's eyes ringed in a faint glow. “He's not – ”

"Sera. Take a deep breath."

"He can't be!" She shoved Ildri aside and charged up the stairs.

Ildri pursued. "Sera! Don't!"

Cat pulled Peter from the bench and followed Kory and Edana into the courtyard. Morning sun reflected off the cloud of twisting smoke overhead and warmed the quiet town. Soft tufts of ash dusted the sleeping Curses in silent vigil outside Tyson's door. Sera jarred them awake with the pound of her fists.

"Ty, are you in there!" she called. "Ty! Answer me!"

"Don't do that!" one of the roused Curses shouted.

Another cried, "Get her!" A knot of teens caught Sera by the arms. She returned to ground level, kicking and flailing.

"Let me go!"

"Sera, stop," Ildri plead. "You'll hurt yourself."

"Hey!" Aiden slipped, soot-stained and exhausted, from the door at the bottom of the stairs. "Keep it down out here."

"Aiden!" Sera yanked out of her captor's hands. "Is he –"

"Asleep," Aiden replied. "I stayed up all night getting him stable; I'm not letting you kill him now."

"So he's alive." Cat's whole body relaxed. "Thank goodness."

"Thank nothing. He's still a wreck," Aiden said. "I had to rip up a couple shirts for most of it. He used our whole box of gauze."

“Tell me the truth,” Sera said with shaking hands. “I can take it if you say it plainly. How long does he have left?”

“Days? Hours?” Aiden sighed. “It's a miracle he made it through the night.”

The Fire Curses exchanged sober glances. Sera staggered and grabbed for Ildri, her face gaunt and haunted. “Hours?”

Sad resolve glowed in Aiden's tired eyes. “Sorry, Sera. He's not surprised. We all knew it was coming.”

“It's not fair!” She grit her teeth and turned on Cat. “Why'd you have to come here?”

“None of that.” Ildri stepped between them. “You won't help Tyson by following his example. Cat's not the enemy.”

“Why are you defending her?”

“I'm not, I mean...” The scars on Ildri's face twitched, growing splotchy around the edges.

Sera stepped away from her. “Wait.” She turned to Aiden who refused to meet her eye. “What were you two talking about before we woke up?”

He struggled to fake indifference. “It was nothing.”

“You sneaked out while we were asleep.” Sera grabbed Ildri's arms and stared into her face. “You were crying, but not about Tyson. What did – ”

Ildri hid her face from Sera and met Cat instead, sadness and determination in her lighted pupils.

"Were you talking about us, Ildri?"

Tears added to the swell around her eyelids.

"Would you like to come with us?"

The crowd was deathly silent. Ildri swallowed and nodded.

Sera shoved her away. "Are you crazy?"

"It's the right thing to do."

"No it's not!" Sera fretted.

The other Fire Curses murmured, each face redder and brighter than the next. Ildri balled her sleeves and buried her face in her hands.

"Aiden, tell her not to go," Sera cried.

His eyes locked to the dirt. "I can't."

"I thought you loved her!"

"I do!"

"Then fight for her!" she demanded. "Talk her out of it! Do something!"

"I tried." A wound in his face kindled orange like embers. "She made a choice."

"It's not fair!" Sera whirled on Cat. "Did you come to take everyone I love? Why are you doing this to me?"

Cat shook her head. "Sera..."

“Sera.” A hoarse voice called from the stairwell. Silence fell again as a hunched man staggered against the open door of the hut. His scarf and clothes were replaced with layers of stained bandages. The bits of skin left exposed were black and gnarled as tree bark. Two eyes blazed from the dark shell, surrounded by fiery cracks that pulsed with the slow beat of his heart.

Sera gasped, “Tyson!”

“For the love of Our God stop yelling,” he rasped. “You'll wake the dead.”

Ildri peeked from within her sleeves as Sera and Aiden helped him climb the shallow stairs. Guilt drew a wave of nausea up Cat's throat. She offered her hand, but Tyson declined and leaned heavily into Sera's shoulder.

“Il,” he coughed.

She bit skin from her lip. “Yes?”

“You sure you want to go on this quest?”

She nodded.

“Even if you won't come back?”

“Yes.” Her voice shook. “I'm sorry if I've upset you.”

“Don't baby me, Il.” He heaved a dry laugh, but faltered with a wince. “You're always babying people.”

“Sorry.” She paused to draw a deep, calming breath. “I know saying 'yes' means I'm going to die, but that's always been a fact, hasn't it? Cat came with real magic and a way to stop this. I knew everyone would disapprove but I wanted to help you all, and I think this will."

Sera blushed bright in shame. Aiden's face twitched beneath new wounds and deep scars. Tyson tightened his hand on Sera's shoulders. "If you really believe that, don't let me stop you."

His profound tone gave Cat chills. She wrapped her arm around Peter as Tyson straightened without a shred of doubt.

"Forget what I said yesterday. I was out of line – " A sharp breath stoked the flame beneath his cracked skin. "Truth is, if I could guarantee I'd live to the end, I'd go myself, because this really sucks. The last six hours..." He flinched and lowered back to Sera's shoulder. "Short version, if you can spare anyone this death you should try."

"Tyson," Cat said. "Thank you."

He nodded.

"Ty." Ildri's voice regained strength. "Be strong for Sera and Aiden, okay? They need you."

"I'll try."

"Ildri." Aiden reached out.

She took his hand, but avoided his eyes and turned to Cat. "Can we leave now?"

"If you want to."

"It'd be best." Ildri forced her pleasant demeanor despite bright, swelling wounds. "Goodbye everyone. Take care of each other. Conserve the water; it looks like a lot, but make it last. I'll miss you."

"Ildri!" Kory grabbed her leg. Other children came forward to join the group hug. She touched their colored scarves, struggling to keep her calm exterior. Heat coursed through her cheeks to her watering eyes.

"No crying, now," she said. "Nobody cry, okay? Be happy we're going to save everyone."

They put on difficult smiles and escorted her to the wagon. She was lifted inside and stood in the bed like a princess in her carriage. The other Fire Curses counted down to a cheer and a celebration started. Cat was troubled and amazed by their practiced grins and the way they each turned flickers of sadness into positive words and encouragement. Even the children would sniff and shout "hooray" or "thank you" to force themselves to smile. It was like a scene from a play. Sera cuddled into Tyson's shoulder, both their tempers suppressed. Edana took cues from Kory, who kept a tight grip on her hand. The sea of colored scarves and varied emotions moved in waves around the wagon, and Cat could only sit in the driver's seat and watch.

Peter joined her. He hid his own feelings behind foggy glasses but managed a reassuring smile. Breaking a family felt awful, but it was not her place to say or do anything. Both Peter and Ildri agreed to this mission. Cat had to trust them and be grateful. She took hold of the reins. “Are you two ready?”

“Yeah,” Peter said.

Ildri beamed with pride beneath her lavender scarf. “Yes.”

“Wait!” Aiden staggered forward. Fear burned hot in his eyes. “Wait, not yet!”

“Aiden.” Her face twitched but she stilled it. “Say goodbye. Don't hurt yourself.”

“Ildri don't...”

“Goodbye everyone!” she called.

“Goodbye!” They shouted back. Cat paused for a second's thought, but gave Strawberry a twitch. She steered the wagon back to the coal field and up the dirt path. The Curses stopped at the fire's edge, removing their colored hoods in reverence. All were bare except Aiden whose eyes blazed with suppressed emotion.

His jaw twitched, cracking blackened skin of his cheeks. Ildri kept smiling, but her strength faltered and she turned away. The flame beneath Aiden's flesh took on new intensity. He shuffled his feet, wet his lips, and ran full speed into the field of coals.

“Aiden!” Sera shouted. Ildri whirled back to see him moving toward her, carving a trail of fire and ash.

"Don't!" she cried, composure forgotten. Bursts of flame singed his pants and bare feet, but he kept running until he reached the back of the wagon and leaped into her arms.

Ildri pulled him into the bed and sobbed as hard as she could into his tattered gray scarf. Cat yanked the horse to a stop. Aiden looked over Idri's head to meet her eye. "Keep going."

"But – "

"Please." His eyes burned. "Just go."

Cat nodded and lashed Strawberry again. The horse snorted and gained speed to the safety of the ridge. The Fire Curses cheered and clapped at the edge of flames. A tiny voice split their noise. "Goodbye, Cat!" Edana waved her blue scarf like a flag. "Bye, Peter! Thanks for everything!"

Kory lifted his orange scarf as well, and the rest followed suit, waving their colors high over the rippling heat. The wind unfurled the colors like flags, whipping and waving until Strawberry cleared the lake bed and Fire Town vanished over the crest of the hill.

They followed Peter's atlas across open country and along the wispy remnants of back roads to avoid other travelers. The foothills changed to withered grassland and stretches of open field that seemed to go on forever. The Fire Curses sat quietly with Ildri's head on Aiden's shoulder. He stared back toward the Western Mountains where a long ribbon of smoke wafted from Fire Town.

Cat let the reins go slack. “How are you guys doing?”

“Fine, thank you,” Ildri said. “Being still helps.”

“Pete has some spare bandages if you need them, Aiden,” Cat offered. “Of course, they're elastic.”

He continued to stare. “I'm fine.”

“Don't act tough,” Ildri chided. “That was a crazy and romantic thing you just did.”

“It wasn't romantic.” His bowed his head. “You said goodbye... and I couldn't.... so I followed.”

Ildri nestled against his shoulder. “Well, I thought it was romantic, anyway.”

He leaned closer. “I'm yours to the end.”

Cat's heart broke as she watched the two Fire Curses together. A horrible sacrifice awaited both of them in the cavern below Lord Creven's manor; one would lose their life, and the other would live on alone. It was hard for Cat to determine which had the worse fate.

Ildri noticed her staring and blushed. “So, Peter, where are we headed next?”

“South to Water Town and the city of Chalsie-Veneer.”

“*Water* Town?” Aiden cringed. “That sounds awful.”

“It's not what you'd call 'Fire Curse friendly'.” Peter propped the atlas on one arm so they could see. “It's on the bank of Lake Veneer – the last and largest body of standing water in God's Valley.”

Ildri bit dry skin off her lip. “It's in a lake? Like a real lake?”

“Don't worry, you guys will be far away from that.” Cat handed Peter the reins and climbed over the partition. “Here.” She fished a water-proof tarp from one of Lady Creven's boxes. “This will protect you from the sun *and* the water.”

“Thanks, Cat.” Ildri stretched it over their heads like a tent.

“You guys had a long night,” Cat said. “Let the Prophet worry about saving the world, you two get some rest.”

They gratefully obliged. Cat waited for them to settle and returned to the seat next to Peter. “I think they'll be all right.”

“And you said you weren't good at this.”

"I'm just being nice. You and Ildri are the real heroes.”

“I don't know if it's heroism, really. She was moved by the truth, like I was. There's no denying you're the real deal – that miracle you made was gorgeous.”

Cat tucked a hair into her bun. “I don't know about gorgeous.”

“Your water magic is really improving,” Peter said. “I mean, that one in Dire Lonato – when did you learn to make a wall like that? It was amazing.”

Fear prickled the back of Cat's neck as she recalled the fire golem and the dark stranger. She swallowed a knot and hugged her arms across her heart. “That wasn't me.”

“What?”

"The miracle," Cat said. "It was someone else."

Peter frowned. "Who else knows magic? A Brushcaster?"

"I don't know. It was a guy dressed in a dark cloak. He had the blackest eyes." Her face flushed as she recalled the way they glittered in the white light of his palm, and the magnetism as they pulled her into their deep, peaceful pools.

Peter tensed. "You mean the guy from Castleton?"

"Yeah." Cat blinked from her reverie. "That's right, you said you felt him."

"Yeah, I felt him." His tone was cagey. "You didn't think this was worth mentioning to me?"

"I was going to, but then with Edana and everything... there's been a lot going on."

"That guy is dangerous, Cat!" Peter said, but hushed with a glance at the sleeping Fire Curses. "You should have told me."

"He saved my life."

"He's bad."

"Why do you say that?"

"I can feel it." A muddy film clouded the whites of his eyes. "The earth... inside... it knew he was watching before I did."

"*It* did?"

"I could feel every bit of it." He shuddered. "My whole life until now I was always just me, but that was the first time I felt like something unnatural – like a person with something foreign inside him. That stranger looked at me, and it was like the stone was scared of him and trying to escape out of my bones."

Cat gulped. "Do you think he was trying to hurt you?"

"Maybe," Peter said. "It sounds dumb, but it felt like hate. Like he hated me and what I was." He shook his head. "I know that sounds like nonsense, but it's what it feels like."

"I believe you." Cat ran a finger under her string. "Do you think he's a Brushcaster? Maybe a rogue one?"

"Could be. He did kill one of their golems."

"He could be on our side."

"You can't feel it like I can." Peter's eyes were skeptical behind the blur of muddy tears.

Cat watched him with tears of her own. "You're scared."

"Yeah, Cat, I'm scared."

"So what are we going to do?"

"Finish the quest," he said. "God's forgiveness will take the magic back from everyone, even this stranger. Whoever he is, he can't hurt you if he doesn't have magic."

She took a breath to steady her nerves and straightened. "No one's going to hurt me. I'm a Prophet. I've got magic of my own."

Peter slouched a bit. "Hmph."

"Yeah, true, this stranger is really powerful. He's got a different kind of magic than Brushcasters do, but it's the same symbols and spells. We can handle it." She took Peter's arm. "Plus we know what to look for, now. Next time your blood gets scared, you tell me. That way we won't be caught off guard."

He cracked a smile. "Like an alarm system."

"More like a lookout."

"More like a lookout tower." The muddy veil lifted from his eyes. "Okay, Cat, don't worry. Your pet rock will keep you safe."

Chapter 15

Clear skies and gentle wind brought the illusion of safety. Although Strawberry pulled the wagon easily across the flats, the midday heat was stifling to the Fire Curses, and they had to stop frequently for rest and refreshment. After dark, they kept Castleton to their left and followed the brilliant ribbon of stars southeast. Darkened towns floated past them like ghosts in the moonlight. Cat couldn't tell if they were deserted, but figured distance was best either way.

The third morning broke in magenta and periwinkle. Thick, twisted weeds had replaced the dead grasses sometime during the night and the gray silhouette of a forest was in view beneath the Southern Mountains.

"What's that?" Ildri pointed from beneath the tarp she and Aiden shared.

Peter lay beside them in the bed with his atlas open. "The Gatekeeper's Forest. See here?"

She compared the page to the horizon. "How far is it?"

"Another full day, probably."

"Feels like we've been out here for ages." Ildri pulled shifted. "I'm restless."

"How's your skin?"

"Hurts. But that's normal." She lifted the tarp to see her sleeping boyfriend. "At least the rest has helped his feet. I was worried."

"Do you heal at all?"

"We can a little with scar tissue. You?"

"Same. The bones are the problem."

"How does that work, if you don't mind me asking."

"Like yours, it's blood based," he said. "The stone's marrow deep. From there it takes over the bones and connective tissue. At this point it's started on the soft parts. A bump or a bruise draws more blood which makes more stone which replaces more things. See, my hands and feet are nearly useless."

She poked his wrist with a fingertip. “I'm sorry to hear that.”

“It's what we are.” Peter shifted to call over his shoulder. “How are you doing, Cat?”

“Sleepy,” she replied. “Do you want a turn?”

“Can I have one?” Ildri peeped. “I feel like a bit of a lump here on my own.”

Cat grinned. “You want to drive?”

“If it's not too much trouble to teach me.”

“Of course not. Climb forward.”

Ildri slipped out from beneath Aiden's arm and slid forward. Cat offered her the reins. She accepted them with her hands balled into her sleeves. “What first?”

“It explains itself pretty well,” Cat said. “Keep them loose. When you want her to slow down you pull back, if you want her to speed up, flick them across her back.”

“You mean hit her?”

“Tap her,” Cat corrected. “Just a tap.”

“Okay, a tap.” She flapped them weakly. They flopped across Strawberry's haunches and she increased her pace by half a length. Ildri's face flushed a bright red. “I did it!”

“You're a natural.” Cat slung a leg over the partition. “Ask Pete if you have any questions. I'm going to take a nap.”

“Okay.”

She stretched out on the bench to Peter's right. He nudged her with his shoulder. "Almost there."

She yawned. "Almost there."

"Hey, healthy girl." Aiden peeked from under the tarp.

Cat raised her eyebrows. "What?"

His orange pupils darted to Ildri and back. "Thanks for that."

"Hey, it's a help."

"No I mean..." He vanished into the dark a moment and reappeared with a softer expression. "Thanks for treating us like people. You're the first person outside Fire Town to make me feel like, you know..."

"You have value?" Peter prompted.

He vanished into the tarp again. "Yeah, that."

Cat regarded Peter warmly and leaned in. "Hey, Fire Curse."

Aiden peered from within the folds.

"You had value either way."

He sniffed. "Thanks, Cat."

They took a break three hours later when Peter took the reins and again five hours after that when they rejoined the South Spoke out of Castleton. Unlike the West Spoke toward Dire Lonato, this road was paved with packed dirt and gravel. An ox cart drawing a long trailer full of water barrels plodded toward them from the forest road. Cat took the front seat and drew the tarp over the three Curses to avoid suspicion. She nodded as the farmer passed them, his eyes bleary and half blind. More wagons followed throughout the day, toting water or furniture; some carried lumber; one held a towns-person's household possessions. Neither he nor his wife made eye contact as they passed. Cat kept watch to the front and Peter behind until night fell and they gave Aiden a turn at the reins.

The moon was past its zenith when they reached the forest edge. Aiden was nodding, so Cat tapped his shoulder and took his place at the reins. The Fire Curse snuggled in his waterproof cocoon next to Ildri and the wagon continued through the drifting shadows of the Gatekeeper's Forest.

Cat watched the woods for hours, expecting every trunk to be a hidden Calligrapher or a dark stranger ready to cast magic on her sleeping passengers. Every now and then, a crack or pop echoed off the shrouded trees. A shrill voice put her heart in her throat, but the flutter of wings against the moon settled her down. They were in a living forest, very different from the acres of dead trees outside Mason Forge. A mouse scurried across the road in front of them and into the tall grasses beside a gnarled fence post.

Dawn broke pale blue through the branches, panting dappled splotches on the mildewed fences lining the road. Aiden and Ildri emerged from their cover and watched the massive trunks pass slowly above them. Their awe reawakened a childish wonder in Cat's heart, transporting her back to a time when the woods in her backyard were huge and magical. They climbed and ran from one imaginary land to another, discovering lost civilizations, finding secret treasure, and slaying ferocious monsters between breakfast and dinner.

The gravel turned to cobblestone as it wound deeper into the forest. The Southern Mountains towered over the leafy canopy. Light glowed in the leaves and spotted their faces with flashes of shadow. Moss-covered stone structures jutted like tombstones from the forest floor; a fallen wall, a freestanding chimney, a foundation draped in decayed beams like dried bones. Chalsie-Veneer appeared like a phantom between the trees.

Cobbled roads and two-story structures built of mismatched lake stone clustered around narrow alleyways. Hand-painted signs advertising restaurants, boat trips, and bait shops peeled in the sunlight filtering through the high canopy. Cat stopped the wagon at edge of town, where early risers waited for shop owners to open their storefronts. The smell of fish and rot hung heavy in the chilled air. The outskirts were crowded with shanty houses and wooden sheds sagging, neglected in the lingering mist. Cat pulled them to a stop beside a crumbling out-building far enough from the main road to obscure them from view.

Aiden shivered with a whistle. “This place is homey.”

Cat handed him the reins. “Move the wagon if anyone comes.”

"You're not coming with us?" Ildri asked.

Cat disembarked. "I'm going to Water Town."

"With me," Peter said.

Ildri bit her lip. "Is that safe?"

"He's my guard tower." Cat smiled.

Peter slid out the back. "We'll be fine."

"You're the boss." Aiden took the front seat. "Good luck."

Cat and Peter continued on foot through the dampened streets, following street signs and tourist posters to the bank of Lake Veneer. They stuck to side roads and mist-shrouded backways, keeping an eye out for strangers around each building and bend. The locals they passed wore heavy cloaks and dark colors. They stared straight through Cat, their downcast faces burdened by exhaustion and distant thoughts. Those who noticed Peter crossed to the other side of the street and stared, wary, until they were safely past.

Peter watched a woman tug her child into a nearby shop. "At least they're not confrontational."

"That's almost like tolerant," Cat said.

"Almost but not quite."

"How much further to the Water Goddess?"

"It should be the next block."

They took a left onto a wide mall lined in wooden billboards and white-washed storefronts. City hall stood a the north end of the plaza. The white stone building sagged beneath an ornate brass clock tower, supported by a line of alabaster columns carved of white marble. One of the four supports had gone missing, replaced by a seated stone golem with a spade-shaped face, long spindly legs and a thick, club-like tail.

Memories of Mason Forge sent a shock up Cat's spine. “What's that doing here?”

“The Elder said they were on a world tour,” Peter said.

She stared into the golem's eyeless face and tightened her grip on his arm. “Let's hope it means they won't come back.”

On the south end was the Water Goddess, stained green and brown by centuries of grime. She held a pitcher of water northward toward Castleton in the same manner as her fire-themed sister, and had the same bit of broken pedestal at the base beneath her feet. Her delicate features were saved from wind erosion by the surrounding forest, as were the details of her billowing hair and knotted shawl. Her eyes stared skyward, striped with rain and distinctly sorrowful.

“Not to give Dolores undue credit,” Peter ventured, “but it does kind of look like you when her face isn't worn off.”

“If by that you mean we're both teenage girls.” She cocked her head to one side. “It's weird she's been vandalized the same way.”

“Yeah, weird.” Peter eyed the growing crowd of morning shoppers and shifted toward the nearest wall. “Let's dwell on it later.”

They hurried past a line of bait shops and fishing supply stores to the bank of Lake Veneer. A line of dry-docked boats sat along a warped gray boardwalk at the edge of a steep dropoff. Below, stretched a musky, mile-wide sink hole, forty feet deep and thick with opaque, rolling fog. Slick, greenish banks dipped sharply toward the lake's surface. Moss-laden trees clung to the slope with exposed roots as if reaching for the standing water below.

A freestanding pier jutted out over the expanse, punctuated by a winding staircase leading down to a floating barge obscured by the fog. Cat pointed. “Is that Water Town?”

Peter peered over the edge with a gulp. “Probably.”

“Quite a drop.”

“Yeah.” His voice quivered. “I can't take those stairs, Cat.”

“We'll go slow.”

“No, I can't.” He shook his head. “I'd never make it back up.”

“Hey you!” A gargling voice called. A boy waved at them from the far end of the pier. “Curse guy! Over here!”

Cat took Peter's arm and guided him onto the creaking platform. The boy leaned on a wooden staff as the two approached. He was soaked head to toe with bloated, bluish skin and unnatural swelling around his face and joints.

Tears streamed from his smiling eyes. “Hey, bud! You're an Earth Curse, right?"

“That's right,” Peter said. “I'm guessing you're water?”

“You bet! Call me Ford.” He extended a dripping hand, but withdrew it with a glance at Peter's bandages. “Sorry.”

“It's fine. We're looking for Water Town.”

“You found it.” Ford gestured to the head of the stairwell.

Cat leaned off the dock for a better view. “That's quite a stairwell you have.”

“Keeps the cityfolk out.” Ford leaned forward on his staff. “Whatcha doin' way out here, Earth Curse? This is the opposite side of the world for you.”

“We're going on a bit of an adventure,” Peter replied.

“An adventure?” The Water Curse winked, forcing a gush of liquid from his eye. “I like your style, bud! Don't let the healthy man, keep you down. This your girl?”

Cat's brow arched. “His *girl*?”

Peter blushed umber and stepped aside. “This is Cat. She wants to talk to you.”

“Sure, you bet.” Ford turned his pooling eyes to her. “Buying water, pretty girl?”

“What?”

“Buy water,” he repeated. “It's what most healthy people come to Water Town for.”

“You sell water from the lake?”

"Bah, no, that stuff's nasty. We sell water from us." He snapped the collar of his soaked tee shirt. "Straight from the source."

Cat grimaced.

Ford laughed and elbowed Peter, leaving a wet mark on his chest. "I love it when they make that face! Don't look so disturbed, Curse water's pure magic! It's the cleanest and healthiest in the world. Not even Lord Creven can give you quality like that."

"I'll take your word for it." She shuddered. "We're more interested in Water *Town*, though. Can we pass?"

"Depends." Ford straightened. "Did the mayor send you?"

"Would the mayor send a Curse?"

"Don't guess he would."

"See, there you go," Cat said. "Pete and I are on a mission and need to talk to Water Town. We think we can help each other."

"Water Town's doing pretty good, thanks," Ford lilted. "Anything we need we can buy from the market."

"You just buy it?" Peter asked. "Like normal people?"

"Yeah, it's where we sell all our water. Makes enough for the essentials. You know it hasn't rained for almost a year down here."

"How about miracles, then?" Cat asked. "I noticed the Brushcasters have been through recently. I'm what they call a Prophet. It's like a Brushcaster for Curses."

“Ain't that special?” Ford grinned. “I never heard of a Prophet before, but I really doubt the Brushcasters have a Curse department unless it's for calling us names.”

“They didn't send me. I'm on a special mission from God – ”

“I'll stop you there,” Ford said. “I believe in Our God as much as the next guy, that doesn't mean we're on good terms, you know? You can be a Brushcaster or a Prophet or whatever you want, but this here is a business transaction. Your money can come in, but only Water Curses beyond this point. Douglas's rules.”

“Who's Douglas?” Peter asked.

“Doug's in charge,” Ford said. “Trust me, he's the best. He made the mayor cry once. Wish I'd seen it, but it was before my time.”

“So Douglas makes the rules?” Cat asked.

“Yeah, his word's the law.”

“Can I talk to him?”

“He'd probably break your neck.”

“I'm not scared.”

“Hah, you're cute.” Ford spat a mouthful of water off the edge of the pier. “I tell you what, come back on market day. If you're lucky, Douglas will be at our stall, although for some reason he's missed the last couple weeks – ”

“We can't wait,” Peter said.

“Is there any way Douglas can see us right now?” Cat asked. “I'm not trying to be disrespectful – we don't have to go to town, he can meet us up here.”

“Yeah, I don't think so.” Ford scratched his bloated neck. “He's not really a talker.”

“But he's your leader.”

“Doesn't mean he's on call.”

Cat pressed her lips. “Okay. How about you? You're a nice guy. Want to help us out?”

“Me? No way, I shouldn't even be talking to you.” He glanced between Cat and Peter with a gargling sigh. “Before Douglas came, healthy folk went in whenever they wanted day or night and took people. Little kids, half dead ones, anybody who could fit in a tank.”

Cat gulped. “A tank?”

“Do you know what water goes for on the black market nowadays?” Ford asked. “One of us in a tower could water a whole field of crops, and we don't have to be alive to make enough of it. When Douglas came, he chased the raiders off. Killed a couple, I'm pretty sure. No healthy people were allowed in Water Town after that. Fear keeps 'em out and keeps us all safe.”

Cat gulped. “I understand that it's dangerous, but still need to speak to your people. If that means talking to Douglas, I'll do it.”

“This must be a real important mission if you're willing to get murdered for it.”

Peter grunted. “In my opinion it is.”

“We're preventing more Curses,” Cat said. “We're collecting volunteers for a ritual that will get God to come back and end magic.”

“End magic? You mean no more Brushcasters?”

“And no more drought,” Cat said. “That means no more people trying to kidnap you.”

Ford gnawed his swollen lip.

“How about this,” Peter said. “What if you had collateral to prove Cat's telling the truth?”

“What's a collateral?”

“An investment. A reassurance.” Peter eyed the staircase. “Something Cat will lose if she doesn't come back.”

She stiffened, suspicious. “Pete....”

Ford's leaking eyes widened. “You mean *you*!”

“If you keep me up here, Cat will come back for me,” he said. “If she's lying, you can push me off the pier.”

“Pete!” Cat recoiled.

Ford cut a smile. “Okay, I'm convinced. She'll come back.”

“Of course I'll come back!” She grabbed Peter's arm. “This isn't Castleton, Peter. The Brushcasters are looking for us, and I'd bet money the local government's got their eyes peeled, too.”

“More reason I'm a good hostage.” Peter leaned close to whisper. “I still can't take those stairs.”

“So I keep Earth guy up here.” Ford stammered. “And you sneak down and talk to Douglas about this mission thing.”

“That's the plan,” Peter said.

“Okay, okay....” Ford hacked a cough and spat a mouthful of water onto the pier. “Maybe it's early enough that everyone's still asleep, but if you get caught don't tell anyone I let you in, okay? Say you swam. Or jumped. Who am I kidding? I'm so screwed.”

“I'm sure Douglas will understand when he hears what I have to say,” Cat said. “You can trust me.”

“Yeah, I know. That's why I'm letting you through.” Ford stepped aside, allowing access to the staircase. “Douglas lives in a houseboat at the end of the floating dock. He won't be happy to see you, so be quick explaining the whole mission thing. I hope it works.”

“So do I.” Cat squeezed Peter's arm. “Don't actually let him throw you off the pier.”

“I'll do my best.”

“Hey.” Ford leveled his staff across her path with guilt in his pooling eyes. “Promise me you won't hurt anyone.”

“I swear on my life.”

Chapter 16

Cat's boot heels slipped on the decaying staircase as she inched her way toward Water Town. Dank air chilled her to the bone and filled her nose with the smell of rot and stagnant water. Lifting fog hugged the grime-coated shoreline as she continued her descent. Morning sunlight pierced the haze to reveal a sprawling labyrinth of platforms, and barges lashed to the legs of the pier.

Cat hid behind one of the wooden supports and checked the surrounding walkways for any sign of Douglas's houseboat. Water Curses trudged along dripping pathways between rough huts built of driftwood and garbage. Cat craned her neck, but the mist was too heavy to see past. She glanced to the pier extending from the boardwalk high above her. Water from Ford's feet dripped through the slats. Peter was waiting. She summoned her courage and crept from the staircase into Water Town proper.

Bowing boards and metal planks bobbed on hollow pontoons. The interlocking pathways branched randomly. Cat kept to the outer path, hoping the houseboat was around each new bend. She stopped short when she found a Water Curse lying face down on the path. Liquid drained from his face and body in a constant trickle as he gargled deep breaths.

"Hey!"

Cat whirled around.

A female Curse stood on a parallel catwalk. "You're not supposed to be down here!"

"S-Sorry!"

"How'd you get here?" The Water Curse frowned. "Did Ford let you in?"

"Uh, no..." Cat swallowed. "I'm looking for Douglas."

"Douglas?" The Water Curse narrowed her tearing eyes. Damp heads peeked from the neighboring huts.

Cat ran a finger under her sting. "I hear he sells water. I really need some water. It's an emergency."

“An emergency?” The Water Curse brightened. “Why didn't you say so? Come with me, I'll get you some.”

Cat gulped and rounded a hut to join the Water Curse on her catwalk. The girl's skin was bluish despite her darker complexion. Her long wet hair clung in crimps and ringlets to the sides of her face and neck, and the heavy flesh on her neck and arms sloshed back and forth as she walked.

They weaved along the interlocking catwalks, winding between driftwood homes where Water Curses fished off the walkways, silhouetted by early fog. A couple of children swam in the lake off the walkway. In the water they seemed normal except for the swelling under their eyes. They scowled when they saw her. One stuck out his tongue.

“It really must be an emergency if Ford let you pass, I didn't that was even allowed,” the girl said over her shoulder. “What's happened? Is someone sick?”

“Yes.” Cat's stomach twisted with the lie. “My friend is. I have to get back to him right away.”

“Don't worry, it's not too far!”

Cat followed close behind her guide, aware with each turn she was growing more lost. They joined a line of younger Curses transporting tar-lined sacks of water to an open metal basin. A pulley system lined with similar bags extended from the container up the bank to the marina at the far end of Chalsie-Veneer's boardwalk. The Water Curses dumped their loads into the trough and padded with their containers back up the walk.

The girl trotted to a table covered with slates and wax pencils. "Okay then, did you bring your own bucket?"

Cat searched the docks for Douglas's houseboat, but the area around the water tank was as samey and maze-like as the rest.

The Water Curse leaned over her paperwork. "Miss?"

"Sorry, what?"

"Did you bring something to hold the water?"

"Uh, no." Cat ran a finger under her string. "I wasn't really thinking about that."

"Don't worry, we stock a couple options." Water escaped from her mouth as she smiled. "We can sell you a bucket for twenty."

Cat wheeled back. "That much?"

"You can't carry the water up the stairs in your hands." She shrugged. "We also have animal skins for thirty-five."

"Forget it, I'll take the bucket." Cat checked the walkways again. "How long will this take?"

"Not long at all, miss, I just have to climb this short ladder."

The Curse selected a metal bucket from a nearby stack and climbed onto the barge. Cat waited until her back was turned and took off at a run.

"Hey!"

"Sorry!" Cat shouted. She leaped over a sleeping child and dashed up a branching path toward the far edge of Water Town. She maneuvered blindly past driftwood sheds, down insecure walkways, and around bloated citizens loitering outside tiny houses. Ten Curses huddled around a trashcan fire at a dead end. Cat met each of their watering eyes as she skidded to a stop and dashed off the way she came with the slapping sound of wet feet in pursuit. Lynn barreled into the whole party at the junction.

"Ahh!"

"Ahh!" Cat was flattened to the boardwalk with three Curses on top of her. Their flesh sloshed like bags of mixed cement, their bones bending like rubber below the thinning skin. Cat wriggled from beneath them, her skirt and scarf soaked from the waist down. The next turn put her on a wide, open platform extending out into the lake past all other buildings. A cabin floated on pontoons nearby.

One of the Water Curses on the platform leaped up at her arrival. He ran to a corner of the houseboat and yanked the chain of a waiting bell.

"Don't!" The Water Curse from the tank burst on the scene. She grabbed Cat by the arm. "What are you doing?"

"What's going on?" A voice gargled from inside the floating cabin. A fierce-looking woman exited onto the platform. She was shaved bald with wrinkled skin and penetrating dark eyes. "Lynn?"

"Brooke!" The girl covered her mouth. "I can explain!"

"That's a healthy girl!"

"Yes," Lynn stammered. "She said she was buying water – "

"You let a healthy person in here?" Brooke shouted. Lynn shrank"Are you crazy?"

"It's not her fault!" Cat jumped between them. "I lied. I came to see Douglas."

"What gives you the nerve?"

"I'm a Prophet," Cat said. "I'm saving the world but I need Water Town's help, so I came to talk to your leader."

"You need what?" Brooke squeezed water from her pursed brow. "You're a who?"

"Brooke! Who is that?"

All the Water Curses on the platform stiffened as a muscular teen exited the houseboat. He was also bald with veins bulging through his translucent skin. Brooke put her hands on his chest. "Doug, go back inside."

"Mr. Douglas!" Cat tightened the comb in her bun. "My name's Catrina Aston. I'm a Prophet – "

“Don't talk to him!” Brooke braced herself between them. “Get lost or I'll bash your head in!”

“I got this.” Douglas dropped a heavy hand on Brooke's shoulder and fixed Cat with a heavy frown. “Did the Brushcasters send you? I should tie a rock to your legs and put in the lake.”

“I'm not from the Brushcasters.”

“The mayor then,” Douglas leaned forward. “Give that slobbering man-child a message from me. I'll see him when I'm good and ready and not a moment before. The next messenger he sends down here, I'll drown in the basin and return to him on market day. Got that?”

“Mr. Douglas.” Cat turned her frustration into courage. “I'm telling you the truth. I *am* a Prophet and I *need* a Water Curse to help me save the world. I know your reputation, I know you're in charge. If you help, I'm sure I can convince one of your people to come with me on this journey.”

“Journey? Why – ” He heaved thick, gurgling cough. Brooke clung to his shoulder as he bent forward and retched a lungful of water into his hand. A glint of fear flashed across Douglas's face. He shot a warning look at Lynn and the other Water Curses, and gave Cat a stern nod. “Let's talk inside.”

Brooke gawked at him. “Doug, but she's – ”

“I said 'inside'.” His tearing eyes sparked as he glared down at Brooke. Cat bit her lip as she waited, glancing between the furious Water Curses. Brooke seethed a gargling breath and stormed past him into the boat. Douglas swept an angry eye over the bystanders, ushered Cat in ahead of him, and shut the door behind.

The main room was a meeting area lined with rough, wooden benches. Brooke kicked open a door on the right, revealing two hammocks over a tarp-lined wooden tub. She slammed the door with a grunt and Douglas gurgled a sigh and opened the door on the left.

Inside was a small office strewn with waxed paper scrolls and folders. Douglas gestured to a chair on the far side of the desk. “Sit.”

“Thank you.” Cat folded her hands in her lap. “I admit, I'm a little intimidated.”

“Of Brooke?” He closed the door. “She's protective. Her husband has a lot of enemies.”

“Her husband?”

He replied with a quick grin.

Cat relaxed a little. “Actually, I was intimidated by you.”

“You've heard stories."

“Any of them true?”

“Every word.” He slouched into the desk chair. “Which version did you get? Did I send a team of horses into the lake? Or break the clock in city hall? Or did I throw the mayor out a second-story window? That's one of my favorites."

She plucked at her string. "It was the one where you killed people for abducting your friends."

His smile faded. "Oh."

"I'm guessing that's the truest one, am I right?"

"I deny nothing." He folded his hands. "Although you probably think I'm a monster."

"People do desperate things when they're pushed to the edge," Cat said. "If what Ford said is true, I understand why you struck back. It doesn't make you evil."

"Interesting sentiment from a healthy person." He narrowed his eyes. "Or a Prophet."

"So you believe me?"

"Let's say you have my attention." His eyes glinted in the weak light. "What's this about a journey?"

"I need a volunteer." She pulled the leather case from her skirt pocket. "This scripture says I'm a Prophet sent to reunite man and God. I'd let you read it but..." She indicated the water pooling on the table between them. "You know."

Humor returned to his veined face. "Go on."

"It describes a ritual required to bring God back. Unfortunately the cost is steep – I need a Curse of each element to die in a sacrifice."

He raised an eyebrow. "You're awful frank asking someone to die for you."

"I've tried the gentle approach with less than ideal results," she said. "Believe me, I don't like it, either. My best friend volunteered to be one element and I found another in Fire Town. I hoped your influence could point me to a willing Water Curse."

Douglas blinked slowly. "How will they die?"

"I don't know."

"When will it happen?"

"Soon." Her throat tightened. "Sooner than I'd like."

"So within the year?"

She gulped. "Maybe within the week."

"Hm." Douglas leaned forward, his face a slab of wet granite. He pressed his mouth to the thumbs of his folded hands. "I'll do it."

"You'll help me find a volunteer?"

"No." He blinked a veil of water. "I'll be the one to die."

Chapter 17

The leader of the Water Curses tapped his thumbs together with a deep, gargling 'ahem'. “Is there a problem?”

“No.” Cat stammered. “I mean...are you sure?”

“Yes.”

“Do you have any questions? Concerns?”

“Nope.”

“What about Water Town? And your wife?”

“They'll have to cope either way.” He paused for another gurgling cough, breathed in through his nose and spat excess water into a waiting bucket. His teary eyes were intense and mournful. “Do you know how Water Curses die?”

“I can't say that I do.”

“We're filling with water,” he said. “It starts in our joints. And bloats the rest until we can't move. Then it hits the lungs. Once your lungs fill, you can count the days until you drown.”

Cat's gut clenched. “How long do you have?”

“Hard to say.” He took a short breath. “Done my best to stay healthy – plenty of food, exercise, rest – but you can't beat fate.”

“I'm sorry.”

“Problem is, I can't die.” He lowered his voice to ease the gargle in his throat. “I'm the thing keeping Water Town safe. I'm their strength. Their direction. What'll happen when the mayor finds out? Will he invade? Will it go back to how it was?” He shook his head. “I gotta stay alive. Leave them powerful.”

“You don't really care about my mission,” Cat determined. “This is about leaving a legacy.”

“Sorry to disappoint you.”

“I'm not disappointed... I mean...” She closed her hand over the scroll. “I came for a willing sacrifice.”

“And I'm as willing as they come.”

“Still, it doesn't seem right.”

“Desperate people do desperate things,” he said. “You get a Water Curse, I get a noble death. We both get what we want.”

“I suppose.” Cat took a deep breath and extended her hand. “Thank you, Douglas.”

“Thank *you.*” He closed it in his wrinkled grip. “You've put my heart at ease.”

The warning bell pealed outside. Shouts filtered through the warped walls of the houseboat. Cat tensed. “What's that?”

Brooke burst through office door. “Douglas!”

He rose. “Is it a raid?”

“Worse.”

Townsfolk swarmed the dock, coughing and gargling. Lynn rang the alarm bell. She spotted the three of them in the doorway and pointed. “The bluff!”

A thirty-foot water golem perched on the boardwalk above the town. Cat recognized its thin legs and club-like tail. Her nerves tingled as its spiraling eyes invaded her mind.

“What is it?” Brooke asked

“It's a Brushcaster golem,” Cat stammered.

“How do you know that?”

“I've seen them before.” She pulled off her string. “That one belongs to the Holy Elder. It chases sin. I can fight it, but you guys need to go.”

“Go where?” Brooke demanded.

“To the boats.” Douglas grabbed her shoulder and barked at the crowd. “Everyone, Cat's a Prophet with power to save the world. I'm going to go with her and help.”

Brooke gulped hard. “What?”

“Get everyone to the south shore – ” He inhaled a watery breath and launched a bout of furious coughing. The panicked Water Curses froze with faces pale and water running in rivers from their widened eyes. Douglas searched their faces, his back bent in shame. He took Brooke's shoulders. “It's up to you now.”

The golem leaped from the bluff and crashed into the lake near the water tank. Dark waves slammed against the beams and walkways, snapping cables, and shaking splinters from the teetering pier overhead.

Water Curses screamed. Brooke searched Douglas's face, emotion twinkling in the excess tears and shouted, “Get to the boats!”

Lynn changed the speed of the warning bell and the Curses throughout Water Town ran for their rafts. The golem crunched through driftwood houses, absorbing muck and refuse into its spindly legs. Cat's hands shook. She threaded the string between her fingers, aimed at the golem, and fired.

A ball of flame broke across the creature's nose. The golem didn't flinch. Its vortex-like eyes stared through the steam rolling from its wound. The spell weakened and a drooling mouth peeled open in its blunted face.

Douglas grabbed Cat's arm. “That was magic!”

“Be impressed later.”

The golem readied another bound. Douglas grabbed her hand and the two ran as the monster crashed through the houseboat behind them. The bell stopped abruptly and Lynn vanished with a scream. Douglas aimed them toward the pier with the golem close behind, churning the maze of walkways to pulp around its legs. Brooke's voice barked over the sound of destruction, directing the stragglers toward the far bank.

Douglas stumbled at the foot of the staircase and clung to the pier support, wheezing heavily. Cat took his arm, but the golem dove toward her. Its legs split the boards, the walk gave way and Cat tumbled into the lake.

The world was a silent green haze. Beams of light illuminated the dirt and rubble like fireflies floating through the depths of a strange forest. Cat blinked. The twisting pillars tied to the lake bed were not trees, but bodies tethered by their feet like stiff, bloated ghosts hovering in the murkiness. Cat released her held breath in a gasp. Douglas grabbed her about the waist and flung her to the stairs.

Cat coughed dirty water. She took Douglas' hand and raced a flight up the stairs. The golem waded around the pier in a wake of floating refuse. Douglas stopped on the landing with a retching cough. "Go."

"But –"

"You're a Prophet." He sputtered. "A real one."

The golem reared onto its back legs. Cat flurried another fire spell, but the weave was loose and slick. Flame hit the golem like a firework and the creature stumbled into the stairwell. Cat pulled Douglas to the next flight, but he was one step too slow. The stairs fell away, carrying Douglas into to the lake, as well.

Cat scrambled up the swaying staircase. The golem snapped at her from the slanted bank, eliminating the path behind her one flight at a time. The planks below gave way and she jumped. A warped, gray quarterstaff caught her across the ribs.

Ford leaned over her. He'd pinned the other end to the deck with his knees. "Climb up!"

He helped Cat drag herself onto the pier. The golem lunged off the slope and snapped at her legs but missed and fell back to the lake. Cat slicked wet hair from her eyes. "Where's Peter?"

Ford sputtered. "I tried to stop them – "

"Who?" She dragged him closer. "Where is he?"

The pier shuddered and a geyser of cold spray and splintered wood exploded from the walk behind them. The water golem breached and scrambled onto the deck. Cat and Ford sprinted for the boardwalk. Ford slipped and fell, but the monster ignored him and pounced on Cat from above. It drove its face into the pavement and caught her in its jaws. Air and sound vanished in an icy, polluted haze as the mouth sealed her inside the wet coffin of its face.

She kicked and thrashed as the creature carried her upward. Its feet fell with heavy vibrations that thrummed in low notes to her dampened ears. Cat scrambled for breath, but swimming was futile. The golem carried her past the weeping Goddess, up the mall, to city hall where thousands of people waited in a cheering congregation. In their midst, an active casting circle shown in radiant splendor. Cat twisted in the liquid, lungs burning, until the golem dropped her with a roll of its icy tongue.

She sputtered on the cobblestone, limbs numb and flailing. Cheers from the audience sloshed a muddied slur through her ears until the Holy Elder's voice cut through the din.

"There you are, Miss Aston."

He smirked at the head of his casting circle, with Paige holding a bucket of white paint at his right hand. Their black horses were held by local police, as was Strawberry, still harnessed to the empty wagon. Aiden and Ildri clutched each other on the steps of city hall, surrounded by spear-wielding local police. Cat reached for her string but Trace caught her wrists and pinned them behind her head.

The Elder smirked and folded his arms. "Can't resist using magic?" He gestured to the water golem. "I expected as much."

She struggled. "Let them go!"

"I don't answer to False Prophets."

"I'm not false!" Cat thrashed. "I'm the messenger foretold by Malachi in his last letter. The one in your highest library."

His eyes narrowed. "How would you know what our highest library says?"

"Because I read it," Cat snarled. "If you really want God back you'll let my friends go!"

"Our God's return is our highest priority. As for your *friends...*" He gestured over her shoulder to a small parting in the crowd. A man in an embroidered waistcoat and tails stepped forward with a bow. The Elder raised a hand to him. "Mr. Mayor."

"Your holy honor!" The man said. "Chalsie-Veneer has been nothing but faithful!"

"Did you find what I asked?"

"Right where you suggested."

He waved to the crowd behind him and another group of spear wielding policemen tugged Peter into view. He was bound in ropes with hair and glasses mussed. A fresh cut oozed brown from beneath his right eye.

Cat's stomach seized and knees buckled. "Pete!"

"Cat!" He moved toward her but was yanked back with a yelp.

"Let me go!" Cat twisted and kicked in Trace's grip.

The crowd snickered and the ropes tightened. Peter struggled for balance, wincing with hurt and shame.

Cat's heart broke into a helpless ruin. "Make them stop!"

The Elder smirked. "Why?"

"Please," she begged, "I'll come quiet. I'll do anything!"

"You had a chance to negotiate in Dire Lonato," the Elder said. "I'm not here to make deals. I'm here to show you and all these witnesses what it means to be pure." He held his glowing brush high. "People of Chalsie-Veneer. This young woman is a knife twisted in the heart of Our God. She chose her fate, but there is still time to choose yours. Catrina Aston comes with me. The Curses are yours."

"Thank you, sir!" The mayor rubbed his hands. "Let's teach that Douglas a lesson – throw the Curses off the pier!"

"No!" Cat shrieked. She and Peter fought to meet each other, but the police holding his lead gave another sharp tug. Peter stumbled to maintain his balance and was herded toward the lake.

Trace tightened his grip on Cat's wrists and wrestled her toward City Hall where officers prodded the Fire Curses with spear points. Aiden's eyes flashed. He grabbed the neck of the nearest spear and took its owner by the arm. The policeman screamed and dropped the weapon to wipe at his sleeve. The Fire Curse took Ildri to his side and turned the spear on the crowd.

Cat drove her heel into the bridge of Trace's right foot and pulled free. He leaped and knotted a hand in the hem of her scarf. The scripture case slid from her pocket and landed between them, with Malachi's name shining in the light of the Elder's casting circle.

The two stared at the case and then each other. Cat followed the glowing line in the circle to the waiting golem and threaded her string. "Ildri! Aiden! Hide!"

Aiden dropped the spear and grabbed Ildri's hand. They took off toward the wagon as Cat knotted a water symbol and blasted a line through the outer rings of the circle. The Holy Elder advanced, snarling, "Get out of my prayer!"

She flashed the water spell into his face and elbowed through the panicking crowd. The Elder charged after. Every word of the half-broken symbol burst to blazing light.

"Master!" Trace snatched the scripture case as he sprang up. The water golem tensed. Trembling light refracted along the length of its body. The creature arched its back and vomited a foaming waterfall of lake debris on the fleeing crowd. Its white eyes blazed like two holes drilling endlessly into its head. With maddened twitching, it tore through buildings and shops, tossing people with its face and forelegs. The mayor ran to city hall. The golem grabbed him on the steps and flung him against the columns where its eyes fixed on the stone golem seated among the supports.

Waves peaked along the monster's back as it rushed the facade and crushed it's inert brother into gravel. The clock tower listed, unsteady, shedding plaster and paint. Trace shielded Paige with his arms as the building came down. Ildri yanked Aiden to a stop as a column fell across their path. The horses scattered. The water golem rose from the ruined building and advanced with it's eyes narrowed to slits. Aiden and Ildri cowered, too frightened to run. Long ribbons of viscous liquid drained from the monster's underside. Trace glanced from the monster to the inflamed circle, grabbed Paige's bucket of paint, and flung the contents in a white ribbon across the glowing water symbol. The spell flashed once and burst from the ground in a flurry of dry flecks.

Light left the water golem's eyes and it collapsed in a heavy sheet of shapeless liquid. Aiden leaped from beneath it but lost grip on Ildri's hand. She fell on the steps. The two exchanged one horrified glance before the falling water smothered her screams.

Trace averted his eyes. Paige watched the death of the water golem, hands clasped and eyes wide. Trace grabbed her arm and followed their Elder into the chaos. Townsfolk, blinded by panic, fought each other to escape the plaza. Trace spotted Cat in the chaos, absorbing stray blows from elbows and knees until she reached the boardwalk at the edge of the lake.

The ruin of Water Town floated in pieces on the surf. Broken struts and ruined buildings jabbed upward like spears. Bodies bobbed amid the loose planks. If they were dead before or after the attack, it was impossible to tell.

Desperation forced tears to her eyes. “Pete!”

“Cat!” Ford grabbed her shoulder, a bloodied staff in the crook of his arm. Behind him, wounded policemen lay unconscious in the street, and behind them Peter stood in the shadow of the Goddess; bloody, haggard, and still bound in ropes.

Cat flew over, heart pounding in a painful ache against her sternum. She blinked through tears and ripped at the knots with her nails. The bonds came free and she pressed herself, sobbing to his chest. Bony knots lurched beneath his skin. He winced. “Cat, you have to go.”

“No.”

“Look out!” Ford shouted. An arm locked around Cat's throat. The Holy Elder dragged her backward toward the broken pier.

Cat grasped his wrists and raked her heels over the splintered wood. “Let go!”

“This was your choice. I gave you the chance to recant...” He held her at arm's length over the jagged shreds of the platform.

Cat pressed her toes to the ledge and stared into the abyss below. “Wait! You're a monk. Think about what you're doing!”

“Oh, I've thought very hard, for a very long time.” He reeled her in, sour breath hot on her face. “I know who you really are, Miss Aston. Do you honestly think someone like you can earn Our God's forgiveness?”

“Yes,” she said. “I'm a Prophet.”

“Then give Our God my regards.”

Trace emerged from the crowd as the Elder flung Cat from the precipice. She vanished, screaming, over the edge. Trace dashed forward with the scripture case tight in his hand. “Master!” He met the Elder with wide eyes. “What did you do?”

“She jumped.” The Elder unsheathed his brush. “Drag her body up, I won't have a martyr.”

“But, sir!”

“That's an order.”

He shoved Trace and stomped back to the crowd. The glowing light of his brush drew their undivided attention as he held it over his head and shouted condolences. Paige emerged from the crowd in shock and confusion. Trace met her eye, turned his back to the scene, and tucked the scripture case safely into the pocket of his tunic.

Chapter 18

Sunlight filtered through the leafy branches to warm Cat's face with fine particles, like fairies, dancing in the beams. She spread her fingers and studied the golden glow through her skin.

"So you're up."

A young man leaned casually against a tree. He was in his late teens with copper skin and black hair, wearing a pale green tunic with strange, side-facing pockets stitched in the sleeves.

He raised his heavy eyebrows. "That was an impressive fall. Are you hurt?"

"I don't think so." The straw bedroll crinkled as she sat up. "How did I – ?"

"Get here?"

"Yeah."

He presented himself with one bronzed hand.

Cat noticed a braided black circle tattooed on his palm. "You saved me?"

"Again." His black eyes glinted. "You're welcome."

"You're the dark stranger." She was instantly alert. "How did I get here? What did you do to me?"

"I brought you here to rest, that's all."

"Where's Peter?" She threw her hands to her face. "Our God... the Brushcasters were right there! They were going to put them in the lake!"

"Shh, take a breath." He squatted by the bedroll and offered her a canteen. "Have a drink."

She sniffed the bitter liquid. "Is this poisoned?"

"It's herbal."

"What do you mean, 'herbal?' Is it drugged?"

"It's tea. It'll calm you down."

She eyed him suspiciously and took a small taste. The liquid was lukewarm, but not unpleasant. One sip was enough to slow the cascade of thoughts. "You saw me fall."

"Yes I did."

"Did you see what happened?"

"I saw what happened to you."

"What about the others?" She persisted. "Peter and Ildri and Aiden? What about the Water Curses, did they get away safely?"

"Yes they did. I'm afraid I can't report on your friends."

"I have to get to them."

"You will. Take a moment to recover your strength, first." He crossed the campsite, lifted a skewer from across a small cooking fire, and placed the end in her hand. Three well-cooked reptiles were speared along the length. "Here."

"Are those lizards?" She studied the tiny legs and tails, curled black like spent matches. "I thought these were extinct."

"They're lunch."

"What? No!"

"Eat it. It's good."

"It's an endangered species!"

"It's fine, trust me." He lifted a second spit and pulled one of the creatures off with his teeth. "Just try it."

Cat opened her mouth and hesitated, but forced herself to bite down. The meat beneath the crunchy skin was surprisingly sweet. She swallowed as fast as she could. "Do you eat lizard often?"

"I eat what I can find." The stranger finished his meal and tossed the spit into the fire. "I can't be seen in town."

"But I saw you in Castleton."

"Obviously you're an exception." His palm glowed and a fountain of clear water extinguished the campfire from below.

Cat dropped the lizards to her lap. "How did you do that?"

"Scoot over, please."

"What?"

"I need the mat."

Cat got to her feet. The stranger knelt to rolled up her bed and strap it to his bag.

"You're leaving?"

"Gotta keep moving," he said. "It's best if we keep some distance between us."

"Why?"

"Don't worry, I won't be far."

"Wait. You can't leave yet." Cat followed him across the campsite. "How do you use magic without drawing symbols? Did the Brushcasters teach you?"

He snorted. "No."

"Then who?"

"I can't say."

"Why not?"

"Because."

She balled her fists. "What do you have against Curses?"

"Did I say I had something against Curses?"

"Peter said you hated him."

"Peter makes a lot of assumptions."

Cat scowled. "Then why are you following us?"

"For your own best interests." The stranger paused his preparations. "Suffice it to say I know more than you think."

She narrowed her eyes. "Know about what?"

"A certain scripture, for instance."

"The scripture –" She threw a hand to her skirt, but both pockets were empty.

"You dropped it in town."

"When did – ?" Cat frowned at him. "You saw that too?"

"You draw a lot of attention, Catrina."

"And you know my *name*?"

"Don't be upset," he said. "I mean you no harm. You're on a journey, and I'm looking out for you. I'm on your side."

"How do I know you're telling the truth?" Cat grabbed his arm. "Why can you use magic? How do you know about scripture? How did you find me before I even knew I was a Prophet – ?"

His eyes met hers and Cat froze, struck dumb by the depth and energy within his dark gaze. The stranger softened and removed her hand from his sleeve. “I can't tell you.”

“Why not?”

“I'm not inclined to say.”

“No,” she snapped, “you can't expect me to take your word when you've left me so little to go on. You have secrets, fine, I respect that, but trust me with something, too. There has to be *something* you can tell me.”

A smile tugged his lip. “Your name is Catrina Aston, your favorite color is blue, the comb in your hair belonged to your grandmother, your best friend is a Curse, you prefer your coffee iced, and you have a short temper – especially when you are denied something you think you deserve.”

She flushed. “I didn't mean 'admit you've been spying on me.'”

“Not spying – watching.”

“That's the same thing!”

“Spies look for hidden truth. I can't find what I already know.”

She pouted, brow furrowed.

The stranger heaved a sigh and hefted his shoulder bag. “Do you know why the golem in Dire Lonato turned wrathful?”

“I upset its Brushcaster?”

The stranger's black eyes softened. “You told it the truth.”

She remembered the argument; she called the Brushcasters villains; she told the living wrath of God they were to blame for Malachi's death. A chill raised goosebumps over her arms.

“Head along this grove north until you reach Logger's Road. Chalsie-Veneer is to the west. The Water Curses are gathered on the boardwalk by the Goddess.” He adjusted his backpack. “It's Joshua, by the way.”

“What is?”

“My name.” He grinned. “You never asked.”

Cat watched, confused and speechless as Joshua jogged away from the glen and vanished like a shadow between the mossy trees.

Cat wandered the Gatekeeper's forest for almost an hour before emerging to a field of severed tree stumps. The Eastern Mountains towered in the distance over empty work yards and an old mildewing lumber mill that gave the road its name. She followed the path west, back into the thick forest until the streets turned to cobblestone.

She crept along the city streets through alleys and shadows. The avenues were mostly deserted. Weeping echoed off the wooden buildings. Loose stone and splintered wood littered the pavement all the way to the open mall. Hundreds of people huddled in shivering groups around the wounded. Dead bodies covered in sheets lined the street beneath the shadow of the Goddess. Cat spotted the embroidered waistcoat of the mayor peeking from beneath a shroud.

The Calligraphers gathered at the remains of city hall. Cat ducked into the hollow shell of a broken building within earshot.

“I'm sorry, sir,” Trace was saying. “I searched thoroughly, Catrina Aston's not there.”

“Impossible,” the Elder said. “No one could have survived that fall. Search again.”

“There's nothing to find.” Trace was tired and hoarse. “My golem pulled dozens of bodies; she is simply not there.”

The Elder thumbed his gray mustache with a scowl. “What of the Curses?”

“Water Town has gathered at the Goddess – ”

“I meant *her* Curses.”

Trace shook his head.

The Elder grunted. He snapped his fingers at Paige. “Ready the horses.”

“But, sir – these people.” Trace gestured to the troubled faces. “We can't leave them like this.”

“They'll manage.”

“At least let me write the monastery for support.”

“I'm done wasting time.” The Elder swung into his saddle. “We will find that False Prophet.”

"But sir – !"

"Do you want to be responsible for more innocent deaths?"

"No, sir." Trace bowed with a hand over his heart. "I apologize."

The Elder spurred his horse and thundered away. Paige brought the second horse forward and gave Trace an unsettled look.

The senior monk combed through his hair and addressed the crowd. "Ladies and Gentlemen." His voice cracked in exhaustion. "I know this looks bleak, but I assure you, we would not take risks if there weren't so much at stake. Our God will come back. Things will get better. Please forgive our haste as we depart. We are not abandoning you. We will send monastery aid as soon as we can."

He mounted his horse, Paige climbed on behind, and the two followed the Elder out of the city. Cat waited for the hoof-beats to fade before venturing into daylight. She crossed the mall at city hall and slipped through the alleys back to the crumbling marina where the Water Town refugees camped.

Water Curses watched with hooded eyes as she approached. Many were wounded from their hurried escape. Their skin hung heavy from their limbs and faces, exposing the pink inner lids and dark veins of their watering eyes. The health she'd observed on the catwalks of Water Town was replaced with hunched backs, matted hair, and taught, stretched skin. She could feel the anger and despair radiating from them as the moved through the clustered bodies. Ford emerged crowd. His staff was missing but the sense of purpose still shone through a veil of tears. “It's you!”

She hesitated. “Yes.”

“Come with me.” He grabbed her by the wrist and led her through the maze of Water Curses to a secluded alley where her wagon waited. Strawberry stood twitching, caked in plaster dust with a mud-stained Earth Curse gently stroking her mane.

A murky film cleared from his eyes. “Cat!”

“Pete!” She sprinted and caught him about the chest, relieved to find all the barbs she remembered in the places she left them. “Are you okay?”

“I thought he killed you!”

“So did I!”

“Are you hurt?”

“No, I'm okay.”

His ribs cracked as he wrapped his arms around her. “Never do that to me again.”

Aiden sat alone in the back of the wagon, his face hidden within his gray hood. A scrap of lavender fabric hung between his limp hands. Dread settled in Cat's stomach. “Where's Ildri?”

Peter lowered his voice. “She's gone.”

The dread tightened to a stone. “You mean...”

He nodded. "When the golem came down."

Cat stepped away from him, mind reeling. An ache spread from her heart through her lungs and back, leaving a sick numbness its wake. She approached the wagon where Aiden sat hunched in a ball against the rail.

"I'm so sorry."

He balled the scarf in his fist.

"We'll take you home if you want."

He gave a raspy snort. "Home?"

"I know you only came as support," she said. "And you probably need time..."

"I came because she was all I had." He turned toward her. Fresh, open wounds swelled beneath his red-rimmed eyes. Cat suppressed a grimace. His breath fanned the coals in the cracks along his jaw. "You still need a Fire Curse."

"Aiden – "

"Don't." He bowed his head again. "I'd rather die than go back without her."

"Hey, Prophet," a weak voice called.

Douglas had his arm around Brooke's. He was sickly pale with dark veins bulging in his slick, swollen arms. "You survived."

"So did you," Cat said. "Are you alright?"

"I live." He heaved another thick cough. "Water Town has been destroyed."

"I know," Cat said. "The golem came for me. It was my fault."

"You're fighting a big enemy. Risks are a given." Douglas sucked water through his teeth. "You're the real deal, Cat."

She wet her lips. "Because of the magic?"

He stared at her through thick walls of tears. "Actually it was the Brushcasters." She felt her own eyes well up. Dark veins pulsed in his temples and over his bloated jaw where flesh sloshed with each breath. "They're afraid of you."

"Me?" Cat tried to suppress a strained laugh. "You didn't see the fight I just lost."

"We heard about it – how could we help it? The size of that golem. The ultimatum. The Elder himself, Cat. The Holy Elder came here to get you. They are terrified."

Emotion fluttered in Cat's chest. She averted her eyes. "I hadn't thought of it like that."

"I need to apologize. I didn't believe when I agreed to come with you. I tried to take advantage of you." His voice gurgled as his head bowed. "Sorry."

"You were doing what you thought best."

"That's not an excuse to be coward." He coughed and stepped away from Brooke. "I'm not a liar, either. I gave you my word. I will be your martyr and go with you on your quest."

"What?" Brooke cried. She inhaled and launched a heaving cough, drawing the attention of the other Water Curses.

Douglas rubbed her back. "I'm sorry I didn't tell you."

"Quest?" Brooke managed her cough. "But your lungs –"

"What's going on?" Ford asked. "What about lungs? What about leaving?"

Douglas sighed with another cough and stood before his people. "I should say sorry to everyone. You've noticed I've been scarce... it's because I'm dying."

Gasps and coughs echoed off the moldy buildings. Ford's lip quivered. "Dude... why didn't you tell us?"

"That was my mistake." Douglas cleared his throat. "I was scared you would think I was weak – that you'd be weak without me. But you aren't. You kept it together, even without me – " More coughing. Another shallow breath. "I'm proud of you."

Light reflected in flickers on the sea of watering eyes. Cat rolled her string against her wrist with residual guilt and regret.

Douglas grabbed her sleeve and pulled her alongside him. "You all saw what Cat did today. She came to me because she was a Prophet and she's going to use a magic ritual to get Our God to come back. She needs a Curse to die though. She's got these other two right here." He pointed to Peter and Aiden. "And now she's got me, too."

"Douglas," Brooke begged. "We need you."

"No you don't." Douglas coughed with a heavy hand on her shoulder. "I was proud of everyone today, but I was really proud of you. You did my job when I couldn't. You've been doing that a lot lately." He swallowed hard. "Water Town won't miss me, because you're the new leader."

"You're wrong." Water trickled from the corner of her gaping mouth. She wiped her eyes on her dripping hands, drawing haggard breaths. "It's not about who's the leader. I've been covering for you for weeks because I want to take care of you. I love you."

Cat's heart raced. The Water Curses coughed and muttered. Douglas swallowed a mouthful of water, his voice low and warbling. "I made a pact."

Brooke straightened. "I'll go instead."

His face rippled. "Brooke, no."

"Then I'll go," Ford hobbled forward. "Today is my fault anyway... I broke your big rule."

"No way, I'll go!" Another Water Curse shoved forward.

Ford coughed. "Hah! With your lungs?"

"Douglas saved my life," the other said. "I'll take his place."

"No, I will!" A third gargled.

A fourth stood. "No I will."

More Curses spoke up. A fist fight broke out. Brooke shouted them to silence as Lynn inched into view at the edge of the group.

Her hair covered a bandaged wound at her neck and shoulder where a bit of debris had punctured the swollen skin. The wound swelled into magenta splotches along its edge, covering her neck and chest with raised patches of puckered skin. Liquid seeped through the linen bandage stained it inky black. "Can I go?"

Douglas staggered. "Lynn."

"Get back in bed," Brooke snapped. "You're not well."

"It's not as bad as it looks." Lynn covered the wound with her hand. "I can still breathe."

"Lynn," Cat covered her mouth. "I'm so sorry."

"It's okay," she said. "It makes this choice easy. I'm already fifteen. This wound isn't going to heal. I can still travel with you, and I'm not important to Water Town like Douglas or Brooke is."

"You are important," Douglas said.

"I didn't mean it like that." Lynn cast her tearing eyes to the boardwalk. "Water Town is the only home I have ever known. You all made me feel safe – safe enough to forget we were in danger, even. I never want something like this to ever happen again, and I can't imagine a Water Town without any one of you... so if leaving means the rest of you can stay, I'm happy to go."

"It's more than just a trip," Cat warned. "If you come, you won't come back."

"I know," Lynn said in an even tone. "You're nice to double check, but you need a volunteer. I'm it, if you'll have me."

"We'll be happy to have you," Cat said. "You're very brave."

She blushed purple. "It's what feels right."

"Lynn, I – " Brooke's throat as she pulled the teen into a hug. "I'm sorry for everything."

"You don't have to be."

"Thank you," Douglas said. "You're a hero."

The Water Curses sobbed amid 'thank you's and 'goodbye's, sorrow twisting their faces, adding gravity to the tears constantly streaming their faces. Lynn sniffled into each of their arms and told them she'd miss them. Cat watched them, recalling Ildri's farewell. The Fire Curse hid emotion beneath calm as she coached her children to smile. It was a trained exercise to keep them safe, but a lie just the same. Did Ildri regret hiding her feelings? A knot tightened in Cat's throat. Aiden curled into a ball in the back of the wagon, stroking the scrap of lavender cloth with his thumbs.

Peter pressed his arm to her side. Cat laid her head on his shoulder and hugged the limb to her chest. The knobs pressed like arrows across her heart.

Chapter 19

Cat rode in the back with Lynn and Aiden as Peter steered up Logger's Road beneath a canopy of trees. Cat was glad to put the events of Chalsie-Veneer behind her, but it couldn't erase the sights and emotions they caused. She avoided Lynn's eye as the Water Curse stroked her weeping wound through its bandage. A constant stream of clear water drained into the storage under her seat. Aiden sulked in the farthest corner of the opposite bench with his legs dangling over the road. He hunched against the rail, petting the scrap of Ildri's scarf tied to his wrist. Stains spread across his tattered gray hood where hidden wounds burned from the fire in his skin.

The trees thinned, revealing the lumber mill a field of severed tree stumps. The midday sun baked the road. Lynn shielded her eyes with a dripping hand. “Wow.”

Cat cocked her head. “Too bright?”

“What?” Lynn asked. “Sorry, there's water in my ears.”

“I asked if it was too bright out here.”

“Oh, no, it's fine,” Lynn said. “I'm amazed it's so flat out here. The other Curses talked about how dry the Valley was, but I didn't expect it to be so... dead.”

“Is this your first time out of the forest?”

“As far as I know. I can't remember very much.”

“You were too young?”

“Oh... no.” Lynn studied her wrinkled hands. “I don't remember anything from before I was abandoned. Douglas called it 'trauma-based amnesia' – he read it in a book.”

“So you don't remember anything?”

“Not a thing.”

“Not your parents?”

“Not even my own name. Brooke named me Lynn. I have no idea what my actual name was.”

Cat paled. “That's awful!”

“No, it's okay.” Lynn blinked tears and smiled. “It's actually kind of a blessing. I don't relive my abandonment the way my friends do and I can remember everything past that just fine. Plus, it's easier to stay positive without that weighing me down."

"Still..."

"It's fine, really. Don't worry about it." Lynn shifted in her nest of wet towels. "What about you? Where do you come from?"

"Pete and I are from the Western Mountains," Cat answered. "The whole Prophet thing's kind of new to us, it's the first time we've been away from home."

"Oh good, something in common! What's your favorite thing about traveling so far?"

"Not a lot of good things have happened, really."

"I bet you've met interesting people."

"Yes, that's true. The Curses we've met are all amazing. I admire them for the strength they show and what they've endured." Cat bit her lip. "I guess I don't need to tell you about that stuff."

Lynn's watering eyes softened. "It's nice to hear, anyway."

Her sincerity tightened the knot in Cat's stomach. She fidgeted. "Thank you again for coming with us."

"It's an honor to take Douglas's place."

"It's still asking everything from you."

"Yes, well..." She poked her bandage, again. "Saving the world is a good way to spend your final days."

A vast, rocky wasteland lay beyond the stump forest with waves of dust rolling eastward toward the mountain. Castleton sat in plain view over the grassless plains. Cat tapped Peter on the elbow. "Do you want me to drive?"

"I'm okay. How about you?"

"Worried about being spotted."

"We should be safe if we go cross-country," Peter said. "If we keep moving due east we might even make it before dark."

"Oh good." Cat slouched.

His brow knit. "What's wrong?"

"Nothing." Cat sat straight again. "We'll take the shortcut."

"Shortcut it is."

Peter gave Strawberry weak flick and they headed into the wastes. The tires rocked over exposed stones beneath the baking heat. Cat's head lolled against her hand, eyes heavy with sleep and stomach twisting in nausea. She dozed, but jumped when a cold cloth pressed her neck. "What was that?"

"Sorry!" Lynn lowered back to her seat. "You looked hot."

"Oh." Cat returned the wet cloth to her neck. "Thanks."

"You're welcome," Lynn said. "Peter, would you like one?"

"No thanks."

"What about him?" Lynn glanced to Aiden slouching in the corner and lowered her voice. "I'm kind of worried about him. He hasn't said anything all afternoon."

"Aiden's... taking some time for himself." Cat replied. "He lost someone he loved in Chalsie-Veneer. His girlfriend."

"That's terrible." Lynn's eyes widened. "Is it okay if I ask how it happened?"

"The golem." Fresh guilt tightened Cat's throat. "Water's dangerous to Fire Curses. It burns them. That's what did it."

"Oh, I see." Lynn swallowed. "Should I say something?"

"I think it's best we give him some space."

"But it must be scary to travel with a Water Curse after something like that. I mean, if I'm really that dangerous." Lynn gathered her towel and scooted along the bench. "I'll let him know everything's alright."

"Lynn, don't – "

"It's okay." The Water Curse stopped across from Aiden with a leaky smile. "Hello, there. We weren't formally introduced. I'm Lynn."

He pivoted away from her.

"I'm sure you're nervous about having me here, but I promise I'll do all I can to keep you safe. We'll stay on separate sides of the wagon and use separate dishes and anything else you think of. Don't hesitate to suggest something, I want us all to be friends. Okay?"

Aiden grunted and ran his thumb over the lavender scarf.

Lynn bent to see his face, but he tugged his hood lower. The Water Curse shrugged and gathered her towels. “If you think of anything, I'll be right over here.” She scooted along the bench. “Bye.”

Cat greeted her with a sympathetic smile. “It was a good try.”

“I hope he doesn't hate me.”

“At least now he knows you're considering his safety,” Cat said. “Let's leave him alone.”

“Okay,” Lynn pulled her feet off the floor. “I think I'll be quiet, too, if that's alright.”

“Sure, Lynn. That's fine.”

They stopped in the early evening to rest and change drivers. Cat took the reins and continued across a rocky wasteland toward a gap in the grayish Eastern Mountains with the sunset at their back.

The lights of New Torston shone through the darkening haze, cradled by a vertical bluff. A metal rail ran up the face from the city on the ground to a high, flat plateau. The silhouette of a windmill turned in a crevice between the peaks.

Cat pulled Strawberry to a stop. “Is that Wind Town up there?”

Peter looked up from the atlas on his lap. “That's where the Wind Goddess is. The city of Torston was up there a couple hundred years ago, but they moved it to ground level for better access. Apparently there used to be a road that zig-zagged up the bluff, but it's been crossed out. Even when my great-grandfather went adventuring, it was already worn away. The elevator is the only way up or down."

"So there's no way to avoid passing through the city?"

"Not according to the map, but I can check it again." He moved his wrist to turn the page, but lost his grip. The book slipped from his hand. "Ah!"

"Oh no!" Lynn reached to catch, but the book flopped open in a puddle of sanding water. She hooked the spine between two fingers and lifted the dripping volume.

Peter beheld the mess and groaned.

"I'm sorry!" Lynn set the book on the bench beside her and searched through her towels, but they were all soaked. Water gathered around the leather cover. Lynn's face paled. "I'm sorry. I'll fix it – "

"Lynn, it's okay." Cat scooped the book from the seat and draped it on the rail. "See? It's just water. Nothing's ruined."

Lynn searched them with a guilty expression. "Are you sure?"

"I promise," Cat said. Peter continued to pout. Cat clapped him on the knee. "How about we stop and talk strategy for a while. We can head to New Torston when the book dries."

He straightened with a heavy sigh. "Sure, fine. Strawberry needs a rest, anyway."

"Great. It's a plan." Cat hopped from the driver's seat.

Aiden dropped from the bench. He and reached for his tarp but snatched the hand back with an, "Ow!"

The dripping vinyl fell to a heap in the dust.

Lynn cringed. "Sorry!"

The Fire Curse glared and left the tarp where it lay.

Peter slid the length of the bench and lowered as slowly as possible. His shaking arms fought against the weight of his legs, but his stiff wrists failed their grip and he hit the ground flat-footed and wincing. Cat dashed around the wagon. "Pete?"

"I'm fine." He staggered against the rail.

Cat took his arm. The wound on his cheek was crusted with dry mud. She reached to straighten his glasses and found the swelling beneath the scab was solid stone. "Oh, Pete..."

"Don't."

"But – "

"I said don't." He shifted onto his right foot and away from her hand. "I'll feed the horse."

Cat's heart fluttered as she watched him limp away. She took a deep breath and spotted Lynn peeking over the wagon rail with troubled eyes. Cat forced another smile. "How about dinner?"

Lynn sat straighter. "I can cook if you want. There's enough water in these towels to make us all soup. I know some great recipes."

Cat grimaced. "Towel soup?"

"We can boil it if that would help?"

"Thanks, but we can't really drink soup around here." Cat gestured to the brooding Fire Curse. "Maybe something drier?"

"Oh," Lynn sank into her towels. "Sorry."

"I'll whip something up, don't worry." Cat reached under the seats for the box of cooking supplies. A chunk of soggy cardboard ripped away in her hand.

Lynn spoke into her knees. "Sorry, again."

Cat fought to keep smiling. "I didn't need the whole box."

"Can I help carry something?"

"No, no, it's okay. You sit tight." Cat gathered all the dry kindling into her checkered scarf and got to work on the fire. Peter struggled with Strawberry's harness a short distance away. Beads of muddy sweat rolled down his powder-pale face as he undid the final buckle and dropped the harness with a crash.

"Ahh!" Lynn jumped.

Strawberry whinnied. Peter stepped into her eye line and calmed her with a stroke of his heavy arm.

Lynn slipped from the wagon. "Is she okay?"

"She's fine," Peter said. He pressed his cheek to Strawberry's forehead. "Sorry, girl."

"You like her a lot."

“She's a good horse. We got her as a gift when Cat and I left home. If I wasn't... well...” He shifted weight with another rattling sigh. “Let's say I wish I could keep her.”

“I've never been around horses before, at least not that I remember. I always assumed they were dangerous and scary.” Lynn inched closer. “Can I pet her?”

“Sure.”

She stroked a damp streak down Strawberry's flank with the back of her hand. “She's so sweet.”

“She's got a good nature, yeah.”

“I'm sure it's because you've taken good care of her.”

“I've tried to. I've only had her a week.” He slouched with another heavy sigh. “Everything's changed so fast.”

“Yeah,” Lynn said. “This morning I was taking amount tallies for the water tank.”

“How's your wound?”

“It's okay.” She touched the bandage. “I can move my arm fine, but I can tell I'm weaker than I was.”

Peter tested his bandaged fingers. “I know what you mean.”

“I'm sorry if I'm a bit of a hazard,” she said. “In Water Town everything was wet all of the time. I didn't realize how much of a mess I made.”

“We know you can't help it.”

She raised her running eyes. “Is there anything I can do to help? Maybe with the horse? I feel like I wouldn't be such a burden if I had a job.”

“No one said you were a burden.”

Her voice lowered to a whisper. “They didn't have to.”

Cat paused her fire assembly. She met Peter's eye and her cheeks flushed in shame. His brow knit. Lynn swallowed a mouthful of water with a defeated slouch.

“You know,” Peter ventured a bit louder. “Taking care of Strawberry isn't only my job. Would you like try?”

Lynn choked out a tiny cough. “Really?”

“I have a feeling you'd be good at it.”

“Okay, what do I do?”

“Follow me, I'll show you where we keep her food.”

Cat rose as they approached. “You two okay?”

“Better,” Peter said. “It's been a rough trip.”

Cat nodded. “That it has.”

“The feed bag and oats are on a shelf under the front seat,” Peter instructed. “Look about waist level where I can reach them.”

“Yes sir!”

Lynn rushed to her task. Peter shifted onto his stronger ankle, and gave Cat an awkward nod. “Can I sit with you?”

“Of course.” Cat settled back to her kindling.

He pressed his shoulder against the wagon and slid to the ground beside her. “Sorry about being short before.”

Cat dropped a match into the wood and folded her hands in her lap. “I worry about you, you know... and not because you're sick. It's hard to read you when you're angry.”

“I'm tired and frustrated – it's not your fault. I'm sorry you get the brunt of it.”

She tucked a loose hair into her bun. “Comes with the job.”

“Are we okay?”

“Yeah, we're okay.”

Peter leaned a little closer. “What did you pick for dinner?”

“Sandwiches.”

“Have you considered something I can eat with a fork?”

“Actually, if you sit tight, I have that covered.” She assembled a sandwich and speared the two slices of bread on a knife like a skewer. “See? A straw for food.”

He pinched the handle between his thumb and forefinger and bent forward for a bite. “This is pretty clever.”

“I learned it from a lizard.”

“A lizard?”

“Yeah.” She glanced from Aiden pouting near the front tire to Lynn rustling through the wagon and whispered. “Actually, I've been meaning to tell you something about this morning.”

“When you went over the cliff?”

“Yeah.”

“I didn't want to come out and ask.” Peter pressed his lips into a line. “What happened?”

“I was rescued.”

“By who?”

She ran a finger under her string. Her heart clenched as the tension between them returned.

Peter dropped his hands to his lap with a rattling breath. “I should have known.”

“He's not what you think he is,” she said.

“He's a magic-wielding stranger.”

“He saved me.”

“He's stalking you.”

“But he's on our side.” She rose to her knees. “He used his magic to help me. He knew about our mission.”

“That's even worse!” Peter snapped. “We know nothing about this guy except he uses evil magic. You said you'd stay away!”

“Would you rather I drowned?”

“No, Cat.” Peter discarded his half-eaten sandwich. “Today was the worst day of my entire life. I thought you were dead. There is this horrible tightness through my whole chest, I can feel it when I breathe." He flexed his back against the tire. "It's stiff, and it hurts, and it's not going away."

Her stomach clenched. "Pete..."

"I don't care what happens to me, I'm dying either way. I'm doing this for you, Cat. You have to live. You're the Prophet."

She averted her eyes.

"What's wrong?"

"Before the Elder tossed me, he said he knew who I was," she said. "That someone like me could never be a Prophet."

"He was trying to rattle you."

"All I've done since Castleton is put us in danger. The Brushcasters are after us, we have magic stalkers – I've destroyed entire towns."

"None of that was your fault," Peter said. "We're trying to change a world built on corruption and cruelty. I'm not surprised it pushed back."

"People were hurt, Pete." Cat bit her lip. "Ildri died."

Peter nudged her with one hand, inviting her to his side. Cat nestled on his shoulder with his arm along her back and her knees against her chest. The hours of guilt and doubt dulled in Peter's warmth as the watched the fire spread from paper kindling to the pale wall of split wood.

He leaned his cheek onto her forehead. “I know it's not the way we wanted it to go.”

“Hmph.”

“I know you don't want to hurt people. No one here blames you. We believe in you. Ildri believed in you, too. That's why she agreed to come with us.”

“Would she, if she knew this would happen?”

“She did knowing she had to try,” he said. “Sometimes trying fails, but not always. We'll succeed for her sake, and for Aiden's, and Lynn's, and Malachi's, too. He's known you were going to succeed for centuries. Pull that scripture out and see.”

Her swelling spirits fell again. “I can't.”

“Why not?”

“I lost it.”

He raised his head. “You lost the scripture?”

“It fell from my pocket in the attack.”

“Cat, that's all the evidence we had.”

“I know,” Cat said. “I'm sorry.”

“All fed!” Lynn threw drops as she skipped over. “What should I do next?”

“There's a bucket we use for her water.” Peter slid is arm out from around Cat's shoulder. “Hold on, I'll show you.”

Lynn gave him a hand and they left with Strawberry's supplies. Cat stayed in the cold void left by her pillow's exit.

"You there!" a woman's voice shouted.

Cat spotted a horse and rider approaching from the darkened road. Starlight reflected off her domed hat and the silver badge pinned over her breast pocket. Cat kicked the logs out of the fire as she leaped to her feet. "Who's there?"

"New Torston Police," the woman barked from her saddle. She nodded to the scattered embers. "What's that about?"

Cat stepped to block Aiden from view. "You scared us."

"Who are you?"

"Travelers from the other side of the Valley," Cat said. "We stopped for the night."

"This campsite is illegal." The policewoman pulled a notepad from her pocket. "State your name."

"I... uh..."

"My name's Lynn!" The Water Curse scooped Peter's half eaten sandwich off the ground and held it forward. "We were having dinner, would you like some?"

The officer grunted. "How old are you kids?"

"Um... teenage?" Lynn smiled and shrugged. "We're sorry to break rules. We were scared to travel by night."

“I see.” The woman stuffed her notepad back in her belt. “Pack your things and come into town right now, and I'll consider this violation a warning.”

“That's very generous, ma'am,” Cat said. “It'll take us a few minutes to pack. We'll finish and come in soon, we don't mean to take your time.”

“It's a precaution, miss.” She pulled a torch and a lighter from her saddle bag. “New Torston's been on lock-down since the Calligraphers arrived. There's a terrorist on her way.”

Cat gulped. “A terrorist?”

“Yeah, a False Prophet. She's already attacked Dire Lonato and Chalsie-Veneer. The Holy Elder says she uses all kinds of evil magic and hoards Curses to fill her heart with sin...”

The torch caught. Light swelled and reflected off Lynn's wet hair and clothing.

“Is that..?” The policewoman raised the torch to see Aiden hiding near the wagon and Peter behind the horse. “Are those..?”

“There's no need to jump to conclusions,” Cat said.

“You're the False Prophet!” She dropped the torch and swung into her saddle.

“No, wait – !”

The officer blew a shrill blast on a whistle. City lights popped on along the outer edge, with more whistles echoing off the sheer rock wall. She reared back in her saddle and thundered back toward town.

Aiden fumed to Cat and Lynn with fire in his eyes. “This is your fault!”

Cat raised her hands. “I tried my best – ”

“Not you!” He wheeled into Lynn's face. “You're an idiot!”

She choked. “What?”

“Stepping in front to offer the cop a sandwich? You didn't think she'd notice you were a Curse? You might as well have turned yourself in – give the Brushcasters our regards!”

“I – I was trying to be friendly.”

“We are wanted criminals!” Aiden roared. “Were you blind for all of Chalsie-Veneer? Do you even know why we're out here?”

“Aiden, stop it!” Cat snapped. “I know you're upset about yesterday – ”

“Shut up.” His face flushed with orange veins. “This isn't about that.”

“You're right. It's about a guard seeing our campfire and coming to investigate,” Cat said. “We've got very little time. Let's pack and go.”

Peter rounded the wagon. “I'll drive.”

“No, you ride in back.”

"But – "

"No 'but's. I'm taking care of you." She pointed to Aiden. "Get the cooking stuff together. The three of you hide under the tarp."

"Yes, ma'am."

"Lynn – !"

"I'm sorry!" The Water Curse trembled with her face in her hands. Liquid gushed through her fingers with each gargled sob. "I'm so sorry. I didn't mean to."

"Lynn." Cat put an arm around her shoulders. "It's okay."

"I was trying to help."

"I know," Cat whispered. "Right now I need you to put the harness back on the horse. Do you think you can do that?"

"I – I think so."

"Good."

Starlight danced in the Water Curse's pooling eyes. "I promise I didn't mean to get us caught."

"I know, it's alright." Cat assured in an even voice. "You did a good job. Aiden was wrong. Keep trying your best and leave the rest to me."

Chapter 28

Trace slipped from his bedroom on the second floor of New Torston's city hall and closed the door softly behind. He crept up the darkened hallway, past the Elder's room, and down the main stairwell to the reception area on the first floor.

Mementos of the Torston family lined the walls of the quiet museum space, including a family tree, a model of the first steam engine, an etching of Old Torston's famous windmill, the first electric generator invented by Reverend Henry Torston, and a book of philosophy written by the ancestral patriarch. The family library waited near the front door below a portrait of Viola Torston, benefactor and final member of the proud Torston lineage. Trace checked over his shoulder and slipped into the moonlit room unnoticed.

The small chamber was lined in book cases from floor to ceiling. Stained-glass windows cast colored swatches over hundreds of leather-bound books. Trace locked the door behind him and exhaled a tense breath. He shrugged out of his leather holster and propped his brush against the wall.

A large felt-topped desk covered in museum brochures dominated the center of the room. Trace slid into the waiting seat, unrolled the portable calligraphy set from his pack, and drew a quick casting circle on the back of a paper flier. The black ink flashed white and raised a tiny fire golem. The creature turned its head toward its master, stretched its oversized arms and curled into a ball at the center of the glowing spell. The Calligrapher moved his snoozing lamp to an ashtray and pulled the water-damaged scripture case from his tunic.

The leather case was dinged and wilted from the events in Chalsie-Veneer, but Malachi's name still shone warm and golden in the weak firelight. Gold leaf meant the scroll was from the highest library, but such a thing was impossible. Trace pulled out his black notebook and turned to the handwritten list of scriptures in the back. The case before him was the youngest of Malachi's writings – the last scripture ever written – and confirmed for most holy. A knot tightened in Trace's throat. Hand shaking, he reached for the case.

"I can't." He drew back. "It's against the rules. It's a sin."

His heart pounded as he recalled the scene of the Holy Elder at the edge of Lake Veneer, holding Catrina Aston at arm's length, tossing her to her death...

His brow furrowed. "There are worse sins."

The scroll inside the case was damp but intact, and the white silk ribbon stained green and double-knotted like a shoelace. Trace lifted the parchment with the tips of his fingers and laid it on the desktop. He coaxed the ribbon loose and spread the parchment with the handle of his pen.

The ink inside was smeared, but Trace recognized Malachi's handwriting as if it were his own. He took a deep breath, said a prayer of repentance and began to read. Each paragraph quickened the pulse in Trace's stomach. He absorbed Malachi's warning of disaster and vision of a future savior with mounting horror. The absence of God, the disappearance of the Prophets, the Holy Elder's feverish search for and most recent murder of Catrina Aston, even her conviction and company made sense in context with the scripture. Trace scrambled for his black notebook for proof.

The handwriting was authentic, the speech pattern coincided with Malachi's other visions, the signature was legitimate. Trace turned to his historical notes. It was dated after Malachi's last public speech. How close was it to his disappearance?

He transcribed the scroll three times, leaving annotations and footnotes as he went. Shafts of colored moonlight mapped the hours in a slow arc across the desk as pages of his notebook, bits of loose parchment, the undersides of fliers filled with asides, hypotheses, and ultimately conclusions. The fire golem shrank in the center of its casting circle until it extinguished with a puff.

A knock scared Trace awake at dawn. He threw himself over the documents on the table. “Who is it?”

“It's me, master.”

“Paige!” He raked the papers into a pile. “One moment!”

Trace put the scripture in his breast pocket, stuffed the stack of notes in his hip bag, pulled on his brush holster, and opened the door.

Paige pouted with her arms crossed. “You look awful.”

“Thanks.”

“Were you in here all night?”

“I was studying.”

She rolled her eyes. “Have you seen the Elder?”

Trace exhaled and joined her in the hall. “I haven't, no. He's probably still asleep.”

“His room's empty. I assumed you were together.”

The double doors at the front of the building burst open and the Holy Elder entered, shoulders back and spirits high. “Hayes! Where have you been?”

Trace shut the library door behind him. “Sir?”

“Catrina Aston's been sighted!” The Elder said. “One of the guards saw the whole party in the desert last night.”

“You mean she's alive?”

The Elder's triumph soured. “You sound relieved.”

“No sir.” Trace set his jaw. “Actually, may I ask a question?”

The Elder's scowl deepened. “You may.”

“How can Miss Aston perform miracles?”

“What?”

“We perform miracles using the symbols passed down from our Elders,” Trace ventured. “Miss Aston used the same symbols against my golem in Dire Lonato.”

“She's a False Prophet.”

“Yes, but how could she know the runes? It's our responsibility as Calligraphers to keep them secret as the Prophets did until Our God's return.”

The Elder narrowed his eyes. “What are you implying?”

“Nothing, sir. Just that if Our God intended the symbols for Prophets – ”

"There are no Prophets!" the Elder snapped. "We are the Prophets – the Order of Holy Calligraphers – of which, I remind you, I am in charge."

"I'm not an acolyte anymore," Trace said. "I've been studying magic and scripture for almost twenty years. I've memorized the lower library from cover to cover. Unless the higher library says otherwise, magic was given to the Prophets. They are the ones to use it, and any others are False – "

With a thwack, the Elder struck Trace in the side of the head with his brush handle. Pain shocked him to silence as the world spun. It settled and Trace saw Paige pale as chalk.

"How dare you try to lecture me!" the Elder roared. "I am the holiest man in God's Valley!"

Trace cringed and straightened back to attention. "My apologies."

"Get to your post." The Elder brandished the gold brush and stormed back outside.

Trace's ears were ringing. He checked his temple for blood and smoothed his black hair back into place.

Paige lowered her hands. "Master? Are you okay?"

"It doesn't matter. Miss Aston is coming."

"But..."

"I am a Holy Calligrapher and a servant of Our God." He unsheathed his brush. The holster strap pressed the scripture against his heart. "I have an oath to keep."

A tarp-covered wagon approached New Torston's north gate. Pots and pans covered in dust dangled from the sides and along the back where they bounced off the rear tires with a rhythmic thud. The soot-covered driver sat wrapped in a muddy blanket with his knees tucked to his chin and a filthy hood pulled low to cover his eyes. He pulled the rattling vehicle to a stop and spoke to the guards through a knotted brown beard. "Excuse me, sirs?"

One of the policeman stepped forward. "Turn around, old man. The city is closed."

He squawked in a raspy voice. "Closed?"

"Yes," a second officer said. "By order of the Holy Elder. No one is allowed in or out."

"Oh, yes, the Holy Elder." The driver coughed, shedding dust from his hood. "The Calligraphers are chasing the terrorist, right? I heard of it in Chalsie-Veneer. I'm a water salesman."

The first policeman propped a short wooden club on his shoulder. "We don't need water."

"Oh, but everyone needs water." The driver gnawed his beard. "Chalsie-Veneer is ruined, you know. You won't be getting another shipment of water from there any time soon. I knew you would need it – I brought what I had to sell, so that your women and children wouldn't suffer."

"The Elder said no one – "

"Hold on," a third officer interrupted. "Check the cargo."

The officers rounded the wagon, lifting the tarp with their clubs and peering through the railings. "These look like boxes," one said. "I thought you said you had water – "

"Oh, yes." The driver coughed. "In jugs. Glass jugs."

"Glass jugs?"

"Bottles. In boxes so they don't break."

"Then why is your cart dripping?"

"One broke."

The officer rolled his eyes. "Don't water salesmen normally use tanks?"

"I'm old fashioned." The driver produced a canteen with one shaking hand. "Try this, Sonny. It's the cleanest, purest, water in the world. Cleaner than the gunk you pull out of the ground, I swear."

The sentry poured a small amount of clear liquid onto his hand. His companions leaped for him. "Don't waste it, you idiot!"

"I wasn't!"

"This guy's not the False Prophet," the stoic sentry said. He waved the driver through. "Go to the inn and stay there. No peddling until the monks say it's clear, understood?"

"Yes sir. Thank you, sir."

The wagon entered the city. The narrow streets wound aimlessly through the crowded stone buildings, every surface coated in a fine layer of dirt. A cold gust rushed down a cavernous alley, raising dust and ruffling the curling paint of the shuttered windows. The hunched driver stopped in the shelter of a building and whispered to the tarp. "We're in. You guys okay?"

The three Curses were packed in tightly between boxes and blankets with Aiden on the left, Lynn on the right, and Peter sandwiched in the middle with the atlas on his lap. "We're good."

"Good job with the guards." Lynn said.

"Thanks." Cat grinned. "Good job with the water."

She blushed bluish. "My pleasure."

"Unfortunately they stole our canteen." Cat combed the knotted hair away from her mouth. "Where to next?"

"Aim for the bluff," Peter replied. "The elevator runs on rails. It won't be hard to find."

"Yeah, and neither will we."

"Don't doubt yourself," he said. "In my opinion, you're a very convincing old man."

Cat smirked. "Let's hope it fools the Brushcasters."

Cat resumed her disguise and pulled from the alley onto a narrow street. The rubber tires bounced in and out of the gutters as they passed clouded windows and faded store signs. Voices echoed off the plaster walls of the bowing houses, growing louder and more raucous as they approached the bluff. They moved from the shadows into to an open square where townsfolk gathered at the foot of the bluffs. Naked rock stretched skyward over a bronze-gilded mansion. The Holy Elder stood on the front step dressed in ceremonial garb.

"Faithful people of New Torston!" the Elder called. "I come in lieu of God!"

The townsfolk cheered. Cat simmered beneath her shawl and steered Strawberry along the crowd's edge as the Elder rapped his gold brush on the marble step.

"You are truly fortunate to witness this day!" he called. "I've received word that the False Prophet has officially been spotted! I, Elder of the Order of Holy Calligraphers, messenger of Our God in this mortal plane, will defeat her using miracles unlike any you've ever seen. These are the powers contained in the highest library. Proof of my worthiness before Our God and mankind!" He flung his robe aside and marched down the stairs where a bucket of paint waited. The Elder lifted the brush over his head and plunged it into the pail with the full strength of his arm.

The bristles streamed paint. He dragged them over the cobblestones in a twenty foot circle. The brush slapped back into the pail and he began writing the verses. Letters filled the ring paragraphs at a time, concluding with a wind rune and a flash of blinding light.

Wind rushed through the audience, gathering dust and garbage into a vortex above the crowd. The cyclone split into three separate spirals and morphed into three golems. The creatures stood forty feet tall with glowing eyes peering westward over the desert. The audience stared, agape. Cat paled and hurried the cart around a corner to the elevator at the base of the bluffs.

The elevator car was an open platform attached to a rail and pulley with steam-powered engine sheltered by a wooden shade. Calligraphers Trace and Paige stood guard at the foot of the access ramp. Cat's stomach knotted. She turned their back to the golems and eased Strawberry forward.

Trace stared into the middle distance, lost in his own thoughts. Paige cleared her throat. “Master.”

He slid the wagon a scowl. “Who's this?”

“Sorry to bother,” Cat rasped through her knotted hair. “I need to use the elevator.”

“The city's in lock-down.”

“I know, I'm, uh...” Cat gulped. “I'm bringing rations to the Wind Curses.”

Trace studied the horse and rider and transferred his brush from one shoulder to the other. “The mayor's office takes care of the Curse Town rations. You don't look like a city official.”

“I work for them,” Cat stammered. “I'm a water salesman.”

“I see.” Trace circled the wagon. “Of course you know Curses are an abomination.”

Cat stiffened. “That's what they say.”

“It's in our scripture. They're sin incarnate and an insult to Our God and his Prophets.”

“But your monastery commands we provide food and water.”

“That's true.” He traipsed back to his spot. “We demand rations to try to ease the suffering, but that doesn't change the cold truth that they're placed here to die – and the sooner, the better. Our God won't return to a world full of sin.”

Her knuckles whitened around the reins. “Let me pass.”

He cut a smile. “I don't think I should.”

“Please.”

“No.”

She closed her eyes and fought to maintain a raspy voice. “I thought you were men of God.”

His smirk vanished. “We are.”

"You always preach about charity. I'm trying to help sick people. That's what Our God wanted." She glared from beneath the shawl. "Or haven't you told us the truth?"

Trace met and held her stare as the Elder's voice echoed off the metal and stone. Cat reached into her cloak and hooked a finger through her string. Trace noticed the movement and straightened, his face stoic and grim. "The old man is right."

Paige glared at him. "What?"

"We are servants of Our God." Trace said, more dutifully. "It's our responsibility as modern Prophets to care for the weak and destitute. Let him pass."

"But Master!"

"Paige." He narrowed his eyes on her. "Let him pass."

She opened her mouth to retort, but stepped aside and let the wagon onto the platform. Trace approached the engine and flipped a large copper lever. The elevator shuddered and began its ascent.

"Master, are you blind?" Paige cried. "That was her!"

Trace released the lever. "I knew who it was."

"And you let her go?" Paige reeled. "You did it on purpose!"

"Paige, do you know what a False Prophet is?" He tightened a fist around his brush. "A False Prophet uses magic against Our God's will. Yesterday, a humble girl fought to save the less fortunate, and the holiest man in the Valley threw her to her death." He paused. "Which Prophet is more false?"

Paige paled. "Master, that's heresy."

"Is it?" Light quivered in his eyes. "I swore an oath upon ordination that I would uphold Our God's law and serve him until his return... or my death, should it come first."

"But if the Elder finds out – "

"I know." Trace hushed her. "If he asks, tell the truth. I made a decision. I'll endure whatever punishment. This wasn't your fault."

"But Master – "

"I'm proud of you, Paige, you'll make a fine monk." He closed his eyes. "I'd rather die a traitor under the Elder's hand than bring you down with me."

Chapter 21

The elevator lifted Cat and her party above the rooftops, beyond the view of the three sentinel wind golems, to a platform atop a sheltered plateau.

Strawberry clopped off the platform into an architectural graveyard. Skeletons of hollowed-out shops and houses caged piles of crumbled brick. Lonely walls and chimneys lined a promenade strewn with boulders. The Wind Goddess waited at the end of the walk with her back to a majestic windmill. The sails turned in the high wind. The rhythmic knocking of the mill echoed off the looming walls of the narrow pass with a hollow clack.

Cat removed her disguise, and peeled the tarp off the wagon. “We're in.”

Lynn beheld Old Torston with a gargling gasp. “What happened here?”

“Time,” Peter said, “and drought.”

Aiden 'hmph'ed. “You mean sin.”

The Goddess sculpture stared mournfully into the center of the valley, slender arms and long hair diminished by the abrasive western wind. A chunk of stone was missing from the pedestal at her feet where two dozen tiny Wind Curses gathered in murmuring clumps.

They were small in mass and stature with sunken faces and long hair. Canvas gowns fluttered about their skeletal limbs, trailing strings and ribbons like wings from the hems and sleeves. A platinum blonde spotted the wagon with wide, clouded eyes. She rose from her seat and pointed. The group flocked, cooing, across the square.

“Excuse me,” Cat started.

The Wind Curses circled the horse with drawn mouths and wide eyes bugging. Strawberry shied from their long, delicate fingers.

Cat cleared her throat. “Hello?”

“Ahh!” The platinum blonde jumped with a hand over her heart. “Who's there?”

“Who's there?” the other Curses murmured. “Who's there, who's there, who's there?”

"Um," Cat grimaced. "I'm up here."

"Oh!" The blonde spotted her with a wide, vapid smile. "Hello, ugly person!"

"Excuse me?"

"My name is Wendy." The Curse curtsied. "Is this creature your horse?"

"Yes."

"So pretty..." Wendy cooed. Strawberry stepped back as the blonde reached for her face.

A young man with flowing brown hair stomped from the crowd. "What are you doing here, ugly person?"

Cat clenched her fists around the reins. "Why do you keep calling me that?"

"Because you're ugly."

"What's ugly?" Wendy noticed Cat a second time. "Oh! Did you just get here?"

"Yes," Cat said. "My name's Cat – "

"You're a cat?" the young man cried.

"No, my *name* is Cat."

"Oh" He rolled his globular eyes. "I thought you were a cat."

Her fists balled tighter. "My friends and I need shelter from a group of angry Brushcasters camped in New Torston – "

"Cat's a funny name!" Wendy giggled. "I'm Wendy."

"So you said."

"And this is Gabe."

He crossed his twiggy arms.

"A pleasure," Cat said through clenched teeth. "Would it be alright if we stayed here a little while?"

"No," Wendy smiled.

"But we have nowhere else to go."

"Ugly people can't stay here," Wendy said. "The Goddess disapproves."

"The Goddess?"

"Yes!" Wendy said. "The Goddess only loves Curses."

"My friends are Curses."

"Friends?" Gabe spotted Lynn, Peter, and Aiden. "Ahh!"

"Ahh!" The other Wind Curses scurried, skirts and hair flying.

Wendy grabbed Gabe's arms. "Why are you screaming?"

"She has ugly things!" he cried. "The ugly girl brought other ugly things with her!"

"It's alright, we won't hurt you." Lynn rose. "We're alike. See? I'm a Water Curse."

A willowy young man with ashy skin and a nest of knotted hair stepped from the turmoil with his jaw slack. "Wow!"

Gabe raised an eyebrow. "Michael?"

"She shines!" Michael whispered. "You're beautiful!"

Lynn blushed. “Thank you.”

“Are you magic?”

“No, I'm wet.”

“I'm Michael!” He extended his bony hand over the rail.

“It's nice to meet you, Michael.” She took his hand and was yanked out of the wagon to the street.

“Gabe! Gabe, look!”

Gabe drew back. “Don't bring it near me!”

“But she's sparkly!” Michael thrust Lynn at the cowering Wind Curses. “Look at her, everyone! She's like us!”

“She is not like us!” Gabe said.

“But she's not ugly.” Wendy poked Lynn's swollen elbow. “A bit saggy, but it's like the Goddess told us. You said you were Water?”

“Yes. I'm a Water Curse.”

“A Water Curse!” Wendy shook Gabe's arm. “The Goddess said there were others!”

“You keep mentioning the Goddess?” Cat gestured to the towering statue. “Do you mean the *Goddess* Goddess. The statue?”

“Yes! The Goddess loves us!” Michael chirped. “She tells us what we should do!”

Wendy rushed past Lynn to the wagon. “Are there more?”

“Wait,” Lynn coughed. “Be careful– ”

“Ahh!” Wendy covered her face. “Oh they're awful!”

Aiden's face reddened. Cat disembarked and stood as a shield between him and their prying eyes. “Stay back.”

“See!” Gabe pointed. “They're not friends. No friends that look like that.”

“We are blessed!” Wendy wailed and raised her hands to the statue. “Thank you, Oh Goddess of Wind, for taking us as your children and granting us such beauty! We are so grateful!”

“We are grateful,” the Wind Curses chorused.

Lynn raised her eyebrows to Cat.

Wendy pranced around the wagon. “These others must be Fire and Earth. Come out of there so we can behold you.”

“Behold!” The Wind Curses whispered.

Peter grimaced to Cat over the rail.

“Come now, don't be ashamed of your ugliness! Let us welcome you with love!”

Aiden leaned to Peter. “We're not doing this, are we?”

“It's alright, Aiden,” Lynn called. “They're harmless.”

Aiden glared at her with a flush of red.

“Come, appeal to the Goddess!” Wendy continued. “She will bless you!”

Peter slouched with a defeated groan. “Fine.”

Cat bit her lip. “Pete...”

"We're not making progress otherwise." The vehicle shuddered beneath his shifting weight as he fought to gain his feet on thick, immobile knees.

Wendy drew an airy gasp. "He can barely move!" The other Curses mirrored her distress. She ushered them forward. "Help him!"

"No, I can do it," Peter said.

The other Wind Curses circled around him. "Help him, help him, help him!"

"Cat..." Aiden warned.

"Hey, stop," Cat said, but was yanked down by her sleeves.

"No, I can do it," Peter said, but the Curses flooded in around him, pushing and pulling. Peter widened his stance in the rocking wagon, refusing to be moved.

Cat elbowed through the sprite-like Curses to support him under the shoulder. "Make room, everyone! One side."

The Wind Curses tugged her sleeves and hair, but her attention was on Peter. He lent her a portion of his weight and the two eased safely to the broken cobblestone. Wind Curses crowded them. Cold air from their skin raised goosebumps up Cat's neck and arms. Wendy stroked Peter's free hand. "You poor thing. Like the mountain itself."

He smirked. "You flatter me."

"You are our friend from here on, Earth. The Goddess will bless you." Wendy spotted Aiden in a corner of the wagon. "Fire!"

His glowing eyes widened. “Stay away from me.”

“Everyone! Retrieve Fire!”

“No, no, no!” Lynn bade, but the flock followed Wendy's pointed finger.

They hooked onto his tattered sleeves and headscarf. He held the hood in place and covered his face with his forearms. Their collective breeze fanned the flames in his open sores. One grabbed the lavender scrap on his wrist.

An orange streak split the skin on his cheek. “Get *off*!”

The Wind Curses scattered like dry leaves. Aiden stood, fists clenched. Steam rose from fresh wounds on the sides of his neck and jaw. The terrified Curses and clustered behind Wendy and Gabe. Lynn raised her hands to him. “Aiden, calm down.”

“Shut up!” He leveled a shaking finger at her. Fire kindled in the back of his throat. “If you dare say another word I'll – ”

“Aiden!” Cat snapped.

He rounded on her, seething, but recoiled from her scowl.

Cat took a deep breath. “Calm down. You're hurting yourself.”

He hugged the bit of scarf to his chest. Another glowing wound ripped open across his temple as he returned to his ball. “I don't need your help.”

Cat exhaled and appealed to Wendy. “My friends are upset. Can we stay?”

“No,” Gabe said.

“Yes!” Wendy grinned.

“No!” He tossed his flowing mane. “Nothing good happens when ugly people come here! We're beautiful, holy, creatures of light. We're made in the Goddess's image!”

Cat maintained her calm. “Wendy says your Goddess respects all kinds of Curses.”

Gabe puffed like an angry bird. “You don't know anything about our Goddess!”

“There are Brushcasters down the hill who want to catch and kill us,” Cat said. “We don't even need to leave our wagon, just let us stay on this plateau for a night. Please?”

“It's what your Goddess would do,” Lynn said.

Michael's smile widened. “Yes! It's what would the Goddess would want!”

The Wind Curses repeated the phrase to each other in a whisper. Wendy considered Michael's fervent nodding and Gabe's glowering disapproval and raised her hands to the statue behind her. “What do you say, oh Goddess?”

Blustering wind whistled through the ruined buildings. Dust stirred in the square. A bit of paper came loose from a rubble pile and rode gusts through the Goddess's arms. The sculpture's face, worn smooth by centuries of abrasive wind, stared mouthless and earless over their heads.

Wendy wheezed through her nostrils. “These Curses are not beautiful, but they are not the ugly sinners from the ground. They are bearing a burden we were spared by our beautiful Goddess. She says they will stay.”

“Hooray!” Michael whooped. He danced circles around a bewildered Lynn, as the other Wind Curses echoed his cheer.

Gabe frowned. “But, these people are ugly!”

“It's alright, Gabe,” Wendy said. “Remember what we do with ugly people?”

A seed of fear planted in Cat's chest. “What do you do?”

“Throw a party!” Michael cried. “Do you like parties, Water?”

“Uh,” Lynn glanced to the others. “I guess we like parties?”

“Yay! Parties!” Michael kissed her hand and hopped away. “Food and music and lights! We should build a stage! Come on everyone, build a stage!”

“Build a stage!” the others agreed.

“Wait! No!” Gabe shouted, but the Wind Curses were swept away by Michael's enthusiasm.

Wendy took Peter's hand. “Follow me, Curses. You can stay in the mansion. It's where the Goddess once lived and where the most honored members of our party get to stay. It's a sacred place!”

"The mansion?" Gabe dropped his hands, weary of outrage. "What about the ugly girl? She's not a Curse."

"I... um..." Cat stammered.

"She's with us," Peter said. "She's our..um... helper."

"That's right!" Cat nodded. "I'm the servant girl. I take care of the wagon and stuff."

"Yeah, we can't take care of it ourselves." He flexed the arm in Wendy's hands. "You understand."

"Oh of course!" Wendy leveled her brow at Gabe. "She is a servant girl, Gabe. She'll sleep with the horse."

Cat cringed. "I will?"

"And she's not invited to the party," Gabe said.

"Of course not!" Wendy laughed. "Come on, this way!"

The Wind Curse drew Peter, Lynn, and Aiden across the square. Cat took Strawberry's reins and followed at a short distance, leaving Gabe fuming on the promenade.

The Wind Curses were busy decorating. Streamers, ribbons, and banners unfurled across the open quad. Cat rounded the base of the Goddess and followed her party past the windmill where strings of electric lights were plugged into a high outlet near an unmarked door. A section of the mill's outer wall had fallen from behind the turning propellers, exposing wooden gears and wires deep inside the ancient building. The mechanics clanked like a heartbeat. Cat stared into the shadows of the open facade and swallowed a knot in her throat. She couldn't shake the feeling she was being watched.

"Here it is!" Wendy cried.

Beside the windmill was a two-story building, covered in crumbled plaster and listing heavily to toward the mill. Time and decay had collapsed the slate shingled roof, giving the whole structure a sad, tired look.

Lynn forced a smile. "It's lovely, Wendy."

"I know." She sighed and rubbed her gaunt face on Peter's arm. "You're going to love it."

A group of giggling Wind Curses fluttered past carrying wads of ribbon. Wendy raised her head and wandered after. "Now where are they off to?"

Lynn gulped and pursed her lips. "Did she forget they were throwing the party?"

Peter shrugged. "Probably."

"Do you think she'll remember to get us?"

"Let's hope not."

Cat tied Strawberry to a loose window frame and led her friends into the condemned building. Exposed beams and splintering supports held the ceiling over one large, empty room. Strips of frayed carpet dangled from the staircase against the far wall. Dust clung to the cobwebs and gathered in the corners full of broken glass and crumbled plaster.

Lynn forced an awkward smile. “This seems nice.”

“Nice?” Aiden rubbed the scarf around his wrist.

“It's thoughtful.”

“Thoughtful?” he cried. “They're brainless!”

“They're Wind Curses,” Peter said. “All our symptoms are different. Maybe turning to air has affected their minds.”

“That's no excuse! They attacked us!”

Lynn bit her lip. “They can't help it if it's a symptom – ”

He rounded on her. “Stop talking!”

“I'm sorry!”

“Shut up!” He covered his ears and backed against the wall.

“Aiden,” Cat said. “Tell us what's wrong.”

“I can handle it.”

“You can trust us,” Peter said. “It's okay.”

“It's not.” He tugged his hood to cover his eyes. “It's her.”

Lynn blinked fresh tears. “Me?”

“You and your apologies,” he muttered. “Trying to look after everyone. Being naive when we're all dying. It's like she's here... but she's not. She's gone.” Fresh wounds broke along the veins of his arms. “I can't stand it.”

“Aiden,” Cat said, but Lynn stopped her.

The Water Curse stepped as close to him as she dared.

"Aiden?"

He puffed hot air through his teeth.

"I want to help you."

"I don't need your help."

"You can't bottle this up. I know our symptoms are different, but I've seen Water Curses drown from sadness. I won't let it happen to you. You have to talk about it."

His voice was hoarse and thready. "I'm scared."

"I know." She kneeled before him. "So I sound like Ildri. Pretend that she's here. What would you say?"

"I can't."

"I'm right here," she said, gently. "What would you say?"

"It's..." He slid down the wall. "It's not fair."

"And?"

"And I'm angry!" A flash of light radiated from his heart, up his neck. "I've been angry since the start. My parents worked for the church. They were ashamed to do it themselves. They shipped me to Fire Town on some merchant's cart like a thing."

Cat's throat tightened.

"I arrived mad and I'm still mad." He dropped his arms. "Ildri calmed me down. She could always do that. I'd get worked up and she'd say something, or just sit and hold my hand. She was perfect that way." He balled a fist. "But she's gone, so I guess I'll die angry, too."

"You don't have to," Lynn said. "You have a right to be upset. I'm sorry this has happened, but you're not alone. You've got all of us. We're going to save the world."

"I don't care about the world," he said. "I promised to stay with her to the end."

"And you did."

Another flash radiated through him, this one weaker and slower to dissipate. He pressed the scarf on his wrist to his eye. "I'm not usually like this."

"It's alright."

"No it's not. We're on a mission." Blistering tear streaks glowed like hot metal in his face. "Can we start over?"

"Of course," she said. "Feel better?"

He drew a long breath. "Maybe a little."

Chapter 22

The Wind Curses moved like spiders across the smooth surface of the Goddess, clinging to her hair and dress folds with fingers and toes. They draped the statue's arms with braided ribbons and streamers. Electric lights flickered on strings above a stage of wooden pallets and moth-eaten carpet. The locals danced with bells knotted in their hair. They draped Peter, Aiden, and Lynn with paper necklaces, and seated them against the base of the Goddess on piles of faded pillows.

Cat pouted in the open door of the Wind Curses' mansion, twisting rows of diamonds in her string. Pairs of Curses carried plates of mushrooms and potatoes from the alley behind the windmill. The dancers cheered and broke to scavenge off the different platters with long, nimble fingers. One of the loops slipped from Cat's thumb and pulled her pattern into a knot. She heaved a sigh and slipped around the square, back to the bluff.

The elevator car was missing from the station when she arrived. Cat peeked and saw it parked behind Trace and Paige, still standing guard. The Holy Elder was a black dot near his glowing circle, waiting patiently for her to approach the town with his three golems staring westward. Their translucent bodies swirled with dust tinted by the sunset.

Cat took a seat on a bit of broken wall and resumed her string game. She twisted a rough wagon shape and paused. Trace was so smug when they rolled up to him that morning. She was certain he saw through her disguise, but if he knew who she was, why didn't he stop her or tell his master where she went? Was Trace holding her captive for some reason, or was he actually fooled by her disguise? Either way, Cat her friends were on borrowed time. The Valley yawned before her. It was like a page of Peter's atlas with Castleton in the center. Destiny waited beneath that burning mountain, ready to swallow everything she loved.

Cat twisted the loop of string back to her wrist and pulled the porcelain comb from her bun. Cold wind ran its fingers through her untwisting hair. Cat closed her eyes and imagined she was flying over

God's Valley; past the Gatekeeper's Forest, around the Outer Bend past Dire Lonato, all the way back to Mason Forge. Peter was waiting for her at the porch table at Brighton's Café. Her coffee was already ordered, all she had to do was sit and the two would spend the whole night there, laughing about their tiny, insignificant lives.

Cat's stomach growled. She opened her eyes and sobered at the ruins around her. She could never go home again – not the way she wanted. Not without Peter there.

The steady thrum of the windmill accompanied the party's bells and bongos. One by one, seated Curses joined the dancers on the floor, singing and twirling with their hands above their heads. Gabe, Michael, and Wendy sat on the stage with the guests. Gabe stood in the midst of an energetic story, including punches, kicks, and what appeared to be a sword fight. Michael listened, transfixed, with one hand on Lynn's wrist and the other shoveling fistfuls of mushrooms in his mouth. Wendy gnawed a slice of potato with her bony cheek against Peter's elbow. She beamed at him. He smiled back down. A knot lodged in Cat's throat.

She crept up the promenade to linger in the rubble on the edge of the decorated square. No one noticed her loitering, which was than better than being called ugly, but not by much. A Curse smiled vapidly at Cat from across the plaza as a new wave of food arriving from the alley. Cat's stomach growled again. She pressed the pink comb to her heart and sneaked closer to the square.

" – And that is how the Goddess fought back the healthy people and gave us our city!" Gabe finished with a bow.

"How interesting," Lynn said. "You told it very well."

He tossed his waist-length hair. "Only the smartest person can be lore keeper."

"Second smartest!" Wendy giggled.

He tensed. "I'll be smartest some day." He offered Michael his hand. "Come on, let's go dance."

"Yeah!" Michael sprang to his feet. "Come on, Water, dance!"

"Oh, I couldn't!" Lynn blushed. "I don't know the steps."

"It's not a dance with steps!" He yanked her to her feet. "Come on, dance with me!"

"Oh, I don't know..." Lynn stroked her bandaged chest. She weighed Aiden's scowl against Peter's nod, looked to Michael and smiled. "I guess it couldn't hurt."

"Yay!" Michael led her into the twirl of tiny Wind Curses.

Aiden snorted at Peter and crossed his arms. "You trust these people too much."

"I'm being diplomatic," he said. "Don't forget why we're here."

"Okay, so let's knock one out and leave."

"That would be kidnapping."

"Like they'd know the difference."

A gaggle of shrill-voiced Wind Curses hopped into their circle. "Fire! Dance with us!"

"No."

"Oh please?" They pawed at his sleeves with their skeletal hands, but he drove them off with a swipe of his hand.

The Curses regrouped and turned to Peter. "Earth, will you dance with us?"

"These arms aren't meant for waving around."

"Of course they are, silly!" one chirped. She tried to lift his bandaged hand, but her tweedy limbs couldn't budge it. The other Wind Curses gathered to help, but their combined strength could only raise his arm to their knees.

Peter tugged the limb free and laid it in his lap. "Sorry, girls."

The Wind Curses turned back to Aiden. "Fire! Will you come dance with us?"

"Again, no."

"Oh please!" They surrounded him. "Please, Fire?"

"No!"

"Aiden." Peter arched an eyebrow. "Diplomacy?"

"Ugh, fine."

The Wind Curses cheered and whisked him toward the procession. Lynn's face swelled when she saw him. Drops flew as she waved at him through forest of waving arms. Peter slouched heavily against the base of the Goddess, alone on the stage with his untouched food bowl and his stiff hands limp and useless at his sides.

An idea rekindled Cat's determination. She pinned her hair back in its bun and jogged to the mansion where the wagon waited with their supplies. Strawberry greeted her with twitching flanks. Cat stroked her mane and found the neck muscles tense and knotted beneath her copper coat.

The warped mansion wall bowed into an archway overhead, the shingled roof of the one nearly touched the brick of the other. Cat ventured to the rear of the wagon and pulled out the kitchen supplies. The thud of turning gears reverberated in the narrow space. A single high window loomed three stories up the crumbling brick wall. A shadow lingered in the frame. A cascade of frightened pinpricks raced down Cat's arms.

She grabbed what she needed and hurried back to the square. Sunlight and music calmed her nerves, but her stomach was in knots. Cat took a breath and slid around the Goddess, onto Aiden's abandoned pillow. “Hi, Pete.”

“Cat!” Peter jumped. “Hi.”

“I brought you a gift.” She flourished a fork.

His smile warmed her heart. “You're amazing!”

“I try.” She grinned. “Allow me.”

She speared a mushroom and pressed the utensil into his hand. He pinched it between his fingers and thumb like a claw and used the other hand to raise it to his mouth. “This is a godsend, I was starving.”

“No one noticed?”

“I didn't say anything.” He loosened his grip to pivot the fork and stabbed another morsel. “These are pretty good. Want to share?”

“Yes, please.” She scooped a handful from his bowl. “So how's the party?”

“Dull.”

“I saw you smiling, you must be having *some* fun.”

“It's nice to feel wanted.” He thumbed the fork back upright and boosted it to his mouth. “They mean well, but Gabe told us the same story four and a half times and neither Michael or Wendy realized it.”

“Did you get a chance to tell them about our mission?”

“We haven't had a chance to say much of anything. At least it's easy to pick out candidates; some Curses are sharper than others.”

“Hmph.” Cat rolled a mushrooms across the plate and nodded to a head of silver hair swirling above the crowd. “What about her?”

“Wendy? She's nice, I guess.”

“She doesn't even use your name.”

“She's lucid. You have to take what you get.”

Cat squashed the cap under her thumb. “She's your pick for volunteer, then?”

“I don't know. She's pretty devoted to their Goddess. Either way it'd be a hard sell.”

The fork clinked against the plat. Cat steered it into a mushroom and righted it in his hand. “What about Michael?”

“Lynn seems to like him. I don't know how he feels about Our God, but he's so spacey, I suspect he'd agree to almost anything.”

“Earth!” Wendy skipped to the stage. “Why are you over here all by yourself?”

“I'm not, Cat's here.”

“A cat?” Wendy's eyes focused on Cat. She jumped back. “Who are you?”

“Nobody,” Cat deadpanned.

“Oh okay...” Wendy gnawed her bony knuckle. “Will you be leaving soon?”

“Hey, ugly girl!” Gabe's long hair rippled off his scalp in waves. “This party's not for you!”

“Let her be,” Peter warned.

“She's not wanted here.”

“I want her here,” Peter said. “I'm your guest so she stays.”

“No, she's ugly and she doesn't!”

"Don't talk to her like that – " Peter used the pedestal behind him for leverage, but his knees refused to bend.

Gabe threw back his head and laughed. "Stupid Earth Curse! You're as ugly as she is!"

"Stop right there!" Cat snarled. She helped Peter upright and stomped to center stage. "You can insult me, call me names, whatever, but you do not under any circumstances insult my friends. They are the best and bravest people I know, and no different than you!"

"We are not *ugly*!" Breeze swirled from the young man's body. "The Goddess made us!"

"The Goddess is a statue!" Cat said. "She's made of stone!"

"You're a *liar*!"

Gabe's cheeks hollowed, tightening skin over his sharp cheekbones. His wind jostled the hanging light bulbs and ripped the paper streamers. The Wind Curses fell to their knees, fretting and clinging to each other with tears in their round, rolling eyes.

"Gabe!" Wendy shouted. His hair lashed and tangled. She slapped him open-handed across the face.

The gusts calmed. Gabe blinked, eyes refocusing as his cheeks warmed to a jaundiced blush. Lynn and Aiden exchanged glances over the field of cowering Wind Curses.

Michael clung to Lynn's dress, ashy face gaunt. "Gabe?"

"It's okay, Mike." Gabe's hair continued to whip, but his voice was steady. "I'm okay."

Michael sighed, stood, and doubled over in pain. "Ahh!"

"Ah!" Lynn recoiled, Michael's fingers clamped, white-knuckled, around her wrist. "My hand!"

All his muscles tensed as he threw himself kicking and thrashing onto his back. An airy scream hissed from his open mouth.

Lynn fought to free herself as the boy twitched. Aiden grabbed Michael's wrist. Drops from Lynn's hair hissed across his upper arm. The Fire Curse leaped backward and Gabe took his place. White froth spilled from Michael's mouth as he writhed. Pencil-thin veins bulged from the yellowed whites of his rolling eyes.

"Michael, no!" Gabe grabbed the boy's dark, knotted hair. "Don't panic! Listen to my voice! Calm down!"

"What's happening?" Lynn stammered. Cat twisted The Water Curse's arm free and guided her back to the stage. A dark bruise swelled on her pale wrist. "Is he okay?"

"He's none of your business!" Gabe snapped.

He bundled the boy close, rocking and whispering as Michael hissed syllables through foam. The spasms subsided. Michael's eyes were glossy and unfocused as he stared at Gabe with a wide, toothy smile. "Who are you?"

Gabe's voice shook. "Who am I?"

“Pretty...” Michael licked spit from his thin lips. “Pretty hair.”

“Michael!”

“Pretty face.” Michael poked the ridge of Gabe's sharp cheek bone. A tear pooled and fell onto the boy's bony finger. “Shiny.”

Wendy put her hands on Gabe's shoulders. “Don't upset him. He's seeing.”

“No!” Gabe turned on her. “He's still here!”

“Hush.” She pressed the palm of her hand to Gabe's face. The other Wind Curses bowed their heads and started a low, cooing chant.

“We are the ones lifted above the ground,” Wendy said. “We are held aloft in the arms of the Goddess. We know the truths that she shared with us and shares with us now.”

Gabe bent, sobbing. Michael stared past him, fully captivated by the twinkle of the overhead lights.

Wendy bowed her head to Peter. “Excuse us, Earth, Water, and Fire. Your welcome party is cut short, but our Goddess calls. Please retire to your mansion. Leave us to care for our own.”

“Of course,” Peter replied.

“Thank you.”

The Wind Curses' chanting grew louder. They laid hands on Michael, obscuring him from view. Cat drew her friends back to the mansion, the unsettled feeling stronger and pricklier than ever.

Chapter 23

Exhaustion drew Cat into an uneasy sleep, stirred by strange lights and sounds. Wind hissed like harsh whispers through the thin mansion walls, filling her dreams with ghosts and monsters. Lynn slept within a fort of rolled towels. The bruise on her arm was nearly black with the same red splotches as her chest. Aiden slept a few paces off, wrapped tightly in his tarp. Cat nestled against Peter's gnarled ribs, desperate for warmth and comfort. The metronome of his heart eased her mind.

Dawn broke dry and chilly. Cat raised her head, hair and arms covered in a thin layer of dust. Sunbeams lanced through cracks in the ceiling. A trickle of dirt fell through the warped ceiling.

The ceiling creaked and another trickle of dirt fell further from the wall. Something rustled above them. Cat slipped from under Peter's heavy arm. The falling dust marked a path toward the old staircase. Soft footsteps patted overhead. Cat twisted the string in her hand and crept up the stairs.

Eighty percent of the roof was missing from the second floor. Thick piles of dirt and garbage hugged the remaining walls, still hung with paper and picture frames. Sun-bleached furniture held old shingles and plaster in piles. Footprints led from the stairs to a sagging scrap of roof to the mill's lonely window. A dark figure filled the window for a moment and vanished inside.

“Hey!” Cat's heart pounded. She dashed forward, but the floorboards bowed and she staggered to a stop. The window ahead of her was empty. She slid her feet to firmer ground. “Joshua?”

“Did you hear something?” Gabe's voice echoed in the alley.

Cat dropped to her knees.

“Are you hearing things?” Wendy asked in reply.

“I heard something.”

“Stop being silly.”

The two were at the front door. Cat surveyed the empty window and crawled toward their voices. Wendy still had bells tied in her hair. Gabe's was tied in a loose ponytail to disguise its excessive billowing. His features appeared sharper and more angular from above. “I still don't think this is right.”

“It's an honor.”

“They're ugly,” Gabe said. “You may not see it, but their skin and their bodies – ”

“Do you remember last night?”

He stiffened. “Yes.”

“The Goddess claims her own!”

“They're not like us.”

“Yes they are. We are ascending, aren't we?” Wendy said. “Shouldn't we give our new friends that chance?”

The dark hollows of Gabe's face deepened. “You don't remember last night like I do.”

“Morning, Curses!” Wendy rapped her bony knuckles on the door. “Are you awake?”

Linens rustled within. Lynn coughed. “Yes!”

“Hush,” Aiden hissed. “Where's Cat?”

“I don't know,” Peter said. “She was right here.”

“Curses?” Wendy knocked again.

Cat watched Lynn move through a gap in the floorboards. The Water Curse straightened her clinging dress and opened the door a crack. “Hello?”

“Ah! You're here!” Wendy said. “Did you sleep well?”

Aiden grunted. “Not really.”

“Where's your ugly friend?” Gabe asked.

“I don't know,” Peter growled.

“Good, she's gone,” Wendy clapped. “We have an announcement. T town had a meeting last night.”

“Yes, I remember,” Lynn said. “How's Michael?”

“Fabulous!” Wendy sang.

Gabe's face darkened. He crossed his arms.

Wendy rocked on her bare feet. “Sooooooooo, the town had a meeting and decided to make you all official members.”

Peter sounded wary. “What does that mean?”

“You'll be Wind Curses like us.”

“But we can't turn to wind,” Lynn said.

“But you'll belong to our Goddess!” Wendy said. “We will teach you the truths and promises, so you can ascend!”

Aiden grumbled. “Forever is a long time.”

“Not between friends,” Wendy lilted. “Do you accept?”

There was a moment of silence as the others conferred. Cat pressed her ear to the floor. She could hear Peter's rasp among the whispers. He replied with an angry tone. “Sure.”

“Good, then it's settled!” Wendy clapped. “I'll tell the others!”

She pranced out the door. Gabe lingered, voice low. “We all talked, but not everyone agreed.”

Gabe slammed the door and stomped away into the square. Cat crept back to the first floor. “What was that about?”

“There you are.” Peter scraped ankle through the dirt, but was too stiff to stand. “What were you doing up there?”

“I saw someone on the stairs.” She hopped the last step and took his arm. “Let me.”

“I can do it.”

“Not without help.”

Cat grabbed his shoulder and hoisted him from the floor. He braced himself against he wall, joints popping, and staggered forward with his arms limp and heavy at his sides. “Fine. I'm up.” He glowered. “You said you saw someone.”

“Yeah, upstairs.”

Lynn gulped. “Who was it?”

“I'm not sure.” Her cheeks flushed. “I only saw a shadow.”

Peter groaned. “Oh, don't tell me.”

“You didn't feel anything in your blood, did you?” Cat asked.

“No, I didn't,” he snapped. “I was asleep.”

Aiden frowned. “What's going on?”

Peter rolled his eyes. “We have a magic stalker.”

“What, another one?”

“He's not a stalker,” Cat said. “He's keeping us safe – ”

“He's been following us for days!” Peter cried. “Magic is a sin, Cat, that's the only thing we know. The whole world is dying because people stole sin from God. Either this dark stranger is a Prophet – which he's not – or he's evil.”

“Joshua's not evil.”

“Joshua?” Peter gawked. “You know his *name*?”

“Hush you two,” Lynn said. “Are we in danger?”

“Yes!”

“No!” Cat shouted. “I talked to him. He's helping. He knows about our mission, he wants us to continue, he saved my life!”

“He uses magic!”

“I don't care!” She took a deep breath. “Your blood's scared, Pete. It feels bad, I get it. But that doesn't mean Joshua's bad. I trust him, isn't that enough?”

Peter's face stayed firm. A film clouded his eyes. “You only trust him because you want to.”

“It's the same reason that you don't.”

Silence settled. Thick guilt like tar swelled deep in Cat's chest. Lynn cleared her throat and swallowed the excess water. “Whether this stranger is dangerous or not is something we can worry about later. We came here to find a Wind Curse.”

“Plus the Brushcasters are waiting for us at the bottom of this hill,” Aiden said.

“He's right,” Cat said. “I think we should split our priorities. I heard what Wendy told you earlier. These Curses won't listen to me, but you guys can use your new status to sway one of them to our side. I'll worry about the Brushcasters and finding a way out.”

Lynn nodded. “Sounds like a plan.”

“Agreed.” Aiden tugged at his hood. “Peter, you in?”

“Sure, whatever.” He shifted weight from one foot to the other. “Let's just go.”

“Pete...” Cat appealed, but he was halfway out the door. Lynn and Aiden followed. The Water Curse gave Cat a sympathetic look, and shut the door behind.

The celebration was more lively than the night before. A parade of Wind Curses led Aiden, Peter, and Lynn on a grand tour of town. Peter's limp was worse than ever. He hadn't smiled once since they argued. Cat watched from a second floor window with her knees hugged to her chest, feeling more lonely and unwanted. Guilt stirred acid in her stomach. Peter had a point – magic was a sin – but if that meant Joshua was evil, her conscience couldn't accept it.

Footprints from earlier were still visible in the dust. Cat followed them across the second floor to the alley, where the mansion's chimney supported a ramp of fallen roof. Cat checked the square for witnesses and ventured up the shingled incline. The old wood shifted. She dropped to her knees and crawled to the apex for a clear view across the alley into the dark, open window.

A strong ammonia-scented wind wafted across the alley. Gears and machinery beat a steady rhythm, illuminated by flashes of sunlight between propeller rotations. Strawberry snorted and pawed twenty-feet below. Cat gulped and called into the mill. “Hello?”

Bits of dust and fiber stirred about the turning gears.

“I know you're in there!”

No answer. Cat glanced to the distracted Wind Curses and adjusted her seat on the roof.

“Listen, you told me to call if I needed you,” her voice faltered. “Please show yourself. I know you're on our side. My friends are scared – I'm scared. I need your help.” She dropped her hands. “I can't do this thing on my own.”

Something twitched in the flashing light. A braided garland fluttered around a stair rail where the silhouette of a figure crouched low in the shadows. It was small and skeletal, with short hair like flames flickering off its tiny head. The figure darted down the staircase, into the mill and out of sight.

"Wait!" Cat reached. The slant of roof shuttered and the old chimney broke beneath her weight. Bricks and mortar fell to the alley. Strawberry shrieked and pulled on her tether as debris piled into the back of the wagon. The wall beneath Cat cracked and shifted. She scrambled back to the mansion as the edge of the roof gave way, taking the ramp to the window with it.

The debris hit the alley with a shuddering crash.

"What was that?"

Gabe's voice echoed against the stone wall. Cat crawled on hands and knees and peered into the alley. The Wind Curse stormed into view, his ponytail whipping behind him. Strawberry shied, stomping and snorting. Cat ducked out of sight.

"Ugly girl!" Gabe scattered bricks as he climbed into the creaky wagon. "I know you're still here! This was you, wasn't it?"

He threw bricks and chunks of plaster toward the second floor. One piece cleared the wreckage and landed at Cat's side while others thudded just below the opening. Gabe grunted and swore over Strawberry's panicked whinnies.

"Damn you!" he shouted. "I'll take off your ugly face! Come out here and fight!"

“Gabe!” Wendy snapped. The activity below stopped. “What are you doing?”

“That ugly girl broke our mansion.” He panted. “She was trying to get in our windmill!”

“What ugly girl? I don't know what you're talking about.”

“The ugly girl!” he shouted. “You have to remember her! She's still here! She'll get inside!”

A slap and he was silent.

“Look at yourself, Gabe!” Wendy cried. “You're going mad!”

He didn't reply. Her voice softened.

“We're children of the Goddess. You know what we have been promised. Set a good example for the new Wind Curses.”

“They aren't like us,” Gabe said. “They're uglier than the girl they're with. We're supposed to be beautiful.”

“And beautiful we are,” she cooed. “Tonight they'll meet the Goddess and know the truth about our windmill.”

“But – ”

“All is as it should be. Come back to the square.”

The alley went quiet. Cat released a held breath and rolled onto her back, heart shuddering with adrenaline. Light flashed within the frame of the high, lonely window. Peter was right – they were in danger. The question was from what.

Chapter 24

Wendy conducted round after round of introductions, her arm firmly attached to Peter's swollen elbow. He kept glancing to the mansion. Cat wondered if he could see her spying from the second story, or if he was still mad about how they parted.

Cat spent the morning sneaking about the edge of Wind Town, searching for exits not marked on Peter's map. The plateau was like a shelf with naked rock on all sides. The remnants of a supply path skirted the range to the south, but the ledge was uneven and too narrow for the horse and wagon. Midday sun baked the valley beyond the bluff, drawing a rippled haze from New Torston directly below.

The wind golems continued to stare westward as the Holy Elder paced the edge of the casting circle, guarded by local priests and policemen. They gave him a wide berth. Cat could feel the frustration boiling from him and stepped back from the edge. She didn't know how long his patience would last, but felt safe to assume that as long as the golems faced westward, his attention did, too.

Cat returned to Wind Town by the main road. Most of the buildings on the outer streets teetered in the wind, reduced to rubble by years of decay. She traipsed one of the side roads and entered the plaza from the north only to find the space below the Goddess empty.

Panic seized her like a cold hand. Cat sprinted to the windmill and threw open the door.

A single naked bulb glowed in the ceiling of a small antechamber, surrounded by a nest of wires and insulation. Two massive electrical generators sat on either side of a second, interior door. The air was stifling hot. Humidity condensed on the metal surfaces, fogging the array of dials and dripping in rivulets to the dirt floor. The inner door was old and metal like the elevator platform. Cat yanked the rusted padlock but it held tight.

The Wind Curses were on the far side of the square when Cat opened the door. The flock moved from building to building with Peter, Lynn, and Aiden following behind. Wendy's voice echoed off the wood and plaster facades. Cat slumped in relief and slipped out to conduct a tour of her own.

In addition to the windmill and mansion, three buildings were still in use by the locals: a communal sleeping room packed with blankets and pillows, a storage space full of spare boards and boxes salvaged from years of supply shipments, and a kitchen near the mushroom garden.

Hundreds of tiny fungi grew on stacks of moist wood behind the windmill. Cat walked the musty aisles, crunching dead weeds under her boots. The garden sloped upward to a narrow crevasse. Thorn bushes and blackened trees curled over the entrance, hiding an overgrown path that snaked northward up the hill.

“And here's where we grow the food!” Wendy sang out.

Cat flinched and dropped to her knees behind one of the garden piles as the tour paraded out of the kitchen building. Aiden and Peter dragged their feet in the middle of the pack, shoulders slumped and eyes half-lidded. Lynn kept rubbing the bandage on her chest as bouncing Wind Curses swirled around them.

“This is the garden,” Wendy directed. “The Goddess gave us the gift of food before she left for the sky. She showed us how to build the sacred towers and nurture the holy crop.”

Lynn forced a smile. “That's very nice, Wendy – ”

“And this is our windmill!”

“We know,” Aiden said. “This is our fifth lap.”

“The Windmill was the prize of God's Valley when it was built by the sinners. It turns day and night in high wind and low to give us power and pull water from under ground to keep our garden alive.”

“And it connects you directly to your Goddess,” Peter said.

“And it connects us directly to our Goddess!” Wendy sang.

Aiden groaned aloud.

The party paraded up the alley to the square. Cat crept around the windmill and hid behind Strawberry along the mansion wall.

“We're thrilled to have you among us.” Wendy took Peter's hand. “The Goddess brought you to us. You'll love being holy!”

“I'm sure.”

“Wendy, where is Michael?” Lynn asked.

Gabe's hair fluttered in its ponytail.

“Michael is wonderful,” Wendy said. “It's sweet of you to worry so much.”

“I didn't ask how he was, I asked where he was.” Lynn said. “We've been to every corner of this town, but I haven't seen him since he got sick yesterday – ”

“Michael's fine,” Gabe snapped.

“And this is our mansion!” Wendy directed the tour forward. “This palace was home to the Goddess when she lived among us.”

"She taught you about the sinners on the ground, and that you were all magic fairies or something," Aiden said.

Wendy whirled, skirts and tresses fluttering. "How did you know that?"

"Guess."

Lynn winced. "Aiden."

"That's correct," Wendy said. "We are made of magic, but there's more to it than that. You'll learn the rest tonight when you become one of us."

Peter's eyes refocused. "You haven't mentioned tonight, yet. What's tonight?"

"The indoctrination!"

The word squirmed like spiders in Cat's stomach. The rest of the Wind Curses bowed their heads. Peter bit his lip. "I don't like the sound of that."

"Stupid Earth." Gabe sneered with thin lips. "You don't get holy automatically, you've got to ascend."

"Don't spoil the surprise!" Wendy cried. "I feel like we were in the middle of something. Were we in the middle of something?"

Lynn grimaced. "The tour?"

"Ah yes! This is the mansion!" Wendy said. "It was home to the Goddess when she lived among us! She taught us about the sinners on the ground and that we were made of holy magic."

Aiden groaned again. The procession continued to the sleeping quarters and on to the storage building for another lap. Cat followed at a safe distance, keeping one eye on her friends and the other on the windmill. The propeller turned in the broken front wall and the high window remained empty. Cat pulled her knees to her chest in the back of the wagon, her heart full of worry and mind full of doubt.

The temperature dropped as night fell. Lynn, Aiden, and Peter were moved back to the stage to eat the evening meal. Faint wisps of cloud hovered at the peaks of the surrounding mountains in the gathering darkness. The moon emerged from behind the sharp peaks. Wendy took Peter's shoulder and stood at his side. “Attention!”

The Wind Curses' soft chatter fell silent.

“The sun is gone.” She raised her hands. “It is time for the indoctrination ceremony!”

The crowd encircled the Goddess, hands clasped and faces stiff amid their fluttering hair. A braided shawl was draped over Wendy's bony shoulders. The Curses took torches and passed fire around the ring, casting Peter, Lynn, and Aiden with flashes of yellow and orange. The light painted golden halos in their frayed hair, emphasizing their sharp skeletal features and wide vacant eyes. Dread twisted Cat's stomach. She climbed out of the wagon and hovered in the shadows as Wendy called out.

“Let the ritual begin!”

The Curses tied ribbons on their guest's wrists and in Lynn's dripping hair. Gabe climbed onto the Goddess's broken pedestal and held a dagger over his head. “Water, Earth, and Fire! You're on sacred ground! We here beneath the sky are not yet perfect. Our minds aren't sharp, but we know this truth: we are holy, we are above the sinners. With this ceremonial knife, you will become holy, too.”

Lynn coughed. “Knife?”

“Children of the Goddess!” Wendy raised her arms to mirror the sculpture's pose. “We gather to hear the voice of our mother. Be still and listen!”

Cat held her breath. Flame crackled. The mill beat its steady pulse. Wind whistled through the ruined buildings, stirring dirt into the square.

Wendy turned to the statue. “She's singing!”

The rest chanted around her. “She's singing, she's singing...”

“We will live forever!”

“Forever... Forever...”

Peter shifted weight. “You believe you're immortal?”

“Shut up!” Gabe snapped. “The truthkeeper is speaking!”

“Generations ago, the Goddess told us we were exalted,” Wendy said. “Her scroll said we were made of nature's magic stolen by the sinners that live on the ground. We are the Goddess's vessels, the ferry that returns power to her fingers!”

“That doesn't make you immortal,” Aiden said.

Gabe dropped to the stage. “Who says?”

“You did in your own story!”

“You mentioned a scroll,” Peter said. “Can we see it?”

Wendy's arms lowered. “What?”

“The scroll from your story,” Peter said. “Your Goddess was right: man stole magic from God. The Prophets wrote it in a letter. It could be the same thing.”

“What are Prophets?” Gabe asked. “What's God? What are you talking about?”

“God is our Goddess,” Lynn said. “He's a person who controlled nature before sin sent him away, and the Prophets were people who use God's power for good – ”

“Ugly people can't use magic!” The hair fluttered from Gabe's face. “We're the magic they stole! We'll ascend like the Goddess did! Like Michael did, too!”

Lynn stepped toward him. “What did you say?”

“Michael is with the Goddess,” Wendy said. “He met her in the windmill.”

“The windmill?” Aiden looked to Peter.

The Earth Curse frowned with a nod.

“He was sick!” Lynn shouted. “You can't lock people up when they're sick, you're supposed to take care of them!”

"Michael saw you were beautiful," Wendy said. "In his memory we honor you. When you lose your beauty, you'll join him as Fire and Earth will tonight."

Peter recoiled. "What?"

She pulled a large key from around her neck. "Prepare the ascendance!"

The circle of Wind Curses converged on the three inductees. Lynn was yanked, coughing, to the stage "Don't do this! Please!"

The Wind Curses lashed the ribbons on Aiden's wrists behind his back. Peter's became leads for clumps of Wind Curses to pull.

Cat rushed from the shadows, her string at the ready. She threaded a wind rune and shot a column of air toward the stage. The blast extinguished the torches.

"Let my friends go."

Gabe's skin tightened over the ridges of his face. "It's you!"

"I'm your new Goddess!" Cat reset her string. "Your magic's under my command!"

She twisted another wind rune and fired it high into the air. The Wind Curses screamed and fell face-down in the dirt.

"You're not the Goddess!" Wendy shouted. "You're a fake! That magic isn't yours!"

"I'll use it again!" She stretched the string between her fingers. "Let everyone go!"

"Cat," Peter said. "Michael's in the windmill!"

"I know," Cat said. "I saw someone through the window."

"No you didn't!" Gabe snarled. "He ascended! Michael's one with our Goddess – "

"You locked him in prison!" Cat aimed the string at Wendy. "Give me the key."

Wendy recoiled. "No!"

"Don't you dare!" Gabe shouted. "She'll ruin everything."

"I – " Wendy's eyes rolled in their hollow sockets. "I don't – " Wind billowed her hair. The key shook in the claw of her gnarled, flesh-less hand. The Wind Curses gaped as their leader crumbled to a heap on the stage, limbs flailing as a seizure gripped her body.

The Curses screamed and swarmed the square, running every direction. Lynn grabbed the key and ran to Aiden and Peter. Cat stowed her string and hurried to untie Aiden's bonds.

"They're insane," the Fire Curse stammered.

"Here!" Lynn pressed the key into Cat's hand. "Let's go!"

"Get the wagon ready," Cat said. "Leave Michael to me."

"Cat," Peter said. "I'm sorry I didn't believe you."

"It's okay. We were both right."

Wendy squawked. She pried herself from the stage, eyes bloodshot. Froth leaked from the corner of her mouth. "Heathen!"

Lynn drew back. "Oh no."

"You'll all die in flames!"

"Run!" Cat shouted.

Lynn, Peter, and Aiden moved as fast as they could toward the mansion as Cat sprinted to the mill with the key tight in her hand. A gang of Wind Curses followed, shrieking like harpies. She threw open the outer door and slammed it behind her.

Hundreds of tiny candles flickered around the antechamber. Wax pooled on the generators and overhead shelves. Two lines of salt lead from her entrance to the inner door, now strung with a garland of braided human hair.

Cat grimaced and reached for the padlock, her hands shaking from adrenaline. The key fit, but dropped as sound flooded the room. Gabe stood at the door, his face tight and skull-like beneath his wild hair. His knife caught the candlelight as it flashed from his robe. "Get away from our temple!"

"Wait!"

"For Michael!"

Gabe leaped, the blade aimed at her chest. She dodged past the salt line and into one of electrical generators. The hot metal burned against her hands. She yelped and whirled, in time to catch Gabe's wrist as it swung another blow. His full strength hit her the heel of her hand, snapping his hollow bones in pieces against her palm.

“Ahh!” Gabe yowled in bitter pain and fell to his knees, the limp wrist pinned tight against his chest. The dagger clattered off the machinery and landed in the salt.

“I'm sorry!” Cat said.

He fell to the dirt before her, his sunken face twisted in hurt and distress. “Please.”

“I don't want to hurt you.”

Gabe doubled over with a breathless sob. “Michael....”

Fists pounded the other door. Bony fingers clawed the doorframe as the outer door creaked open. Cat spared Gabe a pitiful glance and reclaimed the key. She popped the lock and released a howling wind into the room.

Cat squinted into the swirling dust and entered the body of the mill. A cyclone raged in the massive central chamber, carrying dust, hair, and fiber in a column from the ground. Rafters crisscrossed the room, strewn with old nails and loops of fabric caught in the storm. Wind from the maelstrom escaped through the broken front wall to turn the massive propeller rotating above. The gears clunked on a platform near the ceiling, turning a belt that powered a well and a third generator lashed to the base of a long staircase. Cords from the spare generator snaked along the outer wall and into a trapdoor partially buried beneath a heap of knotted rags.

Mountains of burlap and dry hair filled the corners of the room and mounded around the support beams and railings. Several bundles swayed in the wind, suspended from the crossbeams by ropes.

"Michael?" Cat shouted. Something snapped under her boot. A bony limb stuck from beneath the nearest pile.

Cat gasped and stumbled backward, surrounded by heaps of dry corpses sprawled over the floor, stairs and crossbeams. Hundreds of shriveled faces screamed in silence, but only one was familiar. Michael hung in the center of the room, his own coarse hair twisted into a noose about his neck.

Something moved under his feet. One of the corpses rose to its hands and knees and crawled over the pile of bodies. Cat stared in silent horror as the creature inched toward her, the fragile body buffeted by the swirling wind. Gnarled, bony hands grasped the hem of Cat's skirt, as the Curse strained to face her, mouthing words with a colorless wrinkle of a mouth.

"Help me."

Shallow, sunken eyes stared through a mess of closely cropped hair. Cat knelt and took her by the shoulders and shouted into the wind. "I'll help. What happened?"

"Help me die."

"Help you what?"

"I tried." She touched the frayed noose. "I was too scared..."

Cat's shock crumbled into anger. She took the girl in her arms. “It's okay, I've got you. You're not going to die.”

A Wind Curse's hand curled around the metal door frame to their left. Cat gathered the limp girl like a bundle of firewood as Wendy drew herself fully into the room. The Wind Curse's eyes locked on them, silver tresses flapping like wings from her scalp.

“Ugly person!”

Cat rose. Wendy raised Gabe's dagger in her skeletal hand.

“You've angered our Goddess!”

“Hang on!” Cat shouted and ran for the staircase. The weak Curse lolled in her arms as she dodged the corpses tied to the railings and draping steps and landings like heaps of twisted garbage. Wendy followed up the staircase, wide eyes unfocused in rage. The two emerged on the highest platform where the gear mechanism turned with shuddering clanks.

The high, lonely window waited at the end of the walkway with the roof of the mansion visible beyond. Cat noticed Wendy leaping in time to dodge the knife-blade.

Wendy stumbled to the wooden rail. “Heathen!”

“I'm not!”

“Get out of our windmill!”

“I'm trying!”

Wendy raised her weapon and slashed. The point of the knife ripped a stripe in Cat's billowing sleeve.

"Listen to me, Wendy!" Cat stepped backward, toward the moving gears. "I'm not here to hurt you! I'm a Prophet sent by the God of the Valley to fix everything – "

"Shut up!" Wendy's voice was barely audible over the din. "You are not a holy thing. You're a demon – like the rest of the bloated, filthy, ugly monsters scurrying down below."

The wind billowed in their skirts. The heavy clack of the catching gears beat staccato in Cat's ears. Wendy's tiny body was tossed back and forth as she clung to the banister.

"Wendy, please..." Cat glanced between the hand on the knife and the hand on the rail. "It's not safe for you. Go back down!"

"Our Goddess warned us about you." Wendy swayed in the gale. "She said people would come pretending to be messengers. She knew you'd try and redeem yourselves, but you were meant to die suffering – she wants you to – and I will see it done!"

Wendy charged, blade in hand. The wind caught her canvas gown and tossed her into the air. Cat bolted for the windmill as Wendy hit the churning gears. The teeth churned her bloodless body like compost. A metal screech sounded somewhere below. Something snapped and the platform shifted. Cat held the Wind Curse close, got a foot on the windowsill and vaulted from the building.

The propeller kept turning, fueled by the wind from the corpses, as the gears missed their alignment with an ear-splitting screech. The building shuddered as the platform and all attached to it twisted into a splintered pulp.

Cat bundled the fragile Wind Curse against her chest and braced herself for impact. She missed the broken ramp and hit the second floor of the mansion. The old boards buckled under her weight, dumping the two girls and an avalanche of dirt and garbage into the lower chamber. Cat lay on her back in the debris. The Wind Curse whimpered in her arms, frightened but alive.

Screams echoed from the square. A swell of firelight filled the scene through the mansion's front window. Smoke rolled toward the sky from the ruined mill.

Cat rolled to her side, hands covered with splinters and scratches. Peter limped toward her. “Cat!”

“I'm okay,” she winced.

“No you're not.”

He stared at her side. Bits of wood clung to a sticky red stain where a piece of the mansion was stabbed through her leather vest. Cat pulled the stake out with a stab of pain.

“The wagon's ready!” Lynn gasped. “Is she alright?”

“I'm fine.” Cat said. “Where's Aiden?”

“Right here.” He panted. “The town's gone insane!”

“We need to go.”

“We can't. The Brushcasters still have the elevator.”

“There's another way.” Cat gathered the murmuring Wind Curse, but the girl's weight was too much for Cat's wounded side. “Peter, take her.”

He fought to lift his sweat-stained arms. “Cat, I can't.”

“Lynn.” She pressed the Curse to her chest. “Let's go.”

They rushed to the alley. Each step stabbed new pain into her side. Peter offered his elbow and she clung tight. Fire burned within the windmill's broken front, lighting the canvas sails like lanterns as they increased speed. A tornado of fiery dust and fabric rose electric sparks from the generators within.

Strawberry strained at her tether. Cat took the reins and driver's seat with the Curses in back. The wagon burst from the alley, churning debris beneath its wheels. Wind Curses ran in every direction. Several convulsed in the street. Gabe sobbed against the Goddess, his broken arm held tight.

The wagon rounded the goddess's broken pedestal, scattering Curses as it went. Cat ignored the pain in her body as she brought the horse around. They charged back through the alley, into the mushroom garden behind. She took the center path toward the embankment and into the curling brush. Lynn screamed as the wagon rails snapped low branches, but Cat kept the lash strong. Strawberry barreled forward in a panic, dodging shadows and trees until they crested a second ridge and descended into a forest, pursued by the echo of Wind Town's destruction.

The Wind Golems continued to stare westward as the people of New Torston rushed around them to the cliff side. High above, the plateau glowed with a halo of orange light. The Holy Elder painted a slash through his spell and charged to the elevator. The golems died wailing as he seized Trace by the collar. “What happened?”

“I don't know, sir,” Trace stammered. “It looks like fire.”

“Is it her?”

“I don't know.”

“Don't lie to me!” The Elder slammed Trace into the elevator mechanics. Trace gasped. His brush clattered to the platform. Paige stifled a cry as the Elder loomed, scowling over him. “I know your lying tone. This is the only way up or down. Did you let her pass?”

“Sir.” Trace swallowed. “I saw no one of her description.”

“You useless whelp.” The Elder snapped his fingers at Paige. “What did you see?”

“I...” She turned to Trace for instruction but he looked away with a clenched jaw. She squared her shoulders. “I saw no one matching her description, sir.”

"I see." The Elder grabbed Trace by the tunic, ripping the white stole from his neck.

Trace staggered. "Sir!"

"You are stripped of your seniority. Acolyte!"

Paige snapped to attention.

"Bring paint." The Elder barked. "You're my apprentice, now."

Trace paled. "Sir, don't. I beg you – "

"You are a disgrace." The Elder snapped his fingers at Paige. "Now, Apprentice!"

She met Trace's worried eyes and dashed to obey. He clasped his hands before the Elder. "Sir, I beg you. Punish me. Demote me. Just please don't take Paige. I'll do anything – "

"Are you so attached to her, Hayes?" the Elder seethed, "or were you dissatisfied as my assistant?"

Trace gulped. "No, sir."

"Want that girl back? Prove your loyalty," he said. "Get that elevator running. I'm through with regulations and punishment – my grace is all that matters. I want that Prophet dead. Do you understand?"

Trace eyes welled. "Y-yes, sir."

"Good," the Elder said. "Then consider this your trial by jury."

Chapter 25

Strawberry slowed to a calmer pace, plodding between the towering walls of the spire-like mountains. Leafless trees curled black and gnarled in the shallow soil. Thorn bushes scraped the sides of the wagon, catching the rails with snaps as hoof-beats echoed through the sheer crevasse.

Cat bound her wound with her checkered scarf and let Strawberry steer into the darkness. Her injury throbbed as the shock subsided. She hoped it wasn't deep. Exhaustion set in and she dozed with her face buried in her hands, waking only when the wagon jostled a flash of pain from her side.

Twilight broke pale blue against the mountains, casting weak light into a wider canyon further up the path. A dense forest covered the steep slopes with patches of shriveled grass. Cat exhaled a cloud of steam. Her head hurt and her body ached. Nothing about her felt rested. The Curses slept in the wagon behind her; Aiden and Lynn on the benches and Peter propped in the middle with the Wind Curse curled against his chest like a child. Cat watched her short hair wave in the wind from her scalp.

Peter noticed her over his shoulder. “Hey.”

“Hey,” Cat whispered. “You okay?”

“I'm okay. How's your side?”

“Hurts.” She touched her knotted scarf. “The blood's dry. That's good at least.”

“You're lucky to be alive.”

“It wasn't that bad.” She pulled the comb from her sagging bun and scrubbed dust out of her hair. A bit of porcelain fell into her hand. The two middle teeth had broken off her grandmother's comb. Cat sighed and pinned her hair back in a sagging bun. “Something else I've ruined.”

“What ruined?” Peter asked.

“This whole quest is a disaster.”

“How do you figure that?”

“The short list? I got my friend killed. I speared myself on a building. I lost the scripture. There's no way the Brushcasters missed that fire I just set. And this is the second – no the third town I've practically destroyed.”

“Yeah, but this one deserved it.” He regarded the Curse muttering in his lap. “How long do you think she was in there?”

“I don't know. A couple days?” Cat leaned in, but it hurt her side. “I can't imagine what she lived with. You should have seen it, Pete. All the bodies heaped in piles...”

“Piles?”

“They hung themselves.” Her eyes fixed on the noose around the sleeping Wind Curse's neck. “How could they do that?”

“It's what they thought the Goddess needed,” Peter said. “They wanted to die with a purpose. I can relate to that.”

“This girl didn't. She was too scared.” Cat ran a hand over the Curse's blustering hair. “Do you think I did the right thing?”

“We couldn't leave her.”

“You said no kidnapping.”

“I know.” He hung his head. “I thought we could do this with some kind of dignity, but there's nothing dignified about any of this. All the more reason we have to put an end to it.”

“Just because our intentions are good doesn't mean we stop being human.”

"But I'm not human," he said. "The Wind Curses were delusional but they're right about that. I'm a vessel for other peoples' sin pretending to be important. When we're done, I'll die to keep the rest of the world going, like they did with their windmill."

"Don't talk like that."

"It's what I signed up for."

"You are my best friend," Cat said. "Saving the world isn't going to change that. You're mine first and then the world's, no matter what happens."

A thin film clouded his eyes. "I needed to hear that."

The Wind Curse rubbed her face into Peter's mud-stained shirt. She opened her eyes and drew back with an airy scream. "Ah!"

"Shh, its okay. My name's Cat." She took a motherly tone. "I'm your friend. We met yesterday."

"I don't remember." The girl looked from her to the Curses. "What are these creatures?"

"This one's Peter," Cat patted his head. "And the other two are Aiden and Lynn."

"Where did they come from?"

"I brought them with me."

"Who are you?"

"I'm Cat," she said, again. "I rescued you from the windmill."

"The windmill..." The girl felt the noose at her neck. "I'm supposed to be there."

Lynn stirred on her seat. She rolled over and rubbed her eyes. "Did we make it?"

"So far," Peter said.

Aiden yawned. "It's freezing out here. Where are we?"

"We're still in the mountains."

"Better that than caught, I guess." He wrapped his arms around his chest. "How's our new addition?"

"A little disoriented."

Lynn noticed the girl looking around and leaned forward. "Hello there! What's your name, little one?"

"Zephyr." Her wide eyes blinked. "Are we in Wind Town?"

"No, thank God," Aiden grumbled.

"She's lost," Cat said. "Zephyr, is it? That's a very nice name."

Her tight brow furrowed. "Am I dead?"

"No, you're not."

"Then I must go back. The Goddess needs me."

"Your Goddess is a fraud," Aiden said.

Lynn coughed. "What he meant was, you've got an even more important boss, now. Your Goddess wanted you to save Wind Town, but our God wants you to save the world."

"The world?" Zephyr's lip trembled. "I don't understand."

“The whole world,” Peter said. “Wind Town, too.”

“Save Wind Town?” Her eyes shifted out of focus. “I guess that's okay.”

They plodded down an embankment into a grove of thin, bowing, trees. Strawberry was exhausted from a long night of walking. Lynn got her food and water as the others searched Peter's atlas to find their bearings.

“The eastern range is largely unmapped,” Peter said. “My great-grandfather drew this himself, so it was probably too harsh to travel in his day. The path we took isn't even marked.”

Zephyr petted the pages. “Pretty drawings.”

“My ancestors thank you.” Peter grinned. “If only they gave some indication where we were.”

“Well here's Wind Town.” Cat pointed to Torston. “If we've been heading north this whole time, we could be in this spot he called “The Spires,” but it was so dark last night, there's no telling where we've ended up. Strawberry could have turned us around, or taken a fork, or pretty much gone anywhere.”

Aiden puffed steam. “Great, so we're nowhere.”

“Not necessarily,” Peter said. “There's a star map in the back here. We can use it to navigate at night even if the other map has no landmarks.”

“I see one landmark.” Aiden tapped the page. “Though we might not want to follow it.”

His finger left a sooty smear on a city where the Eastern Mountains bled into the northern range. Cat gulped at the label: Calligraphers' Monastery.

A twig snapped to their left. The wagon hushed. Cat held her breath, but couldn't hear past the pounding of her own heart.

“Must have been an animal,” Peter said.

“I don't see any animals,” Aiden whispered.

“Maybe Zephyr knows.” Lynn stored Strawberry's oats and climbed back to her bench. “Do you know what kind of animals live around here, Zephyr?”

“Huh?” Her attention wandered to Lynn. She touched her dripping face. “Crying.”

Strawberry refused to move forward. Hot air puffed in blasts from her nostrils as fog crept toward them from the forest. It weaved between trees, hovering above the thorn bushes and shrouding the wagon in cold, gray mist.

Aiden's skin welled pink in the wet cold. “I don't like this.”

Lynn shivered. “Cat, you're from the mountains. Is it normally misty like this?”

"It probably means there's water around," she replied. "Hopefully it's a river. Water flows downhill, maybe we can follow it back to the valley."

"Hopefully," Peter said.

Fog drifted through the wagon rails. Zephyr's eyes widened as her pupils contracted. "Ghosts."

Another snap cracked to their right, then another, and a third. The sounds moved around the wagon in a tight arc, punctuated by harsh rustles and muted thuds. Cat's knuckles whitened on the reins. She released one to hook a finger under her string. "Pete, how are your bones?"

"Still."

A limb broke and fell toward them out of the fog. Lynn yelped and heaved a cough as Strawberry backed them away. Shadows swirled. A creaky voice whispered out of the fog.

"Make no sound."

Cat froze.

"You are being hunted."

A cloaked figure swept through the near fog and took hold of Strawberry's bridle. Cat held her breath, finger tight in the string, but uncertainty stayed her hand. The horse snorted as the stranger lead her off the path into the woods.

They wove through the shrouded forest, popping twigs and wading through bushes behind their silent guide. Cat checked over her shoulders, but nothing moved in the half-light. They emerged in a wide clearing with mountains on every side. A small cabin stood in the center of a long embankment. Electric lights glowed in the tiny windows and thick cables ran from the structure past their tires and out into the fog-covered woods. A garden sat under the window and an arbor covered the door. Sculptural elements supported the roof, similar to those seen in New Torston.

A ring of white soot circled the cabin fifty paces on all sides. The wagon crossed the powder line and the shrouded figure released the bridle. “You are safe now.”

“Where are we?” Aiden asked. “Who is that?”

“I live here.” The stranger shrugged off the cloak, revealing a hunchbacked old woman with curled hair and a deeply wrinkled face. “I prepared a place for you, Child of Sinners. Companions, sit. There is food for you.”

“You're a hermit?”

“I am many things.” The woman waved a calloused hand. “I was a child, a dreamer, a leader or men, a famous inventor.” She swept into a bow. “Even a Goddess.”

“Goddess?” Zephyr stood with a ripple of her loose clothing.

"Ah, Wind." She took Zephyr's hand. "I see you have already dedicated yourself to me." The woman removed the noose from her fragile neck. "Thank you for your sacrifice."

"But the Goddess ascended," Zephyr said. "She told us we were holy."

"And that you are. All magic is holy. Magic is all that keeps ugly creatures like you alive."

"Excuse me?" Aiden balked.

"You're who Wind Town was worshiping," Cat said. "Why did you lie to them?"

"Because the wind of the dying world has grown feeble and weak. I needed their magic to turn the windmill and power the generators."

"You tricked hundreds of innocent people to their deaths to keep your lights on?" Aiden cried.

"Was it any worse than the fate that awaited them?" The old woman asked. "When I climbed this mountain, Wind Town was full of mindless skeletons. I gave them hope and a truth simple enough for them to hold on to. The windmill gives their town water and power. More would die without it."

"But it's not right!"

"Little is." She fixed her eyes on Cat. "Don't you agree, Child of Sinners?"

"Why do you keep calling me that?"

"It's who you are; Child of Sinners, friend of the earth. The new Prophet who descends to the Valley from the mountains."

"You're quoting Malachi." Peter slid from the wagon. "The Wind Curses said you had a scroll – "

"You mean this?" She drew a yellowed roll of parchment from a pocket in her cloak.

Cat gasped. "Where'd you get that?"

"I inherited it, Miss Aston, as you did." She held it forward. "Read. I'm not lying."

Cat stretched the stiff scroll. The words were faded, but the handwriting looked like Malachi's even without the emotional flourishes she remembered in her copy.

"Is it the one you lost?" Lynn asked.

"Not the exact one, but a copy of it." Cat said. "How did you get this? Are you a Brushcaster?'

The woman chuckled. "God forbid."

"Owning scripture is supposed to be illegal."

"I could tell you, but the Calligraphers you fear are searching as we speak. Why don't you come inside?" the woman said. "I made a meal for you."

"Meal?" Zephyr perked up. "Food?"

The Wind Curse dashed past the old woman and through the front door.

"Zephyr, no!" Lynn called.

They followed her into the house. Simple furnishings and home-made trappings cluttered the tiny foyer space where a pot of bubbling liquid simmered in a stone fireplace. Pots, pans, and other utensils hung from hooks about a single cabinet and a three-legged table. The ravenous Wind Curse crouched over the hearth, scooping handfuls of broth from the pot, slurping rice and vegetables as the soup slipped through her bony fingers.

Lynn crouched down beside her. "Honey, don't do that. You'll burn yourself."

"Good! I knew she would be hungry! There's bowls there on the floor," the old woman said. "There is enough for you too, Water, and some dry goods for Fire as well – and I saw that the Earth Curse had trouble with his hands so I carved some pokers." She gestured to five whittled sticks waiting on the table. "Don't worry, those meant for sacrifice will find no harm here."

Peter frowned. "How did you know all this?"

"I can show you, now that you're in here." She moved from the kitchen into the main room of the house. "Come!"

Cat and Peter exchanged a curious glance.

Aiden shook his head. "This is surreal."

"You guys stay here," Cat said. She gave Peter a tug and the two followed into the musty back room. Empty book cases laced with dust and cobwebs lined the walls. The center of the room was dominated by a circle of soot, sprinkled delicately within a ring of tall, un-fired clay pots.

The hermit plopped cross-legged near one of the basins. "Ask me questions."

"Questions?" Cat asked.

She nodded.

"What is this place?" Peter asked.

"This is my house. I would think your questions should be more significant than that." The old woman pulled a smoking pipe out of the nearest basin. "Like the one you asked before."

"How do you know the future?" Cat offered.

"That one is for later. The one before that."

"You mean how you got scripture," Peter said.

"I inherited a library of scripture from my father on the day of his untimely death."

"Your father?"

"Hanged himself."

"I'm sorry to hear that."

"The truth he read in the scrolls drove him to despair." She reached into the pot again, producing a heaping handful of ash. "Magic is a curse and we've all used it to an indecent extent."

She drew line of powder over the circle, braiding curves and angles together to form a simple fire symbol. The soot flashed white and the rune burst into a carpet of steady flame.

Cat rushed forward. "How do you know the symbol for fire?"

The woman lit her pipe on the open flame and took a long drag. Her sunken eyes narrowed. "How did you know them, Catrina?"

Cat gulped. "They came to me from God."

"How can God send messages when he's been gone for five hundred years?" the woman asked. "No, you stole them, the same as the rest of us."

"She did not," Peter said. "She's a Prophet!"

"Hah!" The crone sneered. "She's no Prophet."

A flutter caught in Cat's chest. "Did the smoke say that, too?"

"That's an accusation, not a question."

"I don't care, just tell me."

The woman dragged a lungful from the pipe. "You are supposed to ask questions. That's how today works."

"So you've seen today before," Peter ventured. "With the food and the fog and all. That's how you could find us."

"That's right."

“So you foresaw this conversation, too?” Cat asked.

“As clearly as my own death.”

Cat's wound ached. She pressed a hand to the bandage. “How can you know this?”

“I am one of the last remnants of a once-glorious age,” she said. “You understand what that's like, of course.”

“I can't say that I do.”

“Then ask a different question; maybe you will.”

Cat breathed again. “How do you know the future?”

“That will be answered by another question.”

“You're horribly frustrating, you know that,” Cat said.

“Where'd you find that scripture?” Peter asked. “If you're not a Brushcaster you must have found it somewhere.”

“Ah, the scripture.” The woman laid the scroll in her lap. “This is the burden of my ancestors. Long ago a powerful man had four powerful sons. They kept four libraries of scripture within their family line. I am the last of the youngest son, Torston, whose lineage formed and founded the Town below this mountain.”

Peter shifted his weight. “You're a Torston?”

“Henrietta Torston to be exact,” she said. “I was mayor, actually, decades ago.”

“Then why are you living up here?”

“This house was my father's library,” she said. “My family harnessed steam, pioneered mechanical engineering, invented the electric generator. We were free-thinkers, but with talent, we inherited guilt. When pain took my father, this house passed to me.”

She blew a ribbon of smoke over the flame. “I thought I would guard it – it is my family's greatest treasure – but I am as weak as my father before me. I read, and the pages fell like years of my life, brittle and meaningless. This scroll is all I have left.”

Cat surveyed the empty shelves around them. “What happened to the rest of them?”

She wheezed a laugh. “I like you, Child of Sinners. We have much in common. We share the same sin.”

The flutter returned. Cat exhaled a shaky breath. “What do you mean by that?”

“Almost. Ask again.”

Cat steeled herself. “What sins do we share?”

A smile stretched the wrinkles of her weather-worn face. “That's the one.”

The hermit tossed another handful of soot on the fire. The flame swelled, painting the walls with shapes and flashes of color. She lifted the scroll to the light. “This scripture speaks of the greatest sin known to man. No less than the outright murder of Our God.”

“You can't kill God,” Cat said.

"But you can kill a Prophet." The fire lit the crone's face, illuminating her bright and somewhat familiar green eyes. "Five hundred years ago, before the drought and the Curses, when civilization was young. Our God lived in the world as pure magic. He conducted the seasons, the animals, the fields, and the four elements. He made mankind to be his companions, but man was not content with that. They wanted to hear Our God speak. They didn't know his voice could melt a man, flesh and bone, into a puddle on the ground."

Cat gulped.

"So Our God chose a Prophet. The people called him the Runian because he was born with the symbols of the elements etched on his spine. The symbols let him survive Our God's presence. He could hear Our God whisper and control magic with his will. Through him, Our God performed miracles and communicated to his people in a way they could understand. But mankind still wasn't pleased. They wanted to be Our God's peer and have all the powers of the Prophet for themselves. And the punishment..."

A lump settled like a rock in Cat's stomach as the hermit heaved a dry chuckle.

"Our God, generous thing that he is, punished us with exactly what we wanted. He gave us control of nature and magic, and we have done a poor job in his stead."

“Man doesn't have power,” Peter said. “The power is in the symbols, not in the users, and they weren't any kind of gift. Malachi was murdered for those symbols.”

“Yes he was.” Fire glinted like brands in her deep-set eyes. “Man can only taste divinity by destroying something holy. ”

She snatched the yellowed scroll and flung it into the heart of the fire. Cat reached, but could only watch as it blackened and curled. Flame reached the ink and the room flashed with white light. Smoke swelled and invaded her nose, mouth, and eyes. The room spun and her senses were whisked somewhere else.

She was in a study full of rich furniture. A young man in white robes sat writing at a desk. His bronze hand scratched a quill across a stretched length of parchment. Tears fell to the page. He paused to wipe his face on his sleeve and signed his name – Malachi – before sobbing again.

The room changed. They were in a parlor. The man in white stood at the fireplace, watching minutes pass on a clock set into the mantle. A pale-skinned stranger appeared. They exchanged words. Malachi turned from the hearth and extended his hand, only for the stranger to plunge a hidden knife into his chest.

Cat blinked and she was in a cavern. A girl stood at the edge of a sharp cliff over a vast chasm of boiling white light. Wind blew her hair and loose skirt as she teetered at the edge. She raised her hands and Cat saw her own face bleached by the brightness. Like a statue. Like a Goddess.

The flash ended with a shock of pain as she hit the wooden floor. Her side burned and the checks of her knocked scarf were wet with new blood. The fire in the room had gone out, but a gritty haze remained. It tasted like chalk on the back of her tongue.

"Cat!" Peter reached out with one hand, unable to bend.

Cat took his arm. "Did you see it?"

"I saw it!"

"That was Malachi!" She pulled herself. "That was me!"

"The past and the future," the old woman confirmed. "This is what happened to my library." She scooped the remnants of the scripture into one of her clay basins. "Now I have finally seen it all."

Zephyr screamed outside. Aiden burst through the kitchen door, cracks in his face blazing. "Cat, hurry!"

"What is it?"

The hermit closed her eyes. "The reason that I found you."

Zephyr collapsed on the front walk. Dust billowed around her body. Lynn hovered over, unable to touch. "Please stop!"

"Burning!" Zephyr clawed the earth. "Fire from the windmill!"

"It's not, Zeph, that's impossible!"

Aiden drew Cat and Peter to the door. “She's sees something, though. Look!”

A button of light swelled over the misty treeline. The canyon walls extending southward glowed orange with strengthening flame. Birds scattered and a twenty-foot fire golem appeared above the trees.

“They caught us.” Peter turned to the old woman. “You saw this in the smoke, too?”

Cat's fist clenched. “Why didn't you warn us?”

The woman blew smoke from her nostrils. “Our God wanted it this way.”

Chapter 26

Heat from the Elder's fire golem burned the morning fog. It dragged its spindly limbs through miles of brush, burning away undergrowth and leaving a path of heat and smoke in its wake. Flame licked the canyon walls. Heat radiated off the stone. The Holy Elder rode behind, bathed in orange light, his gold brush glowing in hand and face creased in a wicked smile. Sweat soaked Paige's collar as she clung to Trace on the back of their horse. He watched the Elder with narrowed eyes. The golem broke the treeline on a long embankment and sprinted toward a tiny cabin with a wagon full of Curses beside it.

The Elder's smile widened. Trace pulled their thundering steed alongside. “Master, we have her! She has nowhere to run. Call the creature off!”

“We aren't here for prisoners!”

“But sir, it's murder!”

Catrina Aston appeared, stained in blood and dirt. She leaped into the front seat of her wagon and steered it toward the far side of the clearing. The Curses in the back of the wagon stared across the glen in horror. Flame reflected off the Earth Curse's glasses. He braced himself against the rails as their wagon jostled. The Wind Curse – a slight, fragile-looking thing – clung to the Water Curse in hysterics. The Fire Curse shielded them, his skin striped with glowing cracks. The fire golem leaped and beat them to the trees. Their horse whinnied and veered left, following the treeline. The golem dragged its flank among the branches. Trace pulled his brush from its holster and passed Paige the reins. “Here!”

“What are you doing?”

He leaped the gap between the horses and tackled the Elder around the chest. The men hit the ground with a crack.

Paige wheeled around. “Master!”

The Elder sprang up, his leg bloody below the knee. “You!”

He reached for Trace, but the senior monk scrambled clear. The Elder limped after, but the younger man was faster. Trace dug the blunt end of his black brush in the dirt and carved a shaky rune within a loose circle.

The spell flashed and a bulbous, misshapen water golem rose from its uneven surface.

The Elder flushed. “What have you done?”

“As you taught me.” Trace stomped a heelprint in the active circle. The line broke under his weight. Its light rippled through the water as the eyes shrank to menacing points. “As I recall, a wrathful golem lives to destroy sin.”

The spell burst in a fiery blaze.

“We were never meant to use magic.” Trace met the Elder's twitching eye. “I hope it comes for you next.”

Madness took the ogre-like water golem. It charged and tackled the fire golem as the wagon dashed past them. The monsters hit the trees, thrashing and lunging in an explosion of hot steam. The wagon veered left in a panic and cut across the field. Catrina stood in the driver's seat, applying all her strength to the reins. Her horse fought her pull and turned them north again. The water golem threw its foe over their heads and into the tiny cabin, crushing the structure to burning pieces. A column of smoke burst from the ruined building, spotted with soot and laced with flashes of white lightning. The wagon vanished in the haze.

Paige steered her horse after them into the expanding fog. The air was bitter. She gasped as a flurry of mangled images overwhelmed her mind. Glimpses of the wagon flit in her peripheral vision. She saw shapes, colors, monsters – unsure which if any were real. Her horse reared. Paige clung tight and spurred it south, away from the smoke.

The wagon emerged from the cloud on the north side with Catrina back in control. The wail of fighting golems echoed in the haze between them, punctuated by the rap of weapons as The Holy Elder struck his brush against Trace's. The gold handle flashed white at every violent impact. Trace struggled to match the superior fighter with dodges and blocks. The Elder forced him backward, off the glowing circle, hooked Trace's brush handle and sent the staff flying.

Trace fell to a knee, arms high to protect his head, but The Elder drove a heel into his ribs. The monk fell and the Elder destroyed his water rune with a swipe of the gold brush.

Trace's golem died in a puff of air and a sheet of falling water. Smoke dispersed as the fire golem wriggled from the wreckage, its body shriveled and concave from the elemental battle. It located the retreating wagon and resumed a limping pursuit.

The Elder returned to Trace, glowing paintbrush brandished in both hands. "You've failed both your mutiny and my test of loyalty."

The senior monk stirred.

“Receive your sentence.” The Elder slammed the gold brush like an axe into Trace's back. The monk cried out and covered his head as the metal struck again and again, battering the helpless man in the head and neck. Trace stopped moving, but the Elder continued, delivering heavy blows. The gold brush blazed white as if in pain. Blood sprayed from the bristles.

“Master!” Paige's stomach clenched. Her hands shook on the reins. Red striped the Elder's face. He swung the weapon again.

Trace's black brush lay discarded in the grass. Paige lashed her horse and charged toward them, leaping from the saddle in time to grab the discarded instrument. She gripped it in two fists and came upon the Elder from behind. “Stop it!”

The Elder struck his victim again. Paige raised the brush over her head like a club.

“Leave him alone!”

With full strength, she drove the wooden staff into the crown of the Elder's head. The brush cracked against the skull, bones buckling around the curve. Across the field, the fire golem exploded in light and flame.

The blast sent a shock wave through the clearing. Trees bent. Debris scattered. Paige fell to her knees. The force threw Catrina's wagon off its wheels and into the trees. Paige heard screaming and cowered. The Elder lay glassy-eyed before her on the grass.

Trace wheezed through bloody lips. “Paige.”

“Master!” Her legs shook as she crawled to him. “You're hurt.”

“Get out of here.”

“You need help.”

“He's dead.” Trace grabbed her tunic. “They know.”

“What are you saying?”

“The Living Golem!” he coughed. “Paige, it's standing in the monastery as dead as the Elder is now.”

“But he was killing you!”

“They'll execute you for this.” His bloodshot eyes welled. “Run. It was my brush, I'll take the blame. Get the horse and go.”

“Not on your life.”

He winced a painful gasp as she dragged him onto their horse. She strapped his brush in its holster. The Elder's body lay face down, the golden paintbrush gleamed with white light in his lifeless hand. Paige wrenched it free, strapped it beside its bloody twin, and steered their horse southward.

Over her shoulder, the toppled wagon spun its wheels. The horse dragged a snapped harness, whining in distress. Its calls echoed like sad ghosts off the scorched canyon walls.

Points of light floated in Cat's eyes. She scraped her hand on packed earth, the cold dull against her numbed skin. A strong ringing muffled her ears. Pungent smoke drifted through the dark tree trunks. Something soft and warm touched her face, followed by a blast of hot air. Strawberry. Cat pet her nose and rolled over, her body loose and foreign like a puppet.

Breathing hurt. Moving hurt. Cat rose to her hands and knees and let the world settle around her spinning head. Burning supplies littered her landing spot. The atlas lay face down in the dirt.

"Peter..."

A man groaned behind her. Cat reached for the book, but her side wound was excruciating. She left it where it was and limped toward the sound. Aiden lay against a tree with his hand against his face. The gauze on his hand steamed as he pulled it from the wound. All the skin from his nose to his right ear was gone.

Cat staggered. "Our God..."

"I'm okay." The inside of his face glowed like hot coals. "I- I think we crashed."

"Yeah..." A tremble stirred her stomach. "Rest here... I have to find Peter."

The wagon was wedged sideways against a pair of trees, the metal rails embedded deep into the trunks. Lynn and Zephyr huddled beneath it, shivering in cold and shock. Zephyr's eyes drifted in different directions. Lynn's face a sickly blue. "Cat, you're okay. Thank goodness."

"Where's Peter?"

Lynn sucked her lip and turned her watering eyes to the mist where he lay on his back.

Cat forgot her pain. "Pete!"

He was ghastly pale. Rivers of dirty blood striped his face and shirt. Broken bones swelled with jabs of growing stone, bending his arms and legs in grotesque shapes and directions. Cat fell at his side, desperate for a sound or sign of life. She pressed her ear to his chest and he flinched.

"Pete." Her voice cracked. She brushed his cheek with the back of her hand, feeling ridges of cold stone. The rim of his broken glasses sliced deep into his face.

Peter's brow twitched, his eyes shut tight against the pain. Cat drew back, shivering in emotion too strong to properly feel. She ached to hold him – to let him know she was there – but couldn't bear to cause his suffering. His face stilled. She hugged her empty arms and choked on a wave of shuddering sobs.

"Catrina."

The voice pricked her heart. Joshua stepped from the fog, his expression passive. She blinked in disbelief. "You..."

"Yes." He knelt beside her.

She grabbed his sleeve. "Please, you have to help him."

"Catrina..."

"You have magic." Tears blurred her eyes and wet her cheeks. "I can't lose him, I can't..." She fell to Joshua's shoulder, weeping and shaking. He wrapped his arm around her, but his hand was barely present and his bones felt small and fragile against her trembling fists.

"I'm sorry, Catrina. I'm sorry this has happened." Joshua cupped her head and met her eyes. His pools of black were gentle, deep and broad as the darkest night. Points like starlight glimmered faintly, gaining strength the more she stared. A tingle rose in her heart and spread in prickles to her feet and fingers. Her vision blurred and she fell unconscious in his arms.

Chapter 27

A flash of light and a strangled roar filled the Hall of the Elders in the heart of the Calligraphers' monastery. Panicked overnight staff gathered in the dusty chamber as the Elder's Living Golem shut its glowing eyes and stilled to a lifeless statue. Senior monk Vivian Arch gathered a troop of mounted Calligraphers and raced daylight across the desert to the central city of Castleton. Lord Creven was in his office when she and her entourage stormed in. “The Holy Elder is dead.”

Lord Creven spilled his morning drink. “Dead?”

“His golem went dormant at sunup,” the senior said. “Tell us what you know.”

“Why do you think I know anything?”

“I have no time for delays,” she insisted. “It's paramount that we find out what happened immediately. Tell me.”

Creven frowned. “And you are...?”

“Senior Vivian Arch.” She tugged the hem of her white stole. “Head of the lower library.”

“Okay, Mrs. Librarian.” Creven rose. “I can understand why you and your group would be upset about this, but charging in here making demands kind of sours your pious reputation.”

The monks gripped their brushes. Vivian set her jaw. “Time is of the essence, Creven.”

“Why bother me about this, anyway? Go elect a new Elder. You do that kind of thing all the time, right?”

“Certainly not,” she huffed. “Elders are elected for life. It is a delicate, scriptural process! And even when a candidate is chosen, we cannot install them without the magic in the Elder's golden brush. It's instrumental in the creation of a new Living Golem. We can't ordain an Elder without recovering the brush, and we can't access the highest library without a Holy Elder.”

“And what am I supposed to do about that?”

"We know the Elder confided in you," she said. "You spoke with him before his disappearance. Did he mention his mission? Did your information network report any sightings?"

Lord Creven leaned forward over the desk. "What will you give me in exchange?"

Vivian frowned. "What?"

"Don't get me wrong, your Holy Elder and I were very old friends, but I am a businessman. What will you give me in exchange for my information?"

"We give you our eternal thanks," she stuttered. "The gratitude of the monastery – "

"I want a political favor," Creven stated. "Exclusive access to the new Holy Elder when you've picked them and an audience before anyone else knows."

"An audience? That's all?" Vivian searched her companions' faces and nodded. "We cannot prioritize you over the monastery, but we can grant you what you ask."

A smile split Creven's face. "Then you are in luck. Not only do I know the ex-Elder's mission, but I'd bet half my fortune the old man was murdered."

"Murder?" Vivian huffed. "Surely not!"

"You can't kill the Elder!" Another monk said. "He was holy."

“He was a man, you moron, not a god,” Creven laughed. “I called him here about a False Prophet by the name of Catrina Aston.”

“A False Prophet?” Vivian balked. “Why didn't we know about this?”

“I guess your elder wanted to handle it himself.” Creven shrugged. “News is only as fast as a horse is. I'm sure you've heard about Dire Lonato, at least.”

“Only that there was a struggle.”

“Then you should pay more attention,” Creven snarled. “That terrorist threatened my house and launched a trail of destruction through the Valley. The Elder took pursuit and now he's dead. If you ask me, the answer's pretty obvious.”

The Calligraphers stiffened, fear in their eyes. Vivian pressed her lips. “So he was killed in a campaign against Our God.”

“A False Prophet is a threat to both your power and mine,” Lord Creven said. “You want my help catching this criminal? I have a militia on hand and ready to go.”

“The Holy Calligraphers cannot take part in an armed act of aggression.”

“But you can assist the public good,” Lord Creven said. “I'm not a religious man; I don't care about your Order, I want to protect my investments. As far as the world knows, Catrina Aston is a terrorist and the Holy Elder still lives. Add your monks to my army and I can take her down."

"That's wicked," Vivian said.

"Hey, you came to me. We wouldn't want God's Valley to find out you are leaderless – half of it's in ruins thanks to your lack of protection." He eased back in his chair. "I'm offering to share power, but I can take it by force if I want to. What do you say, my friends? Do we have a deal?"

The monks conferred in panicked tones. Vivian's heart sank as their voices softened and realization set in. She faced Lord Creven and nodded. "We will do as you say, but only until our golden brush is found. Afterward, the new Elder will discuss it further, and I hope for your sake it isn't me."

A haze of wind and stars muddied Cat's perception. Familiar hints flooded her senses until she couldn't tell what was real or a dream. One moment she was in the desert beneath stars and the next she was in Mason Forge. It was a plain Sunday morning. Peter was waiting at Brighton's to have coffee like they always did. There was no scripture or calling. He was happy and healthy. Not on the floor of a cold glen on the other side of the world. Not in pain.

Cat's eyes snapped open. She rolled to her back in lavender scented sheets. Oil lamps glowed in gold sconces, casting the beaded wall-coverings in warm yellow light. It wasn't home, but it was a stark departure from the forest she passed out in. Was she dreaming? Was she dead?

Cat's muscles ached. She was dressed in a white gown with gold stitching in the cuffs. Her hands were clean, the scratches bandaged, and the wound in her side was dressed and bound. She swung her bare feet from beneath the covers and crossed to a dresser where her pink comb waited on a cushion of blue velvet. The two middle teeth were missing.

It was all real, all of it, from the Calligraphers in Mason Forge to the fight in the glen to wherever she was in that moment, and she had wasted too much time. Cat dashed to the door, but it was locked from the outside. Her clothes were missing. So was her string. She searched the drawers for a replacement when a key turned the lock.

Joshua entered barefoot, wearing a green velvet tunic with two pockets in each sleeve. “Catrina?”

She blushed, feeling exposed, and grabbed the bed sheets to cover her nightgown. “Where am I?”

“I brought you home.”

“Where's Peter?”

Joshua paused for breath. “Resting.”

“I need to see him,” she said. “He's hurt. I should be there.”

“I'll take you, I promise. First you should get dressed.”

She hugged the blanket tighter. “My clothes are gone.”

“I know, I left some out for you. Here.” He moved her comb and unfolded the velvet cushion into a knee-length embroidered gown. “Blue is your favorite, right?”

The soft fabric was embellished with hand-stitched leaves and lilies. The sleeves had pockets like Joshua's, one on each bicep and forearm. The openings pointed in toward the body instead of up and down as they should have. Cat ran a thumb over the lapel and met his eye. “You prepared this room for me?”

“Yeah, just the room though.” He cut half a grin. “In case you were worried... you know.”

She blushed and took the gown. “How long was I asleep?”

“A day.”

“A day...” She swallowed. “What about the others?”

“They're here, too.” His face relaxed, revealing dark bags under his eyes. “I moved you all as quickly and safely as I could. The Holy Elder is dead. The Calligraphers are hunting you across the valley. It's not safe out there right now.”

“And it's safe here?”

“Completely.” He nodded a casual bow. “I know you have more questions. I'll share as many answers as I can, but first you should get dressed. I'll wait for you in the hall.”

Cat sighed as the door latched and traded her nightclothes for the dress. The arm pockets had no pouches. Her fingers caught the open slits as she slid her hands down the sleeves. She tied the sash in the back, pinned her hair in its bun with the broken comb, and joined her host in the hallway.

Extravagant frescoes, chandeliers and plush velvet furniture lined the corridor outside her bedroom. A line of tall windows stretched the opposite wall with a gorgeous view of a lush, green forest. Cat pressed her face to the glass. “Is that real?”

“Yes.” Joshua smiled beside her. “We're high in the Northern Mountains right now. Astonage is fifty miles south with Castleton fifty more south of that.”

“Why haven't I seen this forest from the ground?”

“Height. Camouflage. Astonage took all the rock out of the mountain below us centuries ago, it's impossible to get up or down without magic.”

“Is that how you got us up here?”

“Yeah.” He pressed his lips and took her hand. “Let me show you something.”

They passed through a set of towering double doors and into a grand foyer filled with tapestries and paintings. Joshua stopped them at a banister between two alabaster columns. Below a broad, carpeted staircase descended to a gathering place filled with copper-skinned residents. Men and women chatted around tables or on the stairs. One warmed her coffee with a ball of fire in her hand. A man in the corner conjured gravel into a potted plant as a companion watered it with a jet from his palm. A group of shirtless children propelled a ball with gusts of wind. Cat could see the four symbols of the elements etched on their biceps and forearms.

"These are the Runians," Joshua said. "Descendants of the Prophets from the beginning of recorded history. They've been hiding on this mountain for the past five hundred years."

"And they all use magic?"

"Every one." Joshua rolled his sleeve, revealing the wind rune tattooed onto his left forearm. "Kids are marked with the symbols very young and grow up using the power of nature as naturally as the first Prophet did. It's allowed this mansion to function in isolation."

"They're all Prophets?"

"No, not really. Prophets were born with the symbols in a line down their backs."

She frowned. "But magic when you're not a Prophet is a sin."

"Yes, well, that hasn't stopped them." He straightened his sleeve. "Follow me."

The Runians watched her intently as she descended the stairs. Occasionally adults with other skin tones appeared within the crowd, but all the children were a deep golden-brown with mops of black hair and deep, shoe-button brown eyes. One of the younger men trotted toward them, his red tunic hanging lopsided around his long neck.

"Hey Josh!" He met them on the stairs. "About time you brought her up to the house. Catrina, right?" He shook Cat's hand with a firm grip. "I'm James, Joshua's big brother."

She considered the two. "Big brother?"

James grinned. "You sound surprised."

"I guess Joshua didn't seem the 'baby brother' type."

"He is a stiff isn't he?" James clapped Joshua on the back. "He'll loosen up now that you're here. Sometimes the right girl is all it takes, right bro?"

"James," Joshua said. "She has more important things to worry about right now."

"Oh, sure. Sorry." He gestured absently over his shoulder. "I've got chores anyway. Hope we didn't get off on the wrong foot, Catrina. I'll see you around."

"Sorry about him." Joshua whispered. "James likes attention."

"I can tell."

They crossed the plaza to another set of double doors. Joshua unlocked them with a key from his pocket. "After you."

Cat opened the door to an elegant dining room. Mirrored walls reflected light from a dozen candelabras glowing over a banquet that put Lord Creven's bounty to shame. Lynn, Aiden and Zephyr sat around a circular table. The Water Curse wore a white dress and her hair in a ribbon. “Cat!”

“Lynn!” Cat took her clammy hands. “Are you guys okay?”

“I'm fine. Anxious.” She ran a hand over her freshly bandaged shoulder. “We wanted to find you, but they locked us in.”

“I'm sorry about that,” Joshua said. “You four are my guests, but that won't stop some of my family members from treating you poorly. If there's anything you need, I'm your servant.”

“We need you to let us go!” Aiden rose, dressed in white wide-legged pants and a hooded shirt. A patch of gauze covered his right cheek and the lavender scrap of Ildri's scarf was still tied to his left wrist. “This is kidnapping, and we won't stand for it.”

“It won't be for long.”

“I don't care!”

“Aiden,” Lynn bade. “Your face.”

The blackened skin under his eye glowed with deep fiery cracks. He tugged the hood tighter.

“I apologize again,” Joshua said. “I'm doing all I can.”

“Then tell us how we got here!” Aiden growled. “And what you want with us. And what you've done with our injured friend.”

“Aiden, it's okay,” Cat said. “Joshua's not our enemy.”

“Peter thought he was!”

Cat flinched.

Joshua raised his hands in surrender. “It's fine. I'll step. You three can catch up. There's something I need to check on, anyway.”

Cat's brow knit. “Something?”

“Trust me, Catrina.” He eyes glinted. “I'll take you to him when I get back. I promise.”

The door shut and locked behind him. Aiden pulled off his new hood, revealing the patched and bandaged scalp beneath. “How can you trust that guy?”

“He's keeping us safe...”

“You're making excuses,” Aiden said. “That guy is bad news. His eyes make my skin crawl.”

“Peter said something similar about his bones.” Cat reached for her string but it was still missing from her wrist.

Lynn softened her gargling voice. “Have you heard anything about Peter?”

“No.” Cat's throat tightened. “I was asleep until now.”

“Same,” Aiden said. “We woke up in separate rooms with these clothes laid out. I don't even know where we are.”

“It's the home of the Runians,” Cat said. “They're what's left of the Prophets. They've been living up here for centuries.”

“They've been hiding that long?” Lynn asked. “Why?”

"Because God left," Cat said. "Without God there's no Prophets. It's as much a risk for them to trust us as it is for us to trust them. If the rest of the Valley knew there were here..."

"They'd be running the place." The Fire Curse crossed his freshly-bandaged arms. "More reason to ask why they hid."

"I don't know, Aiden, I can't think that broadly right now."

"We ascended because we were better than them." Zephyr sat curled in her seat, mumbling into a half-eaten loaf of bread. Her hair was trimmed to a couple inches over her patchy scalp. Her vacant eyes strained to focus on Cat. "Who is the ugly girl?"

"This is Cat, remember?" Lynn grimaced. "You met her yesterday?"

"If you say so."

The door opened again. James slipped in with a toothy smile. "Greetings all."

Zephyr's brow furrowed. "Who's the ugly guy?"

"Call me James." He smirked. "Boy, you guys are a sight. I've seen Curses in God's Valley but never this close. It's pretty bad out there, huh?"

Aiden tugged his hood back up. "What do you want?"

"To welcome you all." James held the door for a woman with bright curly red hair and an infant in her arms. "This is my wife Marianne and our son, Silas."

“Baby!” Zephyr's gloomy demeanor flipped with a squeal. She climbed onto the table and pranced over plates of food to loom over the baby with bright, attentive eyes. “Can I hold him?”

“I-I don't know...” Marianne stammered. “James?”

“Ah, let her, she's not contagious.”

Zephyr plopped onto the end of the table and wrapped a squirming Silas in her bony arms. She hummed and rocked him, blush rising to her cheeks.

Cat exhaled a held breath and sweetened her voice. “You're very good with him, Zephyr.”

“I love babies!” She grinned. “When I was little, Mama had two babies at once. She always asked me to hold one while she took care of the other.”

“You remember your mother?”

“Yes! She was so nice. She called me Zephie.” The depth in her eyes faded with her smile. “She called me Zephie and took the baby. Zephie it's not your fault. Zephie be a good girl. The floor rose.”

“Zephyr?” Lynn inched closer.

Her voice cracked. “I don't remember why.”

Wind picked up, ruffling through mesh panels in the sides of her white jumpsuit. Silas cried and waved his bronze fists in her failing grip.

Marianne scooped him up. “Is she okay?”

Tears wet the Wind Curse's gaunt cheeks. Cat gripped her knee. “Zephyr, it's okay. You're with us.”

“Zephie.” Lynn's voice eased the tremor in Zephyr's lip. The Water Curse wrapped an arm around her back. “Look at my face. Do you remember me?”

Zephyr blinked glaze from her eyes. “Water?”

“That's right!”

Zephyr slouched, eyes unfocused. “Who's the ugly girl?”

“Your friend,” Cat said. “You sit quiet, okay?”

“Okay.” She stared at her hands. “Why am I shaking?”

“Well then.” James cleared his throat. “That was kind of a thing, wasn't it? Being a Curse is more than getting your face messed up, I guess.” He referred his wife to Cat. “Marianne, this is Catrina – the one I told you about.”

“It's good to finally meet you, Catrina.” Marianne shifted her child to shake hands. The baby calmed and grasped his tiny fist in Cat's direction. His mother smiled. “Silas is happy to meet you, too.”

“See? I knew she'd fit in!” James gave his wife a nudge and gestured to the Curses. “Marianne is here to keep you company while I take your friend upstairs. My father would like to see Catrina in private, if that's alright.”

“I can't,” Cat said. “I'm waiting for Joshua.”

“Joshua was called away.”

“He said he'd be back, though.”

“Trust me, it's fine.”

“You're very lucky, Catrina,” Marianne said. “Joshua has a good reputation around here. The ladies and I think he'll take his father's job as our leader in a couple years. He is very wise.”

“He's a pain in the neck is what he is,” James dismissed. “Come on, Catrina, your boyfriend will know where you are.”

“Boyfriend?”

“Take care of our guests, Marianne! We'll be back!” James pressed his fingertips between Cat's shoulder-blades and steered her back into the hallway.

She spun to face him as he locked the door. “I'm not trying to be rude about this. Joshua said he'd come back right away and take me to see my friend Peter. Do you know about him? He's hurt.”

“Yeah, I know. News travels fast.”

“Then why are you taking me somewhere else?”

“I don't bite, Catrina. I'm helping you out.” He led her up a branching hallway to a secondary staircase. “Our father's the patriarch. When the patriarch wants to talk to someone you take them there. I'm scoring you a good impression.”

“What if I have different priorities?”

“Tell him about it. See what he says.”

They wound deeper into the mansion. Each room was more extravagant than the next. Gold leaf and intricate detail covered every surface, including floors, walls, columns, ceilings and furniture. Runians cared for every inch, dusting and polishing the stone to a mirror sheen. They slipped their hands into the openings in their sleeves to fill buckets with water or dry paint with wind. Cat poked a finger into the pocket on her left forearm and felt her skin beneath. "Joshua said you all use magic here."

"Everyone born here, yeah, it's our inheritance. See?" James showed his hand. "The circle on our palms fit over the rune and complete the spell."

"Like the Brushcasters."

"Yeah, I guess." He shrugged. "We train the way the Prophets did though, practicing spells and taking classes until we come of age – usually sixteen, but Joshua graduated early, the little showoff."

"If you're not a Prophet, using magic is a sin."

"We're God's people, I doubt he minds."

"No, I've read Malachi's scripture. It seems pretty clear – "

"Listen, Mountain Girl," he snapped. "If it wasn't for miracles we couldn't survive up here. You've got a fancy thing going with your string tricks and your Curses, but don't ride in here on Joshua's back and think you can tell us what to do."

“I've seen what's happening in God's Valley. Magic's destructive, my friends are proof.”

“The Valley doesn't have this.” They mounted a final flight of stairs and stopped near a set of wooden doors. “The Runians' library.”

“I've seen libraries before.”

“Yeah, but this one's full of scripture.”

“I've seen scripture too.”

James tightened his grip on the door handle. “You're not the only one who's toured the Valley, you know. Joshua and I traveled it together when we came of age. We took a pilgrimage from town to town; observing, staying hidden, gathering resources. I found my people food, technology, materials... I even found Marianne working as a nurse, but all Joshua found was you.”

Her face flushed.

“Joshua's always been the level-headed one, but something about you got to him. He's waited four years to grab you out of that dumb little town and I'm having a hard time understanding why.”

“He's been watching me that long?”

James's bronze face darkened. “My family's important to me, Catrina. I'm helping you because you're my sister-in-law. You should be a little more grateful.”

“Now wait just a minute.” She flushed in anger. “I'm nobody's sister-in-law, and I'm not here to play games with you. I'm the New

Prophet – that should mean something to you people – and my best friend is somewhere sick and dying in this house. I care about that!"

"And I care about Joshua." James yanked the door open. "Dad's waiting."

Cat crossed her arms and refused to move. James grabbed her by the arm and shoved her in, slamming the door behind.

Shelves of gold-etched leather cases lined the walls surrounded by books, charts, and artifacts on alabaster pedestals. The back wall was a solid pane of clear glass through which the whole valley unfolded like the pages of Peter's atlas. A middle-aged man stood before the window, the floor and ceiling reflecting the sky around his darkened silhouette.

"Catrina Aston, I presume?"

"That's me, what do you want?"

"Respect, to start." He turned with a limp. His sloping jaw and high cheekbones resembled his sons' with blazes of gray at his sun-damaged temples.

Cat faltered beneath his gaze. "Sorry. That was rude of me."

"I understand your frustration, Miss Aston. You've had quite the week." The patriarch struck a match to light a lamp on one of the reading desks. "Would you like to sit down?"

"I'd prefer to stand."

"Indulge me, please."

She eased into an antique armchair near the desk, her hands folded stiffly in her lap. The old man kept his right knee straight as he eased into a matching seat.

“Maybe now we can continue more amicably,” he said. “Please call me Isaiah.”

“Cat,” she said. “I'm sorry again for being impatient. I'm anxious to see my friend.”

“The Earth Curse. Yes, I've heard about him.” Isaiah adjusted his leg. “I'm familiar how a loved one's illness can make you feel helpless. I lost my wife to illness not long after Joshua was born. His delivery left her weak – a problem we sometimes have up here.”

“Was she from the Valley?”

“No.” His wrinkled face pulled tight around deep-set black eyes. “Don't worry too much about your friend. I'm sure our healers are treating him with the same diligence they did my beloved, although I confess we aren't used to treating Curses as patients. We don't get them here.”

“You don't *get* them?”

“We share the blood of God's Prophets. We're immune.”

“But that's not fair!” Cat said. “You use more magic than anyone does!”

“I know, I know.” Isaiah's brow pinched, emphasizing the age and worry about his eyes. “Joshua told me you've read Malachi's scripture. He is my direct ancestor. I know you think you are the Prophet from his vision."

She set her jaw. "I more than think it."

"I see." He cleared the books cluttering the desk. "There was a time not long ago when this world was our kingdom. The Prophet was a ruler, and his relatives advisers. We still care for God's Valley in a small way, moving in secret on the wind and through the shadows, but it no longer belongs to us, and we are not welcome. Instead, we sit patiently here on this mountain, waiting on God's inevitable return." He leaned forward. "Joshua said you spoke with Hanrietta Torston."

"You mean the old woman in the mountains."

"She's the last living member of the Torston family."

"Not living any longer." Memory of the glen stabbed knives in her chest. "She was killed by the Brushcasters."

"I see..." Isaiah slid a thick leather book across the table between them. "This is a history of God's Valley compiled by our young people over centuries of pilgrimages. It maps the chain of power, the rise and fall of leaders, and specifically lineage of the four founding families. It is a joy to know another of these lines has come to end."

"A joy?"

"I have watched this valley die, Catrina. Grass still grew on the western plains when I was a child, but the use of magic has killed almost everything below. When Malachi lived, God's Valley was a garden of life. Forests and rivers bred hundreds of different animals. All humanity lived in a city at the center until Malachi's death when a white chasm swallowed the Prophet's temple and the city around it."

"A white chasm?" Cat's mind flashed. "I think I've seen it."

"The city?"

"The chasm," she said. "When I was with the hermit in the mountains, she set a scripture on fire and Peter and I saw a vision of a cave with a glowing canyon. She said it was the future."

"It was."

"Have you seen it?"

"No, but others have," Isaiah said. "When the Holy Calligraphers grew to power they hoarded scripture. When their library was complete, they destroyed the excess and the visions received by those witnesses have rippled through history as a sign of the Calligraphers' prophetic power."

"No one thought burning something so important was wrong?"

"That is but one event in a long line of sins." Isaiah patted the thick book. "We've logged them for posterity so someday they'll learn about who they trusted and what they've done."

"Is that why you called me?" Cat asked. "To tell you about Harriet Torston so you can add her to your book?"

"Among other things."

"Well, I thank you for the opportunity." Cat said, flatly. "Maybe when this is all over I'll give you the answers you need, but God sent me on a mission, so I'm going to have to pass."

"Who are you to say what God wants?" Isaiah rose, favoring his left leg. "Why would someone like you be the New Prophet instead of one of us?"

"Because of the scripture," she said. "Because of everything I've seen."

"Then let me relay a bit of context." His voice grated beneath a piercing stare, his starless eyes flat and hard as steel. "Five hundred years ago a young man named Uzzah lived in the Prophet's Temple. He was the holy architect – a sculptor and scholar raised in scripture – and Malachi's dearest friend. But he wasn't a Runian. He was common, and selfish, and jealous of the Prophet's magic. And when the opportunity presented itself, Uzzah murdered him."

Cat cringed.

"You've read Malachi's final letter. You understand what I'm saying." Isaiah's voice rose. "Uzzah killed the man who trusted him most and took God's power for his own. All magic in the world resulted from him, but more than that, God was with Malachi in the moment of his death."

"With him?"

"The Prophet was more than a messenger!" he shouted. "The Prophet was God's residence while in the mortal world. He felt Prophet's pain – not just the blade but the emotion. God felt the heartbreak of that betrayal. It broke his heart, so he left us. He left us because of you."

"Me?" Fear lanced her heart. She backed away from his fierce expression. "What do I have to do with it?"

"You are the result!" Isaiah roared. "Uzzah was never punished! He died important and wealthy. His four sons divided God's Valley in quarters as if it was theirs! They named their cities after themselves – Torston, Chalsie, Lonato," he thrust an accusing finger across the desk, "and *Aston*."

Cat paled. "Me?"

"Astonage! Your ancestral home."

"I didn't know – "

"Your ancestor murdered mine in cold blood!"

"It wasn't *my* fault."

"You are Uzzah's heir!" He slammed his fist on the book. "You have the flesh that drove the knife into my grandfather's chest! Someone has to pay!"

"Father!" Joshua barreled into the room. He tugged Cat from her seat and tucked her behind his back. "What is this?"

Isaiah stumbled back into his chair. "Son, I – I was sharing what needed to be known."

"Not now!" Joshua's face flushed umber. The air chilled as his palm glowed around Cat's wrist. "Not like this."

The old man's hand shook over his heart as the two stared through the tension. Isaiah broke eye contact and buried his face in his hands. Joshua relaxed. His palm faded and the room warmed with the smell of spice and incense.

"Don't burden this girl with your sorrow." Joshua's eyes sparked. "Do you understand why this was inappropriate? Why your impatience creates more victims? Catrina's here to help."

"If you say so." Isaiah steeled. "I will meditate on it."

"Do." Joshua took Cat's hand, again. "I'm sorry about this. It's okay, don't worry. I'll take you to your friend."

Chapter 28

Cat kept hold of Joshua's hand as they moved through the mansion, avoiding crowds and workers by narrow hallways and hidden steps to a blue-painted corridor. The air was cold. Joshua steered her up the hall to a set of unmarked double doors. Cat could hear people moving inside. “Is this...?”

“The infirmary.” Joshua released her hand.

She shifted weight and clawed at her naked wrist. “I know I wanted to see him, but now that I'm here, I'm scared.”

“I don't blame you.”

“My head's so full of questions,” she muttered. “I don't know how to feel, so I'm feeling everything all at once.”

“That's understandable as well,” Joshua said. “Listen, before anything else happens, let me apologize on behalf of my father. You deserved to know the truth, but it should have come at a better time.”

“Is he right?” she asked. “Am I Uzzah's descendant?”

“You are.”

“Then...” Her voice shook. “I'm literally the worst person in the world.”

“No you are not.” He stepped closer. “Uzzah's your ancestor, not your alter ego. It doesn't change who you are.”

“But he broke the valley over his knee. My family started the Curses. Everything that's happened is our fault.”

“You are more than a name, Catrina. You a full and complex person who can make her own choices. Don't doubt yourself because of what you've learned; absorb it and accept it like you have so many things on this trip. Use it to the completion of your mission.”

“My mission?” Cat said, aghast. “My great-something grandfather murdered God's dearest friend. How am I supposed to talk to him?”

“Like you are right now.”

“That's a joke.” Tears brimmed her eyes. “I know what having a best friend feels like. And losing one. If God felt about Malachi the the way I feel right now... why would he listen to anything I say?”

Joshua's frame relaxed. “There.” He brushed the wetness from her cheek. “That's why.”

Cat bowed her head, lip twitching in shame.

“Events in the past cannot be changed,” Joshua whispered. “What matters is the present. Right now, the person you love most needs you. Focus on that. The rest can wait.”

She took a deep breath, heart aching. “Alright.”

“The fall has accelerated the stone growth. You may not like what you see.”

“It's okay, I'm ready.”

He nodded and led her inside. Six caretakers crowded a slab-like metal bed. Peter lay beneath a thin sheet, dressed head to toe in white with his glasses folded on a table full of medical instruments. His arms, legs, and chest bulged with jagged crags. Thick outgrowths from his cheekbones and forehead swelled beneath ash gray skin, warping the features of his bruised face into an unfamiliar mask.

Cat's stomach dropped, taking her heart and breath with it. Shock trembled in her chest as she leaned into the mattress. “Pete?”

She muffled a sob and waited for a response, but his face remained still. She brushed her fingers against the club of his hand as his massive chest struggled to rise.

"He's sedated right now," Joshua said behind her. "We didn't want to hurt him more."

She brushed Peter's blonde hair. "How long does he have?"

"It's hard to say. The stone is growing everywhere, but it slows when he's asleep."

"I wanted to save him." She sniffed. "I knew it was impossible, but I wanted it more than anything. We agreed to start this mission because he wanted to die as a man."

"He will," Joshua said. "You've helped assure that."

"I'd like to take him home."

"Home?"

"Mason Forge," Cat said. "If he can't save the world, he should to be with his family."

"He's very sick, and it's a full day's ride from here."

"Is that too long?" she asked. "Will he make it?"

"I can give him more time."

"Really?" She met the weariness in Joshua's dark eyes. "You can do that?"

He nodded.

The exam room door opened behind him, revealing James with a scowl on his face.

Cat bristled. “What's he doing here?”

“He's your guide,” Joshua said. “James, lead Catrina back upstairs, please.”

“No!” She clamped her hands on the edge of the metal slab. “I'm not leaving.”

“Catrina...”

“He needs me. I'm staying here.”

“Please trust me on this,” Joshua said.

James scoffed. “Enough coddling. Are you coming or not?”

Cat lingered on Joshua's eyes, studying the lights and stars within. She cleared her throat and shifted away. “I'm coming. Not because I like it, though.”

Joshua nodded. “Thank you.”

She stomped after James up two flights of stairs, through several crowded hallways to the dining room. Aiden, Lynn, and Zephyr sat with Marianne and little Silas. Lynn was laughing with little hiccups as the baby grabbed food from her hand. James yanked the door closed behind them and made them all jump.

“Oh!” Marianne fluffed her hair. “Look, Silas, Auntie Catrina is back!”

"Did Joshua find you?" Lynn's cheeks dimpled in a smile. "Did you see Peter?"

His name hit like a punch to her chest. Cat opened her mouth to reply but had no breath.

Aiden rose. "Cat, are you okay?"

"I guess the meeting went sour," Marianne said. "Don't worry, Catrina, Father Isaiah will come around. Jim had to talk him into me when I first arrived, too."

"Annie." James snapped. "Get Silas, we're going."

"But he's having so much fun!"

"Just do what I ask."

"Oh...okay." She took her son from Zephyr and left without another word. James ushered her ahead of him locked the door loudly behind them.

"Jerk." Aiden glared. "Okay now, Cat, tell us what happened."

A wave of nausea rolled through her. Cat gripped the back of a chair. "Joshua took me downstairs. They've got a clinic or something down there. That's where Peter – " The name caught in her throat.

Fire flushed through Aiden's face. "Is he dead?"

"No, but he's bad." Her voice shook. "It won't be very long..."

The confession broke the last of Cat's resolve. She dropped her face into her hands, shaking so much she could barely cry. Lynn pulled her into a hug, the Curse's chilled body was like a cold compress on her heart. Cat let Lynn's water wash her face until she was calm.

Aiden leaned on the table cleared his throat. “So what now?”

“I want to take him home.” Cat sniffed. “To Mason Forge.”

“You mean the mountains?” Aiden asked. “That's out of our way, isn't it?”

“I know it sounds selfish,” Cat said, “but I promised he'd die a person. If it can't be on his feet it should be with his family. We'll have to find another Earth Curse to take back to Castleton.”

Aiden frowned. “That's a whole other town! We just got the four of us together – ”

“And we can do it again,” Lynn squeezed Cat's hand. “We'll go wherever you need to, Cat. I know we haven't known each other for very long, but I consider you all family as much as I did Water Town. All we've got is each other, and we know what's important. Curses stick together in times like these.”

“Times like these times.” Zephyr said in monotone. “Windmill times.”

“Windmill times...” Aiden considered the Wind Curse and bowed his head with a sigh. “Okay, so when do we leave?”

“When Joshua says we're ready.” Cat's breath shuddered through her. “Thanks you guys.”

They returned to the circular table to wait. Cat picked at a slice of toast and told them everything she'd learned, from the vision in the hermit's hut to the sight of Peter on the slab. She stumbled as she mentioned her ancestry, expecting Lynn and Aiden to flinch, but they averted their eyes and sat quiet. The mirrored walls reflected their sad expressions.

Lynn gargled and shifted in her seat. “I suppose this puts your mind at ease about the whole Prophet thing, at least.”

“What do you mean?”

“The old woman called you Child of Sinners,” Lynn said. “That's what Malachi wrote in the scripture you had, right?”

“Yeah, that's right.”

“Well, your ancestor was a sinner,” Lynn said. “And you said you saw yourself at this white chasm. That must be you giving magic back. It's more than we knew before, at least.”

Cat took a deep breath. “Yeah, I mean... I guess, you're right.”

“Jumping into a chasm doesn't sound like such a bad deal,” Aiden said. “Better than slitting our wrists or something.”

Lynn grimaced. “Slitting our wrists?”

“That's what I was imagining.” Aiden shrugged. “What did you think was going to happen?”

“I don't know. I hadn't given it a lot of thought – ” Lynn flinched and went silent as Joshua slipped into the room.

The young man's bronze cheeks were hollow and his sunken eyes heavy. He leaned on the closed door before addressing the crowd. “Sorry for the wait.”

Cat wet her lips. “Peter?”

“Sleeping. I've got your travel preparations under way, but it will take a few hours. Please rest in your rooms until we're ready.”

“What preparations?” Aiden asked. “Why the wait?”

“Just a vehicle. And supplies.” Joshua drew a couple tired breaths. “It's going as fast as I can manage right now, I'm sorry.”

“It's okay,” Lynn said. “Thank you for helping us.”

“It's the least I can do.” He pulled the door open with a meager smile. “After you.”

“Come on, Zephyr,” Lynn said.

The Wind Curse perked up. “Where are we going?”

“Upstairs. You should take a nap.”

“I am a bit sleepy.” Zephyr took her dripping hand. “Do I have a room?”

“Yes, Joshua will show us where it is.”

“Oh good.” Zephyr's tight lips whitened as she grinned. “This place is so nice!”

The Curses slipped past Joshua and into the foyer full of disapproving Runian onlookers. Aiden eyed him with glowing pupils and kept close to the girls.

Cat tarried in the doorway. She whispered to their host. “Are you okay?”

“I'll be fine. I forget how much magic takes out of me.” His voice softened. “I did what was possible. The stone is growing fast, and I redirected it where I could, but I can't take it away and I can't make it stop.”

“Is he in pain?”

“Not while he's sleeping, and he'll sleep the whole way there.”

“Thank you.” Cat bowed her head, heart quivering against her diaphragm. “Are you coming with us?”

“I can't.”

“Why not?” She asked.

The stars in Joshua's eyes glimmered faintly to match his exhaustion. “I would like to, but I don't belong in this world.”

“Because you're a Runian?”

“Something like that.”

“Joshua.” Cat stared at her hands, a final question still nagging. It felt petty, and worthless, but she couldn't let it go. “James said you found me out on your pilgrimage. He keeps talking about a marriage.”

Joshua rolled his black eyes. “Of course he does.”

“Is that why you're helping me?” She braced herself. “I'm your claim?”

"No," he said. "There's a lot James and my father don't understand. They have no idea what's at stake, here. The Runians have lived in this mansion for nearly five centuries, and in that time, their world has grown smaller and smaller. You and I know what's important and it's not the Runian gene pool. I help you because I want to. I'm telling the truth."

She clawed her wrist for the missing string. His bronze hand closed around her fingers.

"Have I ever mentioned a marriage before now?"

"No."

"Would you say yes if I had?"

"I barely know you."

"Exactly." He stepped close. "I'm not hiding things because I like it, I'm doing what's best. When this is all over, the laws of Runians and Calligraphers won't matter. The world is changing, and you'll be there in that moment. That's what I care about."

She wiped her eyes. "I want to believe you."

"It's the truth." He waited for her attention and cut a weak smile. "Your friends are waiting. Go back to Mason Forge. Return Peter to his family, like he would have wanted. I won't be far away, I promise."

She leaned into his velvet tunic, wetting the embroidery with quiet tears. Joshua tightened his arms around her.

"It's going to be all right."

Paige descended the eastern mountains by the condemned road outside Wind Town. They'd been moving since sunup after a restless sleep in the ruins. The Wind Curses cried over their windmill all through the night. Paige did her best to tend Trace's wounds, but his strength failed by the moment. The unconscious Calligrapher leaned heavy on her back as they descended inch by inch along the side of the mountain. The horse struggled for balance in the harsh wind. Her left leg scraped the naked wall as her horse struggled for balance. Bits of stone broke under its hooves, falling hundreds of feet to the valley floor.

They crept around the bluff, out of sight of the New Torston elevator and continued past noon until they reached level ground. The other Calligraphers were moving. Paige watched their specks on the Outer Bend and shifted Trace on her back. The metallic scent of blood filled her nose as it smeared on her cheek. He was fading. Paige spurred the horse and charged toward Castleton's glowing peak.

They crossed the Outer Bend hours after the other Calligraphers and approached the towering city by the southeast. Her horse foamed and panted, sweat gleaming on its neck. She took the East Spoke past the electrified fence and veered left into a lettuce patch. They hid in an orchard as mounted Calligraphers pounded past them toward the desert. Paige waited for them to pass and kicked her horse again. The heat and distance had overwhelmed the exhausted creature and it refused to move another step.

Trace's body weight shifted on Paige's shoulder. His arm went slack and he tumbled sideways to the dirt.

"Master!"

His face was pale. Blood trailed from the loose bandage at his forehead, down his cheek onto his neck. Paige dropped beside him and found a pulse fluttering weakly in his wrist.

"Hold on, Master." She hooked her hands under his shoulders and tugged him back to the horse, but the ride had exhausted her strength as well. Her knees buckled and her arms shook. She dropped him with a grunt.

A woman in a Castleton uniform rushed from the gate on a spotted brown horse.

Paige broke a cold sweat and rose to attention. "This is no time to panic," she muttered to herself. "They won't know what happened. Monks get free lodging, and we are just monks"

"Our God!" The uniformed official dropped to her knees at Trace's side. "What happened?"

"Are you police?"

"Checkpoint guard." The woman stopped short when she spotted the glowing brush strapped to their black saddle.

Paige side-stepped to hide it. “My master is hurt. Can you point us to a hotel or – ”

“Stay quiet.” The guard snapped and grabbed Trace under his arm. “Let's get him on my horse.”

“We can use our own.”

“Yours is spent,” she said. “If you don't want to get caught, do as I say.”

Paige's heart pounded. The two draped Trace across the guard's saddle.

The woman covered his head with her jacket. “Hide that brush and bring the horse with us with us.”

“Where are you taking us?”

“Someplace safe,” she check the road either direction. “Now act normal.”

Paige tugged the reins. The horse resisted, but followed the spotted mare's lead. They passed a long line of farmers and slipped through the each checkpoint, into the shelter of Castleton's high city wall. Squads of Calligraphers walked the streets of the sloping city. A knot tightened in Paige's stomach. “Why are all these monks here?”

“The Elder's dead.”

They stopped at a small guard house near the public stable. The woman tied the horses to a hitching post. “Get him inside.”

“He needs a doctor.”

“He'll get one, I promise.”

“Hey.” Paige grabbed the woman's shirtsleeve. “Whatever you think you know, you're wrong. We're monks in the Holy Order, you're supposed to do what we say.”

“You have the dead Elder's paintbrush.”

Paige blanched but stayed diligent. “That's not your concern.”

“I answer to a higher power than your monks or your Elder,” the guard said. “Your colleagues are not the only ones who are looking for you. I'm not going to turn you in. Get those brushes and anything else you need from the saddle. I'll hide the horse in the stable and be back with help.”

Full of regret and panic, Paige unstrapped the two brushes from her holster along with food and water, Trace's saddle bag, and her supply of paint. The guard dragged Trace from her horse to a cot in the back of the shed and laid him flat.

“There's an antiseptic on that far shelf,” she directed. “Stay away from the window and don't open the door until I get back.”

“Okay.”

The guard pulled on her jacket and slipped back to the street. Paige shut the door and watched through the small window as the guard deposited their tired horse and her own steed up the hill.

Paige released a held breath and propped the brushes against the wall. The single room was cluttered with hanging clipboards and loose paper. She found the medicine in a first-aid kit near a grimy sink. Paige opened the glass bottle and pressed a rag full against the gash on Trace's forehead.

He winced.

“That sting?”

Trace groaned and wrenched his eyes open. “What the...? Where are we?”

“You passed out.” Paige returned to the sink and twisted the handle. The water was clear and cold despite the rusty faucet. “I drove us to Castleton.”

“Dangerous choice.” He tried to sit up but couldn't manage. “My head hurts.”

“It was smashed with a brush handle. Then you fell off a horse. Plus you're pretty anemic.” She applied a cold cloth to his neck and released a heavy sigh. “I've doomed us.”

“You what?”

“I was trying to get you help.” She puffed her black bangs. “Now we're stuck here.”

“Why stuck?”

“There are monks all over this place. Plus, I trusted this guard woman and she's probably getting the cops.”

“Cops are better than monks.”

“Was that supposed to be a joke?”

His reddened eyes looked sidelong. “Does this look like the time for sass to you?”

Paige lowered the damp cloth to her lap. “Sorry.”

“What did you say?”

“Nothing.” She wet the rag. “Forget it.”

“You apologized. You've never done that before.”

“I never killed anyone before, either.”

“Telling that one came first.” Trace released a heavy breath. “It was my fault, not yours. I knew he would kill me if I didn't overpower him – he was never the forgiving sort – but I couldn't let him kill her.” He met Paige's eye. “Thank you for saving me.”

She blushed and tossed her bangs again. “Whatever.”

“Now, that sounds more like my apprentice.” Trace closed his eyes and lay silent.

Paige swallowed, a knot of guilt in her stomach, and dabbed his head again. “So what do we do now?”

“Keep running. Change our clothes, change our names.... what was your natural hair color before the Order made you dye it?”

“I don't want to say.”

“It can't stay black.”

“Then I'll dye it something else. Blue.”

“Because that'll help us blend in.”

“Fine! It's red,” she groaned. “Bright, orange. Like a carrot.”

"Honestly? You?" He laughed with a wince. "Ow."

"Serves you right."

"At least no one will recognize you." He held is ribs, smile fading. "Mine is brown. Flat, boring, brown. A metaphor for my life, really. I was unremarkable in every way until I joined the Order. I worked harder than anybody, trained under the best instructors...I wanted to be the elder. Now I'm bleeding in a closet."

Paige hung her head. "Sorry your dream got ruined."

He sighed. "It ruined itself."

A flurry of hoof beats thundered outside. Paige sneaked to the window and peeked sidelong around the frame for a view of the street.

"Attention! Guard!" A senior monk in black travel garb and a white stole sat on a dusty horse. A group of seven monks waited behind him, escorting a metal cart draped in heavy black cloth. It was the size and shape of a human body. Paige's blood ran cold.

"Checkpoint!" The senior turned to a man at his left. "Check the guard house."

Paige braced her back against the door. A knock sounded near.

"Guard! Come out, in the name of Our God!"

Trace rose to his elbows. Paige gestured for him to stay. A carriage rattled toward them down the hill.

"Parden my absence, sirs!" the guardswoman's voice called. "I was called away."

“You are not to leave a checkpoint unattended!” the senior said. “There's a murderer on the loose!”

“It was my fault, your grace,” a young man answered. “I'm Lord Creven's attendant.”

“Good, take us to your master. We have the Elder's body.”

Paige shot Trace an anxious glance. Trace nodded to the gold brush. She hugged it across her body and listened through the door.

“I'll take you, sirs,” the guardswoman said. Horses clattered and grunted away up the hill, leaving the gatehouse in heavy silence. Paige exhaled and relaxed.

A small knock tapped at the door.

“Sir? Miss?”

It was the lord's attendant. Paige hissed, “Stay back!”

“Paige,” Trace bade. “Open it.”

“But – ”

“He already knows we're here.”

The young man wore a blue waistcoat, with his brown hair pulled into a low ponytail. Behind him, a horse and buggy waited in the street. He swept a bow. “I am Kaleb, first attendant to Lady Orella Creven. She offers her protection. I will take you somewhere safe.”

Chapter 29

Lord Creven's office was a mess of open maps and empty wine bottles. The master of the house was decked in full parade attire, his long coat covered in cut gems and gold cords. An audience of Calligraphers waited as he paced the head of the room.

Lady Orella Creven waited in the corner, stiff and lifeless as a statue. She watched the crowd closely. The monks shifted weight, thumbing their over-sized paintbrushes and fidgeting. The senior monk, Vivian Arch, had deep-set eyes and tightly curled gray hair. She searched to the maps on Creven's desk while his back was turned.

"Senior!" The Lord slapped the broad side of a gold-plated sword cross the desk. "How many monks are left in your monastery?"

The senior's brow twitched. "Enough."

Her tone was unsettled. Orella cast her eyes to her husband. It was clear early in their marriage that the lord lacked certain social perceptions – the ability to read people, the capacity to empathize, the impetus to accept others as human. It was his greatest weakness and Orella's greatest strength, considering it allowed her access to his political meetings.

Lord Creven met her stare. Orella raised her eyebrows and he snarled at the Calligraphers. "Are you holding out on me, Ms. Arch?"

"You ask too much from us," the senior said. "We can't leave our monastery unguarded. It's our home and our library. Many of our acolytes are young children. The building needs protection."

"I want all magic painters here, protecting my interests!" Creven snapped. "Bar all four gates. Seal off the roads. Occupy every city in the Valley until the terrorist is found!"

"What makes you think a False Prophet would strike here and not the monastery?"

"I have my reasons." He slapped the map again. "She's attacked Dire Lonato, Chalsie-Veneer, and the curse town above New Torston. The only place she has yet to hit is Astonage. We should fortify our base here and send occupying forces there to wait. "

“Do we know why she's attacking these places?”

“Because she's an anarchist!” Lord Creven's face reddened. “She killed your Holy Elder and crippled your government, what more do you need explained? This city is the dominant economic power in the Valley – I should have killed her a week ago!”

Kaleb slipped in from the hall. The young man glanced to Orella. His eyes were nothing like her husband's. They were wide and intelligent with a full understanding of those around him. She saw love there, too, and respect. He'd do anything Orella asked – all the more reason to protect him.

“Excuse me, sir?” Kaleb said.

Lord Creven slashed the air in a rage. “What?”

“The eastern scouts have returned. They request an audience.”

“Fine. Show them in.”

Kaleb bowed his head. “They're in the morgue, sir.”

The gathered Calligraphers paled. Creven sheathed his ceremonial sword. “Well, it's about time.”

“Lord Creven.” Ms. Arch caught him at the door. “This is a monastery matter. Let us see him first.”

“So you can light candles and pray on him? This isn't a holiday, it's a crime scene. Get out of my way.”

He stormed from the office with the crowd of monks close behind. Kaleb waited at the door. Orella motioned for him to stay close and followed the procession to the basement where a small morgue waited deep in the service corridors.

The room was cold. Water dripped from freshly wiped counter tops. Instruments soaked in disinfectant solution sat in jars beside the sink. A senior monk waited outside a drawn curtain, his black robes still wrinkled and dusty from travel. He bowed as Lord Creven entered. "Thank you for coming."

"Get on with it."

The monk pressed his lips and opened the drape, revealing the Holy Elder's still body, now dressed in black and white ceremonial robes. He lifted a black veil from the figure's crushed head. The other Calligraphers turned away in horror.

"So it was murder," Ms. Arch shuddered.

Creven grunted. "As I told you."

"We found him deep in the eastern mountains." The senior monk replaced the veil. "There were signs of a battle with footprints of three horses and at least two golems. Witnesses in New Torston report two other Calligraphers with the Elder when he ascended the elevator but we couldn't find them. They were either killed, kidnapped, or escaped in the chaos."

"And the terrorist?" Creven demanded.

"Gone."

Vivian Arch ground her teeth. "Where is the gold brush?"

“We couldn't find it, either,” the senior said. “I left men behind to search more thoroughly.”

“Stolen no doubt!” Lord Creven said. “See what I mean? Catrina Aston wants to destroy your order of ascension or tradition or whatever. That's why we should act now.”

“We need to get the Elder back to the monastery.” Vivian said. “There are ceremonies and procedures – ”

“Listen to yourself!” Creven snapped. “Your criminal is at large and you waste time on stuffy old traditions. This is the reason I took charge! Call all of your monks and acolytes here to guard Castleton. We'll flood the roadways with magic users until we ferret Catrina Aston from her hole and snare her where she stands!”

“This is not the way of the Holy Order!”

“Would you let murder and destruction go unpunished?” Lord Creven drew his sword again. “You'll have plenty of time to cry over the dead when we're done! Stick the body on ice – this is now an offensive.”

The monks' breath hung in the cold air, their faces twitching with sorrow and anger. Disgust, confusion, and rage creased Vivan's weathered face. She set her jaw and smothered the expressions one after the other. “We are not a militia. We are a holy order.”

“You are the law.”

“We are emissaries of Our God.” She looked up, eyes flat, soul closed. “What must we do to stop this False Prophet?”

“Call your forces out. Send them to the north.”

“I will send word as soon as possible.”

The group filed back to the hall, leaving Kaleb and Lady Creven alone with the body. Kaleb tried not to stare. Sweat shone on his forehead. It was the death, not the Elder, that upset him. Orella had not forgotten about the young servant's brother.

He kept his voice low. “My lady, I have more news.”

“Yes?”

“Follow me.”

He led her up the hall to the manor's infirmary. Two of her loyal guards waited outside an examination room. They both stood tall and confident, eyes full of the same fervor as Kaleb's. They stepped aside and allowed the two of them to enter.

Two more Calligraphers waited inside; a young man wrapped in bandages and a pig-tailed girl holding two brushes – one black and one gold.

Orella drew a sharp breath. “What is going on here?”

“Forgive me, ma'am.” The male Calligrapher slid off the table into a wincing bow. “I am Senior Calligrapher Trace Hayes, this is my assistant Paige. We killed the Holy Elder. ”

The confession sent her reeling. The lady betrayed a moment's surprise, but trapped it beneath a scowl. “An army of Calligraphers and a well-armed militia are hunting an innocent girl for that crime!”

“You mean Catrina Aston.”

“How do you know that name?”

He reached a hand to his assistant and received a battered leather case. The gold letters were dull and damaged, but Malachi's name shone boldly in the bright overhead lights.

Lady Creven snatched it from him. “Where did you get this?”

“From a Prophet in the town of Chalsie-Veneer, before I learned the difference between true and false.”

“Is she dead?”

“Not if Our God is to be trusted.” His face wore evidence of a fight, but the soul was fierce and unbroken. “The Holy Elder tried to kill her twice. I fought him to protect her. The Calligraphers have no idea who they've been following. We think we're holy, but we sin more than any other. I see that now.”

“You read this scripture?”

He nodded. “I get the impression you have, too.”

Orella tightened her fingers on the scripture case and spoke to Kaleb. “Clear the route. The two of you come with me.”

Trace leaned on his assistant and limped along the labyrinth from the infirmary to the hidden library. Orella turned the key over in her pocket. These two were Calligraphers, but if either one were lying, they were masters of the game. Kaleb undid the padlock on the exterior door and locked it again after the three entered. Trace revealed his first doubt in the stone antechamber before the ancient library doors. His assistant clung more tightly to his chest. "What kind of place is this?"

"A sacred one," the lady said. "I can tell you're a man of faith, Mr. Hayes. You say you're chief of sinners but I regret it is not the case. My husband uses magic to control his empire from deep inside this mansion. The amount of raw holy power moving through these walls has turned God's Valley into a wasteland. He knows Miss Aston is a Prophet and that her quest will remove his power. He'll be ruined, so he hunts her with all his resources."

"I suspect our elder felt the same."

"And so I am willing to protect you," the lady said, "but I ask something in exchange."

"What do you ask?"

She unlocked the bolted doors and led them to the inner chamber. The Calligraphers gaped at the shelves of scripture gleaming in the low light. Lady Creven cradled Malachi's scripture and slid it back into its shelf, filling the void it left less than a week before. "Do you recognize it, Mr. Hayes?"

"Every inch," he said. "This is the sacred library. I know every name and date. Even the leathers smell the same."

"It is an exact replica of the one in your monastery."

He breathed sharply. "Exact?"

"Both higher and lower. All of it is here," Lady Creven said. "I've seen the types of miracles your Elder can perform. Your people are formidable, but with your training as a senior monk and the secrets of these scriptures, we might stand a chance against both my husband's armies."

His brow leveled. "What you ask of me is sin."

"Is it?" She approached the center desk. "In the name of Our God, and in exchange for your health and protection, I ask you protect Catrina Aston. We are grossly outnumbered, but have never been closer to success. The Prophet and her party must reach this chamber at any cost."

Trace's eyes did not waver. He touched the stack of waiting scripture and pressed his hand over his heart. "You have my word, good lady. I will defend her with my life."

Emotional exhaustion drew Cat into a restless sleep. When she woke, her travel clothes were clean and folded on the dresser, with all evidence of her journey repaired. Even her checkered scarf, last seen soaked with blood from the wound in her side, was spotless with no evidence except fading at the old stains. The wound, itself, was healing quickly as were the marks on her hands and knees. Whether through magic or science, the Runians had a gift for restoration. Cat buttoned her boots, zipped her vest, knotted the scarf back to her waist, and stepped out into the hall.

Aiden paced before the windows. The soft soles of his new slippers clapped his heels in a steady march. “You're finally up.”

“Didn't you sleep?”

“Can't.” He was missing his face bandage. The flesh beneath was ridged and twisted like the bark of a burned tree.

Lynn slipped from Zephyr's bedroom. “I thought I heard your voice.” The Water Curse cleared a wet catch in her throat. “Do you feel better?”

“Not really.”

“I don't blame you.” Lynn shrugged. “Has Joshua come by?”

“No, he hasn't.”

“That guy gives me the creeps,” Aiden grumbled. “A couple days ago you and Peter were fighting about how evil he was. Now you're engaged.”

“No we're not.”

“You trust him enough.”

“He's helping.” Cat groaned and leaned against her door. “I don't want to think about it, I just want to leave.”

Aiden crossed his arms. “Sounds good, so do I.”

The three stood in silence until the door opened at the end of the hall. James appeared, dressed for travel. His brow furrowed over hardened eyes. “Sun's setting. Let's move.”

Cat narrowed her eyes. “I thought Joshua was coming.”

“Josh is busy. He sent me.”

“Last time you said that you told me a lie,” Cat said. “How do I know you're not leading us off somewhere?”

“Because last time I was trying to help you,” James said. “Now I just want you to go.”

Lynn slipped into Zephyr's bedroom. The Wind Curse emerged smiling. “Good morning! Were you waiting for me?”

Cat tried to smile. “Did you sleep well?”

“I did! Although I have no idea where I am!”

Aiden grunted. “It doesn't matter, we're leaving.”

“Aw! Do we have to?” Zephyr whined. “Shouldn't we visit a while first? Who invited us here?”

“James did. See James?” Lynn pointed Zephyr at the Runian. “He's going to escort us back to our wagon.”

“Oh okay.” Zephyr waved. “Hi James.”

He snorted and led them back into the foyer where Marianne waited with Silas asleep on her shoulder. “Hello Curses.”

“Hello!” Zephyr sang.

“It's been a pleasure meeting all of you today,” Marianne said. “I've never spoken to your kind before. You were delightfully normal. Thank you for the opportunity.”

“You're...welcome?” Lynn's brow pinched with a trickle of water. “It was nice to meet you, too.”

“Goodbye!” Zephyr cheered again.

James left his wife and led the group down the stairs. The other Runians watched the Curses sidelong, hiding disgusted faces behind their hair and shoulders. James ignored them and headed across the marble foyer to the massive, hand-carved front doors. Beyond, a lush, sloping lawn thick with grass extended toward the treeline, spotted with brush and tiny flowers. Zephyr 'ooo'ed and 'ah'ed, her hand in Lynn's hand.

“No one in the house is allowed past this point.” James said over his shoulder. “There's no path, so stick close. It's going to be a long walk.”

“How long?” Aiden asked.

“Not far enough to kill you.”

They entered the treeline. Tall and green trunks towered overhead with narrow leaves and bushy crowns. The branches swayed, scattering tiny shafts of light over the floor. Zephyr reached with bony hands to catch the flashes. Birds chirped near the house, but quieted the deeper they went. The last time Cat heard a real bird was in Mason Forge when she and Peter were kids playing adventurers. The memory shot a pang through her stomach. She trained her eyes downward and watched James's heels crunch the fresh grass.

Zephyr clapped her hands over a bit of dust and laughed. “This is fun! Did the woods change? I remember them being black and twisty. Are we near the mushroom patch?”

“We're not in Wind Town, Zephyr,” Lynn answered.

“No?” The joy evaporated from her voice. “Where are we?”

Aiden stumbled and wheezed through cracked lips. “Hell.”

He slowed as they continued, hampered by dry breath and coughs. James charged on, unrelenting. Cat fell back and met Aiden's pace. “You alright?”

“Fine,” he snapped, but apologized with a glance. A line of moist sores glowed in the shadow of his hood. “Give me a moment.”

“Sure. You rest.” She left him against a tree trunk and jogged ahead. “James!”

He ignored her.

Lynn stopped to heave a thick, heavy cough into her hand.

“James, stop.” Cat matched his pace. “The others need a rest.”

“We're losing daylight.”

She grabbed his arm. “I said stop.”

He yanked it back. “Don't touch me.”

“Then listen when I talk to you.” She glared. “My friends are sick. They're going to rest if you stop walking or not.”

“Fine.” James put his hands on his hips. “We're stopping for one minute! One! If you need water or something, I can make some.”

Aiden glared at him. “I'll pass.”

“Forgive us.” Lynn breathed a gargle and spat clear water on the ground. “We can't help what we are.”

James rolled his eyes. “I'm sorry, I know.”

Their break lasted ten minutes until Lynn could breathe without coughing. Aiden kicked off his loose sandals and resumed the hike barefoot over the soft, mossy soil. Zephyr took the lead for Lynn, but her spryness was gone. She ignored the play of light and shadow as the two trudged along.

The terrain leveled as the evening grew darker. Living trees changed into imposing white behemoths, with branches too high for the rustling to reach the ground. James threaded them through the forest, banking left and right around trunks. Sunset stretched the shadows like prison bars across their path.

Cat looked back to find nothing familiar. “Are we lost?”

James snorted. “I don't know, are you?”

“You're supposed to be the leader.”

"And that I am." He sobered. "I had two jobs today; see you safely out of our forest and keep you from finding your own way back. Looks like I accomplished both."

"You tricked us?"

"This mansion's our shelter from the eyes and sins of the world. Letting you go is against all our laws, so forgive me for keeping you from coming back."

"You could have said that instead of tormenting my friends." Cat scowled. "Joshua got us here without us knowing. If you were scared, why not do what he did."

James sobered at his brother's name. "I can't."

"Not your style?"

"I don't have that much magic," he said. "I can't do what my brother can, Catrina. All I can do is make you trust me and hope you learn something as I lead you astray."

Cat gaped, heart pounding in hurt and outrage. She peeked over her shoulder at her friends stumbling through the woods, their pristine white clothes stained with dirt, water, and pus. She held her tongue for another half-hour as the sun dipped past the horizon and deep blood-red colors stretched in a bubble from the west.

The forest trees grew shorter and more sickly. Fallen timbers swollen with knots lay rotting on the parched ground. Leafless branches, knotted trunks, and peeling bark dominated the forest until only the husks of dead trees remained standing. They emerged from the forest at the edge of a stone quarry. Vertical cliffs chiseled by human workers extended straight down for hundreds of feet through striations of red, brown, and gray. Joshua waited on a flat outcropping with Strawberry, her long pale mane braided back away from her eyes, and a canvas-covered wagon packed with sacks of supplies.

"Oh my goodness!" Lynn gave the horse a wet hug. "You saved her, too?"

"I thought you'd appreciate having a friend." Joshua smiled. He took Cat by the hand. "I'm sorry for the walk. I didn't intend it."

Cat tensed in his grip. "Say sorry to them."

He nodded to the Curses. "I'm sorry."

Lynn shivered under his eye. Aiden peered from the shadow of his hood and crossed his bandaged arms.

Joshua sighed and returned his attention to Cat. "My people repaired your broken wagon. It's fully stocked. I included as many of your personal things as I could find. We also added a cover. Hopefully it'll make you a little more discrete."

"You brought the wagon across the mountains by yourself?"

"Magic's an incredible tool." He lowered his voice. "Peter's already in the back."

She gulped. "Can I see him?"

"Of course."

The canvas tent covered the bed from one rail to the other. The front and back were sealed by zippers with four mesh windows snapped into the sides. A knot tightened in her throat as she stared at the entrance, her pulse rushed in her ears. Joshua unzipped the curtain and waited for her to breathe before drawing it wide.

Peter lay as if in a casket on the cushioned floor, supported by pillows on all sides. His expression was peaceful, but his face was still foreign with fresh lumps and protrusions. The atlas sat on one of the seats with his folded glasses wrapped in a handkerchief.

Cat wrapped the cloth around the metal frames and tucked them in her vest pocket, heart breaking all over again. “I still can't believe this happened.”

“You're doing the right thing.” Joshua took her wrist and pressed the missing loop of string into her hand. “You can do this. Stay strong.”

Cat wound the thread around her wrist as she fought to keep her composure. Lynn and Aiden came alongside. Aiden winced with a hiss of steam. “You weren't kidding.”

Lynn swallowed. “Is he in pain?”

“Not while he's asleep,” Joshua answered.

“We'll take care of Peter, don't worry.” Aiden touched Cat's shoulder and shot Joshua a suspicious glare. “Let's get out of here.”

Aiden, Lynn, and Zephyr took the seats on Peter's left and right. Cat took the atlas and climbed into the driver's seat. Joshua stood at the running board. She searched for comforting starlight in his eyes. “Are you sure you won't come?”

“I'll follow as soon as I can,” he said. “I won't be far.”

Joshua motioned James away from the bluff and slipped a hand in one of the sleeve pockets. His free hand swelled with light and the ground beneath the wagon shook. The chunk of the hillside dislodged and slid over the carved rock face. Joshua cradled the light like a bowl in his fingers and the platform beneath the wagon descended like a stone version of New Torston's historic elevator.

Strawberry snorted and pawed the moving earth. Cat kept the reins tight and watched Joshua recede. His eyes hardened to piercing black disks. They drew Cat's mind toward them, stilling her breath. She stared, knuckles whitening, as the cliff rose between them and didn't inhale until it obscured him from view.

Chapter 38

Cat drove for hours beneath silver moonlight, her eye on the western mountains and her mind on nothing else. Strawberry plodded off-road over miles of packed dust. The beat of her hooves formed a lulling rhythm. Cat tried to stay alert. Calligraphers could be anywhere and her cargo was both precious and extremely fragile.

They reached the head of the mountain pass at sunrise and wound their way toward Mason Forge. The dead forest closed in around her, shrouded in deep silence. The curled branches shielded the wagon from view, and reminded her how quickly God's Valley was dying.

Mason Forge appeared as a sliver of color tucked in the crevasse ahead. Cat kept her eyes squarely forward. She'd never come home before. In stories it was always happy, yet her heart was cold as a stone in her ribs.

The town felt smaller and more cage-like than it had before. Noontime workers gathered in the street, curious to meet the new visitors, but sight of the weary driver kept the locals at a distance. Faces last met in fear and anger now followed her up the hill toward the intersection of Main Street and Cross. Cat barely acknowledged their presence, too tired and sad for anger, as she turned the horse toward home.

Mona Aston was changing a lightbulb on the front porch.

Cat cleared her throat. “Hi. Mom.”

“Cat? Oh, my goodness!” Her mother leaped the stairs. “What are you doing back? Where's Peter? Where'd you get this wagon?”

“Mom...” Her voice strained. “Something happened.”

“Mom, its Cat!” Peter's younger brother Alan shouted from his living room window. Cat saw the curtain flutter and Sheila Montgomery appeared at the top of her front ramp. Cat's chest pinched tight. Nausea bubbled under her ribs as she climbed from the wagon and took careful steps to Sheila's front door.

The woman was already shaking. The speech Cat rehearsed over hours of empty desert stuck like a knot in her dry throat. She reached into her vest pocket and pressed Peter's folded glasses into his mother's hand. “I'm sorry, Sheila.”

Sheila stared at the frames, her face contorting in sadness. She held tight to Cat's wrist as if it was all that kept her upright. Tears welled and Cat pulled Sheila close, the two shaking and sobbing into one another's shoulders. Alan watched from the doorway, frozen in grief. Mona came close, muttering weak assurances and petting Cat's head through the loose hair of her sagging bun.

Aiden climbed out of the wagon to a chorus of gasps. The gaggle of townsfolk had doubled in size. They watched from a distance as if witnessing a stage play. The Fire Curse scowled and waited for Lynn and Zephyr to disembark. Mona backed away as they approached.

“Hey Cat.” Aiden cleared his throat. “I know this is tough, but we should probably get him inside.”

Cat found strength in the determination in her companions' eyes. Even Zephyr was bright and aware of the crowd around them. Cat sniffed into Sheila's shoulder and stepped out of the hug. “Yeah, you're right.”

“Wh-who is this?” Mona asked.

Cat cleared her throat and spoke to everyone gathered at either end of the street. “Don't be scared, these are my friends. They helped me bring Peter home. He's in the wagon and he's hurt. I know how we left, but I hope, if you'll let him, he can die here peacefully with his mom and his brother. Is that okay?"

To her surprise, tears glistened on their guilt-ridden faces. Men removed their hats. Women dabbed their eyes. Mayor Young stepped forward, wearing the same hat and overalls as the day he drove Peter out of town. "Cat, this is our fault – "

"Don't," she interrupted. "I don't want your speeches. Apologize with your actions if you're going to do it at all."

"We can help you get him inside." Mr. Brighton edged out of the crowd. "If we all help it'll be easier. We... We don't want to hurt him any more than we have."

"Thank you." Cat deferred to Sheila. "Is that alright?"

The woman sniffed and nodded. Alan's twelve-year-old face flushed red. "No!"

"Alan," Mona hissed.

"I don't want them to help us!"

Sheila glared. "Alan, go inside."

The boy fumed and stomped up the ramp, his anger lingering in the air. Cat guided Sheila to the wagon for a look at her son, and kept a tight grip as the rest of town approached. Mayor Young, Mr. Brighton, and other local men and women used Peter's sheets as a stretcher to carry him to his bedroom. People bowed their heads as he passed them, paying respects as if to a casket. No one spoke. No one made eye contact. It didn't undo the betrayal, but it helped Cat see them as human. She recognized regret she felt reflected in each of their down-turned faces as she, Lynn, Zephyr, and Aiden followed the Montgomerys into their house.

Peter's bedroom was off the main living room in a space once used as his late father's study. Sheila moved him there five short years ago when his knees got too stiff to take the stairs. It had a set of double doors and a custom-made bed wide and long enough to fit the over-sized young man. The townsfolk counted to three before lifting him into it. Sheila tucked him under the covers and followed the rest to the living room where Alan sat, red-eyed, in the front window.

Cat sat on the couch, her limbs heavy and weary. She watched in silence as Mayor Young tarried at the threshold. “Will you be alright, Sheila?”

“Yes,” Mrs. Montgomery peeped. “He's home now.”

“Is there anything else we can do?”

“You can get out,” Alan snapped.

His mother's face scrunched with fresh tears. Mona Aston put an arm around her and hissed across the room. “Apologize, Alan.”

“No,” Alan said. “Without him, Peter would still be alive.”

“He *is* alive!” Sheila shouted.

Mona petted the sobbing woman's back and addressed the mayor with a heavy sigh. “You'd better go.”

"We really are sorry." Mayor Young stared deliberately into Cat's eyes. "We were wrong."

He left with the rest of the volunteers. Mona Aston snapped at Alan. "Don't raise your voice like that! You respect your elders even when you don't like them."

"Leave him alone," Aiden said. Mona jumped and went quiet. The bit of lavender cloth peeked from his sleeve as the Fire Curse put a bandaged hand on Alan's shoulder. "I know how you feel, kid. Yell and scream all you like, you've got a right to, but don't let the anger take you over. It's addictive and it'll burn you up."

Alan shrank under the orange glow of his eyes. "You're a Fire Curse, right?"

"Yeah."

"Are you friends with Peter?"

"We're brothers in arms." Aiden's rasping tone softened. "The name's Aiden."

"I'm Lynn." Water leaked from Lynn's smile. "And the Wind Curse is Zephyr. Forgive her if she's a little spacey, her symptoms are confusing."

Sheila took a deep breath, her voice shaking. "Hello."

"I'm sorry for surprising you at such an emotional time," Lynn said. "I know we're a bit shocking to look at. We're happy to stay in our wagon if it will help."

“No, no, no,” Sheila said. “I won't let Peter's friends sleep in the yard. You stay here with us.”

Lynn curtsied with her dripping skirt. “Thank you, Mrs. Montgomery.”

“Call me Sheila, please.” She wiped her hands on her apron. “You'll need food and proper bedding – what is easiest for the three of you? I know each Curse is different.”

“We have supplies in the wagon,” Aiden said.

“Good. Very good.” Sheila touched Peter's closed door. “Alan, help them unpack so I can sit with your brother.”

He pouted. “I don't want to.”

Mona seethed. “Our God, Alan, just do it.”

The boy grumbled under his breath and hung close to Aiden as the party filtered back to the street. Sheila slipped into Peter's bedroom, leaving Cat alone with her mother.

“Phew, I'm so tense,” Mona Aston said. She touched Cat's shoulder as she took a seat beside her on the couch. “Are you okay?”

“No.” Cat's voice cracked. “No, I'm not.”

“Would you like to talk about it?”

Cat watched the door to be sure the others were still busy outside. She leaned forward over her knees. “This is my fault.”

“No it's not, Cat,” Mona said. “We all knew this would happen at some point.”

“I was supposed to take care of him.”

“You can't blame yourself.”

“Yes I can,” Cat said. “We were on a mission. I didn't have to say 'yes' to it, we could have stayed behind. It was my decision.”

“Mission? What mission? I don't understand.”

“It's too much to explain.” Cat leaned into the armrest. “And I know I'm being the victim. He's yelled at me for that before. I'm just... it's not fair.”

Mona bit her lip and adjusted her seat on the couch. “Listen, Cat. You're exhausted. Go lay down in your own bed. I promise, I'll wake you if anything happens.”

“I can't.”

“Catrina...”

“What if he – ” she swallowed a lump. “What if it happens while I'm gone?”

“Sheila will let us all know.”

Cat's heart and eyes ached. Her head spun as she stood. “Wake me when Dad comes home. I've got some things to ask.”

“Okay, honey. Sleep well.”

Cat left through the back door. Summer sun warmed the brown grass of the dying back yard. Her bedroom window looked eastward toward the Valley. The young peach tree under her window sat withered in the parched soil under her window, surrounded by a sprinkling of fallen brown leaves. Anger boiled from somewhere deep as Cat grabbed the dead tree and ripped it out of the ground. She tossed it out into the yard, stomped into the house, and fell face first onto bed.

Injustice, guilt, and nausea swelled through her chest and stomach, bringing new dread with every wave. She released the torrent of emotion as sobs into her pillow, choking on the fabric case between her shuddering breaths. Sleep took her unawares and when she raised her head, the sun cast beams of orange light onto her bed.

Hours had passed. Her empty stomach clenched like a fist in her gut. She lay in the fetal position, feeling carved out and hollow as footsteps moved up the hall to her doorway.

"Hello, Cat."

She soaked her voice in acid and refused to raise her head from the pillow. "Hello, Dad."

"I'm sorry about what's happened," Raymond said. "It's still good to see you."

She returned her face to her soggy pillow. "Right."

"I sense the feeling isn't mutual."

"No it's not."

"Will you tell me what I've done wrong?"

“I don't know, Dad. How about you tell me?” She sat up. “Was I going to know about my great-grandpa Uzzah at some point, or was that going with you to the grave?”

Raymond Aston's face flushed. “Who told you?”

“Several people.” Cat shoved herself to the side of the bed. “Lady Creven told me I was a Prophet, then a crazy hermit in the woods called me a sinner, and finally Malachi's great great great great-something grandson told me I was the root of all evil.”

“Calm down, Cat. I can explain – ”

“How could you look Peter in the face every day knowing his sickness is our fault?” Her lip quivered. “How could you sit here in this nowhere town and do nothing?”

“What was I supposed to do?”

“I don't know, try and fix it!”

“Cat, I'm one man!” he cried. “I'm not a scholar or a monk, I'm a business clerk! I inherited this guilt out of the blue, the same as you did! What was I supposed to do that all our grandfathers haven't already tried?” He ran a hand over his graying head. “All I wanted was to take care of my family. We're the last of the Astons. The line's almost gone. If you were boy it would be different, but at least you'd be spared. With any luck you'd marry out of our name and when I died it'd be over.”

"No it wouldn't," Cat said. "My blood is still yours. God's Valley's still dying and only I can stop it." She released her anger with a sigh. "When I got to Castleton, Lady Creven gave me a scripture written by the Prophet Malachi."

"I know the one."

"It was about me."

He shut his eyes. "I was afraid of that."

"I'm going to apologize to God," she said. "I'm giving back the magic our family stole. That's why I have these powers, God gave them to me for this purpose."

"That's not how it happened."

Cat frowned. "What?"

He shuddered and hung his head. "It's easier if I show you."

Raymond led her from her bedroom to the hall closet. The tiny space was packed tight with hats and coats. He moved a couple heavy boxes from the overhead storage, revealing a trap door built into the ceiling above.

"I bet you don't remember the attic, do you?"

"No..." Cat bit her lip, oddly uneasy. Raymond yanked a hanging cord and a hidden ladder unfolded. It slid on rails with a metallic whoosh and clanked into place. The sound rang eerily familiar in the back of Cat's head. Something squirmed inside her. "Was this always here?"

"We don't really use it. I told your mother the floor was weak." Raymond climbed the rungs and slid the trap door open, dislodging a thick cloud of dust. Raymond extended his hand. "Come on."

Cat backed away. "What's up there?"

"It's okay. You've seen it before."

She set her jaw and followed him into the dark and musty loft. The low ceiling met at a slant beneath the apex of the roof. A claustrophobic feeling closed in from the shadows, leaving Cat small, helpless, and anxious to leave.

Raymond retracted the ladder and closed the trap door, removing the only light source for the tiny room. He flipped the switch on an electric lamp hanging from a loose wire. Homemade bookshelves hugged the sloping walls, packed with leather books and bound packs of loose paper.

Unexplained fear raked down Cat's spine. She fought the urge to flee. "Dad, what is this?"

"Your inheritance." Mr. Aston put his hands in his blazer pockets. "What's left of it, anyway."

Leather cases filled the shelf directly behind him, marked with gold and silver inlay like veins of ore in a cave wall. Cat recognized Malachi's name as if it were her own. "Is that scripture?"

“Yes, among other things. A lot of our collection was destroyed when the Brushcasters raided my father's house in Castleton. I saved what I could.”

“Is that when you found out about it all?” Cat asked.

Raymond nodded. “Just before your grandfather died. Since then, I've read through most of it, but I only come up at night or when Mona's out so she won't know its here.”

“Why keep it from her?”

“Because it's a filthy secret.” Anger edged his tone. “Your mother's a good person. She respects the Brushcasters. I was afraid of what she'd say if she found out who she married.”

Cat tightened her arms around her chest. “Why did you keep it from me, then?”

Raymond shifted away from her toward a shelf packed with old textbooks. He reached to a high shelf and pulled out a leather volume decorated in silver and jewels. The glittering baubles sent a fresh chill down Cat's spine. Raymond blew dust from the cover and held it toward her. “This is why.”

She drew back.

“Go ahead. Look inside.”

Her subconscious begged her to not to, but she took it in her arms. It weighed less than she expected. Cat opened the cover and found the symbols of the four elements burned inside. “These are...”

Raymond's voice was a whisper. “Yes.”

Portions of the runes were repeated throughout the volume, embedded in page after page of dense handwriting. Cat flipped through diagrams, schematics, notes, and experiments marked with the symbols of water, earth, wind and fire. The hand-written passages were not scriptural or reverent. The language was strict, sometimes profane – the scrawl of a desperate man grasping for power. The nagging fear vanished as Cat met her father's eye. “I've been up here, haven't I? I've seen this book before?”

“Yes.”

“How? When? Why don't I remember?”

Raymond closed the book and took it back. “When you were six years old, you came up here while your mother and I were asleep. You were a clever kid, you must have seen me unfold the ladder at some point because you stacked your toys to get to it.”

His face twitched. He faced the bookcase. “I heard you clunking around in the ceiling and ran up to find you reading through this book.”

The memories resurfaced as he spoke; the excitement of finding a hidden door, the size of the room compared to her tiny body, how the sparkle of the cover drew her to one of the middle shelves, her father's eyes so full of rage he turned into a monster.

Cat hands were clammy with cold sweat.

"I lost my temper," Raymond's shoulders shook as she breathed. "And I struck you. You hit your head. I was disgusted and horrified – I never wanted to hurt you. I couldn't imagine I'd ever be capable..."

He shook his head and spoke more strongly. "I took you downstairs, laid you by your bed, and told your mother you fell. She called the doctor and he said you had a concussion. I hated myself so much, I prayed at the church for an hour even though I knew no one was listening. I swore to God I'd never raise a hand to you again."

Raymond cleared his throat and wiped tears on the cuff of his sleeve. "When you woke up you couldn't remember what happened. I thought maybe Our God actually heard me, but I guess the sight of the runes got stuck in your head. In hindsight I'm not surprised, the symbols are the written language of the divine. They drove our ancestors mad.

"You were a stubborn kid. I told you not to draw them, so you wove them in your string games and set the back yard on fire. Mona thought you were a genius. I couldn't tell her what really happened, and I couldn't punish you for what you didn't remember, so I voiced my disapproval and prayed you wouldn't draw attention to yourself." He put the book back on the highest shelf. "I guess it didn't work."

Cat ran a finger under her string.

"I hope you don't hate me now that you know."

Years of guilt and regret saturated his strangled words. His shoulders hunched, ready for an overdue punishment. Cat's heart rattled in her chest. She'd never seen him so broken. She reached out and touched his arm. “Thank you for telling me.”

Raymond's tear-streaked face raised and hope.

“I know you didn't mean to hurt me.”

“You aren't angry?”

“I've got a taste of that guilt you were talking about,” she said. “It's potent stuff.”

“It is.” He exhaled with relief. “How did you get so wise?”

She grinned and shrugged. “In the genes I guess.”

“That's a lie and you know it.” Raymond pulled a half grin. “It's good to finally be honest with you about that night... and all this.” He gestured to the bookcases. “I haven't shared this with anyone. Not since my father died.”

“Then tell me everything,” Cat said. “It'll help us both.”

Chapter 31

Cat leafed through blueprints with designs for schools, churches, and government buildings, each bearing Uzzah's seal. She unfolded a large page and found a cross-section of Castleton, with details of Lord Creven's mansion and the network of stairs and passages underneath. “Did Uzzah build this, too?”

“He was the Prophets' Holy Architect.” Raymond traded the blueprints for a heavy textbook. “An historian, too. He kept a careful log of everything he did with his magic. His son Aston picked up where he left off and our family's kept the tradition. Your grandfather only wrote a couple pages. I'll add my piece someday, I'm sure.”

“I guess I will too.” Cat flipped through the blank leaves. “Do you think there's enough space?”

“Depends on what happens.”

“Hmph.” She set the book on a growing pile and pulled a bundle of envelopes from the nearby shelf. The yellowing parchment cracked as she peeled open a letter and read the opening line. “To my friend Uzzah.” The handwriting was familiar. She turned the page and gasped. “It's from Malachi!”

“Yes.”

“Look at the dates!” She flipped the loose papers. “There's hundreds of them! Personal papers, well-wishes, reports from Malachi's ministry....”

“All lovingly preserved.” Raymond put his hand over hers. “He wasn't evil, Cat, at least not when these were written. He lost his mind to greed, and tried the rest of his life to redeem himself. He even tried Malachi's last prophecy. See?”

Raymond handed Cat a sketchbook. Inside were production sketches and scale drawings of the four Goddesses sculptures, complete with the billowing skirts and plaintiff expressions she recognized from her journey. Intricately decorated stone placards were drawn at the foot of each statue, bearing one of the symbols for wind, water, earth, or fire.

“These were his life's work,” Raymond said. “He wanted them sealed in his tomb, but his sons each took one when they split his estate. That's how God's Valley learned about the symbols... the rest is pretty obvious.”

“Why haven't I heard any of this before now?”

“The Brushcasters. They're also children of Uzzah in a way; his son Lonato started them way, way back when. They hid the scriptures and history in their monastery and destroyed everything else. This library's all that's left outside their walls.”

“Not all,” Cat said. “Lord Creven has a library in Castleton, and there was a hermit named Torston in the eastern mountains... but hers burned.”

His smile faded. “Another tragedy for the history book.”

“Hello?” Mona's voice echoed in the hallway below them. Raymond waved for Cat to be quiet. “Raymond? Cat? Are you here?”

Raymond pressed a finger to his lips and doused the light. The two tiptoed across the attic to the back of the house where something resembling an old mattress was pressed to the wall. Behind it, a small hidden door was cut into the exterior wall, complete with hinges, handle, and lock. Raymond opened it outward and dropped from the attic onto the wood pile in the back yard.

Cat gawked. “You have an escape route?”

“Please, I kept this a secret from your mother for thirty years.”

“Is that my window down there?” She hung her legs out. “Is this why there's a draft?”

“Hush up and jump down.”

She fell into his waiting arms and hopped safely to the yard. Raymond closed the hidden door with a rake handle half a second before his wife appeared at the kitchen door. “There you are!”

“Ah!” Raymond jumped and tossed the rake into the alley. “Don't scare me like that!”

“What are you doing out here?”

“Nothing!” Cat pressed her lips tight. “Just catching up.”

“Good, I'm glad you're feeling better.” Mona paused. “Sheila says it's time for dinner. She wants us together as a family.”

Reality crashed over Cat like a wave. “Oh, okay.”

“We'll be right there,” Raymond called. Mona went back inside and he raised his eyebrows to his daughter. “Are you okay?”

“Yeah, I just....” She tugged the string on her wrist. “I'd stopped thinking about it for a minute.”

“I know how that is.” His arm tightened around her shoulders. “Let's go in together.”

They headed back to the Montgomery's and found the dining-room table overflowing with casseroles, sympathy cards, and silk flowers. Aiden dumped a load of tokens in an empty chair and sat near the other Curses. Alan paced the kitchen, his eyes manic and his arms full of serving dishes.

“This one mom made in ceramics club, and this one she made from an old lamp we had – everything here is recycled or something. This one my dad found. I was too young to know my dad when he died. I've never seen anyone die before...”

He trailed off. Lynn coughed and cleared her throat. “It sounds like you have a very creative family.”

“Yeah, we never had a lot of money... especially after... you know.” He put his armful of things on the table. “Can I get you anything else? What do Water Curses need? Like... a sponge or something?”

“I'm fine, Alan, thank you.”

“Why's that boy talking so much?” Zephyr asked.

Alan's face flushed bright red.

“He's alright, he's just nervous,” Lynn said. “Eat your dinner.”

“Dinner?” The Wind Curse sat, puzzled. Her eyes focused on the table a moment before she let out a squeal and descended on a full casserole dish like a vulture from above.

Aiden grimaced. He spotted Cat and Raymond at the door. “Look who's back!”

“Hi, everyone,” Cat said.

Lynn sucked water through her teeth. “How are you?”

"The same."

Raymond gaped at the three Curses in shock. "What is this?"

"Oh, I'm sorry." Cat cleared her throat. "Dad, this is Aiden, Lynn, and Zephyr. Guys, this is my dad. He's had a hard day."

"Haven't we all?" Aiden scoffed.

"It's okay, Mr. Aston," Lynn said. "We came with your daughter. We're saving the world."

"Good, I'm... uh... glad," Raymond said. "Where's Sheila?"

Aiden replied. "She's in with Peter."

The name dismissed all shred of humor from the room. Alan's face twitched. He returned to the kitchen to hide the tear in his eye.

"She wanted us to send you in when you got here, Cat," Lynn said. "Do you want to eat something first?"

"No." She swallowed hard. "Thank you, though."

Cat slipped from the warm electric light into Peter's darkened room. The walls were lined with well-read books. A large hand-drawn map was tacked to the ceiling, lit by the shuttered window above Peter's bed. The Earth Curse lay motionless against a mound of pillows, wrapped in blankets and quilts with his mother seated beside.

Sheila's eyes were red and pooling. "There you are." She pulled Cat into another hug. "Are you okay, hon? I know this is hard."

"I'm okay."

“I need a moment. Can you sit with him? I'd feel better knowing you're here in case he – ” Her voice faltered.

Cat swallowed hard. “I'll be here, don't worry.”

“Thank you, dear.” Sheila sniffed and returned to the living room. “I'll be back in a little bit.”

Cat closed her eyes and inhaled the earthy musk of the quiet space. It was as much home as her own bedroom. Her gifts and drawings covered the walls. Mementos of childhood adventures sat like trophies on the shelves. They belonged there, together. Cat drew the chair and sat down. “Hi, Peter.”

He didn't stir. Rattling breath whispered from his constricted chest. The mask she saw in the Runian mansion looked more familiar in the light of his bedroom window. His cheekbones were the same, and the arch of his brow. She touched his hand and watched his chest rise and fall beneath the covers.

“So you'll never guess what Dad just told me,” Cat whispered. “Apparently there's been a library of scripture in my attic this whole time. Crazy, right? And my great-something grandfather stabbed Malachi in the chest. I guess the Astons have been breaking other people's stuff for centuries, huh?”

She paused to let him reply. He didn't.

Tightness squeezed through her chest. “I'm sorry about all this. If I hadn't let my guard down.... If the Brushcasters didn't catch up to us, then we wouldn't have crashed.”

Going back hurt too much. She started again.

“We were wrong, Pete. God didn't give me powers like he did the Prophets. I stole them the same way Uzzah did... he killed Malachi to get magic, and how many people have I killed when my magic made them Curses – ?”

The word cut like a knife. She leaned forward, hands shaking. Everyone they'd met on their quest would die because of what her family did. How much magic did it take to make a Curse? Was it enough to start a camp fire? Or water her garden? She bit her lip to keep herself quiet as tears streaked her face.

Fabric rustled on the bed. “Cat...”

The voice sent a chill through her. Peter winced against the pillows. Cat fell from her chair to her knees. “You're awake!”

His eyes pried open. “I'm trying to be.”

“No, don't talk.” She inched forward. “Don't move. Don't do anything. Just... look at me a minute.”

His muddy eyes cast toward her, shallow and unfocused without his glasses. Cat held her breath, frightened by the pain and exhaustion she saw in them. “Pete, I'm so sorry – ”

“Don't.”

"Shh," she said. "Talking sounds like it hurts."

"All I can do is talk." He focused on the ceiling with another long blink. "Talk and listen to you blame yourself."

"You heard all that?"

"This isn't your fault."

"Yes, it is," she muttered. "It's all still true. Dad said it. Joshua said it. His dad said it. Even that woman in the mountains said it. My family got rid of God. If it wasn't for us you wouldn't...."

"Stop it."

"Pete."

"I'm the one dying, here." He paused for a ragged breath. "If I don't blame you, it's not your fault."

Cat stared at her lap, miserable and convicted, as her heart throbbed in the pit of her stomach. Each labored pull of Peter's breath raked a gash across her guilty soul. "I owe you an apology."

"For five hundred years ago?"

"For the years leading to right now." She stared at the floor. "I wanted to save your life. I knew I couldn't, but I insisted, even when you told me not to. It wasn't fair to either of us."

"It wasn't easy, either."

"But you were struggling more than me." She laid a hand on his arm. He winced and she jumped back. "Sorry!"

He cracked a tiny smile. "Don't worry about it."

The grin faded. Cat swallowed hard. “I still don't want you to die, Pete.”

“I know.”

“I'm sorry I never let you talk about it.”

“It's alright, I'm not mad. I always figured this is how it was going to end.”

“But... our mission.” She tugged at her string. “You wanted to die a whole person.”

“I am,” he said. “I had a great life. I had love, and family, and an adventure.” He closed his eyes “And I had you.”

Her heart skipped.

“Saving the world was a dream, but it'll happen without me.” His voice grated. “I see now what I really wanted was the two of us exploring together like when we were kids. I didn't mind being a Curse when you were around. I wanted to spend the rest of my life with you... and I did. So it's okay.”

“I wanted that, too.” She brushed the back of his hand with her finger. “I'll stay here the whole time. I won't leave for a minute.”

“No, Cat, I'm done,” he said. “Don't wait for me. You've got a world to save.”

“I'd rather stay with you.”

A sharp cough constricted his chest. His stiff ribs refused to bend as the muscles strained between bruised skin and jutting bone. He braced himself against the pillow with a wince. “Sorry.”

She bit her quivering lip. “It's okay.”

He relaxed again. “Seriously, Cat. It doesn't matter what your dad and all those people said. You're a Prophet. You're going to make all that stuff right again.” He paused for breath. “Don't sit here and watch me fade out, I never wanted you to do that. Finish this for Aiden and Lynn and Zephyr. Their time is as short as mine is, and they've already given so much.”

“I know.” Tears burned in her eyes. “You're right.”

“Thanks for being here, Cat – and not just right now, but all of it, now that it's over.”

“Pete, don't...”

“You were the best part.” His expression went slack. “I still believe in you.”

Cat listened for breath, but couldn't hear past the pounding in her ears. She rose to her knees. “Pete?”

His skin was thin and cold against the stone beneath it. She couldn't see a pulse, and was too afraid to touch. She sat on the side of the bed and hovered close to hear his lungs. He remained still as the bed rocked. Cat scooted to his shoulder, slid her hands behind his head, and leaned in until she felt a puff of warm air on her face.

Fresh tears brimmed her eyes. “Don't give up, Pete. You have to hold on. I can't leave and miss saying goodbye to you. If I go, I have to come back.” She kissed his forehead and pressed their brows together. “I love you so much.”

“Love you, too, Cat.”

He strained to press back. Cat took the weight of his heavy head in her hands and held their faces together for as long as the moment could last.

Sheila knocked on the door. “Cat?”

She straightened, face wet and heart broken. “Yes?”

“Is everything okay?”

“Yeah. Just a minute.” She leaned back toward the bed. “You still with me?”

Muddy tracks pooled in the bags below Peter's eyes. “Yeah.”

“I should tell her you're awake.”

“Okay.”

“And Alan. He's scared for you.” She dabbed his tears with the hem of her loose sleeve. “Promise you won't give up, okay?”

“I promise.”

“Wait for me?”

“As long as I can.”

Cat kissed his brow again, as lightly as she could, and combed his blonde hair with the tips of her fingers. He relaxed at the soft touch, and sank into the bed. If she could occupy the moment for the rest of her life she would have, but there was more to the world than her one broken heart. She left him on the pillows and paused at the bedroom door to watch his shallow breathing, afraid if she left it would come to a stop.

Sheila drew her hand from the doorknob as Cat pushed it open. She met the worried mother's eye. “He's awake.”

“He's what?”

“You should go in.”

Sheila brightened with rekindled hope. “Alan, come here!”

The boy paled.

“Don't worry,” Cat said. “He's still your big brother. Tell him how you feel.”

“Okay.” Alan rose with a nervous gulp and did as he was told.

Cat shut the door behind them and joined the others at the table. Mona Aston occupied the seat closest to the door. She turned with a pinched brow. “Did you talk to him? Is he okay?”

She steeled herself with an anxious shudder. “He's tired.”

“What did he say?”

The shaking intensified. “He said we should keep going.”

“Keep going?” Mona asked. “You mean leave? And miss his – I mean it won't be – ”

“I know, Mom!” Cat snapped, louder than intended. She clawed her loose bangs and fought to calm down.

Lynn cleared her throat. “Don't worry, Cat. We can stay.”

“If anyone knows what it's like to lose a loved one, it's us,” Aiden agreed. His pulse glowed orange in his ruined face, betraying emotion he dared not show. Lynn had one hand on her bandaged chest wound, her skin heavier and blotchier than ever. Zephyr sat beside her, studying her own knuckles, too fascinated by the tendons to notice how emaciated the rest of her body appeared.

All three would trade their lives to end magic. They had suffered so much pain and grief, and managed to keep going. Cat couldn't risk losing them. “We'll do what Peter says.”

Lynn nodded. “If you're sure.”

Cat's weary heart fell to pieces. “There's no time to wait.”

Chapter 32

Dawn broke in stripes through Peter's shuttered window. Cat drew her head from the cradle of her arms and untwisted herself from the side of the bed. The Curse lay peacefully in the blankets. Cat waited for his chest to rise and slipped her hand into his. “Peter?”

He drew another breath, but didn't stir. Cat rubbed her thumb across his gnarled palm.

“I'm with you, Pete. Don't worry.”

The bedroom door opened behind her. “Cat? You in here?”

“I'm here, Aiden, come in.”

He, Lynn, and Zephyr tiptoed into the room. They looked ragged, but rested. Zephyr flew to the bookshelves to examine the trinkets and play with the toys.

"We have the wagon packed," Aiden said. "Your folks helped us last night."

"I slept through it?"

"You were distracted." Lynn regarded Peter and swallowed a mouthful of water. "Are you sure you want to leave?"

"No." She laid her hand on his forearm. "But he asked me to."

"Peter was always putting other people before himself," Aiden said. "I wish he could come with us, but it's time to say goodbye."

Cat gulped. Even if she returned before Peter's passing, the others wouldn't be with her. Reality sank like a rock in her gut. "Do you want to say a few words?"

"I'm not a words guy," Aiden said.

"I'll say something." Lynn cleared her throat. "Peter was a very sweet person to me. He tried to make me feel welcome when I was lonely, and he loved you very much, Cat."

"Yes he did." She tugged the broken comb from her bun and pressed it into his swollen hand. "Here you go, Pete. You've been looking down on this since the day I started wearing it. It's a part of me you can hold on to. I'll make it back, I promise."

"Wow, who's that?" Zephyr leaned over Peter's headboard. "He's like a statue!"

"Yes, Zephie," Lynn took her shoulders. "Say goodbye. He was your friend."

"Oh, okay," she grinned andwaved. "Goodbye friend I-don't-remember-who-you-are!"

Lynn bowed her head. "Goodbye, Peter."

"See you sooner than later," Aiden dug his hands in his pants pockets. "Okay, time to go."

"Where are we going?" Zephyr asked.

Cat suppressed a sob. "To find you a new friend."

She forced herself out the bedroom door and through the living room to the front yard. The neighbors were still indoors, and Cross Street was clear. Strawberry tapped her hoof in the dirt, rested, harnessed and ready to go. Alan hopped from the wagon's driver seat. "Cat, I've got it all set! I restocked your food and water – Lynn said I didn't have to, but it doesn't hurt to be prepared – and there's clean blankets and dry towels and all kinds of stuff in the back."

"Good work," Cat said. "Are you feeling better?"

"Yeah. Last night Pete told me to take care of you." He blushed. "You know, in his place."

Her eyes welled. "Thanks, kid."

Sheila stored Strawberry's feed bag and came close, head bowed. “How is he?”

Cat pressed her lips. “The same.”

“I don't understand why you're leaving,” Sheila said. “You mean so much to him.”

“I know.” Cat steadied her confidence. “I don't want to, but Peter understands.”

She hunched, crestfallen. “If you say so.”

“I still have Peter's atlas. You should keep it – ”

“No, no!” Sheila said. “If Peter wants you to go, you take it with you. That way he can guide you.”

Cat's heart swelled warm in her chest. “He always has.”

She gave Sheila a farewell hug. The grieving mother felt fragile, but gained strength in her arms. She kissed Cat on the temple and stepped back as the Astons joined them from their house. Mona met her daughter in tears. “I never thought I'd lose you twice.”

“You never lost me.”

“It still feels like it.” She sniffed. “But I trust you. I know you'll be safe.”

“Thanks, Mom. That means a lot.”

“Take this with you.” Raymond pressed a familiar leather case into her hands.

Cat turned it to find Malachi's name on the spine. “Is this...?”

"Aston's copy," her father said. "It belongs with you."

"I'll keep it safe." She tucked the scroll in the pocket under her scarf. "Tell Mom everything you told me. All of it. Alright?"

He paused, and nodded. "I will."

"And take care of Peter," she told the group. "If the Brushcasters come looking, don't tell them we were here."

"No one will. We'll make sure of it," her father assured. "Please be careful."

Aiden, Lynn, and Zephyr took their seats in the back. Cat set the atlas on the driver's seat beside her and took the reins. The leather felt stiff and hard in her worn hands. She gave Strawberry a flick, her parents a goodbye wave, and with a final glace at Peter's window, put her home town behind her a second time.

Dawn light stretched shadows across the mountain road. Cat tried not to acknowledge the doubt gnawing her heart. She promised to make it back, but time was her enemy as much as the Calligraphers. At least he wasn't alone, she told herself. He had his family, like his father did when he died ten years prior.

Lionel Montgomery had a weak body, but a big heart and a strong will. He lay in bed for three days before sickness overtook him. Cat remembered waking up to the adults crying. Her father said to stay inside, but she slipped out her window and tossed rocks at Peter's bedroom until he opened the shudders in tears. It was the first time either had seen death up close.

Six short months later, he was diagnosed as a Curse. Everyone knew that meant banishing him, but with Alan as an infant and Lionel lost so soon before, Mayor Young told Sheila he could stay. It wasn't an easy decision. Cat recalled the adults yelling at each other in the town square. Her father stood in Peter's defense – it made perfect sense, in retrospect. He was fighting a guilty conscience. But Cat was grateful, regardless. If it wasn't for him, her life would have been different, and Peter would have gone to Earth Town to die all alone.

It was hard to imagine seven year-old Peter walking into to Earth Town with his over-sized glasses and well-combed blonde hair. All the Curse books Sheila ordered said Earth Town was a fortress. Kids were only allowed inside once the parents were long gone. Cat shuddered at the image and forced her attention to the road. Peter wasn't in Earth Town, but she and her wagon soon would be.

They wound through the forested pass and reached the open valley by mid-morning and arrived at Cartographer's Junction. Cold wind buffeted the directional sign, pointing them north to Astonage and Earth Town. Castleton blazed like fire in the distance. Groups of tiny black dots moved along the Outer Bend. Calligraphers. They were hunting her like Joshua said. A streak of panic prickled the skin on Cat's neck and arms. She took a calming breath, opened Peter's atlas, and steered her wagon northward, where the rolling hills hid them from view.

Sagging, sun-bleached cabins pockmarked the level landscape where fence posts and fallen slats mapped property lines of ancient farmlands. The Curses chatted in the covered wagon. Their words were muffled but their voices were light. Cat heard them laughing. She didn't know how they could smile when her soul still felt so weak.

She kept Strawberry turning eastward and watched for activity on the road. She added a bit of speed and forged onward through the wasteland. The day wore long and hot over the wagon. As hours passed, a pale haze gathered at the foot of the Western Mountains. Aiden unzipped the tent flap behind her seat. “Are you seeing that cloud back there?”

“Yeah.”

“It looks like a storm,” he said. “We should stop.”

“We can't stop,” Cat said in monotone. “We have a mission.”

“The mission's not getting done if we get stuck. Dust storms can kill people.”

“We can make it before it hits.”

“Storms are faster than they look.”

“We have the wind at our back.”

“It does, too.”

“We have to hurry,” Cat said. “Brushcasters are everywhere.”

His brow leveled over glowing eyes. “Is it the Brushcasters or is it Peter?”

She flinched. Bile rose to her mouth. “It's a lot of things.”

“Listen, I've lived in the desert most of my life. That wind will take the skin off me, and I'm not going to think about how it'll affect the others. Breathing it alone – ”

“Then you guys stay inside,” she said. “If it's really that scary, the Brushcasters will stop and give us the advantage.”

“Cat.” Aiden's voice was firm. “I know it feels bad – I lost someone, too – but hurrying isn't going to change facts. Peter's gone.”

“No, he's not.” Her knuckles whitened on the reins. “And we aren't stopping.”

They doubled their pace, crushing dry weeds. Cold wind chased them into crumbled prairie land where the industrial city of Astonage waited like a predator on the horizon. A dull roar filled the air. Cat leaned around the wagon to see a wall of rolling brown dust racing toward them from the mountains. The storm absorbed the farmland, tearing apart the aged buildings and adding debris to the barreling tower of dust. Fear flooded Cat with adrenaline. She lashed Strawberry to a gallop as the sky turned from blue to an ominous red.

The storm struck the wagon broadside like a mallet. Strawberry shrieked as the wheels skidded sideways, and the world plunged into ruddy darkness. Grit flooded Cat's eyes. It filled her lungs as she breathed. Peter's atlas flipped its pages and was tossed across the seat. She released the reins and caught it midair.

Cat pressed the book to her heart and hunched forward, wind whipping her loose hair and raking her exposed skin like sandpaper. Tears caught dust and grime as she shivered from panic and cold. The whole valley had vanished with no sign of Castleton or Astonage to help mark the way. The storm howled like a furious monster with the sun its single red eye.

The loose reins whipped the air as Strawberry reared and tugged her harness. Cat reached for the strap, but it broke painfully against her raw hand. Cat secured the atlas under her seat and tied her scarf over her nose and mouth. The Curses were sealed and protected inside the tent. Overhead, the afternoon sun sat right of its zenith. As long it was at their back they were pointed eastward, and as long as they were moving, they would make it to their goal.

She climbed from the driver's seat, skirts billowing, and grabbed the feedbag from its hook. Strawberry's nose was bleeding. Cat walked her hands up the horse's heaving flank and secured the empty bag over her mouth.

"I'm sorry, girl," Cat muttered, more to herself. She grabbed the reins where they met the bridle. "Do the best you can."

Cat put the sun behind them and forged into the storm. Strawberry moved faster with her mouth protected, but the trail was arduous beneath the lash of dust and wind. The lack of horizon closed the valley into a bubble around the wagon. The space beyond was surreal and foreign, cloaked in shades of rust and red.

Night plunged the storm to blackness, stealing any sense of direction. Moonlight scattered into a fine haze before it could reach the ground. The temperature dropped to almost freezing. Cat slowed Strawberry to a walk and huddled, numb and shaking, in the front seat of the wagon.

The storm drained the dregs of Cat's stubborn soul. She blinked grit from tearing eyes and puffed air through her scarf. The fabric smelled like incense from the washrooms in Joshua's mansion. She remembered when he held her, warm and safe, against his velvet shirt. She wished he was there with her. The incense smell dulled and soured as dirt muddied the damp fabric. It was Peter's smell. The earthy scent spun her heart into a spiral. Peter was too hurt to hold her again. She'd never bury her face in his chest again, or hold his stony arm to her cheek. She left him. She left both of them.

She was alone.

Aiden was right about the storm, and Peter, and her stubborn ignorance. Not wanting to hear the truth didn't make it magically false. Miserable and ashamed, she sobbed into her lap and screamed as loud as she could, but her voice was lost in the storm.

Cat felt the wind shift. The howl quieted, and she could see a faint glow radiating like a halo from the horizon ahead. The light beamed through the dust cloud in shining rays of gold and copper. A figure emerged from the glow with hands stretched toward the sky.

"Joshua?"

Cat rubbed her muddy eyelids but the vision didn't change. The silhouette reached through the darkness, tossing starlight like lighted bits of confetti from its hands. Cat didn't know if she was dead or dreaming, but steered Strawberry toward the shine.

The figure grew in size and stature as they approached. It was a woman, facing toward them, her skirts frozen in the wind. To the right, the dark towers of a hidden city appeared from the moonlit haze. The starlight she saw revealed itself as lighted city windows. Warm color caressed the brick along the outer wall and touched the girders and smokestacks of the factories inside.

It was no mirage, it was Astonage. They'd crossed the desert moving eastward and reached their destination. The Earth Goddess towered above them, holding a block of uncarved stone. The holy glow behind her was a massive cauldron of billowing flame. A door stood open in the front of it, surrounded by ogres with bent backs and misshapen limbs.

The storm glowed with heat and fire.

Earth Town was in flames.

Chapter 33

"FIRE!" Zephyr shrieked and thrashed within the wagon.

The commotion rocked the vehicle and drew Cat from a daze. She unzipped the tent flap. "What's going on?"

Lynn's red eyes poured tears over the panicked Wind Curse, kicking and screaming in the bed. Zephyr ripped at her short hair. "Don't make me go in, Wendy! Don't make me!"

"What's happening out there?" Aiden asked. "Is the storm over? Are you okay?"

"Earth Town's on fire!" Cat tossed him the reins. "You guys get some distance. I have to help them."

"Cat, wait – !"

She leaped to the ground and charged full speed into the raging inferno. Hot air rippled above the boulders of the sloping outer walls. Every breath burned in Cat's dust-damaged lungs, yet she sprinted past the staring Earth Curses into the heart of the fire. Her cold-numbed fingers tingled as her eyes adjusted to light.

Dust from the persisting wind storm poured over the slanted outer wall, tossing embers from patches of wildfire burning in the crevices between the stacked boulders. Twelve ignited huts glowed like lanterns, their open doors like screaming mouths between small, misshapen windows. A bonfire of stacked supplies blazed against the far wall, spitting embers and fibers one-hundred feet into the sky.

Cat's sweaty hands shook with exhaustion. She knitted a loose water rune and flashed a fountain of cold liquid into the nearest house. Steam burst from the hot stones, filling the hut with white smoke. When the first spell weakened, Cat released it and moved to the next house. Wood popped and crumbled as burning thatch fell to the dirt. Cat's arms ached from the strain as she extinguished each house.

A lone Earth Curse bustled around the last house in the circle, flinging buckets of water through the doorway as the roof peeled and burned. The man was dressed in ragged pants with hair down to his waist. His left shoulder swelled from his torso in a shelf of layered tumors. Cat recognized the way the skin stretched over his afflicted skeleton and shivered despite the permeating heat.

The young man hobbled to the well in the center of town and cranked the low handle to refill his bucket. Flame rolled from a pile of crates and firewood, downwind of his house. The pile teetered over his head as he hobbled back to the hut. Cat drew a breath readied her string. “Move!”

The young man turned in a splay of singed hair. For a moment she saw Peter in the swollen bones around his eyes, but blinked the image away.

The Earth Curse stumbled back to the well and Cat hit the flaming tower with full-powered spell. The waving stack of crates and boxes shuddered under her assault. Steam wrapped the tower in glowing clouds. Cat felt her strength fade. The light in the string dimmed. She paused for breath, reset the string, and hit the tower again, this time aiming along the right side to guide its collapse.

“Whoa!” The Earth Curse shouted over the storm. “How are you doing that?”

“I'm a Prophet.”

The tower tipped toward the wall, shedding bits over the town like glowing hailstones. Cat shoved the Earth Curse toward the entrance and re-positioned herself on the weakened side. She sent a spray of water into the collapsing structure, but cut the magic short, nausea snaking up her throat. Her head was swimmy and feverish. Her throat was dry, her limbs weak and shaky. The string blurred in front of her but she forged ahead by memory – her fingers knew the symbols better than both her head and heart.

Water bathed the lower boxes and bent the tower northward, away from the town proper and against the perimeter wall. The structure collapsed into a burning carpet. Cat aimed her symbol at the flames, but her arms were so heavy, she could barely hold the string taut. The water rune shook out of her twitching hands as her vision clouded into a dizzying tunnel of fire and dust.

Her knees failed and she tumbled backward into a frigid pair of arms. Lynn held her close, liquid gargling in her chest. "Cat!"

Cat leaned in, the water was refreshing on her flame-chafed cheek. "I'm okay."

"I'm sorry!" A wet cough chopped Lynn's words. "Aiden said the storm – we couldn't open the tent – I called but you didn't hear – "

"It's okay, Lynn... you did the right thing."

"How is she?" Aiden limped to them with Zephyr close behind. Light from the fallen tower illuminated his face where glowing veins pulsed in the corners of his eyes. "You hurt?"

"No." Cat lifted her head. "Just weak."

"What is the meaning of this?" A gravelly voice roared.

Earth Curses gathered around, their deformed bodies draped in simple clothing and their matted hair down to their waists. Flame reflected off faceted stone barbs protruding from their flesh where stripes of crust and mud traced paths through the knobs.

An eight-foot woman approached, supported by two other Curses like a pair of living crutches. Her right leg and arm were a single motionless chunk bound to her side with cloth bands.

“Monsters!” Zephyr squeaked.

Aiden grabbed her arm. “Hush!”

“My name is Catrina Aston.” Cat staggered up using Lynn's shoulder and held her head high. “I came to your town as a Prophet from God.”

“I don't care about preachers, what do you want?”

Cat faltered. “What?”

“Healthy people don't come here without a reason.” The woman loomed over them. “Are you here for a shock? Or a laugh?”

“No,” Cat said. “I saw the fire and came to help.”

“No one helps Curses unless they have to.”

“But she did, Georgia!” The young man from the bonfire hobbled into the group, the well bucket clenched in his fairly normal right hand. “I was doing what you told me, then WHOOSH – water out of nowhere! She saved all the houses and probably some of the boxes, too – ”

"Shut up, Will," Georgia snapped. The young man ducked behind the other Curses as the hulking woman continued. "Alright, so you put out the fire; it's too late to refuse help. Name your price."

Cat frowned. "Price?"

"Earth Town doesn't take charity," Georgia said. "Everything's paid in equal measure. What do you want? Food? Water? Stone? We can't get you what you ask for until tomorrow morning. The town's in shambles. We have a lot of work to do, so make it quick."

"What I... want?" Cat looked to Lynn and Aiden and pulled her father's copy of the scripture from her skirt pocket. "I'm a Prophet foretold by Malachi to bring God back to the world. This letter describes the process it takes – you can read it if you want. It needs volunteers from each of the elements, and I've traveled God's Valley to gather them. You see Aiden, Lynn, and Zephyr from Fire, Water, and Wind. They've agreed to give their lives to give God back his stolen magic."

"And now you've come here?"

"Yes." Her heart trembled. "We need an Earth Curse willing to be a sacrifice."

Georgia's heavy brow furrowed across a broad tumor. She shouted over her useless shoulder. "Will! Get up here!"

The young man with the bucket peeked out of hiding. "Yes?"

"You're leaving with these people."

“Wait a minute.” Cat glanced between them. “I didn't mean for you to *give* me someone! It has to be willing volunteer.”

“Are you a willing volunteer?” Georgia asked. Will nodded vigorously. “See? Then we're even. Do you need to kill him now?”

“What? No!”

“Good, 'cause we need the hands.” Georgia nudged her crutches and they shifted her to face the townsfolk. “Everyone see to your houses. If anything's still burning, scrape it out. I want the kids to hit the stockpiles. Find whatever's salvageable. Break up boxes for new roofs.”

Will perked up. “Me too?”

“I think you've done enough,” Georgia huffed. “Get these outsiders out of the way. This is Earth Town business. They're your problem, now.”

“Yes, ma'am!”

The Earth Curses broke to follow Georgia's instructions. Cat stammered. “Wait! It's not that easy. It can't be that easy, can it?”

“Looks like it was to me,” Aiden said.

“Hey Prophet!” Will dragged his misshapen left leg toward them. “Name's Will. Good to meet'cha. You all hungry?”

Zephyr brightened, skirt billowing. “Yes!”

“Great, come home with me! The building's pretty ruined but the food should all be cooked!”

Will led his guests across town at an uneven gallop. The limbs on his right side maintained a degree of function, but the left arm and leg were three times normal size. He dragged the stiff half past several fire-damaged houses to the black ruin Cat saw him defending moments earlier. “Here we are, home sweet home!”

Aiden eyed it from a distance. “There isn't much left.”

“Yeah, it's cool, though, we can still have a good time.” Will bumped his left shoulder on the door as he entered. “Sorry there's no furniture, that was the first thing to catch. We don't sit very well, anyway, but we do the best we can. I don't know what Fire People and Water People eat, but Wind Girl looks like she could eat anything.”

Zephyr was already digging through debris. She found a smoldering broom handle and admired the ember. “Shiny!”

“Zephie, no!” Lynn wrenched the stick from her hand. “Why don't you wait in the wagon?”

“I don't want to wait in the wagon!”

“C'mon, she didn't hurt anything.” Will tossed a blackened chair past her out the door. “Here's my portion of the veggie rations! The lettuce is a bit gone, but peppers are good blackened! Here!” He shoved a splintered box toward Zephyr, who dove in.

Cat cleared her throat. “Thank you for the hospitality, Will, but I don't think you understand what Georgia's signed you up for, here.”

"Eh, don't worry about Georgia. Trust me, playing host is way better than putting out fires."

"Yes, tell us about the fire," Lynn said. "Did it start because of the wind storm?"

Will shoveled dirt with his club-like left arm. "Kinda?"

"Did a torch or something blow over?"

"Not exactly." He grimaced. "See, I was trying to cook up a little something for dinner and... you know.... these big limbs of mine. I might have accidentally cooked up a lot of other things instead."

Aiden raised a scabbed brow. "Your neighbors' things?"

"A few?"

"Uh-huh." Cat bit her lip. "Is that why you got volunteered?"

"I can't really say that kind of stuff. Georgia's the one who makes the choices; she's the leader." Will grinned. "I'm just glad she gave me another job! I thought that last screw up ruined me!"

"I see." Cat beckoned Aiden and Lynn out of the hut. The moon dipped low in the storm overhead. Earth Curses shuffled in the light of the remaining fires, dragging bits of their ruined belongings into a pile in the center of town. Strawberry huffed and snorted along the wall to their right, her coat matted with scales of dirt.

The cold air ached in Cat's lungs. "We can't take him."

"Because he didn't volunteer?" Lynn asked.

"Because he was volunteered as a punishment," Cat said. "That's not what this sacrifice is for."

"You can't say a full understanding of the theology is a requirement at this point," Aiden said. "Zephyr doesn't know where she is half the time and you were okay bringing her."

"I – I know." Cat watched the Wind Curse through the doorway as she handed Will a broken table one piece at a time. "But this mission is more than a checklist. Lives are at stake."

"We know, Cat." Lynn sweetened her gargling voice. "We're the lives. When we finish this mission we'll die, but the world will be better for it. Will will understand that once we explain it to him. Remember what we came here for."

Illness and exhaustion tightened their grip on her guts. "Remembering doesn't help."

Chapter 34

Cat spent the night in the back of the wagon thinking about Will and coughing brown mucous into one of Lynn's soggy towels. Strawberry lay on the ground outside. Breath wheezed through her congested chest, punctuated by snuffles and snorts. Cat's stomach rolled with guilt. What would Peter say if he knew she'd hurt her trying to keep their promise. Cat closed her eyes and imagined the muffled wheezing was the sound of his heavy chest. The thought calmed her mind enough to sleep a couple hours.

Dawn broke on a hazy sky diffused in red light through the lingering dust. A subtle uneasiness permeated the town as she slipped from the wagon bed and tiptoed to Will's hut where Aiden, Lynn, and Zephyr slept along the walls. The Earth Curse sat propped against the empty door frame with Zephyr curled in a ball around his healthier arm. Sadness pierced Cat's chest. She left the Curses sleeping and crept further into town.

Earth Curses were still at work rebuilding the previous night's damage and doing meager chores. Older Curses sat against the charred houses or on shelves along the outer wall as younger ones scurried about delivering rations of food and water. A blonde boy rushed past her. She thought she saw glasses and stopped where she stood. The boy delivered a piece of bread directly into the mouth of an older Curse and returned to the supply pile. A bulbous stone tumor warped the right side of his face.

Georgia leaned on a large rock in the center of town, observing the piles of ash and debris collected from the houses. The young woman's disfigurement was more pronounced in daylight. Giant knots of stone hooded her eyes and burdened her neck and shoulders. The growths sliced through her dark skin and rose naked like silver mountains behind her head. A sheet of coarse fabric covered her useless limbs like a cape.

“Stop where you are.” One of her crutches, a pale-haired Curse of indiscriminate gender, approached as Cat neared. “What are you doing?”

Cat tried not to stare. “I'm just walking.”

“Walking or gawking?”

“Walking.”

“Is that the Prophet Girl?” Georgia barked. “Bring her here!”

The Earth Curse grumbled and brought Cat to the leader.

Georgia shifted her lean against the standing stone and leveled her heavy brow. “The storm's passed. Why haven't you left yet?”

Cat steeled. “I'm still looking for a volunteer.”

“I gave you one.”

“That was because Will started the fire,” Cat said. “He made a mistake, so you're getting rid of him.”

“You're the one who asked to be paid in a life.”

“That doesn't make me your executioner.”

“You're a healthy person, so I don't expect you to understand,” the Curse replied. “We're Curses, we have no value, our only worth is our contribution to this world while we're alive. If it wasn't him it would be someone else. This way our cost is minimal.”

Cat pressed her lips. “Will may not be perfect, but he's still a person. He has value.”

“Do they look like persons to you?” Georgia nodded to the laboring townsfolk. “They are stones. Things.”

“That's not true.”

"I have no delusions about what I am." Georgia's expression darkened. "My blood is dust, my skeleton clay, my heart a stone. When I die I'll fill my place just like Will. He is a resource, like any other. I hope you find a use for him."

"It won't be as an object."

"Do whatever you like. Just do it somewhere else."

Cat stormed back to her wagon. Will gathered food rations from the singed supply pile. Unlike Georgia, daylight revealed how healthy he appeared. The skin over his misshapen ribs had a warm tone, and his face was full of character with a scraggly beard and a large nose she guessed had nothing to do with being a Curse.

"Hey Prophet Girl!"

"Hey."

He dropped the vegetables and bread from waist height. "You doin' alright? You look pissed."

"I was talking to Georgia."

"Ah, yeah, that'll do it."

"Say Will...." She cleared her throat and gripped the scripture case in her pocket. "How old are you?"

"Fourteen-ish?" He shrugged his uneven shoulders. "My birthday's in fall. How about you?"

"Sixteen." She bit her lip. "Look, I know I asked you this before, but are you aware of what you've been volunteered for?"

"You said it was a suicide mission, right?"

"Are you okay with that?"

"Sure, everyone has to die sometime." He stooped to grab the bread with his healthier hand. "We've all got a purpose – or don't Prophets believe that?"

She smirked a little. "We do."

"I know Georgia's gruff and all, but she's not a bad person. She makes sure everyone here has a role to play, that's what keeps us all going. Stuff can't be too bad if we can still be useful." Will handed her the dusty loaf with a grin. "Before you showed up I was supposed to shore up a weak spot in the wall, but this new job's tons better. Being a wall sounds so boring."

"Being a – " Cat stammered. "You'd actually *be* the wall?"

"Yeah, where did you think the wall came from? Don't worry, not all of us have to be walls. My old roommate is a house!" His smile drooped. "I hope he wasn't burned too bad."

Cat stood frozen as he returned to the house. Her heart pounded as the lumps in the buildings took the likeness of heads and torsos. An older Curse sat alone on the ground with mud-glazed eyes and shallow breathing. Another leaned against the wall with it's legs tied together. Empty eye sockets watched from faces full of pain and exhaustion. Broken limbs overgrown with facets of stone gripped door frames and houses. Every stone in the complex, from the scorched perimeter wall to the mound Georgia leaned on was once a person, and Cat could see Peter's face in every one.

She dropped the loaf of bread and ran for the town gate. Bile burned a hot path in her throat as she stumbled into the desert. The Earth Goddess emerged from the passing storm, lifting her stone block southward toward Castleton, hidden by miles of haze. Cat tread the blustering wind to the pedestal below the statue.

Emotion rattled her every nerve. She hugged her arms to her chest and sobbed. “I can't – I can't do this.”

“Yes, you can.”

Joshua sat crouched in the folds of the Goddess's dress. He hopped down and Cat leaped into his embrace. His warmth and the scent of incense filled her fractured heart like glue. “Where were you? You said you'd be close.”

“I'm here, aren't I?” Joshua's arms tightened around her back. “Don't cry. It'll be okay.”

“No it won't,” she mumbled into his tunic. “Peter is... he's...”

“Just breathe.”

“I made him promise to wait for me.” Her voice shook. “He was hurting so much and I made him hold on... and I'm not going to make it in time.”

“You don't know that.”

"I miss him so much." She stepped back, wiping tears. "How am I going to do this? Losing Pete hurts so bad, and this mission is going to kill all of them. Aiden, and Lynn, and Zephyr and now Will? I don't care if they agreed. I can't do this to them. It's not fair."

"It wasn't meant to be easy," Joshua said. "Everything happens for a reason."

"Maybe God wants us to suffer before he comes back," she spat. "Maybe these five hundred years were supposed to torture us."

"That's not true."

"Your dad seems to think so. He said all this destruction is us getting what we deserved."

"Look at me a moment." He locked his sparkling eyes with hers. "I wouldn't encourage you if this journey was meant to be a punishment. It serves a purpose. If you could see things the way I do, you'd understand."

"Aiden and Lynn aren't just Curses, they're thinking, caring people," Cat said. "Zephyr doesn't even know what's happening to her, and Georgia paid us with Will like he was money. His life matters – they all matter – and I'm leading them to their deaths."

Joshua shut his eyes and breathed a moment. The wind around the sculpture dulled long enough to hear him whisper. "five hundred years ago, death tore this valley apart. It takes life – pure life – and magic to put it all back in place."

“Why, though?”

His eyes opened, the pupils deep and dazzling. “Everything is connected through people and time. Your friends were cast out, but understand the value of life and love more than all of humanity. You are your ancestor's daughter, but are braver than any of the generations before you. You all have faith when it's hopeless – that's why you'll succeed.”

Cat bowed her head. “I'm scared.”

“I know.”

“Stay here with me?” She plead. “I know you can't be seen by people, but maybe by Curses? I don't want to be alone.”

“You're not alone.” He brushed the loose hair from her eyes. “You have a whole party of friends. Don't shut them out in an attempt to protect them. They're here for you. You strengthen each other.”

She glanced to Earth Town. “I don't want to go back in there.”

“You don't have to if you don't want to.”

“Don't tease me; you know I have no choice.”

“You always have a choice.” The muscle in Joshua's jaw flexed as he took her hands. “Say the word and I'll carry you back to my mansion where we can live peacefully in the mountains like none of this ever happened.”

She paused. James said the two were betrothed. She couldn't imagine it with Peter hurt, but now that he was gone.... Her stomach lurched. She freed her hands to untangle a knot in her string. “I'm sorry Joshua, maybe someday... but Pete's dying for this mission. I can't give up because I'm scared. It's too important for that.”

He relaxed with a smile. “And that's why you're going back.”

“Yeah.” She snorted a bitter laugh. “I guess it is, isn't it?”

“It's okay to be scared, be strong anyway,” he said. “I'm sorry, I've got to go.”

“Go where?”

“To do my part for the mission.” He kissed the back of her hand. “See you soon.”

Joshua slipped past and vanished into the rolling dust. Cat cradled the hand he kissed to her heart all the way back to Will's hut. Lynn brushed mud from Strawberry's mane. “Cat! There you are!”

She touched Strawberry's panting chest. “How is she?”

“Better after resting. She's breathed a lot of dust.”

Cat dropped her gaze. “Aiden told me it was dangerous to drive through.”

“Dangerous for both of you!”

“I know,” Cat said. “Let's give her another night, I don't want her pulling the wagon until she's well enough.”

“Are you sure?” Lynn blinked tears. “I thought you made Peter a promise.”

"I made you guys a promise, too." Cat took a deep breath. "This is the right thing to do."

"Good." Lynn stored the brushes and got Strawberry a bucket of water to drink. "I've been worried about you. You've been so quiet."

"This place is... overwhelming."

"Do you want to talk about it?"

"Not yet." Cat forced a smile. "But I will."

"Whenever you're ready." Lynn gargled a relieved sigh and wiped her muddy hands on her dress. "Come inside. We made breakfast."

"I'm not really hungry."

"Then come for the company. Will's a very nice person, if you give him a chance."

Cat tried not to look at the walls as Lynn led her into the ramshackle house. Aiden, Zephyr, and Will sat around a stony fire pit, eating dry meat and bread. Will noticed her and struggled to stand. "Hey, you're back!"

Cat waved. "Stay, please. That looks hard."

Will obliged with an apologetic smile. "Aiden and Lynn were telling me about your trip so far. I'm sorry about your other friend. A fall is a rough way to go."

"Thanks." Cat sat between Aiden and Lynn, on the floor. "It was rough on all of us."

"Not that it helps, but from a fellow Earth Curse, going quick is better than waiting around. Some of us take the leap on purpose around here, not that I'm recommending something like that. Still, it sucks making it to fifteen or sixteen and picking a spot."

Cat feigned a smile. "Silver lining, I guess."

Lynn settled on a pile of towels near the fire. "Tell us about yourself, Will. Where were you born?"

"Right here in Astonage. I'm a factory brat born and raised. Mom was a textiler, Dad was a smelter. That's how this happened." He hoisted his over-sized left arm onto his lap. "I smacked it on some rebar by accident and it swelled like a melon. When it turned to stone, they dropped me out here."

Lynn sucked her lip. "Do you ever see them?"

"Nah, but Earth Town never lets normal people in. You guys were lucky the door was open. Usually folks drop their kids, knock, and leave."

"That's what the books said, too," Cat said. "Peter's mom bought a bunch when he was diagnosed."

"Man, he's lucky," Will said. "Wish my mom had ignored the Brushcasters and bought a book."

"He's lucky in general," Aiden tossed a stone into the fire. "Mine didn't even dump me themselves."

“I like this sharing circle thing we're doing,” Will said. “New topic, though! Worst thing about your particular curse. I'll go first; aching. Everything aches all the time. Aiden, you're next.”

“Itching. I can avoid water fairly well, but I can't escape the itching. Plus if I scratch, it'll rip more holes in my skin.” He glanced across the fire. “Lynn, what about you?”

“Definitely the cold. I can never get warm, and I can't feel my toes.” She wiggled them in the pool gathering around her feet. “It was nicer in Water Town when we could pack in close on cold nights, but if I do that around here, I might kill someone.”

Aiden picked at the scar on his cheek. “Sorry.”

“It's not your fault.”

“What about you, Zephyr?” Will asked.

The Wind Curse stared into the heart of the fire. Her short hair kept time with the pulse pounding in her temple as it moved in waves over her head.

Cat leaned around Lynn, brow raised. “Zephyr? You okay?”

“What?” She started as if waking from a dream. “Who was that? Where am I?”

“There's your answer.” Aiden said to Will. “That's the worst part of being a Wind Curse.”

“It's a symptom,” Lynn said. “She's not trying to be difficult, she can't help what she is.”

Zephyr frowned, exposing tendons and veins across her forehead. Her eyes darted, focused and alert with thoughts racing behind them. “I don't recognize any of you. This isn't Wind Town, is it? The temperature's wrong. The air feels thick.”

“Wait.” Cat sat forward and met Zephyr's eye. The two studied each other, searching their eyes for clues. Cat dropped her tone. “Do you remember leaving Wind Town?”

“No.” Zephyr noticed Lynn between them and drew back. “Oh my goodness!”

“It's okay!” Cat assured. “That's Lynn. She's your friend.”

Zephyr's wide eyes deepened in fear and confusion. “I'm sorry. I'm having trouble... thinking...”

“It's okay, Zephie,” Lynn said. “Your curse affects your mind.”

“My curse?”

“You're a Wind Curse,” Cat said, gently. “We found you in the windmill, do you remember that?”

“The windmill?” Zephyr bit her knuckle. “Yes.... I remember. But if I was in there, then that means – ”

She drew her bony hands along her scalp, through her short, blustering hair. “Oh.” Heartbreak darkened her pale face. “Oh, I see.”

Cat lowered her voice. “I'm sorry.”

“It's okay,” Zephyr said. “Where am I now?”

"Earth Town," Lynn answered. "We came here for Will. He's volunteered to come with us so we can save the world."

"Will?"

The Earth Curse waved his stiff right hand.

"Holy moly!" Zephyr rubbed her eyes. "Are you okay?"

"I'm good, Zephyr, don't stress," he said.

"Oh... okay... I'm sorry." Her eyes glassed. "It's hard to think."

"Just relax. We're all friends here."

"I want to remember... but it's like fog." She forced her eyes back into focus. "Quick, how are my friends back home? Wendy, Gabe, Michael – did you see them? Are they okay?"

Lynn shot Aiden and Cat a panicked look. The Fire Curse cleared his throat. "They're fine, Zephyr. We saw them when we left."

"Good!" Zephyr collapsed in on herself like an old umbrella. "I remember their faces surrounded by smoke and fire. They had torches..." Her pupils contracted to specks. "Wait! No, I don't want to remember! Make it stop!"

"Think of something else!" Cat urged. "Something happy! Anything."

"They're coming for me!" Zephyr clamped her hands around her head. "Don't let them cut it. I'm still me, I swear!" She screamed, hands tight in her short hair, until she was out of breath and fell silent. A heartbeat later the light was gone from her eyes. "Where am I?"

Lynn sniffed. “It's okay, Zephie, you're with us.”

“Who's us?”

“Your friends,” Cat said. “We're all friends.”

“Oh good,” Zephyr stared back into the flame. “I like friends.”

“Okay, I give. She's got it worst.” Will whistled. “That was a trip and a half.”

“We haven't seen her snap in and out like that before,” Cat said. “Most times she's in a daze. I don't know which is better.”

Will winced. “From all that, it sounds like it's better to forget.”

“I disagree,” Aiden said.

“You'd rather relive that nightmare every day?”

“It's my life, I don't want to lose it,” Aiden said. “I've seen my share of tragedy, sure. Losing Ildri was the worst thing that's ever happened to me, but if I forget her, it's like she never existed. I can't forget it, even if it hurts. She meant too much to me.” He touched the scrap of lavender cloth on his wrist. “You agree with me, right Cat?”

She tightened her hands in her checkered scarf. “Yes.”

“I know what it's like to forget,” Lynn said. “I'm missing all memory from my childhood.”

“And are you happier?” Will asked.

Lynn shifted in her wet towel. “I guess so? It makes me treasure the memories I do have, but I do wonder who my parents were and where I came from. It sounds dumb, but sometimes I wish I had someone to miss."

Aiden tossed a bit of wood into the fire. "In the end all we have is each other."

A smile lit Will's face. "Absolutely right! From now on, you guys are my Curse Siblings and Cat's our Prophet Cousin. We'll be the Holy Five and they'll raise statues and write history books about us. That way we'll be together forever."

"Wow," Lynn said.

Zephyr gaped in wonder. "Together forever?"

"Yeah, Zeph, forever." Will grinned. "How lucky is that?"

She giggled. "I do feel lucky! I don't know why, but I do."

Cat marveled at the four Curses. The smiles on their faces un-knotted her heart like fingers in the string on her wrist. "Wow, Will, you're really something."

He shrugged. "Isn't everyone?"

Chapter 35

The time had come to leave. Strawberry was breathing normal and eating well. The sky was clear and blue once again. Cat packed with a sour taste in her mouth. The last leg of their journey would be the hardest both physically and emotionally, yet her friends were resolute. She tried to mirror their confidence as they drove the wagon toward the gate.

"Goodbye everyone!" Will waved out the open back to the Earth Curses watching from the surrounding homes. "Remember me when the plants start growing again – that's right, we're gonna make plants grow again! You're welcome in advance!"

Georgia watched from the backs of her living crutches. Cat made eye contact, but saw no regret or compassion. The misshapen woman was as cold and lifeless as the stone inside her, hollowed by a world equally heartless and unfeeling. She nodded to a group of Curses near the town gate. The door, open since the fire, was a slab of recycled metal in a trench along the wall. The Curses put their shoulders against a metal slab and slid it through the dirt, shutting the wagon out with the thud of metal on stone.

The wind-swept northern desert behind Astonage was smooth as a riverbank. A heap of dirt sloped against the industrial city's outer wall. Ribbons of white steam and exhaust fluttered from a man-made forest of spires and smokestacks beyond. The Earth Goddess pointed them southward, past Astonage to Castleton waiting in the distance. An ugly gash, like Uzzah's signature, marred the front of the pedestal where the earth rune once was. Cat recalled her father's attic with a deep, ragged breath and searched the Astonage skyline. It was her ancestral home, but compared to the forest and mountains of Mason Forge, felt more foreign than any place she'd ever been.

They made slow progress across the desert. Cat cut a wide path to avoid possible lookouts and travelers moving carefully along the dust-covered roads. She found the rivets of an old path and headed southward. Gusts of wind rolled waves of dirt like wagon wheels across their path. By noon, Strawberry was wheezing again. Cat stopped the wagon to rest. “Be careful everyone. We don't know who's watching.”

“It feels good to stretch.” Lynn slipped from the wagon and filled a bucket for Strawberry from the water tank under her seat. “I can tell from here she's doing better.”

“That's good,” Cat said.

Will limped around the wagon with Zephyr wrapped around his right arm. She let go and ran to Lynn. “What's wrong with him?”

“With who?”

“Him.” She pointed a shaking hand to Will's arms and legs. “Is he sick? Is he okay?”

“He's fine, Zephyr,” Lynn said. “Will's an Earth Curse. Like Peter was – ” She coughed and shot Cat a worried glance.

Cat cleared her throat and tried to ignore the sour gurgle in her stomach. “That's right, you've known Earth Curses a long time, Zephyr. You don't have to be scared.”

“I don't?”

Cat climbed from the wagon and ruffled her blustering hair. “Everything's okay.”

The message sifted into Zephyr's broken mind, stretching her tight face into a smile. “Everything's okay!” She hooked herself back onto Will's right arm.

He smiled. “Not so tight, Zeph. That one still works.”

Cat bit her lip. “Are you sore?”

“Yeah, but what else is new?”

“Come over here.” She pulled a thick roll of elastic bandages from their medical supplies. “Our previous Earth Curse was the best friend I've ever had. ” Cat stretched the bandages for Will to see. “We used to wrap his arms and legs in these to help with the pain. Want to give it a try?”

“Uh, sure. Why shrug experience, right?”

His left arm and leg were mostly stone with a thin layer of skin and little to no soft tissue beneath. The bones were unrecognizable and unlike Peter's limbs, there were no joints left to wrap.

Will cocked his head to one side. “Am I too stony?”

“No, no.” She shook her head. “I was thinking about Peter. He was three years older than you, but his symptoms were a lot less.”

“He got to stay home,” Will said. “I bet he ate as much as he wanted and slept on a real bed and didn't bang himself on weird-shaped doors his whole life.”

“You're right about that,” she said. His right arm still had bend, grip, and a little torque. Cat bound it from wrist to shoulder with an extra layer about his elbow. “How does that feel?”

Will flexed his fingers. “That does help a little, I guess. Bandages – who knew?”

“Let me know if you need them tightened.”

“Ah!” Zephyr dropped to her ankles and pulled her shaking knees to her chest. “What was that?”

Aiden frowned. “What was what?”

“An awful feeling!” She cringed. “Like my bones squirmed.”

Cat's heart leaped. “Your bones?”

The others flinched. Lynn's skin rippled over her swollen face and limbs, and a wave of light coursed up Aiden's face and down his arms. He hugged his arms. “It's him.”

A man dressed in a black cloak marched toward them from the desert with a knapsack on his shoulder. A familiar peace washed Cat like a cleansing slower. “Joshua!”

“Good morning,” he called as he neared. “Going my way?”

Cat smirked. “I thought you weren't allowed to travel with us.”

“I'm not allowed to be seen among the people.” Joshua pulled his hood back with a smile. “But you're actively avoiding people, aren't you, Catrina?”

“That's the plan.” She grinned. “Welcome to the team.”

Lynn and Aiden exchanged glances as he stored his pack in the wagon. Will looked him up and down. “Joshua huh? You're the weirdest looking guy I've ever seen.” He offered his right hand. “I'm Will. Pleased to meet ya.”

“The pleasure is mine.” Joshua shook, and Will yanked his hand back with a start.

“Ow!”

“Ahh!” Zephyr yelped. “What's wrong?”

“I don't know. He shocked me or something.”

“Sorry about that,” Joshua said. “It's a side-effect of the magic. My body's marked with the holy symbols. I'll try not to brush up against anyone.”

Lynn forced smile. “We appreciate it.”

Aiden tugged his hood to mask the glowing scar in his cheek. “Whatever. Let's go.”

The group resumed their positions with Joshua joining the Curses in back. Strawberry kept a steady pace across the smooth desert, kicking clouds of loose dust with her thick, powerful legs. Cat sensed the tension mounting behind her. Lynn cleared her throat with a cough. “So Joshua... what's it like to have the power of Our God in your hands?”

“It's its own burden, and a lot of responsibility.”

“From the little time we've spent together, I think you handle it very well.”

“Thank you.” He perked up, but his eyes made her flinch and he cast them back down. “Sorry.”

“Everyone else seems to know you already,” Will said. “Are you part of the mission?”

Joshua cut a smile. “I'm along for the ride.”

"Cool, the more the merrier!" Will's leg shifted into Joshua's line of sight. "Yow!"

"Sorry! Sorry again!"

"Can you wear a blindfold or something?" Aiden groaned.

Lynn sucked her teeth. "He didn't mean to."

"It's fine." Joshua closed his eyes and raised his tattooed hands. "I don't want to hurt you. I'll ride up front."

"Okay." The Water Curse shivered as he passed. "But don't feel like you have to."

He climbed over the partition into the seat next to Cat. She grinned with a shrug. "Sorry about Aiden. He's protective."

"I don't blame them at all." He slouched in the seat. "It's a weird situation, and they've tolerated a lot, already. Your friends are rare people."

"They're better than this world deserves."

"I agree. Few people are willing to give their lives for others."

Cat lowered her voice. "What's going to happen to them?"

"You mean at the chasm?"

"Lady Creven told us it's under her mansion, but other than that I don't know anything about what will happen there," she said. "Do you know anything? Are there any clues in the Runian history Malachi didn't write in his last letter?"

Joshua's dark eyes stared into the middle distance. “I know there's a long stairway that descends into a cave, and the void below is full of wrath and magic.”

“And that's where I talk to God?”

“Yes.”

“What about the sacrifice?”

“You'll know when you get there.” He cleared his throat and leaned closer. “I'm sorry that's not very helpful, but what I know only matters if you're there to experience it. Rest assured, you've all come here for a reason. You can find comfort in that.”

“I guess,” she said. “It's scary to think about.”

“You'll be all right.”

“Thank you for being here.” Her eyes stung. “I had a vision of me standing alone at the sacrifice. Now I know there will be somewhere there with me when it's all over.”

“There will be.” His starry eyes glinted. “I promise.”

Haze from the storm shrouded the horizon to the northeast. Strawberry forged a path across the flat country between Astonage and Castleton. Hours passed without a sign of life, save a team of mounted travelers barely visible at a distance. Cat whispered. “Are those Brushcasters?”

“Yes, they're on their way to their monastery.”

“How do you know?”

"I scouted the area earlier." He hopped from the wagon. "The monastery's mostly empty save the very young and very old. The rest of the Calligraphers are in Castleton where they're apparently following Lord Creven's orders. His militia forces have sealed the city gates on all sides. He has to know you're coming. We may have to improvise."

"Improvise?"

"Don't worry. I'm an expert at going unseen." He pulled his hood back up. "When you reach the Outer Bend, get on it going east. It'll be easier on the wagon to take the paved road. I'll hop out and cover our tracks."

"Are you sure it's safe?" She eyed the specks again. "They can see us from there."

"We'll be alright, trust me."

He walked beside the wagon until they came upon the beltway marked by treads from previous travelers. Cat fit the tires to the ruts and resumed the trek eastward with Joshua behind, blasting wind from his open palm. The spells stirred the layer of dust, erasing their tracks. Curses watched out the open tent flaps.

"So you use magic, too, huh?" Will asked.

"That's right."

"Up to now, I thought only Brushcasters knew magic."

"Technically no one should know it," Joshua said. "It's not meant for mortal use."

"I'm surprised to hear a Runian say that." Aiden snorted. "Aren't you guys supposed to be holy?"

"The Runians are special, but that doesn't make them holy," Joshua said. "The Prophets could use magic because they were partially divine, but magic in the modern sense is sinful. Heritage has muddied their judgment."

Will frowned. "Muddied it?"

"Time erodes everything, even ideals. The same thing happened to the Calligraphers." He turned his hand and erased his footsteps with a swirl. "five hundred years ago, everyone knew magic was a sin. Now only the rich and the powerful know, and they don't seem to care."

"You seem to care." Lynn swallowed. "You know, but you're still using it."

Joshua shot another blast of air. "That's very true."

"You're aware you're making Wind Curses, right?" Aiden said.

Zephyr snapped from a daze. "Wind Curses? Where?"

"Not here, Zephyr," he said. "Sorry."

She settled. "That's okay."

"Hopefully no one will be making Curses of any kind after tonight," Cat said.

"After tomorrow," Joshua corrected. "We'll have to camp before Castleton."

"Camp?" She stopped the wagon and waited for him to appear around the side. "Shouldn't we go in tonight? Use the cover of dark?"

"Rest is going to be more important than cover." He climbed back into his spot beside her. "That said, we still have to get in the electrified fence."

Cat smirked. "Do you have lightning powers, too?"

"Would you be surprised if I said yes?"

"At this point, probably not."

Joshua grinned. "We'll see when we reach the Spoke."

They crossed open country for the rest of the afternoon and reached the edge of Castleton's farmland just before dark. Warning signs hung on the electrified fencing, reminding the Valley who owned the land inside. Sunset wreathed Lord Creven's mansion in a halo of blazing light and cast a long, tapered shadow over the acres of farmland beyond.

The electric fence was closed across the East Spoke. A fuse box stood open on the inside, where the gate itself was latched with simple hinge.

Lynn leaned out of the covered wagon with a gulp. "I guess they want to keep us out."

Aiden slouched with a pout. “If by 'us' you mean Curses, then probably yeah.”

“It's a property line,” Joshua said. “Creven uses it to keep normal people from stealing his crops. He closed the fence when he sealed the gates. They'll know if we break it.”

Cat frowned. “So what do we do?”

“Make it look like an accident.” Joshua hopped from the front seat. “Want to give me a hand?”

“What do you need?”

“More dirt.” Joshua's palms glowed with white light. “Enough to pack a punch.”

Wind from his hands stirred the powder on the ground. Cat handed Lynn the reins and climbed down beside him. She twisted an angular earth rune out of her string. The thread flashed, tugging an uncomfortable knot in her stomach. Soil and gravel spilled from the surface into Joshua's whirlwind. He kept the wind low. “Open the gate on my signal.”

Cat sneaked across the open road and hovered near the gate's entrance. The East Spoke extended all the way to Castleton's wall five miles away. The fence hummed in her ear as Joshua drew the twisting air in a broad circle, mimicking the birth of a real dust devil and gathering more powder from the surface.

“You ready, Lynn?”

“Yes, sir.”

“Get the wagon through when it's open.” He swept the twisting dirt toward the fence. The twister rustled a wheat field on the other side of the fence. Stones clinked off the metal links. Joshua took a deep breath and swept it over the open road to the fuse box where the stone battered the works.

There was a spark. The fence powered down. Joshua released the storm. “Now!”

Cat unlatched the gate and slid it wide. Lynn gave Strawberry a lash and the wagon hurried inside. Joshua jogged past it.

“In this field!” He removed two slats from the chest-high wooden fence. “The wheat's high enough to hide in.”

Lynn shook her head. “It's too thick.”

Joshua waved his hand. The earth wriggled and churned over, folding the stalks down into a woven mat of living plants. He gestured again and the carpet extended ahead of them into the field.

Aiden puffed steam. “Showoff.”

Cat locked the gate back where it was. A warning light flashed in the dusty electrical box. Cat checked over her shoulder and snapped the fuse lever. The fence hummed back to life and the warning light switched to a peaceful green.

She walked behind the wagon as Joshua led them in gentle curves behind the falling grass. The living mat was stiff and springy under her boots. A quarter mile in, Lynn drew Strawberry to a stop. Joshua spread his hands wide and the wheat fell in a spiral to form a wide clearing with a patch of fresh soil at its center.

Will winked at Cat from the wagon. “He sure is handy!”

Joshua snapped his fingers. A campfire sprung to life.

Aiden climbed down. “He's a magical one-man show.”

“We'll definitely be safe in here!” Lynn said with a leaky grin. “Thank you, Joshua! I'll make us dinner. What would you like?”

“It's been my pleasure, Lynn. Your favorite is fine.”

“My favorite is soup.”

“Then we'll have that.” Joshua met her eye. She shivered and he looked away. “Sorry. You guys lower the canvas on the wagon. I'll be right back.”

He left up the folded path. Aiden's cracked face pulsed within his hood. “I don't like him.”

“Don't like who?” Zephyr popped her head out of the wagon. “I hope it's not me.”

“No, not you, Zephie,” Lynn said. “You're being protective, Aiden, and thank you, but Joshua has helped us a lot today.”

“He's plotting something, I can feel it.”

“Who is?” Zephyr asked. “Do you mean me?”

“No, Zephie,” Lynn said again. “How about you find our soup pot for us? It should be under one of the benches.”

Zephyr bit her knuckle, thinking hard. “Soup pot? Okay.”

She vanished into the wagon and Aiden stormed to Lynn. “You're actually making soup?”

“Joshua asked – ”

“I don't care about Joshua!” He raged. “I can't eat soup – Will can't eat soup!”

“I can try to eat soup!” Will called.

“Hush, you guys,” Cat bade. “We're supposed to be hiding.”

“No, we're supposed to be storming Castleton,” Aiden said. “Why are we stopping? Because Joshua said so?”

“Because after this, it's over,” Cat said. “Tomorrow we go face-to-face with God and I know as much about what to do now, as I did when I started. Joshua's the only resource I have. I have to trust him, I'm sorry.”

The light in Aiden's face dulled.

Cat took a breath. “Let Lynn make her soup, I'll fix something else for you and Will.”

She returned to the wagon. Zephyr sat in the far corner, staring at her shaking hands. The Wind Curse unfocused her eyes with a sob. “Where am I?”

“You're with us, Zephyr.” Cat pulled a strained smile. “Lynn sent you in here for a pot.”

Tears filled the girl's eyes. “Who did?”

"It's okay, come here."

The Wind Curse crawled into Cat's arms. Individual ribs pressed through the Curse's thin skin as she lifted the girl from the wagon like a child.

"Give her here." Will slid to the ground against the wagon's right tire. "She can sit with me. I'm not doing anything."

"Thanks." Cat draped Zephyr against his healthier right arm. The Wind Curse leaned into his shoulder and stared into the low fire. Cat pulled the canvas from the covered wagon and assembled sandwiches in the bed as Lynn assembled a stew using dry meat and lemongrass. The Runian mansion provided them with new flatware and utensils. Cat examined the bowls in the firelight – white porcelain with gold inlay and a delicate floral pattern.

Joshua returned to the clearing, righting wheat stalks as he went. "That covers our exit. We're practically invisible."

Aiden bit into his sandwich. "So no one's going to see this fire you started?"

"Not if we keep it low."

"What about the smoke?"

"It's magic. Nothing's burning."

"Okay, smart guy." Aiden vented steam through his nose. "If you're so strong, what's stopping you from conducting this whole mission yourself? You can make a dirt wagon and wind horses and parade us all into Castleton shooting fire from one hand and water from the other."

"That would break my own rules." Joshua met Aiden's eye and stared as he flinched. "I'm sorry you're intimidated, but I'm doing all I can to help you – probably more than I should. Magic is the tool I have. Forgive me if I use it."

"Fine. Sure. Whatever." Aiden shuddered.

Joshua sighed. "I'm sorry if I've upset anyone else. I'm powerful, but I'm still bound by the limits of my body and the rules of my house. Once you get into the city, I can't be seen. Let me help you while it's possible. I'll do whatever I can."

"Thanks, Joshua," Cat said. "Really."

He beamed gratitude and took a seat at her side.

Lynn filled the bowls with soup and Cat passed them around. Zephyr ignored hers to continue staring into the fire with a vacant expression. Cat set it at her feet and offered one to Will. "Are you sure you want to try? Spoons were the first thing Peter had to give up."

"I won't know until I give it a shot." He freed his arm from Zephyr and pinched the spoon in his hand. Cradling the shallow bowl in the crook of his left arm, he dipped the utensil but lost his grip and knocked the rest of the bowl to his lap. "Ahh!"

"You okay?" Joshua asked.

"Yeah, it's this hand..."

Joshua rose to his knees. “Let me see it.”

He removed the elastic wrappings and pressed his fingers into the stony growth at the base of Will's right thumb. His palm flashed white and Will yanked the hand back. “Whoa! What'd you do?”

“Try it now.”

The thumb flexed easily across his palm. “Wow!”

Lynn's watering eyes widened. “I don't believe it.”

“It works again, see!” Will flexed his thumb at her.

“You healed him?” Cat grabbed Joshua's arm. “Teach me how to do that!”

“It's not healing. Not really,” Joshua said. “I moved the stone that was there, I didn't change it back to flesh.”

“You shifted his insides?” Aiden asked. “That's impossible.”

Joshua smirked. “I can help you, too, if you'll let me.”

“No way!” Orange light pulsed through Aiden's face and neck.

Lynn sucked her lip. “He helped Will. Let him try.”

Embers burned deep in Aiden's wounded cheek. Joshua cracked his knuckles and met Aiden on the far side of the fire. His palm glowed. He opened his hand and slapped the Fire Curse across the side of the face. The flesh hissed under Joshua's hand.

Aiden leaped back. “What the – ” The open wound on his right cheek was cauterized flat. Smooth skin reflected the firelight without wrinkle or scab. Aiden stroked it, dumbfounded. Embers caught at the corners of his eyes. “How did you...”

“You're welcome.” Joshua cut a grin. “Anyone else?”

“Me?” Lynn cleared her throat. “If it's alright, I mean.”

“What would you like?”

“I don't know if I should.” Lynn coughed. “See, when I was abandoned, I lost my memory.”

“And you want it back?”

“No! I mean....” She cleared her throat with another cough and squeezed water from her dress. “My friends in Water Town could remember being healthy. I can't recall a time when I wasn't already sick and I've always wondered what it was like to take a deep, clear breath. Is that in your ability?”

He smiled. “Sit up nice and straight.”

She blushed purple but did as she was told. Joshua placed his glowing hands on her back.

“Whenever you're ready.”

Lynn drew a lungful of air, her chest expanding without a sputter. She breathed out and back in, holding the breath as long as she could as veils of water streamed from her hair and closed eyes. Joshua removed his hands. She exhaled with a cough, tears of emotion reddening her pooling eyes. “Thank you.”

Joshua squeezed her shoulder. “I'm sorry it was temporary.”

"What about Zephyr?" Will asked. "Don't forget her!"

"Yes." Lynn wiped her dripping face. "Do something for her."

"What do you suggest?"

"Let's ask!" Will nudged the Wind Curse beside him. "It's your turn, Zeph! What do you want?"

She didn't respond, her mind held captive by the fire.

"She's not like the others," Cat said. "Her body is turning to air. Her mind has...evaporated."

"My hands can't put back what's not there," Joshua said.

"Try anyway," Lynn begged.

Aiden's eyes glowed from beneath his hood. "There has to be something you can do."

Joshua regarded him with a meager smile and knelt in front of Zephyr. She stared through his chest toward the hypnotizing flame. He brushed through her billowing hair, tipped her chin and looked deep into her eyes. Zephyr stared back as he sank down on his ankles and pressed his hands gently to the sides of her head. His palms glowed. Zephyr gasped.

"Our God!" She blinked in wonder. "What beautiful stars!"

Chapter 36

Joshua's palm glowed against Cat's shoulder as it maintained the campfire. She cuddled under his arm, warm and grateful. Night passed in a moment. He shook her gently. “It's time to go.”

She buried her face in his shirt and inhaled the smell of incense. “Do we have to?”

“Having second thoughts?”

“Always.” A ribbon of dawn spilled color over the eastern mountains. Cat resigned herself with a sigh. They roused the others and ate a silent breakfast around the fire. Melancholy lingered on the Curses' faces. Cat wet her lips to speak, but was at a loss for encouraging words. Speaking to Joshua was easier. “So how are we going to get into Castleton? Lady Creven said the checkpoint guards were her agents, but that won't help us if the gates are locked.”

“Leave that part to me,” he said. “You five should concern yourselves with what you do once you're inside. Yesterday, patrols walked the major roads. You can't take your wagon, you'll have to use the alleys.”

Aiden's eyes steamed. “We have to walk?”

“Unless you want to brute-force it. Of course, every Calligrapher in town will find you if you try that.”

“We're slow enough, they'll catch us anyway.”

“Not if you are careful.”

“He's right, Joshua,” Cat said. “It's an ascent on hard pavement. There's got to be another way.”

The light in Joshua's hand dimmed as the campfire died. “Can you fight off a city full of monks on your own?”

“I won't be on my own,” she said. “I'll have you with me.”

“I'll be with you, but not how you're thinking.” His brow knit. “The Runians don't 'exist' in this world until the sacrifice is complete. I can't be seen by the people, I've told you this already.”

Cat stiffened with disappointment and a touch of shame. “I thought maybe because this was the end...”

"This IS the end, but not until you get to the heart of that mountain." Joshua smiled. "I'll wait for you there. For now, we should get going."

The Curses didn't argue. They piled in the wagon as Cat took her spot in the driver's seat. Joshua righted the wheat behind them and jogged forward to lead them down private roads and driveways, deeper into the farmland as the city loomed closer. Sunlight slanted over the mountainous city, crowning the mansion above in white and casting shadow across the party. Joshua stopped Strawberry at a gravel road along the base of the city wall. "Leave the wagon here."

"Leave it?" Lynn stopped stroking Zephyr's wild hair with a cough. "What about Strawberry?"

"She'll be fine."

"How do you know?"

"Trust me," he said.

Lynn gulped with a glance to Aiden. Will cleared his throat and swung his stiff left leg to the ground. The other three followed, uncertain. Cat hated to leave their traveling home behind. She made sure Peter's atlas was safe under the front seat and the scripture was safe in her pocket, and tried to calm her nervous stomach with a deep breath of cold air.

Joshua flexed his back and arms as he approached the whitewashed outer wall. He shut his eyes and pressed his glowing palms flat to the stone. The bricks shook beneath his fingers, shedding mortar and paint. Sweat broke along his brow. Every muscle tensed as Joshua drew his hands apart. The layers of brick shifted and folded back like bark from an old tree, until a gap large enough for Will's massive shoulders opened in the barrier. Cat stepped close and peered through to the city street beyond.

"Go on." Joshua grit his teeth, every muscle in his upper body tense and his eyes as hard as flint. "I'll close it behind you."

Cat swallowed hard. "Okay, I'll go first."

"It was an honor to meet all of you." Joshua strained. "Peace and great love."

"Peace and great love..." Zephyr muttered.

Aiden nodded farewell. "Thanks, Joshua."

"Thanks, Josh." Will knocked his left shoulder on the exposed brick as he passed through the gap.

Cat whispered back through the opening. "Be careful."

"I'll see you at the top." He relaxed his arms and the doorway closed between them without a seam. The whole of God's Valley closed and Cat and the Curses were sealed within the occupied city.

Vending carts and silent storefronts lined the streets leading upward, their owners preparing for another normal day. Sunlight crept along the eastern curve of the hilltop and reflected harshly off metal roofs. Tiny black-clad Calligraphers marched between the buildings on the streets above. Cat steeled her resolve. “Get to the alley.”

They slipped into the sheltered narrows and began the ascent. The naked backs of the buildings were red like the quarry below the Runian mansion, spotted with gray and white brick patches. Wires snaked from the walls to the ground where massive copper pipes carried water to the fields. The group matched Will's labored pace as they inched up the hill, pausing at every shaft of daylight to check for witnesses. Early risers in suits and dresses walked the main streets on either side of the alley. Cat held her breath whenever one paused, but the shadow of early morning protected them from view.

Will panted and heaved, Zephyr tight on his arm with the bones of her forehead pressing hard against her puckered brow. Lynn coughed into the meat of her swollen arm, thick lungs forcing air in through accumulated water. The bandage about her chest wound was stained brownish. She put the others between her and Aiden, who was moving well despite his ruined feet. Cat could feel his body heat on the back of her sweaty neck as they paused for breath at the first cross-street.

When Cat and Peter first arrived, Castleton was full of shoppers. The bustle masked their progress, and those who noticed she had a Curse with her kept their distance. With three more Curses and wide empty streets, there was no way to sneak across open road without being seen. Teams of Calligraphers walked the boulevard on either side. Their simple black collars marked them as low-level monks, but the brushes on their backs meant they were still dangerous. A knot tightened in Cat's throat.

"We need a diversion." Aiden whispered.

Will wheezed. "Diversion? Like what?"

Cat ground loose hair between her teeth. It had to be something to draw both Calligraphers and commoners. She un-spooled her string. "Cross when the coast is clear and keep going as long as it's safe. I have an idea."

Aiden nodded. "Good luck."

Cat tapped each of the Curses as she sneaked back down the alley. Zephyr's breath quickened. "Is she leaving?"

"She's running an errand," Lynn choked. "Stay close to Will."

Cat trotted back through the alleys until she spotted a newspaper stand parked at the edge of the street. An artist's rendering of a young woman filled the front page. Above her menacing stare read the headline "WANTED: FALSE PROPHET. LORD CREVEN OFFERS REWARD." Cat sneered, readied her string, and blasted the news stand with a torch of red flame.

The thin paper ignited in a flash. Pages peeled in layers of black tinged with orange, tossing ragged bits like dying moths. The fire spread to the wooden stall and up a nearby shutter to the building behind. The shop owner screamed. Cat raced back up the alleys as a pair of Calligraphers arrived. The monk slapped her wet brush on the pavement, painting a casting circle with a water rune that birthed a ten-foot water golem. The creature resembled a lizard with a long, undulating body and spindly legs. Cat gulped and jumped a pile of garbage on her way up the hill.

The Curses were gone when she reached the cross-street. People trotted past, drawn by the commotion. Cat joined their throng long enough to reach the opposite block of alleys. Apartment buildings towered on either side of the narrow path, the copper water pipes rose from the ground to the roofs, making way for trashcans and general clutter behind the residences. Cat kept an eye on the alley-facing windows. Common townsfolk moved behind them as shadows, unaware of the chaos downhill from them. A door opened ahead. Cat ducked into an adjoining alley as a housekeeper emptied a dustbin into the road.

“Eeeeeeek!”

A girl's scream reverberated between the buildings. Cat recognized the airy tone and bolted back into the alley. “Zephyr?”

“Hey!” The woman with the dustbin went white. “You're the False Prophet!”

Cat dodged her doorway and raced toward the screaming. Warm light lit the bricks ahead. It was too intense for daylight. Cat hooked her string around her palm and dodged another knot of commuting locals to reach the sharp incline. The Curses were trapped in the open along the next road. A fire golem shaped like a bird towered over them, its massive body supported on two spindly legs.

"Stand back!" Cat wove a water rune and bisected the monster's legs above the knee. The golem's flailing body dropped. Cat pushed the Curses ahead of her into the next block of alleys. The space between the buildings was narrower than ever. Flags and clotheslines stretched from rooftop to rooftop. Cat kicked over a pile of boxes and assessed her group. Will and Aiden were panting. Fresh cracks laced the Fire Curse's face, glowing bright and steaming with each breath. Brown sweat coated the Earth Curse like a second layer of skin. Lynn coughed into her forearm and pressed Zephyr's screaming face into the front of her wet dress.

"I'm sorry!" Lynn sputtered. "We tried to hurry."

"I know you did." Cat said. "They know where we are, now. We have to move."

The party doubled their pace, burdened by hurt feet and heavy limbs. Cat kept her string ready and her eyes keen for golems. White light flashed on the painted houses on the left and right. A swell of flame boiled to life behind them, revealing a squat fire golem with eight ropy legs that filled the space with waving fire. Cat fired water, severing the legs on its right side.

Another fire golem rode in on the left, its head like a battering ram. The monster tossed a waste bin into the party. Cat deflected it with her water spell. Aiden leaped away from the spray. “Ah!”

Lynn coughed. “Aiden!”

“Sorry!” Cat cried.

“Do your thing, Cat!” Will shouted and bent his bulk around the three other Curses. She reset her string and hit the fire golem with a water spell. Pain swelled behind her eyes. Her energy drained through the glowing string. The water spell began to fail as it bored a hole in the creature's broad forehead. Arms shaking, Cat bent the stream left and diverted the golem head-first into the wall.

Zephyr screamed and pointed downhill where more golems of all sizes and shapes charged between the towering buildings. Drying clothes caught fire. Glass cracked in the windows. Trash fluttered from their pounding feet and charging legs. Cat dropped the knots of her water spell and wove another as fast as she could.

She hit a human-shaped fire monster square in the chest. The golem reared back and a lanky, lizard shaped one to sneak under its leg. It was the same shape as the water golem painted to extinguish her newspaper fire. The monks were massing against them. Cat shouted over her shoulder. “Run for it!”

Aiden and Lynn took Will's arms hurried past the branching alleys. Cat blasted the fire golems as they came in range. Each flash from her string drained her strength. The wound in her side ached and spread warmth under her vest. She trotted in spurts up the hill as fire golems flooded in from the sides.

The birdlike golem with the spindly legs appeared. Cat aimed for its knees, but her water spell was too weak to cut through its legs. She focused on the knee of its right leg and the creature stumbled against the overhead roof. The affixed copper irrigation pipe puckered at its touch, spraying a cold mist onto the howling golems below.

Cat trained on the crumpled pipe like a magnet. She checked that the Curses were a safe distance and wove a hasty fire rune. The symbol flashed white and she aimed the flame at the sweating copper tube. The metal warmed a rosy pink and burst in a frigid explosion.

Golems screeched and withered under the falling liquid. Cat cut a self-congratulatory grin and raced after her friends, bursting pipes as she went. Fire golems swung in from the side alleys to be met with sparkling fountains of water. A river of ash and garbage ran downhill behind.

She rejoined the Curses at the next crossroads where a team of white-wigged militia men met them in the road. The lead soldier drew his sword. “Stop in the name Lord Creven!”

“Nope, sorry!” Cat blasted the attackers with a wind spell and hustled the group forward into the next alley. Lord Creven's mansion gleamed on the hilltop straight ahead. One more block and they'd be at the summit and on their way to God.

Cat's string knotted spell after spell. Her muscles strained but she plowed forward, tossing guards and breaking water pipes. The regular hiss of steaming fire golems followed her up the street. Water soaked her hair and clothing, adding weight to her weakened legs.

The militia soldiers ceased pursuit. Cat counted it a blessing and fell back to rest her limbs and cover their flank. Pale flashes of swirling light passed the alleys on either side. Cat set her string at an opening stage and raised her hands to the streets beside her. Nothing. Her heart 'woosh'ed through her ears and pounded in her neck. She checked the alley and locked eyes with a wind golem. Its snakelike body rolled in fine wisps from two piercing white eyes. Cat's weak soul wavered, drawn to the holy light. The wind golem broke her gaze and dashed off to scout the pathways ahead of her.

“They're surrounding us!” Cat called. She urged her friends onward, but their drawn faces were haggard. Will's front leg shook as he dragged his useless left half after Lynn and Aiden. Sores from the earlier splash branched like lightning over Aiden's face and neck. Lynn's coughing echoed about them as water poured from her eyes. Zephyr darted between them, absorbed in the panic. Lynn called for her between violent coughs.

The wealthy homes of the higher elevations waited at the end of their alley. Cat wedged under Will's left arm. “We'll do it together.”

“What's that?” Zephyr asked. Fear flashed in Aiden's eyes. A towering earth golem blocked their destination from view. The creature towered on its hind legs with a bent, muscular back and long sickle-like claws on its spindly forelegs. More stone golems appeared in the alleys on either side, their faceted bodies scraping paint off the brick walls as they squeezed past. A fourth earth golem emerged from the wall of water behind them, liquid streaming like a fountain between its shining white eyes.

“We're trapped!” Lynn sputtered. “What element kills earth?”

Will winced and shrugged. “Gravity?”

Cat slipped from beneath his arm and readied her string, but the combination of fear and exhaustion kept her fingers from obeying. She knitted a wind spell and thrust it at the golem blocking their exit. The magic wafted off its pointed face. The monster's eyes flashed and it shook the alley with a deep roar.

“You made it angry, at least,” Aiden said, but the sarcasm quivered in his throat.

Cat tried a fire and water rune with no obvious affect. The earth golem scraped its claws as it closed in. The earth golem behind them swiped with a barbed fist like a cudgel. Will pivoted to shield them. The blow grazed his over-sized left shoulder, ripping shreds of his leathery skin from the stone. Zephyr gripped his arm as brown blood swelled over his back.

Golems beat the walls of the alleys, slowed by the tight quarters and their own excessive bulk. Cat threw earth, wind, water, and fire at each of their shapes, but none of the elements damaged the stone. Like the golem under the waterfall, these creatures were meant to be permanent.

Cat's sight fizzled. A tone rang in the space between her ears as she threw a weak earth rune into the nearest golem's face. The light of the string drained the dregs of her strength. Her knees buckled. Lynn caught her from behind, but the comforting words she mouthed were lost in a high, persistent ringing.

A black shadow flashed overhead. Something tingled in the air and the stone golem bearing down on her reared back, clawing the air. Its bladed forearms raked the walls as its feet left the ground. A crack opened between the monster's blazing white eyes. The break radiated down its front. The creature screamed and broke into two equal parts. A figure leaped away as its eyes faded and died. He landed on a nearby roof, his hand glowing white beneath the fluttering edge of a hooded cape.

Cat gasped. “Joshua!”

He saluted with his shining palm and vaulted toward Lord Creven's manor, propelled upward on a puffs of magical wind.

Chapter 37

Cat hustled Aiden, Lynn, Zephyr, and Will through the side yards of the wealthy neighborhoods. Her heart pounded like a warning drum as they flit from drive to drive. Shapes moved between buildings. She searched the rooftops for dark shadows or hints of white light but found only shuttered windows and clear morning skies.

Will leaned heavy on her shoulder. His right leg was swollen stiff from the sprint up the mountain. Zephyr steadied his right arm as they padded the cobblestone. “Is he okay?”

“I'm cool.” Will winced. “It's fine.”

“Hush!” Aiden threw a hand out to stop them. “What's that?”

Breath caught in Cat's throat. The road was empty. The rooftops were clear. “What's what?”

“That!” He pointed up an empty side street.

Lynn gulped. “I don't see anything.”

“There!” He spun on his blistered feet. “It's gone again.”

“Lynn, help Will.” Cat ducked from beneath his shoulder.

“No, I'm okay.” Will shifted weight to his heavier leg. “Zeph will help me.”

Zephyr's worry vanished. “I'm helping!”

Cat pulled a knot from her string and stretched it between her hands. Her muscles were weak and rubbery from the charge up the mountain. She edged between Aiden and Lynn. “Where is it now?”

“Over there,” he pointed to an empty gap between mansions. “It's moving too fast.”

“What did it look like?”

“I'm not sure. By the time I notice, it's always gone – ”

A strange pull nagged her from somewhere on the right. Cat raised her hands to the source, but there was nothing.

“You saw it?” Aiden asked.

“No. I felt it, though.”

The pull drew again on the right. Cat knit the body of a fire rune into the string, holding the final exchange like a trigger. A pair of tunneling white eyes shone beneath a hanging balcony, but vanished before she could fire.

"They're wind golems," Cat said.

Lynn gargled. "Why aren't they attacking us?"

"I don't know." Cat lowered her arms. "Let's move."

Wind golems surrounded the party on all sides, appearing and disappearing in brief flashes. A rat-shaped golem bounded into the road and vanished in a puff of air. One of the lizard creatures snaked from behind and did the same. More bodies emerged. Cat counted twenty different animal shapes; rodents, birds, reptiles, even a fish-shaped one with three legs like a tripod. The magical bodies shimmered like swirling mist in the slanted light. A horse-shaped one charged the group. Cat unleashed her loaded fire rune, but the creature vanished before the flame could touch it.

"What's happening?" Lynn shivered.

"We're being hunted," Aiden said.

"Worse." Cat set her string again. "Being herded."

Another golem dashed along their left. The wind from its body threw Will off-balance. Zephyr clung to his lumpy torso as a second dashed near. Cat shot a fire spell as it passed and caught the creature between the eyes. The golem burst on impact with a high-pitched squeal and a flash of white light. The other golems converged, encircling Cat and the Curses in a whirlwind. Cat threw fire spells into their midst, popping one or two like balloons. The number of golems increased faster than she could destroy them and the world beyond the tornado blurred into a pale curtain of thickened air and dust.

The temperature dropped. Cat's fire spells were sucked into the cyclone and extinguished. Weakness and nausea clawed her throat. She shut her eyes to fight dizziness and started the next figure from a new opening stage. Wind golems blurred past, their shining eyes a streak of magic. Cat threw an earth rune into their midst, showering the wall of golems in fine gravel. The stones whipped through the racing air and scattered the pavement. Bits struck the golems in their glowing eyes. The creatures burst in puffs of wind and flashes of light.

Shapes moved beyond the thinning wall of golems. An army of monks gathered above them on the street. The wind golems dispersed as an older woman wearing a white stole over her black tunic stepped into a massive casting circle. The verses coiled from an empty space where the elemental symbol was missing. The senior monk stopped before the blank cobblestones, the bristles on her weathered brush gleaming with wet paint. “False Prophet!”

Fear prickled Cat's spine. She stretched the loop of string between her hands.

“I am Senior Monk Vivian Asher,” the woman said. “For the murder of our Holy Elder, the defilement of holy scripture, and the perversion of nature in the form of unordained magic, I find you guilty of the worst crimes known to the Order of Holy Calligraphers."

The monks beside her tightened their grips on their brushes. Hatred and disgust smoldered in their eyes.

"As written in our scriptures, I offer a chance to repent," Vivian said. "Submit yourself willingly to punishment, and you will find redemption in our monastery. Refuse and be imprisoned."

Cat's palms were wet and clammy. Exhaustion from the climb ached in her arms and lungs. The scripture deep in her skirt pocket lay heavy across her hip. She tightened her fists around her string and took a deep breath. "Ms. Vivian Asher," her voice evened with each word. "I'm Catrina Aston, descendant of the man who killed the Prophet Malachi. I am a child of sinners who has come down from the mountains. My friends are the human embodiment of magic. I have the power of our absent God stretched between my hands. I didn't kill your Elder, I have fulfilled your scripture, and your magic is every bit as sinful as mine."

Vivian's knuckles whitened around her staff. "Repent!"

"I will," Cat said, "but not to you."

She balled her string in one hand and pulled the scripture case from her pocket. Malachi's name glinted in the morning light, its gold script flashing recognition across Vivian's face.

“I know you haven't read this,” Cat said. “It's from your highest library. If you give me a moment, I'll prove I'm a real Prophet, not a false one. God's coming back. Your Elder knew. He tried to kill me to prevent it.”

Vivian's eyes slit. “Our Elder was a wise and upstanding man. You are a criminal and a liar, and you stole our holy magic to defeat our leader and bring us to ruin!”

“You're right.” Cat clenched her chattering teeth. “I did come to defeat you, because you're destroying the world and causing Curses. In the name of the Prophets and the one true God, I demand you let me pass!”

“You blasphemer!” Vivian shouted. “Have it your way!”

The senior monk swirled her brush and slapped the bristles to the pavement. In a single swift motion, she knotted a perfect water rune and lit the open street with a flash of holy light. A ball of liquid formed above the center of the ring. It gurgled and swelled, growing four legs and a tail, like a twenty-foot wildcat poised over the painted scripture. The spell burned like a cursive fuse as the creature opened its eyes and arched waves along its sleek, powerful back.

Aiden froze before the towering water golem, horror slicing cracks of fire about his flaming eyes. Zephyr's bugging eyes rolled back as she screamed and fainted into Lynn's arms. The Water Curse sputtered syllables through wet coughs. “Cat!”

Cat thrust the scripture back in her pocket. “Run, you guys!”

The army of Calligraphers wet their brushes and painted circles on the ground. Golems of all four elements knit together out of nothing and followed her water monster down the hill. Cat blasted earth spells at the wind golems and water at the fire golems. An earth golem raised its fist and she ducked left to avoid the blow. The creatures followed her across the street, away from the Curses. An army of white-wigged soldiers blocked her path.

“Miss Aston!” Lord Creven sat on horseback with his sword high over his head. “Give up, you're surrounded!”

The feline water golem pounced and knocked Cat backwards onto the stone floor. Impact rang like a bell in her ears. Creven's soldiers pressed he Curses to a garden wall.

The feline golem closed its frigid mouth around her waist. Water soaked through her vest and skirt. The wound in her side screamed in the icy cold, the shock drawing memories of Chalsie-Veneer where the Elder's golem nearly drowned her in the waters of its face. Vivien's pinned her arms and legs together but kept her head free to the air. She screamed and grunted as it lifted her skyward and returned to its master's right hand.

“Make it kill her!” Creven shouted.

“No,” Vivien said. “She's coming with us.”

“That's not the plan!”

"It was our plan. You thirst for blood, but we are holy messengers, not executioners." Vivian sheathed her brush. "The heretic comes with us. The Curses are yours."

Cat thrashed. Lord Creven grunted and snapped his fingers. The soldiers drew their swords. Lynn clutched Zephyr's limp body as she and Aiden backed into Will. The Earth Curse moved his stone arm to shield them as blades flashed on every side.

A massive earth golem leaped over the nearby mansion and crashed into the street above the gathered Curses. The impact scattered Lord Creven's forces and rippled through Vivian's water golem. Cat sloshed and rolled in the creature's mouth. Shouts from monks and soldiers muffled Lynn's panicked coughing as the earth golem caged the four Curses within its thick, club-like forelimbs, short squat back limbs, and deeply swayed back. White eyes searched the crowd from deep between massive stone shoulders.

Vivian gasped in shock. "That's – "

A fire golem with the same swayed back and thick forearms bounded over the rooftops to confront the Castleton forces on the earth golem's left. A water golem followed, hedging the monastery forces from the south. It raised its mallet-like fist and struck at the field of active casting circles. A dozen golems wailed and perished. Broken flecks of white paint from their ruined circles floated through the water golem's legs like confetti.

"Retreat!" Creven shouted, but the monks and soldiers forgot their orders in the confusion. Cat took a deep breath and tucked into a ball within the water golem's mouth, freeing her arms from her sides. The chaos warped within the waters of the creature's head. Cat pulled her string loose, fingers numb and stiff from cold, and worked a sloppy wind spell. Light flashed in the rippling water. The creature's face exploded with the force of a small bomb, destroying one of the water golem's blazing eyes, and expelling Cat at speed. She tumbled toward the pavement when a cold wind rushed beneath her.

The air was soft and solid like a pillow. She stared through thin air to the ground ten feet below where people and golems dashed. The invisible platform lifted her higher, over the assembly, to the eyes of a massive wind golem with the same wide shoulders.

Trace Hayes stood, brush drawn, on the golem's transparent back. "Miss Aston!"

Cat sat in the creature's fist. "You!"

"Yes!" He saluted with the handle of his black brush. "Your escort has arrived!"

Vivian's ruined water golem twitched, its remaining eye tunneling deep and wild as righteous anger overwhelmed it. The casting circle that bore it burst into white flame as the water golem roared and bounded toward Cat and Trace with strength and madness.

“Lower!” Trace commanded. The wind golem bent on one elbow. Trace grabbed Cat on his way to the pavement and swept his brush across the yard. “Attack!”

All four of his matching golems charged the wrathful creature. Monks and soldiers cleared as the battle filled the street with steam, dust, and cold wind. Cat raced to the Curses, still huddled against the garden wall. Aiden reached to grab her shoulder but winced and recoiled from her wet sleeve. “Are you okay?”

“Yeah...” Cat's voice shook with cold and adrenaline. “You?”

“Terrified,” Will answered.

Lynn swallowed and held a sleeping Zephyr tight. “Alive.”

“Hayes!” Vivian's voice boomed. She swept her brush through her own blazing water spell and killed the wrathful golem in a wave of steaming water. Trace's four identical golems returned to their master. Vivian's eyes widened. “What have you done?”

“Stand down, ma'am.” Trace stepped between Cat and the senior monk.

“You raised multiple golems!” Vivian shouted. “They obeyed your verbal command! You've read the highest library!”

“I said stand down.” Trace held his black brush in both hands. “The Prophet is in my protection.”

“*False* Prophet,” Vivian hissed. “She killed the Elder.”

"She did not," Trace said. "The Elder fell by his own hand. I saw it. He used a miracle to kill another and met death himself."

"This is treason, Hayes!" Vivian roared. "You are a Holy Calligrapher! You've violated your oath!"

"My oath was to serve Our God and protect his scripture to the time of his return. This is the time. I defend his scripture with my life. If you challenge me, I will fight."

"Challenge is all you've left me," Vivian said. "Calligraphers!"

The monks behind her pulled their brushes.

"Defend our order!"

"Forgive me for this." Trace raised his brush. "Attack!"

New creatures rose from circles of white paint. Elements clashed and monsters swarmed. Each broken spell was painted anew as Trace's golems formed a line of defense.

"They'll cover us," Trace said. "Can the five of you move?"

"We're okay," Will replied.

"Lady Creven is waiting." Trace beckoned. "This way."

They slipped past a towering mansion into the sheltered garden behind, where four massive casting circles glowed with shimmering light. A carriage was parked along the inner wall where Paige waited with a pail of paint. One of the casting circles flashed and broke to ribbons on the ground.

Paige spotted Trace. "Master!"

"Ready more paint!"

"Yes, sir!"

Paige returned to the carriage. A young man with mousy brown hair climbed down from the driver's seat, wearing the same powder blue uniform as Lord Creven's soldiers.

Aiden halted. "Who's that?"

"Don't worry, it's Kaleb," Cat said. "He helped Peter and me through Lord Creven's mansion. He's working for our contact."

"Welcome back, your honor." Kaleb bowed. "The lady is waiting in the library. I have to get you back."

"We'll buy you some time," Trace said. "Speak to Our God. Set the world right again."

"Thank you." Relief and gratitude swelled in Cat's chest. "I never thought I'd owe a Brushcaster so much in my life."

"No thanks needed." He smiled. "Just put in a good word for me with the almighty."

"Master!" Paige emerged from the cab of the carriage with a fresh skin of paint and the Elder's gold brush strapped across her back.

Cat gaped. "Is that what I think it is?"

Trace frowned. "Paige? Why did you – ?"

"Because." She gripped the brush tight to hide the tremor in her arms. "You should have it."

Trace's brow furrowed. "What are you saying?"

"This was your dream! There's no one more qualified." She pressed the brush forward. "Please, Master. It was meant for you. I'll follow you anywhere. Take it before magic ends."

"Paige..." Trace glanced to Cat and the Curses, his eyes wet and humbled. The sound of battle raged beyond the garden grounds. Trace laid his hand on the gold brush. The light inside swelled and his whole countenance changed.

"I will take it on one condition." He set his wooden brush in Paige's empty hands. "Will you fight with me?"

Paige clutched the handle to her heart. "Yes, your honor."

Chapter 38

Kaleb rushed Cat and the Curses through the maze of hallways beneath Lord Creven's mansion as fast at the party could move. Servants wearing blue waist coats and powdered wigs ducked out of the way. Cat tried to ignore their stares as Kaleb made a beeline for the secret library.

"Lord Creven will know you're down here," Kaleb told Cat over his shoulder. "He'll know where you're heading as well. That's why we have to hurry."

"How do we get to the chasm?" Cat asked.

"The lady will show you."

They hurried up the dead-end hallway, through the padlocked door, into the stone antechamber. Cat stopped below the ancient stones, awash with memory. Kaleb hurried to the decorative library doors. “Lady Creven is waiting within.”

“What even is this place?” Will panted.

“Holy ground.” Kaleb's hands were shaking. “The stones that make up these walls and the door you see before you are all that is left of the Prophet's Mansion after Our God swept it from the land five hundred years ago.”

“God destroyed the Prophet's home?” Aiden asked.

“He destroyed their entire city.” Kaleb opened the lock and bowed to Cat. “The lady will escort you from here. I will stay here and guard the door.”

“You said Lord Creven will know where to find us,” Cat said. “What if he comes here with his army?”

Kaleb's sword clattered as he drew it from its sheath. “Then I will die to defend you.”

“Die?” A chill like a million needles stabbed down Cat's back. She grabbed Kaleb's shoulders. “No! Don't martyr yourself for me!”

“But your honor – !”

“Don't.” She looked to the others, dread gurgling through her gut. “There will be enough sacrifice today. No one else needs to die.”

Lynn swallowed a mouthful of water. “Cat...”

Cat took a deep breath and relaxed her grip. “Kaleb, do you remember what you asked me when I left? About your brother?”

His youthful eyes widened. “You saw Kory?”

“He told me he missed you,” Cat said. “You should go to Fire Town and get him.”

“Get him? But the law – “

“Is over,” she said. “When my friends and I are finished, God will be back and all the rules the Brushcasters used to control everyone will end. Go get your brother. Lady Creven says this prophecy isn't going to take away his illness; you should take care of him. Treasure the time you've got together while it lasts.”

Kaleb straightened and sheathed his sword with a determined nod. “Yes, ma'am, I will.”

“And when you get there – ” Aiden cleared his throat, his face flushed with smoldering embers. “Tell Sera and Tyson what happened to me. Tell them what we've done here. And...” The Fire Curse bit at the dead skin on his lip. “And that I'm sorry about Ildri.”

“Consider it done, your honor.”

Aiden returned a grateful nod and Kaleb hurried from the room. The exterior door locked with the snap of a padlock, cuing a flight of butterflies in Cat's stomach. She looked into the eyes of her four companions. “Thanks you guys. I can't believe...” Heart-sickness tightened within her, forcing breath from her lungs and tears from her eyes. "I doubt I'll be able to say this when you get downstairs..."

"It's okay, Cat," Lynn said. "We agreed to this, remember?"

Aiden's eyes gleamed as he nodded. "We do it together, like we promised."

"Songs and statues, right?" Will grinned.

Zephyr cheered. "Songs and statues!"

"They'll pale in comparison." Cat blinked back her tears and pulled open the library doors. Warm candlelight spilled into the cold antechamber. The library was more lived-in than she left it; leather boxes sat crooked and empty on the shelves. Parchment scrolls and note paper covered the center desk. Stumps of melting candles cast shadows across the Curse's faces as they stepped into the heart of the mountain.

Zephyr wheezed and clung to Will's heavy left arm. "I don't like it in here."

"Your honor." Lady Creven rose from a seat near the fireplace at the far end of the room. She wore a blue gown with a ruffle at the collar. The color gave life to her skeletal face. "Welcome back."

"Lady Creven," Cat said. "These are my friends."

"Four Curses." The lady's hand shook as it rose to her face. "I can scarcely believe it. The four elements. Here at last."

"They're Aiden, Lynn, Zephyr, and Will," Cat said. "They all know why they've come here. They're ready to give their lives to put magic back where it belongs."

"So what's next?" Will asked. "I mean, there's a lot of guys out there chasing us, what do we do, your grace? Your majesty? What do we call you?"

"Call me your servant, my friends," Lady Creven said. She touched a decorative clock on the mantle, triggering a hidden switch. The mantle swung aside, revealing an elaborately decorated elevator car attached to a pulley system in the ceiling. The shaft was carved of course, gray stone and extended deep into the bowels of the mountain with no visible bottom. The steady clank and thrum of machinery echoed deep within the cave. The lady opened the gilded door. "If you would, your honors. Our God awaits."

All six slipped into the carriage and began the journey downward. The lady kept her head bowed and her hand on the controls. Electric lamps in the walls popped on as the car descended past them. Zephyr whimpered like a lost child in the dark between the light bulbs. Will held her to his side with his heavy left arm. Cat tucked her loose hair behind her ear, wallowing in a mixture guilt and grief. The pound of metal on metal reverberated on the stone walls.

The elevator stopped at the mouth of a large, flame-lit stone cavern filled with clanking machinery. Pistons pumped water through a network of sweating pipes. Turbines spun and electricity arced from mechanism to mechanism. Modern technology built of steel, copper, and bronze rattled against the rough walls. Condensation dripped from stalactites along the roof as steam exploded from vents above a massive furnace where smokeless flame burned behind dusty glass.

At the center, surrounded by densely packed machines, stood a finely crafted pavilion. Delicate branches of braided stone lattices stretched between columns carved with rosettes. Vine-work similar to the motifs carved below the Goddess statues adorned an altar enshrined within the arbor.

Waxy circles and odd stains marked the surface of the altar. Cat touched the cold stone, drawn by a strange pull, like staring into the eyes of a Calligrapher's golem. It tugged her to the spot in the center of the archway where a thick metal slab was bolted to the floor.

"This path was built by Lord Uzzah," Lady Creven said. "It was intended to be his tomb."

Lynn swallowed hard. "Tomb?"

"Now it's my husband's factory. He uses the magic below to fuel his empire above." The lady pulled a lever grafted into the back of the altar. Steam puffed from surrounding pipes as the metal slab split and slid open in two parts. The metal vanished into housings beneath the polished marble, revealing a wide staircase curving deeper into the dark mountain.

The pull on Cat's consciousness increased exponentially. The tunnel whispered with muffled voices over the sound of the machines. She leaned against the altar to keep from falling. “What's this?”

“The path to the heart of the world,” Lady Creven said. “The last scrap of Our God left in this dying world.”

Will stood at the head of the steps with a low whistle. “Long way down.”

“I don't like it here.” Zephyr shivered. “Is this the windmill?”

“Yes,” Aiden said.

The reverence of the moment broke with a sudden crash. The clatter reverberated off the sweating machinery, followed by an alarm that echoed off the rounded walls. Lady Creven's face went white. “You must go.”

Aiden's eyes flashed. “What's that sound?”

“The service door,” the lady said. “My husband is here.”

The clamor sorted into clattering buckles and dozens of boot heels. Figures filtered through the machines. Cat ushered Will and Zephyr downward, assisted by Aiden and Lynn. She stretched the string between her hands. “Do we fight or run?”

“You run.”

“I won't leave you here.”

"I will seal the door behind you," Lady Creven said. "My husband trusts me, but not if he sees you. Speak to Our God. Finish what we've started."

The soldiers neared. Cat nodded. "Good luck."

Lady Creven pulled the lever once Cat was on the stairs. The stone doors puffed steam and inched from their housings. Cat tarried below, watching Lady Creven as the hatch closed between them.

Lord Creven's voice boomed off the copper piping. "What in Our God's name are you doing here, Orella?"

"Guarding the altar, Horace," she replied. "You told me it was in danger so I hurried – "

"The girl is in the building! Get back upstairs!"

The stone doors were still a foot apart when Lord Creven stomped into view. A filigreed sword hung at his hip. His vast stomach was covered in medals and golden seals. Cat ducked as he rounded the altar. The lord stopped short. His beady, hate-filled eyes snapped to the closing metal door.

His gaze struck Cat like lightning. "It's her!"

"It's not!" Lady Creven cried.

He tore his sword from its hilt. "Soldiers! Get the door."

"No!" Lady Creven shoved him back and jammed her foot into the side of the altar. The lever broke under her heel, jamming the metal doors with inches left to close.

"Orella, you witch!" Lord Creven regained his footing. "You've betrayed me!"

He thrust his sword into the lady's back. Lady Creven went rigid, pain and shock stretching lines across her face. Cat froze, heart pounding. The blade forced upward through the lady's ribs and out of her breast into the heated air. The lady's skin paled. Her arms went limp. Lord Creven removed his sword and she collapsed. Her body fell across the metal doorway. Cat backed against the wall as splatters of steaming blood dripped onto the cold stair.

"Get the crowbars!" Lord Creven kicked the body clear of the door. "The heretic can't be far!"

Chapter 39

Cat hurried her friends down the darkened stairs, away from Lord Creven's booming voice and the clank of tools on the metal door. She tried not to think of the blade bursting through Lady Creven's chest. The first death of many – the thought made Cat sick.

Lynn, Aiden, Zephyr, and Will puffed along the shallow stairs, heaving and coughing with each step. The wide path curved left with no landings or floors. The hand-carved path bent deeper and deeper into the cold mountain, lit by a string of naked light bulbs on wires overhead. Four copper pipes sweated in the chiseled walls, leaking a fine mist from the brackets to the gray stone floor.

The tug Cat felt from the top of the steps drew her like a magnet along the gentle curve. Energy drained from her, as if she was using magic, leeched into the walls and through the floor as she stumbled in a daze. The clinking of tools and thrum of machics faded to a faint echo behind them. The dark stairwell continued bending and descending until time and distance were irrelevant. The Curses started trailing. Lynn's coughs echoed like a bell toll, pulling Cat from sleepy melancholy. She stumbled to a stop against the wall. Shock sent lightning through her as the Curses inched into view.

Aiden clung to the wall as he descended, his exposed hands swollen with blisters and broken skin. The flat scar on his right cheek was ringed in fire where blackened skin curled in strips from his face. His quickened heart pulsed light down his limbs and up his neck where heat from the blood opened deep cuts. Stains from weeping sores spread steaming blotches through his white shirt. He staggered against the wall.

Cat reached for his arm, but his skin burned her fingers. He winced and jumped back.

Lynn's bare feet slapped the stone. She took a sharp breath and surrendered to a thick, gurgling cough. Each heave shook the water beneath her thin skin in waves about her bones.

Zephyr and Will moved the slowest. The Earth Curse scraped his heavy leg behind him, his body doubled in size. Stone bloomed in fractals from his injured shoulder. Brown tears zig-zagged his crooked face, but his eyes were determined behind a veil of mud. Zephyr clung to his right arm, her frame willowy and stiff. The Wind Curse's mouth opened and closed without speech as the bones of her skull pressed tight against her papery skin. He wide, unfocused, eyes sat deep in their sockets. She walked off the stair and toppled forward, the wind of her body swirling the mist as she fell. Cat caught her before she hit the stairs. The Wind Curse curled her gnarled hands in Cat's loose sleeve, her body light and thin as a bolt of sheer fabric.

Cat stammered. Wind from Zephyr's scalp stung tears from her eyes. “I'm so sorry.”

“Cat...” Aiden's voice rasped. His breath lighted the back of his throat like a furnace. “Don't.”

“But – ”

“I –” Lynn was interrupted by a fit of wet coughing. She covered her mouth and retched a gush of water between her bloated fingers. “I can't breathe – ”

“We'll rest here.” Cat trembled.

“No.” Will forced each word from his constricted lungs. “Gotta. Keep. Going.”

“I can't – ” Lynn collapsed on the stair, expelling more water. Aiden stepped away from the river, his brow creasing into deep cracks.

Cat cradled Zephyr in one arm and rubbed a hand across the Water Curse's back. “Maybe five minutes and you'll be better?”

“Don't be stupid.” Aiden's eyes glowed with fire. “There's no 'getting better.'”

“Then we'll take it slow.”

“I can't.” Lynn's eyes flickered behind walls of rippling tears.

Aiden cringed. “If we wait, we won't last.”

Lynn nodded, wiped her mouth, and used Cat's shoulder to stand. “Okay.”

“Lynn...” Cat's voice trembled, but there was nothing to be done. She hefted Zephyr's tiny frame and resumed their descent. The mist thickened as they went deeper. It rose past their knees until they found themselves wading waist-deep in white clouds. Aiden's pace slowed to a stumble in the damp air. Lynn hugged the opposite wall, heaving water between steps. The copper pipes hummed in the walls like a swarm of caged insects. Pressure muffled Cat's ears. The staircase continued downward in an endless spiral.

The pace slowed as the Curses worsened. A strange glow shone ahead of them, illuminating the mist into a white sheet of moving light. The light bulb chain ended in a single dangling wire.

Zephyr lay open-mouthed against Cat's shoulder, her lungs inflated and twitching within her withered body. Light from the swirling smoke cast through her skin, illuminating hollow bones beneath her paneled dress. Lynn coughed constantly, punctuated by choked breath and occasional sobs. Will's feet scraped the staircase with the grate of stone on stone. Cat pushed on through an emotional bog of sadness and guilt until she reached the final stair and stumbled into a blaze of white light.

A massive door stood in a tiny domed chamber. Rolling fog lapped the walls, lit by blocks of glowing text. Cat's heart trembled, pulled in all directions by sentences too bright to read. The copper pipes from the tunnel arched over their heads to the iron door where four oval-shaped plaques twitched in glass housings. The marble disks were each carved with an elemental symbol, surrounded by chisel marks and broken ornamentation.

A flush of hot rage welled in Cat's chest. Uzzah carved the Goddesses with the elemental symbols at their feet. The statues were in the valley, but his apology stood before her, bucking and writhing like pained animals within their metal fixtures. Flickers of flame, condensation, dust, and fog flicked the glass on their way into the copper piping toward the surface.

Aiden stopped on the step, orange light glowed through his closed eyelids. “What is this feeling?”

“Pain.” Cat set Zephyr on her feet and approached the vault door. The metal was icy cold. It breathed against her hand, bowing in and out within its frame with no hinges or handle.

Will wheezed from the steps. “Locked?”

“No.” Cat searched the cracks for an opening and found a spot on the right side where holes had been soldered closed. “Vandalized.”

Lynn swallowed. “Creven?”

“I don't know.”

Cat pressed on either side, knocked and pounded her fists, dug her nails in the cracks, and threw her body weight into the door, but the panel didn't budge. Her sweaty hand stuck to the metal. She peeled free with a grunt and unfurled her string.

Aiden's face flashed. “What are you doing?”

“Getting inside!” She knitted the first steps of the fire rune and aimed it at the door. The thread glowed white, releasing a column of flame with a size and power Cat was unprepared to hold. Her hands burned and arms shook. Mist swirled around her chest and channeled into the string, adding strength and power to the flame as it beat against the door. The ensconced fire symbol vibrated in its housing. The pipes whined overhead.

The temperature rose around her as Cat squared her stance. The metal frame expanded, cracking the wall in snaps and pops. The pipes burst and buckled. Water spilled from overhead. Aiden shouted and dodged away as stone broke fell from the walls.

The marble tablets bucked in their frames, the symbols beaming through the rioting cloud. Glass shattered. Copper pulled and twisted, ejecting the marble within. The symbols burst from the walls like freed doves, fell, and shattered on the floor. Spotlights of white light poured through the voids left by the tablets, adding strength to the spell. Every muscle in Cat's body fought to control the bucking string as her fingers bowed and blistered in the rumbling jet of flame.

Slabs of rock fell from the ceiling. Lynn coughed a muffled scream. Aiden shouted through the chaos. “Cat! Stop!”

“Not yet!” She shook, sweating and panting, and slid her feet toward the door. Mist cascaded around the frame, feeding light into her active spell. The string ground between her fingers, pulled tight by the excessive power. Blood ran across her palms as her arms shook, uncontrolled. She bore down all her will, tears streaming down her face. The string snapped. Cat flew backward in an explosion of light.

Cat lay prone, her skin hot and stinging as she drew deep breaths of cold air. Smoke and silence hung in the air. She pulled herself from the mist and faced an empty doorway filled with rolling, silver fog.

Chapter 48

A vast cavern extended beyond the broken door, too deep to see the back and too wide to see the sides. A jut of stone extended for a dozen feet past the iron door frame and into thin air above a white chasm rolling with ethereal light. The canyon stretched down for miles through layers of smoke and light into blackness. Magic resonated within the pit, expanding and contracting like a heartbeat in the center of the world.

Lynn's thick cough echoed into the distance. She collapsed to her knees before the doorway. Will struggled to shift his weight, brown blood streaming down his face. “Cat. Help.”

"Will..." Cat took his right arm but it was fused solid at the shoulder. She urged him forward. "Can you move?"

"Not," he gasped. "Not on my own."

"Here." Cat braced his chest across her back. Will yelped at the pressure but gave her his weight. She hooked her hands in the bandages around his swollen elbow. "Aiden, can you move?"

The inside of his head glowed like a lantern through the husk of his face. "Yes."

"Lynn?"

"Yes." She coughed up more water. "Slowly..."

"It's okay, we're almost there." Cat inched Will toward the door. "We'll do it together."

Will's damaged rib cage grew spines against her back. Fractured bones within his body sprouted with calcified tumors. Mud smeared across her face as sharp edges split skin and grew out toward the pit. Will's hips refused to bend. She dragged him to the open door frame and paused a moment for breath. Will groaned a low moan in her ear. "It hurts."

"I know." She rubbed his arm. "I'm sorry."

"We should be dead." Aiden drug his wounded feet through the mist, his breath steaming in a thin cloud from his mouth. "Anyone else would be dead. How can we live – "

He stepped into a pool of Lynn's water. His food crackled with a flash of light that lit his pant leg on fire. Aiden leaped against the wall, face burning in agony. The wound carved a path up his leg like a burning match. He stepped down on it with another cry.

"Aiden..." Lynn gargled, water pouring from her eyes, nose, ears, and mouth. She coughed and collapsed in a puddle of her own water. "I'm sorry..."

"Not now." He winced. "Keep going."

"Can't breathe..." she coughed. "Can't see."

"Can you see me?"

She met his lantern-like eyes, speaking in waterfalls. "Yes..."

"Then take my hand."

"No!" She flopped away from him, water sloshing inside her. "I'll hurt you – !"

"Lynn." He reached toward her. "It doesn't matter now."

The Water Curse groped for his light. He grabbed onto her hand with a billow of steam. Aiden cringed, but held tight. Lynn heaved lungfuls of water from her open mouth as she dragged herself to her feet. They crossed the threshold and ventured into the cave.

Zephyr hadn't moved from the staircase, her mouth agape and her eyes unfocused. Cat leaned Will on the door frame and took her by the hand. The Wind Curse toppled, collapsing like a rag doll into a pile of bones and skin. She stared ahead of her unblinking, without evidence of thought or feeling in her shallow, clouded eyes.

"Cat..." Will heaved. The stone grew spires into a thick yoke across his neck. Cat lifted Zephyr in the crook of one arm and wedged herself back under Will's chest. He took a step and snapped the bones in his shin.

"Ahh!"

Cat staggered under his weight, hugging Zephyr in both arms. Sobs echoed in his ribs. Cat pressed her cheek to the craggy cluster that once was his shoulder. "I've got you."

"It hurts."

"I know." She tried to sound calm. "I won't drop you."

Lynn's hand slipped from Aiden's grip and she fell with a slap on the ground. He reached after her. His outstretched hand burst into full flame. Fire crawled through his skin and clothes, burning the lavender cloth on his left wrist to a cinder. Aiden's glowing eyes widened, his mouth hung in horror as he cried out and collapsed in full flame an inch from the ravine. Lynn heaved a weakened cough and did not move again.

Cat held her breath to keep from screaming. She shut her eyes and tugged Will forward. His arms and legs fused in position around her, growing larger by the second. The weight folded her in half. She cradled Zephyr's body, trembling from emotion and exhaustion. Her boot slipped on the wet stone and all three went down. Will hit beside her, physically breaking to pieces. His right arm snapped off and knit together at an odd angle. He closed his eyes and lay quiet. Cat cringed and looked away.

Zephyr was nearly translucent within the baggy folds of her dress. Cat lifted her with ease and laid her with the other three, feet from the misty edge. Dizzy from the horror and burdened with guilt, Cat trudged to the lip of the chasm and dropped to her knees on the crumbling bit of stair.

White light swirled over the darkness below. Tiny points of light flickered in the depths, as if she were looking through the earth into a night sky beyond. It was quiet and peaceful. She considered releasing herself into its embrace, but forced herself to stand. Cat raised her head and shouted. “I know you're here!”

Her voice echoed into eternity.

“I know you can hear me! This is where you said you'd be waiting!” She pulled the scripture case from her pocket and held it toward the abyss. “I did everything you told me to. Come take your magic back.”

The chasm said nothing. Her fingers tightened around the leather box. “Did you hear me? I said I did it! I sacrificed my friends for you; it's time to come back!”

Still nothing. Cat's brow furrowed. She threw the scripture on the ground. “Do you need an apology? Is that what you want? Fine, I'm sorry! I'm Uzzah's descendant, what he did was wrong. He sinned when he killed Malachi. He sinned when he used your magic. We've ruined everything, just like you said we would. Now come back here and fix it!”

Nothing changed. Fear seized her heart with a cold fist.

“Why won't you answer?” She backed away from the edge. “Where are you?”

“Right here.”

Cat spun. A man stood silhouetted in the frame of the open door. The mist parted as he stepped forward and pulled back his hood. Joshua peered sheepishly through his wind-swept black hair. “I said I'd meet you at the heart of it. Sorry it took me so long.”

“Joshua?” Cat gaped. “How did you get down here?”

“I have ways.” His footsteps echoed but his voice did not. “It's okay, Catrina, it's not every day a person meets their maker. It's alright to be a little overwhelmed.”

“But... no.” She shook her head. "You can't be God. God is – ”

“Gone?” Joshua cut half a smile. “And where do you think I went? Another place? Another time? Maybe, say, five hundred years in the future?”

"But you can't be *God.*" A new, more personal fear clawed through her chest. "You're here. You're a human and God is...is..." She gestured to the chasm below them. "This!"

Rolling silver clouds reached from the chasm as Joshua approached the edge of the ravine. They wrapped his legs like grasping fingers. He dispersed them with a wave. "This is not me. This is my magic."

"What?"

"I couldn't take it with me when I took a human body. It was too powerful. It all wouldn't fit." The mist rose about his torso. He breathed it into his chest and released it with a sigh. "I've dreaded coming back here."

"You knew all along." Cat backed away toward the wall, reality blurring. "Why did you do this?"

Joshua's face hardened as more tendrils reached toward him from the pit. They scattered at a wave of his hand. "You know what it's like to have a true friend, Catrina. Someone whose soul moves in you as yours does in theirs. My Prophets were like that. We were perfect companions. They could hear my voice without harm, perform miracles without consequence, and sense my presence without fear. Malachi even laughed at my jokes." He wore a sad smile. "I experienced creation through them. Every moment of their lives... and then Uzzah happened."

Cat gulped.

"It hurt so badly." He pressed his lips tight. "Not the knife, although I did feel it. I've died with each of my Prophets and some were extremely painful, but the heartache... Malachi and Uzzah were closer than brothers. I knew their hearts. They trusted each other implicitly, but the jealousy... Uzzah couldn't control what it did to him. It wasn't Malachi he hated. It was me. I'd picked a favorite. It's only natural to be drawn to power. I knew the Prophet arrangement made it inevitable, but I'd gotten too close. I had to go."

"You left because you were guilty," Cat said.

"I left because I was sad." His voice was ragged and raw. "It wasn't supposed to be like this, Catrina. There weren't supposed to be Prophets. When it started, I was in perfect harmony with everything I'd made. The whole world was my body and I could move it at a thought. I knew the future and the past. I even knew the way Malachi would die, but the experience – " He stopped short. "Brother against brother. Malachi's betrayal. Uzzah's fear and hate and guilt. It was so potent and terrible, it hurt me and that pain shook the world. It created this pit, and would have destroyed everything if I gave it the chance, so I left. I knew how long the world could survive on this pit of residual magic, so I quieted my mind until it was safe to return in order to keep my heart from destroying everything I've ever made."

The starlight in the chasm reflected in his eyes. Cat inched forward. "Why turn yourself into a man?"

"Because it was like being with my Prophets again," he sighed. "You all have a limited perception. Time, for instance – every moment is precious. I needed some of that. To remind me."

"Remind you of what?"

"Why you're worth it."

His eyes steeled. The sparkle and depth collapsed into cold, shallow disks lit only by the rolling fog. The mist boiled in time with the pulse at his temples. Cat's heart doubled speed. She felt the anger reverberating off the stone walls.

"Five hundred years," he said through clenched teeth. "You think that'd be long enough but no, they learned nothing. The magic I left drained out like a sieve. Nature driven into the ground. My children dying in horrible ways with no one to help them."

"I tried." Cat's voice echoed louder and harsher than she expected. "I followed your instructions to the letter."

"Catrina..."

"I don't understand what more you want from me."

"It's not what you think."

"Not what I think? Look at them!" She gestured to the four bodies like pillars lying prone on the floor. "They died for you! The magic's there, take it! If you want revenge for Malachi, I'm standing right here. I'm Uzzah's blood, punish me. It's what I deserve."

"No!" His eyes flashed as he grabbed her wrist. Cat jumped and stumbled away.

He released her arm, brow knit. "Are you scared of me?"

She wet her lips. "Yes."

"I won't hurt you." His eyes swelled to pools as mist twisted ribbons around his empty hands. "I'm sorry."

"Why did you lie to me?" Cat asked. "All this time you told me to keep going, all the pain my friends and I went through, Peter and Ildri and Lady Creven.... You made me think it was for a reason."

"It was. It is," Joshua said. "I couldn't explain it before because I needed you to be here. If it was just me, it'd start all over. James told you back in the Runian mansion that I chose you for a reason. He was right, but not in the way he thought. I didn't pick you for a wife. Despite your heritage, your magic, your naiveté... in this dying world, you were someone worth saving."

Cat stared, speechless. She let Joshua's hands rest on her arms.

"I know you're not perfect," he muttered. "You're defensive and confrontational with a bit of a temper, but the choices you make and the love you have for the less fortunate set you apart. You're important, Catrina, You're precious to me."

"Then why did you let all this happen?" Cat's fear flared to anger. "Do you realize how many people have been hurt? Have died? You're God! How dare you hold my hand and say it'll be okay when you knew it wouldn't from the start. You lied to me!"

"Not a lie," Joshua said. "I can never lie."

"But you let me believe I could change things!" she roared. "I thought I was a Prophet. I thought God would forgive us but no – you're *upset*."

"Are you saying I didn't have reason to be?" he countered. "Everything I've done I did for my people. They're the ones who asked for a Prophet – I didn't design it this way! I wanted to make them happy and I was rewarded with insults and betrayals and real pain over and over again. Man thinks he's so powerful but he's a splinter compared to me. I could grind this world to powder between two fingers!"

"And what's stopping you?"

He dropped his face to his hands and snarled in frustration. The mist about him dimmed and sank back to the floor. Joshua drew a breath, emerging measured and calm. "Do you remember our conversation outside Earth Town? I told you we could run away together: retreat to the mansion and watch the world die around us. I can still do it, but you know that I won't. I can't turn my back because I'm afraid. It's too important."

Cat's heart quaked as she met his sparkling, star-filled eyes. "You're afraid?"

A faint ring of white light glowed along the rims of his eyes. He stooped and lifted the discarded scripture case from the ground. "I am the New Prophet; man and miracle in one. I was born in the mountains to a tainted tribe of once-holy men. With your help, I befriended those suffering most without my care. I returned to the spot I was betrayed to face the truth that has eaten away at me." He stared back into the chasm, his dark face heavy in heartbreak. "And meet a painful death in the face of my own forgiveness."

"What?" Cat stepped forward. "Death?"

He swallowed hard.

"But you're God."

"Not right now. Right now I'm flesh and bone with only as much power as a Prophet. If I pick up this mantle, the force of my own voice will rip me apart." He looked back at the scroll in his hand. "From the first dawn, all I wanted was to bond with my people as a father and a friend, but all it created was jealousy and pain. I can't let it go on like this. I have to take control, even if it hurts … and leaves me lonely."

Joshua backed toward the edge. Cat watched him teeter and grabbed his arm. "Wait."

He turned, face drawn and eyes sparkling.

She tightened her grip on his arm. “I don't care who you are or what you can do; you're important to me. I've lost too many people. There's got to be another way.”

He smiled. “Thank you, but I can't stay here and be God at the same time.”

“But the sacrifice – ”

“It's me, Cat,” he said. “It was always me.”

The mist swelled, overflowing the chasm in a blanket of white. Dust and stone fell from the ceiling into swirling smoke. Cat tucked into Joshua's shoulder, the smell of incense still strong on his skin. “Please don't leave.”

“Don't worry. This isn't the end.” He took her hands. “Things will change, but I'm not leaving you alone. Your job this whole time was to be my witness. You saw the valley at its most wicked, found humanity in the rejected, and learned the whole truth right from the source. Speak for me to the people, tell them everything we've done. Your happiness is waiting on the other side of this moment. Enjoy it. Live in it until we meet again. Love and be loved just as I love you.”

Cat's eyes welled, stirred by the pools of wisdom and love staring back at her. Her lip trembled. “What should I do?”

“Be here with me,” he said. “Remember everything you've seen and heard on this journey including this miracle, because both your path and mine have led to this moment.”

He leaned in and she met his lips in a kiss. Warmth spread through her body, seeping into her soul. She held his heart to hers and he held back. The moment lasted, sad and soft, until he broke it with a wince. He buried his face in her shoulder with a small, strangled cry.

Waves of pain shuddered through him. Light glowed from his core and filled the cavern with whiteness Cat could see through her eyelids. Beams burned through his skin. They tingled beneath her palms and into her chest where her heart fluttered in compassion and fear. Joshua pressed his cheek to hers, seeking closeness and comfort. She pressed a hand to his cheek as a tear rolled down and as his flesh warmed and tattered to ribbons. His body evaporated in brilliant light.

Whiteness filled the cave, piercing the stone. Clean air poured, warm, into the dank cavern. Lord Creven's manor crumbled as the hillside dissolved, throwing mortar and stone as holy light raced over the land. It destroyed the warring golems, tore pipes from the farmland, bent crops, and toppled houses on its way toward the mountains. The light swept the desert through villages and towns, covering God's Valley mountain range to mountain range in a sparkling blanket. The wave climbed the mountain ranges, cleared the many peaks, and faded into sparkling silence.

Soft rain, like music, fell over the land.

Chapter 41

Trace lay half-buried in dirt and debris. Castleton was obliterated, its pieces scattered over the farmland like islands in a lake of waving, green crops. Trace crawled out of the rubble, dazed and unarmed. The mountain below the town was flattened to nothing. Green shoots of young grass poked from the damp soil.

He wiped rainwater from his brow. The bandage on his forehead was missing, as was the wound beneath it. He checked his bruised ribs, but all signs of damage were completely healed. The sheath on his back was empty. A voice echoed in the chaotic terrain.

"Master?"

"Paige?" His heart quickened. Trace ventured into the surreal landscape. Whole buildings lay tossed at odd angles through the colorful fields. Streams of water trickled over vertical slabs of paved road and naked rock. Humans wandered the crops looking healthy but dazed. Trace cupped his hands and called again. "Paige?"

"Master?"

Trace rounded a chunk of white wall and found a full, intact church, ripped from its foundation and lying whole on its side. Paige stood on the roof, her black paintbrush in hand.

"Paige!"

"Master!" She skidded over the shingles and threw both arms around his chest. "I tried painting a wind golem to find you but it didn't work. The symbol didn't even flash. Does that mean what I think it does?"

"I hope so."

Dust-covered Calligraphers joined the growing crowd of soldiers and townsfolk, eyes hungry for answers. The congregation parted and senior Vivian Arch appeared. Her tight curls frayed about her head like a halo. In her hands, the golden brush lay dull. The light at the heart of the scripture was out.

"What does it mean?" Vivian looked to Trace with tears in her weary eyes. "What's happened?"

"It's alright," Trace assured. "Magic is gone."

“Gone?” Vivian gaped. The Calligraphers behind her exchanged anxious mutters.

Trace raised his hands for attention. “There's no reason to be afraid. You've all witnessed a great miracle – today is the day we've prepared for for five hundred years. Our God is back. He's taken magic for his own. The world is made well.”

“You sound so certain,” Vivian said. “How do you know?”

“The Prophet,” Trace answered. “It's as Malachi foretold.”

Vivian bowed her head over the gold brush. A tear fell to the grass. “We should have listened to your words, Trace. I led us the wrong way... against Our God.”

“Don't be ashamed,” Trace said. “We were kept ignorant on purpose by a long line of corrupt rulers. You served scripture well, and did what you thought was right. The proof was in the highest library, but our Elders chose to ignore it.”

“Not all of them.” Vivian inched forward, the gold brush in her hand. She offered it to Trace. “You saw.”

“Me?”

“The Order has changed. Without magic, we have no purpose,” she said. “You fought for the truth using all the spells required of our elders. Your grasp of scripture is more complete than any who have come before you. I trust you to keep leading us with the wisdom you have gained.”

"Agreed!" Another Calligrapher called.

"Seconded!" A third answered back.

"Thank you all." Trace beamed to Paige and pressed the brush to his heart. "I accept your commission with humility, honor, and honesty. You have my word."

"May it be so." Vivian rose. "Well, Elder Hayes, what is your first order?"

"First?" He slid the staff into the holster on his back. "We are Holy Calligraphers; our commission as always been to serve the people. There are more people in this rubble. I want a calculated sweep of the surrounding area. Leave no stone unturned."

The monks snapped to attention. "Yes, sir!"

"I will organize a center of operations," Vivian said.

"Very good, Ms. Arch. I trust your direction."

"Master," Paige interrupted. "What about the Prophet?"

Trace's brow knit. He stared over Castleton's broken outer wall to the heart of the ruined city. "Let's start in the middle."

He gathered a party of monks and followed a trail of loose bricks up the West Spoke to the freestanding city gate. A massive crater lay where the city used to stand, as if a giant fist punched the mountain into the earth. The walls of the depression were marbled with lines of slate gray and reddish brown. Sharp cliffs stuck like stairs from the side. Trace and his party used them as a path through the jagged boulders. A silver lake rippled at the bottom of the hole, stirred by raindrops and loose stone.

Trace stopped a moment in awe. “It's hard to believe we were just on a mountain.”

“How'd we survive?” Paige asked.

“A miracle.” He pointed to a rise of stone in the center of the lake. “That's the heart of it. We'll start there.”

Rain trickled over the faceted rock as Trace and his party snaked along the crater wall. Tiny streams grew to rivers, washing stone and dirt from the sides. The Calligraphers searched the crumbling bank for survivors but found only rubble. After an hour's descent, they arrived at the water's edge.

Musical drops pattered across the lake beneath a faint mist. Trace stepped in – the water opaque with dark silt and staggeringly cold. He waded waist-deep and headed to the island.

The mound of naked rock jutted upward at an angle, crowned by an empty iron door frame. Trace climbed out of the water and searched the isle for life signs. Paige joined him, wet and scowling. “She's not here.”

“She must be.”

“Why are you so sure?”

"It's a feeling." A curved ledge drew his eye downward to a raised platform near the water. A scrap of pink and yellow fabric fluttered at the water's edge.

Senses returned one at a time; first the patter of rain, followed by wetness and cold. Cat thought she smelled incense and raised her head. Someone lifted her body. "Joshua?"

"Miss Aston!" Trace held her close. "Catrina. are you alright?"

Her limbs were stiff and heavy and her heart was numb with loss. She closed her eyes and focused on the warm embrace. "Yes."

"Praise Our God. Can you tell us what happened?"

Cat touched a hand to her lips. A tear joined the rain on her cheek. "God took back the world."

Trace helped her stand as the other Calligraphers joined them on the bank. Cat felt their eyes like a dozen spotlights.

"She's alright." Trace kept a supportive arm around her back. "Search the area for survivors."

Cat's voice caught in her throat. "There are no survivors."

"Master!" Paige called from the edge. "I found something!"

She waded into the lake and lifted a head of dark hair to the surface. Lynn. Another Calligrapher helped her pull the body to the shore. Cat covered her mouth, throat tight. She could hardly stand to see her, but couldn't look away. Lynn's arms hung limp, the skin dripping wet but tight and a warm shade of brown.

Paige waved. “She's alive!”

Cat staggered against Trace's arm. “What?”

“She's okay! Look!” Paige helped Lynn to her feet. The young woman blinked through dripping hair and spotted Cat with a pair of clear brown eyes.

“Cat!”

“Lynn!” Cat met her in a hug. “How are you here?”

“I don't know!” Lynn laughed. “I was listening to you and Joshua, then saw a light and I woke up!”

“Sir, another!” Two Calligraphers called from a couple yards off. They pulled a young man from the water. Lynn clapped her hands over her mouth. “Is that Aiden?”

He staggered, his shirt in tatters, wiping water from his unblemished face. “Our absent God...” He noticed his own hands and took a start. “What the? I'm – ”

“Alive!” Lynn leaped into his arms. “It's a miracle!”

“Zephyr and Will.” Cat grabbed the nearest monk. “There's two more! Go find them!”

Someone flailed in the water to their left. Cat ran to help and found Zephyr with full, healthy cheeks and an inquisitive look in her eyes. “Where am I?”

"It's okay, Zephie," Lynn smiled. "You're with us."

"Lynn?" Zephyr searched their faces. "Cat?"

"Yes!" Cat cheered.

"Is that Aiden?" Zephyr turned in the water. "Where's Will?"

"Over here!" The teen waded over with elastic bandages hanging from his scrawny arms. "Hey everybody! Fancy meeting you all here like this!"

"Will!" Zephyr clapped for him.

"Hey Zeph! How's it going?"

"Wonderfully!" She hugged him around the neck. "Everyone's together, like you said!"

"Not exactly like I said, but way, way better."

"These are the Curses?" Trace watched the four in wonder. "The ones you were with?"

"The same ones," Cat beamed. "I can't believe it, either."

"How did you do it?"

"I didn't. Joshua – " She gulped. "I mean God. He promised to show me a miracle."

"You spoke to him?"

"Yes."

Trace's eyes lit, awestruck. "What did he say?"

"He said that he loved me," Cat replied. "Then he let me go."

Morning broke over the Calligraphers' camp with the most brilliant sunrise Cat had ever seen. Light rain continued to fall from a cloudless pink sky, painting rainbows in wreathes around the sun as it crested the mountains. Cat watched the dawn from the rocky bank of the crater, now filled to the brim with the miraculous rain. She tucked her knees under her chin and spoke to the sky. “Settling in okay up there, Joshua?”

The rain calmed to a drizzle and a brilliant new rainbow reflected in the rippling lake like a smile.

“I'll take that as a 'yes.'” Cat tucked her loose hair behind her ear. “You feel really far away right now. I mean, I know you're everywhere, but... it's not the same. I miss having you with me.”

The rainbow faded as the clouds spread, channeling the sun past the valley to illuminate a path toward the western mountains. Cat followed and saw Lynn approach through the Castleton's broken west gate. “Hi, Cat.”

“Hi.” She made room for Lynn on the bank. “You're up early.”

“It's hard to sleep with so much excitement.” The former Water Curse straightened the folds of her skirt and sat. “You okay?”

“Yeah. How does it feel to be dry?”

“I wouldn't know, this is as close as I seem to get.” Lynn shook the drizzle from her curls with a laugh. “I don't mind though.”

“What about the others?”

"They're anxious." Lynn took her arm. "Are you really okay?"

"Of course." Cat's smile faded. "Maybe a little worn."

"We've had a crazy week." Lynn drew her from the ground. "Come on, the Elder says we're ready."

The citizens of Castleton huddled in huts and tents within the farmlands. There were no injuries, but homelessness weighed heavy on their hundreds of faces. The Calligraphers prepared wagons for supply runs to the neighboring cities. Refugees loaded in the open beds, carrying what few possessions they still owned. They watched Cat with fear and fascination as she passed.

Trace oversaw the preparations from the top of a rubble pile with Paige taking notes on one of the checkpoint guards' old clipboards. She cupped her hands around her mouth. "All headed for Dire Lonato board the marked transports!"

Aiden stood near one of the front wagons. His face was foreign without the burns, but his impatient posture was impossible to mistake. Will and Zephyr ran circles around him, laughing like the fourteen year-olds they were.

"Hey there, sibs!" Will waved a lanky arm to Cat and Lynn. "Good morning!"

"Good morning to you," Lynn smiled.

Aiden wore a clean white shirt two sizes too big. He crossed his arms in the wrinkled sleeves. "Cat, you okay?"

“Do I look that bad?” She lilted. “What's it like being wet?”

“Weird.” He wiped his bald head. “I miss my hood.”

“I miss my hair.” Zephyr combed her uneven bangs. “I remember it being long and beautiful. Now it looks like something died on my head.”

“I like it.” Will said. “It's edgy.”

“Am I edgy? Like, do I seem like an edgy person?”

Lynn smiled. “What do you think?”

“I don't know.” Zephyr shrugged. “I just met me yesterday.”

“There you all are.” Trace slid from his podium with Paige close behind. He gave Cat a pat on the shoulder. “Are you alright?“

“You're worried about me, too?”

“Yes,” Trace replied. “I expected a smile from the girl who saved the world.”

“God saved it,” Cat replied. “I didn't do anything.”

“If you say so.” Trace turned to Paige. “Is everything ready?”

“Yes, Master.” She flipped through her stack of handwritten notes. “All we need are the liaisons.”

“I guess this is it, then.” Trace addressed Cat and her companions. “Thank you all for doing this. You were already heroes, but as witnesses to the events, your testimony is invaluable. When people find out you are healed Curses... let's just say I can't imagine this effort succeeding without you.”

“We have our own reasons for going back,” Aiden said. “I need to know if Fire Town is safe. The Curses are my family, and with all this rain I'll find them either healed or dead in their homes.”

“Of course. I'm sorry,” Trace grimaced. ”I apologize on behalf of the Holy Calligraphers for the centuries of wrongs we've committed against the Curses. We were blind to our own cruelty. I ask forgiveness especially for any offense I, personally, committed in the last week, month, and twenty-seven years of my life. If you need anything, ask and it's yours.”

“We appreciate it.” Lynn swept a small curtsy. “Thank you, your honor.”

“Please, I'm only a man. The honor is mine.” He bowed. “Miss Aston, I have a present for you.”

“Present?”

Trace signaled to Paige. She rushed to the far side of the rubble and returned with a copper-colored draft horse, her mane still braided with flowers from the Runian's garden.

“Strawberry!” Cat cried. “Where did you find her?”

“Hiding in a farmer's shed,” Trace replied. “She was eating his sunflowers.”

“That sounds like her.” Cat petted a hand down the horse's neck and hurried to the wagon and checked the under-seat storage. Peter's Atlas was tucked inside. “Thank goodness for that.”

“It's good to see you smile.” Trace said. “She's ready to take you home.”

“Home?” Cat hugged the atlas to her pounding heart. “Actually, I was planning to stay here and put myself to good use.”

“You'll be of much better use after a little rest,” Trace persisted. “You've done enough for one week, Catrina. Take some time for yourself. I'm sure Mason Forge is anxious for your return.”

“It's a good idea, Cat. You did say you were tired.” Lynn patted her shoulder. “We'll all meet back here soon, I promise.”

“Promise.” Cat's stomach turned at the word. She glanced to Aiden's sympathetic brown eyes and put the atlas back under the seat. “I suppose I should at least visit.”

“Good,” Will said. “Just a visit, though. We can't break up the Holy Five!”

“We better not,” Zephyr said. “You're the only people I know.”

A line of wagons waited behind them, the drivers all monks with brushes on their backs. An open seat waited for each of her friends. Cat swallowed hard, her throat tighter than expected. “I guess this is goodbye.”

“For now.” Lynn hugged her. Cat sniffed and held tight. Zephyr joined, followed by Will, and finally Aiden, who strung his arms wide around the outside. Cat cherished the moment and released them to their wagons before taking the driver's seat of her own.

“You know, Catrina,” Trace ventured, “it's not too late to join the Order. I think you'd make an excellent monk.”

“I don't like black.” She grinned. “But I'll think about it.”

“Please do.” He nodded a bow. “Our God be with you.”

“He is.” Her smile faded. “Take care, Trace. Good luck.”

Strawberry pulled the covered wagon westward toward the mountains. Colorful crops glowed with vigor, the artificially watered plants swollen with fresh rain. Copper pipes lay broken beneath strewn bits of mountain. The wagon crossed the twisted remains of Creven's electrified fence, rolling over a warning sign as it passed into the desert where prairie grass blanketed the old landscape with a thin carpet of new life. Pieces of Castleton littered the desert like the bones of an ancient monster. Cat watched it all pass in a fog.

It was strange driving alone. Her thoughts drifted back over her journey. Were the coals around Fire Town still burning? Was Lake Veneer at full capacity? Did Wind Town have power? Were the Curses of Earth Town healed? It was entirely possible Aiden, Lynn, Zephyr, and Will's restoration was a reward for their sacrifice and the rest of the Curses were still sick, like Lady Creven assumed. Cat couldn't believe Joshua would let them all die. She hoped he wouldn't. Her friends deserved happy reunions when they returned to their homes.

Thoughts of home made her nervous. Peter was so sick when she left. There was no way he held on for three days without her. Still, the tiniest hope remained, and it hurt most of all. Fear of disappointment clamped her heart and lungs. Cat breathed deep and resigned herself to an exhausted, emotionless blank.

Strawberry reached the mountain pass at sunset. The rain had passed and brilliant colors danced against lines of cloud. Trees swayed in the rich light, their gray limbs dotted with fresh buds, as if all nature had waited patiently for God's return. The trees reached down, welcoming. Cat kept staring forward until Mason Forge inched its way into view.

She stopped Strawberry at the entrance and led her in on foot. The street was quiet for a summer evening, restaurants and shops deserted. The clock in the town hall tolled the late hour. Cat gulped and guided Strawberry up the hill to the square at the intersection of Main Street and Cross. Electric lights extended along the residential side streets where shadows moved in the homes. Brighton's Café near the waterwheel bustled with people. Cat turned toward her parents' house when the church door burst open. Raymond Aston stood silhouetted in the entrance. “Cat!”

“Dad.”

“Our God!” He jumped down the church steps and yanked her from the wagon into a hug. Cat leaned in, glad for the comfort. She snuggled in his arms. His cheek pressed to her forehead as they rocked back and forth. “When that white light came through I didn't know what happened. If it meant you were... that you had...”

“I'm fine, Dad.” She stared into his watering green eyes. “Magic is where it belongs.”

“You've been so strong.” A tear fell as he cupped her face in his hand. “For the first time in my life, I'm proud to be an Aston.”

“Raymond? Is it her?” Mona Aston's eyes welled. She leaped down the church steps and embraced her daughter. “My hero! My little Prophet. I *knew* you were destined for greatness!”

The town came alive. Men and women poured from the church sanctuary. Neighbors came from their homes, clapping and cheering. The crowd from Brighton's abandoned their tables and ran up Cross Street to join the welcome. The Astons beamed and presented their daughter to the celebrating crowd. Cat couldn't help but smile.

Mayor Young took her by the arm. “Welcome home, Catrina! Your father told us all about your mission. Did that white light mean you won? Did you talk to Our God?”

“I did.”

Gasps filled the square. The mayor gaped. “What did he say?”

“I'll tell you everything, but first I have a promise to keep.” Cat's voice quivered. “Is Peter – ?”

“Cat!” Alan Montgomery burst from the crowd.

Cat's heart raced. "Alan? I was just... Is your brother...?"

A pair of strong arms scooped her off the street from behind. Cat tensed, feet dangling, heart in her throat. The crowd watching smiled. She landed and turned. Peter stared back at her, an image of pure joy. "You did it!"

"Pete!" Her knees failed her. She staggered forward and steadied herself on his healthy arms. She was holding his hands – touching real skin with no stone growth or bandages to get in the way. She let go to bury her face in his chest. His heart beat a strong rhythm within his smooth rib cage without a rattle or echo.

He stooped to see her, brown eyes clear behind his glasses. "You alright?"

"I – I'm..." She threw her arms around his neck and cried as hard and loud as she could. She couldn't believe he was real, yet his touch, smell, and warmth were all there. The only thing missing was the stone.

"You'll notice I kept our promise." He grinned. "Although I slept through most of it, I saw that white light and when I opened my eyes, I knew you'd saved me."

"Not me." Tears streamed down her cheeks. "Joshua did it. He was God the whole time."

Peter smirked. "That figures."

"Don't be mad. He saved all of us – Lynn, Aiden, and Zephyr, too. And Will – you have to meet him. We all thought you were dead." Her throat tightened. "He gave you back to me."

"Then I guess I owe him for that bit, but I owe this to you." Peter pulled her pink comb from his back pocket and pinned the loose hair from her eyes. "Thanks for everything, Cat. Welcome home."

She threaded her fingers in his. "I'm never leaving you again."

Peter kissed her forehead and pressed the mark between their brows. She pressed back, heart soaring, her hands tight in his.

The crowd cheered. Their joyful noise echoed within the western mountains and soared over the budding trees, into the sky where the faint twinkle of evening stars peeked through the last wisps of sunset. Velvet sky stretched to enfold the valley like a blanket, shimmering with the light of hope and a deep, comforting peace.

THE END

Acknowledgments

Eternal thanks to God and my supportive family, especially Mom and Dad for your faith, Olivia for your patience as I talked about this thing for years, aunts, uncles, and cousins who read it in its different drafts – especially Catherine for her incredible interest, investment, and insight, and my grandparents both Myles and Stolzers for their faith in my potential and making this book possible, even if they cannot celebrate with me now.

A big shout out to Megan Geeck for believing in the book and reading almost every draft. Thanks to Meredith Tate and Amanda Blair for late-game CPing, Kathleen Kayembe for boundless encouragement and enthusiasm, the members of the Write Pack for knowledge and experience (I love you guys! I couldn't do this without you), and all my many beta readers who kept my chin up in the eleven years I've worked on this project.

Threadcaster was a dream I refused to let go of. It wouldn't have come true without all your help!

Made in the USA
San Bernardino, CA
11 March 2017